Nantucket
Sawbuck

Books by Steven Axelrod

The Henry Kennis Mysteries
Nantucket Sawbuck

Nantucket Sawbuck

A Henry Kennis Mystery

Steven Axelrod

Poisoned Pen Press

First Edition 2014

10 9 8 7 6 5 4 3 2 1

Library of Congress Catalog Card Number: 2013941160

ISBN: 9781464200878   Hardcover
      9781464200892   Trade Paperback

Map: David Lazarus
Cover photo: Cary Hazlegrove

Poisoned Pen Press
6962 E. First Ave., Ste. 103
Scottsdale, AZ 85251
www.poisonedpenpress.com
info@poisonedpenpress.com

Printed in the United States of America

To Annie Nick and Caitlin:
Family given and chosen.

Acknowledgments

Thanks to my brilliant editor Annette Rogers, and the faculty of Vermont College of the Fine Arts, where I finally learned how to write: Chris Noel, Domenic Stransberry, Diane Lefer and the inimitable Douglas Glover. Cheers also to my astute and merciless writing-group beta-readers, Neil Brosnan, George Murphy and Kathy Butterworth. My argument with Neil about Henry's final disposition of the case made it into the book almost verbatim. I'm grateful for the advice and guidance of the real Nantucket Police Chief William Pittman. He would want you to know that Henry's poetry and procedural mistakes are all my own. Finally, thanks to Suellen Ward for jump-starting this project over soft-shell crabs ten years ago. And to my Mom and Dad, Ed Breeding and Mimi Beman, true blue supporters who will have to miss the launch party.

Contents

Part One: Premeditation

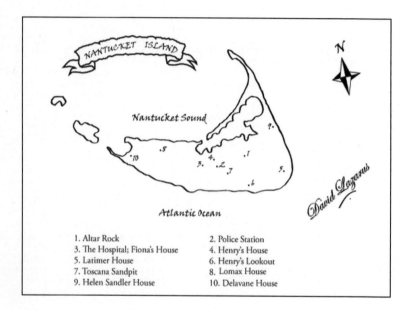

1. Altar Rock
2. Police Station
3. The Hospital; Fiona's House
4. Henry's House
5. Latimer House
6. Henry's Lookout
7. Toscana Sandpit
8. Lomax House
9. Helen Sandler House
10. Delavane House

Chapter One

Preston Lomax

Just before two a.m. on a Friday morning three weeks before he was murdered, Preston Lomax was making a list of all the people who wanted to kill him. It was a long list. First of all, there were his three sons, whom he had humiliated for most of their lives. They naturally assumed they would be inheriting an almost incalculable fortune. He heard them joking about it: how to commit the perfect crime. Of course they would be the primary suspects if he were found dead, so they toyed with the idea of making it look like a suicide. Danny's handwriting was virtually identical to his own, which meant faking a suicide note would be no problem. They often entertained themselves devising drafts of this document: "I can no longer live with myself," the best of them began. "Wives can divorce me, children can run away from home. Friends can shun me. And they do. Everyone can flee the foul putrid horror that is Preston Lomax. Everyone except myself. For years I have had to live with this tedious, conniving self-centered monster twenty-four hours a day. At last I have found my own way to escape."

Of course the boys had no idea their apartments were bugged.

Preston Lomax didn't believe in anyone's privacy, except his own. Secrets were a luxury that you had to earn.

His wife and daughter would no doubt like to get rid of him, also. He had cheated on Diana with every one of her friends, all three of her sisters, two of her business partners, and the few attractive members of her support group: Women Who Love Men Who Hate Women, or Women Who Hate Women Who Love Men Who Love Hating Women Who Hate Men, or whatever the hell it was called.

If they needed someone to love and hate at the same time, he was happy to oblige.

His daughter hated him too. He had the tapes from her psychiatric appointments. He was apparently a demanding, unappeasable tyrant who forced her to play a game she called Guess My Mood. His rages and silences were as unpredictable as the occasional moments of warmth. She had never felt loved. She had "abandonment issues" and "anger management" problems. The hundred-and-fifty-dollar-an-hour shrink was supposedly helping her to "own" them. Lomax smiled. That girl could hardly even afford the down payment. If she ever did take full possession of all those pent up resentments, she might become dangerous. But that was at least a million dollars' worth of therapy away. Right now, she could barely look him in the eye over breakfast.

Who else wanted him dead? His drug dealers, his bookies. Several dozen top-of-the-line call-girls. None of them had been paid for months. There was a string of bad business deals going back fifteen years, dozens of people he'd left owing massive amounts of money while he disappeared with various companies' assets. It was mostly legal, or close enough to legal, and the lawsuits that would have disentangled the criminal from the legitimate would have been too time-consuming, and too embarrassing, to pursue. He knew his victims. He was shrewd about people, but one thing you could never predict was when someone was going to snap. Many of these fools had threatened him with bodily harm over the years. Lomax sighed. He brought out the Kamikaze in people.

Then there were the servants.

He had fired so many, tormented so many more into quitting. Desperate fringe people, bitter and unemployed, could easily feel that they had nothing to lose. Murder might seem like a reasonable option. Lomax generally wore thousands of dollars' worth of jewelry—his Rolex watch alone would make the killing worth the trouble for any of that rabble.

And think of all the kitchen maids, secretaries, and au pairs over the years. Some of them had fallen in love with him, some had gotten pregnant. Many of them had friends and family members as disgusted as they were. Why, the murderous potential of just the siblings of the girls he'd used and discarded multiplied the threats he faced exponentially. He had a brief chilling vision of a veritable army of hate-filled, cheated, abused, furious people, like the villagers in those old Frankenstein movies, storming the castle with their torches.

He walked to the window of his study overlooking Central Park. Fifth Avenue was almost deserted at this hour and the quiet soothed him. All day long he had heard the children in the playground across the street. He still had the remnants of a headache from that clamor.

Walking back to his chair he sat down and went over the list again. It was incomplete. He had ignored a vital segment—the people who would want him dead in the near future. Most of those new victims lived on the island of Nantucket, thirty miles off the coast of Massachusetts. They were tradespeople and retailers, professionals who relied on home owners like Preston Lomax for their sustenance. They saw the huge trophy fortress he was building on Eel Point, they noted his urgent attempts to gain admission to the ever so particular and stuffy Nantucket Yacht Club, chuckled over the way he had insisted that the residents whose house he had leveled to build "Sea Breeze" give him their 228 exchange telephone number and their two digit, in-town mailbox—small but significant indicators of "old" Nantucket money; an aura that instant millionaires like Lomax craved.

They assumed he was there to stay. The gossip mill ground out its formal conclusion from the benches of Main Street to the counter at Crosswinds, from the Wharf Rat's club to the editorial offices of the *Inquirer & Mirror.* Lomax was another fat cat who would plunk his slab of property tax money down every year. In return he'd spend four weeks out of fifty-two in his shingled palace, call himself a "native" and grouse about the "new people", especially the ones whose houses, no uglier or more ostentatious than his own, blocked his ocean view. He'd be a regular at the most expensive restaurants, running tabs at Topper's and The Pearl, and the cops would offer him a lift home when he got drunk. In other words, he was a type, a part of the island landscape, as unremarkable as the successful Irish contractor building a house in Tom Nevers, or the hard working Jamaican riding to work on a too-small bicycle, or the old lady from Greenwich volunteering at the Hospital Thrift Shop. He was common as mildew, regrettable as red tide, inevitable as fog. And that was just the way he wanted it.

Because none of it was true.

The reality was that Preston Lomax's company was under investigation by the Attorney General's office. And he knew exactly what the audit would show. He'd been robbing LoGran Corporation blind for years. No matter how well he covered things up, some ratty little accountant would turn State's evidence and screw him. But he was going to escape long before that, and Nantucket was the perfect staging area for his embarkation to parts unknown. All he had to do was keep things running normally and make no obvious moves. He had to keep building his house, for instance. That was fine, it would cost him nothing. He had paid everyone their first third, so they assumed he was good for the rest. Together they had donated hundreds of thousands of dollars in free labor and materials to the Preston Lomax fund. They just didn't know it yet. Appearances were everything and he appeared to be the safest bet around.

Well, let that be a lesson for them. And if the tuition at this particular school bankrupted them and ruined their lives, so be it.

Everything had worked perfectly so far. One of his bookies had even told him to start thinking about a second mortgage. His cocaine dealer was worried that he might find a cheaper on-island connection. The camouflage was perfect. And at the other end, there was enough money to keep him fat and happy in Central America for the rest of his life. All he had to do now was disappear.

He crumpled up the list of possible assassins and threw it out. They were all too late: in a month he'd be gone.

He poured himself a glass of neat Lagavulin single malt, walked to the window again. Looking down on the dark trees beyond the Park wall, he toasted the shadows.

"One month," he said aloud. And he drained the glass.

Chapter Two

The Scene of the Crime

Preston Lomax was found murdered at home in the early morning hours of December 16th. The body was discovered by his daughter Kathleen, after returning from a party in Wauwinet just after 1 a.m., according to her initial deposition, which I took on the scene. Her mother had been off-island, and her two brothers maintained separate residences, Danny in a renovated second floor condo in Freedom Square, Eric in a converted garage apartment on Helens Drive. So Lomax had been alone in the house for the evening.

"I knew something was wrong before I even got inside," Kathleen told me.

I watched her, letting her take her time. We were sitting on one of the two big couches that flanked the fireplace, in the great room of the Eel Point mansion. If she had been drinking at the party she held it well. If her father's death affected her, I saw no sign of it. Maybe she was in shock. Maybe she didn't care. Maybe she had killed Lomax herself, and was still in some nerveless fugue state. I didn't want to rule anything out. But she seemed smaller than she had the previous night, when she had danced happily into her father's Christmas party and disappeared upstairs a few minutes later. She was pulled into herself now, crumpled like a plastic bottle when you suck the last of the water out.

"The house was quiet in this odd way," she said. "I mean…
Dad usually listens to music when he's alone—he always has his
Frank Sinatra CDs with him. Francis Albert, Dad calls him. The
Chairman of the Board. I always thought it was funny because
Sinatra was just this old singer and Dad actually was the chairman of the board, you know? Anyway…I had downloaded like
fifty of those songs onto an iPod. I was going to give it to him
for Christmas and I—" She stopped talking, pulling herself back
from the brink of tears.

I began to relax—this was the kind of response I'd been
waiting for. "Walk me through it slowly. You pulled up in the
driveway. Did anything strike you as unusual?"

She nodded. "The lights were on. I mean—all the lights in the
house. Which was bizarre, because my dad is always like 'turn out
the lights, I don't own the electric company yet.' And the door
was open. I mean…closed but not latched. I didn't need my key.
That really freaked me out. I had reset the alarm before I went
out, so I figured maybe friends had dropped over. Except it was
so quiet. Then I thought, maybe Dad went out, but there's no
way he wouldn't have locked up. He's paranoid about burglars,
even on Nantucket where's there's totally no crime, right?"

I shrugged. "I wish that was true."

We fell silent for a moment. The tragic absurdity of her last
comment seemed to roll over her like a breaking wave. Nantucket would never be her safe, idyllic island again. She pulled
her pony tail loose and was wrapping the hair elastic around
her fingers, binding three of them together, doubling the band
twice, cutting off her circulation.

I could hear my men moving upstairs, taping off the bedroom. I had sent Barnaby Toll back to the station for the dental
stone casting kit. We'd gotten lucky—I saw that as soon as we
arrived. A brief late December thaw the night before had left the
lawn and driveway muddy, the perfect medium for absorbing
footprints and tire tracks. Then the weather turned cold again,
the temperature must have dropped twenty degrees in the last
few hours. That meant the impressions stamped into the wet soil

were hardened into ice and easy to preserve. I only wished my detectives had understood the situation. Kyle Donnelly actually tripped on the icy ridge of a footprint and wound up on the ground staring at it. I had to smile when he stood up, cursing about the slick soles of his police brogans. The print he'd been staring was some kind of ridged vibram type, exactly the kind of footwear Donnelly had been requesting since the first dusting of snow in November: a man's print, but not a policeman's. And the Lomax clan didn't strike me as work-boot people. This could be our intruder, but Donnelly hadn't made the connection. That's why I go to every crime scene, when the Board of Selectmen would prefer to keep me sitting in my office fiddling with paperwork. There was no point in giving my detectives on-the-job training if there was no one on the job to train them.

I pointed out the obvious and I could see his face light up, as the synapses sparked. It reminded me of my kids' Lego blocks. With enough time and patience they could build the rocket ship or skyscraper pictured on the box. Kyle was building something much more important: the working police officer's opportunistic style of perception, always hunting for the odd detail, the small anomaly, and the connections between them.

He had a way to go, but he was getting there. One block at a time.

The state police would be arriving soon. The C-Pac unit would be on the first flight over from Hyannis. Four other officers were securing a wider perimeter around the house. One of two big red garbage cans was sitting on the front walk; the other was upstairs. I always brought them to a crime scene. It was a trick I had learned from the lead homicide detective I'd worked with in L.A. The cans were for police trash: cigarette butts, coffee cups, candy wrappers, tissues—anything that could confuse the SID people and contaminate the scene. People got careless, even cops, and especially after a late night. The trash cans helped.

Kathleen was fading. Her fingers were turning white. "I have to call my brothers. They don't know what happened. I have to tell them, I need them to be here. They—"

"You have three brothers, is that right?"

"What? Oh—yes, that's right. Timmy's in Dubai, he works for BP. But Dan lives here now. He dropped out of law school to write a memoir. Life with father? Or something like that."

I knew Daniel Lomax. I had arrested him at a beach party the summer before and watched while his father paid off everyone to drop the charges. The money must have been pretty good because a lot of furious people turned sweet and warm way too fast, like dumping sugar into day-old coffee and popping it into the microwave. I had hauled Danny in again a few weeks ago, after a fight at the Chicken Box, and Daddy had taken care of that problem, too. The gravy train was permanently derailed now. Every tragedy has a bright side. I pegged the kid for a spoiled arrogant little bully. He didn't strike me as the literary type.

I turned back to Kathleen. "And the third brother? The youngest one? Eric, is it?"

She nodded. "Poor Eric. He checked himself out of Riggs two weeks ago. The Austen Riggs Center? In Stockbridge? It's a rehab clinic. Daddy made him go. They had a huge fight but it didn't matter. He checked himself out like two days later."

"So he was back on island?"

"He has a crumby little garage apartment in towney-ville. You know—off Bartlett Road? Near the high school. Dad pays the rent. I mean—the company does. LoGran? Eric gets an allowance, too. He's just a tax write-off, that's what he always says. Eric's always kidding like that—kidding on the square, that's what my grandmother called it."

"Kidding on the square?"

"Yeah...like it's a joke—but you really mean it. Except... not totally, Just—"

"Somewhere in between."

"Yeah."

"Kidding on the square. I like that."

She fell silent again. I backed things up. "So Eric didn't want to go to Riggs."

"It was horrible. They were screaming. Eric was like, 'Why aren't *you* going? This is your fault, I learned this shit from you.' He called Daddy a hypocrite and—and other things. As if Daddy was some kind of crazy drug addict or something. And that was the last time they ever saw each other. Daddy didn't even know he was back. Eric was hiding out but—now he…he'll never be able to say he's sorry. He'll never be able to say anything to him ever again and he— he…" She started crying again.

I reached out to squeeze her shoulder. "Kathleen, I'm sorry. But I have to ask. Do you know his whereabouts last night?"

Her face pulled tight around wide eyes. "Oh no. He could never—he…the boys used to joke around about killing Daddy, but there's no way…I mean, they couldn't kill anyone. Except maybe each other. It was just—"

"Kidding on the square?"

She smiled nervously. "Exactly. My grandmother was tough. 'Doing does it', she always used to say."

I sat back. "All right. Let's do this, then. Can we go back to last night, just for a few minutes?"

She looked up, pushed the tears down her cheeks with the heels of her palms. "Okay."

"So…you came inside," I prompted.

She looked up. "What?"

"Last night. You came into the house. Did you—?"

I could see her starting to focus again. "The desk was missing," she said. "This kind of slant top desk where we put our keys when we walk in? It was right under that painting of the black lab with the tennis ball."

She flicked her head in the direction of the front door. I took out my spiral pad and made a note. "So you thought there had been a robbery?"

"I didn't think anything. I just…I started losing it. I was calling Daddy, but I knew he wasn't going to answer. You know when you're on your cell and you're talking and the other person's phone cuts out, like they're going through a bad reception area or something? You don't notice at first, you keep talking but you have this funny feeling because there's no response at all, and then you figure it out and you're embarrassed because you've been talking to yourself even though no one heard you, I mean obviously, since no one was there, but…anyway. That's what it was like. But a thousand times worse. Like the whole world had cut out. Like there was no one anywhere."

"So, you went upstairs?"

"I—yeah. I was sure I was—I don't know, like someone had slipped me some bad drugs or something at the party. I figured I'd wake Daddy up and he'd, you know, I could …"

"Tell me what you saw in the bedroom. Take a few breaths, Kathleen. There's no rush. I know this is hard. But anything you tell me may help us catch the person or people who did this."

"I knew he was dead. Does that sound crazy? I knew it. The whole house felt dead. The air felt dead. And there was this smell. I got to his door but I couldn't go in. I called out again. I knocked. The door opened a little when I knocked on it and I thought, Everything will be okay if I don't go in there, if I just pull the door shut and go to bed, this will all be gone in the morning. But the smell was worse. I realized I was breathing through my mouth. I just stood there for, I don't know. A long time. Finally I went in, though. I mean, I had to. I couldn't just…"

I reached over and pressed her shoulder. "Do you need more time? Because we could…"

"No, sorry, I'm okay. I need to…I have to get this over with. He was on the bed. There was blood everywhere and there was some kind of…tool. It was in his chest and his mouth was stuffed with money. Someone had—his eyes were wide open, they were bulging out like he was trying to say something, like he was trying to talk with his eyes. No one had even shut them. Don't you think they could have at least shut his eyes?"

"These people, Kathleen…"

"I know, I just…it seemed so…" She exhaled a long tired breath. "I don't know. I don't know what I'm talking about. I'm just babbling. I'm sorry, I wish I could be more helpful."

"You're helping. But I have to ask, did you touch the body or move anything in the room?"

"I never even really went into the room. I just ran out of there and called the police. I could never…ugh. No way."

I tried a different approach; lingering over the horror she had just witnessed wasn't doing either of us any good. "Did your father have any enemies that you know of? Anyone who might have—"

"—been willing to kill him? To do—that…what I saw? To just—"

"Kathleen. Listen to me. There was a lot of anger in that room. It wasn't some cold-blooded contract killing. And it wasn't a heat of the moment outburst, either. Whoever did this came prepared."

"So who had a motive, is that what you want to know?"

"Well—"

"Who didn't have a motive? That's the real question."

"Kathleen, maybe we should—"

'No, I'm fine. This is good. Get it all out there. No more secrets." She gave me a crooked little smile "Let it rip."

"So you believe that there may have been—"

"Do you have any room left in that pad? You're going to need it."

I tipped the notebook at her by way of invitation.

"Fine," she said. "First of all there's my Mom. Dad was going to change his will in January. He was cutting her out. He practically dared her to kill him before New Year's. He knew about her boyfriend and he was pissed."

"He said that to her?"

"Right after the Christmas party. I was there—snooping. In the den." She twisted around to point out an unobtrusive door at the other side of the fireplace. "I wasn't even hiding. They were so oblivious. I could have been dancing over there."

"Did you know about the boyfriend?"

She stared at me. "I caught them together. He was—I thought…"

"Kathleen? If you're not—"

"He was my boyfriend, too. At least, I mean…I thought he was. Until last night."

"Busy boy."

She laughed, then clamped down before it turned into a sob. "I'll say. His name is Kevin Sloane."

Of course; I'd seen her mother with the kid. I'd pulled them over on Milestone Road, a couple of weeks ago. It was a small island and that made it tough to do anything unobserved. People worry about our new "surveillance state." The social panopticon of Nantucket made the NSA look puny by comparison. Half the island probably knew about Diana Lomax's love affair. "So you think they might have done this?"

"Not my Mom, not directly, not stabbing and that stuff with the money and all that. She'd get Kevin to do it for her. She always gets someone else to do her dirty work. I bet he jumped at the chance."

I scribbled Kevin's name, circled it and added a question mark. "You indicated that there might be other people who—"

"I wasn't the only one eavesdropping last night."

Charlie Boyce closed his phone and started toward us. I held up a hand to stop him. He met my eyes, nodded and faded back to his position by the front door. Whatever he had to say could wait.

"Who else was there?" I asked Kathleen.

"The paint contractor, Mike Henderson. And he was with that girl."

"Mike is married." I said it automatically, but it sounded foolish even to myself. So Mike Henderson was cheating on his wife? Well, who wasn't? Extramarital sex was the island's primary indoor sport. I might as well have gotten huffy at people letting their dogs off the leash.

"He's not going to be married for long," Kathleen said. "Not when his wife finds out."

"Who was the girl?"

"Her name is Tanya Kriel." She must have caught my startled look. "You know her?"

"We've met. Your brothers were fighting over her at the Chick Box a few nights ago."

"That sounds right."

"And you think she's a suspect?"

Kathleen took a deep breath and let it out with an exhausted shudder. I knew that particular fatigue: the dread tedium of explaining the obvious. How often had I said to one of my officers, "I shouldn't have to tell you this. You should know this stuff! You tell me!" That was the vexed impatience I heard in Kathleen's sigh. Maybe I was pushing too hard. Maybe we should continue this later, at the station.

But she forged on. "Her sister used to work for my family. I was away at school so I wasn't sure what happened. But there were fights about her. She got pregnant. Then she went away. Anna Kriel, that was her name."

"Did she quit or get fired?"

"She died. I heard Dad say, 'She went to the wrong abortionist.'"

"I'm sorry."

"It was creepy. But that's how things happen in this family. You cause a problem and then you're gone. I could have told them it was crazy having her around. Dad was too rich, and she was way too pretty, especially in those little maids' outfits. She looked like a porn star. Seriously. And there's a word my dad invented, he was pretty funny sometimes. Nonogamy? He was like, 'I don't do nonogamy.'"

"I'm not sure …"

"It means being sexually faithful to a woman who's not… you know. Who's not interested."

"And your mother wasn't interested?"

Kathleen looked down. "She was interested in Kevin."

I had to get her back on track. "So the sister gets knocked up and dies and then Tanya shows up. What? A year later?"

"Six months."

"Quite a coincidence."

That got a laugh out of her. "Right. What are the chances? She wasn't even trying to hide it. I heard her talking to Danny and Eric about how to kill people. She knows all the techniques. Poisons and stuff."

"But your father was stabbed. So it was more likely to be Henderson."

"Oh yeah, sure. That makes sense."

"But why would he do it?"

"Well—Dad was going to stiff everyone—take off without paying. He was gloating about it after the party. We all heard him. Henderson freaked out. So I don't know. That's a pretty good motive. If Dad was dead, the estate would have to settle the outstanding bills."

"Not in time to help anyone. If they were living paycheck-to-paycheck."

"I guess."

I flipped a page in my notebook, mostly for effect. The message was, we're moving on. "Was there anyone else who might have held a grudge? Your father seems to have made a lot of people angry."

She nodded. "You know how some people need to have harmony at any cost? I'm like that. I hate confrontations. But my dad was the opposite. He loved to fight. He loved pissing people off. He never lost an argument. He always had one more fact, you know? One more little piece of information. Even if he had to make it up on the spot."

"So who was he fighting with?"

"Lately it was mostly the tradespeople. Pat Folger? Do you know him?"

I knew Pat, and I'd seen him rip into Lomax at the same Christmas party. That was one argument the tycoon didn't win. I nodded, scribbled the name. The notes made some people nervous and I used them that way when I needed to. But they were calming Kathleen down. She needed to know what she said was important.

"Pat has to pay all his sub-contractors, so I guess money is pretty tight for him right now. But some of the worker people are independent. Mike Henderson, and the plumber, and the electrician. They had to go to Dad directly. He was bragging about it at dinner one night—not having to pay Pat Folger his percentage, cutting out the middleman. Dad hates the middleman. I feel bad for those guys, asking him for money directly. I could barely get my allowance out of him. The electrician, Tom Danziger? He's a total sweetheart, despite the 'I stand with Arizona' bumper sticker and all his second amendment blah blah. It just goes to show—politics don't mean anything. Some of the ickiest people I know are Democrats, sorry. Anyway, Tom helped me change a flat tire one day, in the rain no less, and the next time he saw me he said 'you've cut your hair'. I took like two inches off. No one else even noticed."

"He sounds like a good egg."

"He told me, 'If I don't get paid soon your Dad's going to own my company.'"

"Did he seem angry?"

"He seemed sad. He said people do this stuff all the time, they brag about not paying the final bill. I guess the idea is, like, all the tradesmen are ripping them off and over-charging, and the final bill is pure profit."

"Right. Can't have mere tradesmen making a profit."

That earned a quick brittle laugh. "Exactly. The plumber was really mad one day. I saw him slam the door on the way out but I don't even know his name. He's kind of scary, though. Can you tell who might have committed murder by things like that?"

"Not really. I wish we could." There was a pause, then. She squinted in thought, like she was trying to remember a line from a movie or the tune of a song. "What?" I said.

"Speaking of scary guys ..."

"Go on."

"A big mean-looking guy came to the house last week and then drove off in this big black pick-up truck. I'd never seen him before."

"He wasn't working on the house."

"No,"

"Would you recognize him? Pick him out of a lineup?

"Oh yeah. Totally."

"I may ask you to do that later. He won't be able to see you."

"Okay."

I was done. I closed the notebook. Charlie Boyce hoisted his phone and said. "Fraker's ten minutes out, Chief. More like five minutes, now."

"I think I need a glass of water, or an aspirin or something," Kathleen said. "Percocet would be good. No, seriously. Would that be all right? My Mom has some in her medicine chest."

"That's fine. But I'd go easy on the Percocet, if you've been drinking."

"I had like one glass of wine. And that was hours ago. I wish I had been drinking. I could use a drink right now."

"That's probably not the best idea."

"I know. I'm just going to get the stuff, okay?"

"Sure. But I'm going to send one of the officers up with you. If that's all right."

"Sure, fine. Whatever."

She pushed herself off the couch. I nodded to Charlie and he started upstairs behind Kathleen.

Kyle Donnelly came inside and walked over to a hutch with beveled glass doors. Various pieces of silver were displayed inside. "You'd think a burglar would take some of this stuff, Chief."

I got up and walked over. "Tough to fence."

"Still. Looks tempting to me. And no one says these boys were especially bright. You know what I mean? Chief?"

I was staring into the hutch. Something bothered me about the collection of silver pieces. They were laid out on four shelves: tankards, a tea service, bowls and spoons, little engraved boxes. The arrangement wasn't quite symmetrical. It was as if someone had shifted things around and failed to put them back properly.

"Something wrong, Chief?"

"I don't know. Make sure all this stuff gets printed." I turned away from the hutch. "Let's see what else we've got here. I want to be ready when the state police show up. Any sign of Barnaby?"

"Not yet. But we got the break-in site. In the basement. Come on. I'll show you."

We went down the basement steps. All the lights were on. At the bottom there was a small landing, with a storage area to the left and a big garage on the right. There was a window on either side of the garage door. The one on the left had a broken pane in the top sash, in front of the lock. "One of them could have gotten in here, a thin one." It was a small window. "Then run upstairs and opened the place up for the others?"

I shook my head. "Where's the broken glass?"

"He picked it up?"

"Maybe."

I hit the garage door control and it started grumbling up on its metal tracks. I pulled a flashlight off my belt and ducked outside. The light hit the shards of broken glass on the brown mulch below the window.

"I don't get it," Charlie said.

"Sure you do."

It took another moment, but finally Charlie nodded. He was a little sharper than Kyle Donnelly. "Oh. Yeah, okay. That's why the alarm didn't go off."

"Talk to the girl. Get the mother on the phone. I want a list of everyone who had access to that alarm code."

"Maybe it was just off for the night."

"It's the most expensive system Intercity sells. It's wired with Cat-5 networking, motion detectors, glass break monitors, and they just got it hooked into the station. You don't have a system like that and not use it."

Charlie shrugged. "I got a four hundred dollar a month gym membership and I don't use it."

I stopped myself from making the obvious uncharitable reply. Instead I said: "I don't watch much cable TV, either. But this is different. Get me the names."

"Okay."

I patted Charlie's arm. "It's getting late. Let's check out the bedroom."

I shut the garage door and we went back upstairs. The bedroom was closed off with yellow crime scene tape. I ducked under it, pulling on a pair of rubber gloves. Charlie followed me.

"Move anything?," I asked. "Touch anything?"

"Chief."

"I mean it, Charlie."

"So do I. This ain't Podunk."

I smiled. "People who actually live in Podunk must spend their whole lives pissed off. The name just means hick town full of rubes and retards. There must be some bright people there thinking, 'Hey, Des Moines ain't exactly Paris, either.'"

Charlie laughed nervously. It seemed disrespectful, but I knew better. In these death chambers you worked quickly and you made bad jokes. One SID tech I had known in L.A. sang Puccini arias while he worked. Death may have won but you wanted life to make a showing. That was what dignity meant to me. No puke, no despair, just shrug it off and do your job. Measure the spatter patterns. Examine the ligature marks. Check the hands for defensive injuries. Pace the scene off for droppings, for the bits and pieces the perpetrators left behind. It was Locardo's Exchange Principle, the fundamental axiom of police work. I had studied it at the Los Angeles Police Academy; Charlie had written a paper on it at John Jay College. Events leave traces, things rub off on each other, nothing moves without leaving a trail. So I always looked and then I looked again; and again. Sometimes I found nothing, or a weird little scrap of information that didn't fit, like the extra screw left over after assembling my son's Christmas bicycle. Other times I got lucky.

Like tonight.

I pulled a tweezers and a plastic evidence bag out of my coat jacket pocket, kneeled down and plucked the cigarette butt from where it was lying on the carpet, half-obscured by the dust ruffle of the king-sized bed. I stood, and extended it to Charlie. You could see the thin gold ring just above the filter.

"Look familiar?"

Charlie squinted at the cigarette. "I don't smoke, Chief. You know that."

"But you think. That's what I pay you for."

The edge in my voice seemed to wake him up a little.

"Lattimers'," he said. "It's like the cigarette we found at the Lattimers'."

"Exactly. Camel Lights. If the DNA matches, we're closing in on them."

"Thanks, Chief."

"Thanks?"

"For not riding me about that comment I made at the Lattimers' house. 'What are we supposed to do with that piece of information?' or something. Like it was nothing."

"—I said 'Remember it.' And you did."

I looked around the room, noted the packed suitcases, three Louis Vuitton bags lined up in the corner of the room

Charlie followed my gaze. "Looks like this guy was getting ready for a trip," he said. I nodded, walked to the closet and opened it. We both stared inside. It was empty.

"What the hell—?"

I smiled. "A little trip? I'd say he was making his getaway, Detective."

I returned to the bed. "That's a screwdriver in his chest. It looks like one of those four-way tools they sell at the Marine Home Center front counter. Two sizes of flat head and Phillips on either end of a shaft that fits into the handle."

"So?"

"So...for one thing this was a big strong guy because he only had one shot. It's in there deep and the screwdriver bit would have pulled loose coming out of the chest cavity. For another thing...Lomax owed a lot of people money, Charlie. Hundreds of people worked on this house. I've heard them talking: everyone's waiting for their last payment. And he's clearing out? Someone must have known he was splitting. Someone in the trades." I thought about Mike Henderson, eavesdropping after the party. If he had told even one person what he'd heard, the news would have spread across the island like a case of strep throat through an elementary school. "Problem is, it could have been anyone. Everybody has a screwdriver in their toolbox. And that makes everybody a suspect. We need a list—everyone who worked on this house. Masons, plumbers, electricians, drywall hangers, plasterers, floor finishers, painters, the people who install the granite countertops and the custom cabinetry, landscapers, the people from Intercity alarm, the people who put in the sound system, the decorators, the wallpaper hangers…and am I forgetting anyone?"

"The house cleaners?"

We stared at each other for a second.

"Sorry, Chief."

"No, you're right, Charlie. Thanks."

It was true. I was going to have to investigate Fiona Donovan. I was going to have to grill her about her whereabouts and her alibi and her motives. Either that or let the state police do it. But I wasn't alone. This crime and the waves of suspicion and animosity it generated were going to touch everyone on the island: all the friends and families of all the suspects and the victims and the police. The contamination would linger after everyone had moved on, like the faint tang of smoke damage in a newly painted house.

I stared down at the body, pulling a small jar of Vick's Vapo-Rub out of my jacket pocket. It was an essential tool for this kind of crime scene work. I unscrewed the cap, got a dollop on my finger and smoothed it under my nose. The sharp smell of menthol didn't do much to clear my sinuses, but it cut the smell from the corpse. Charlie was watching me. I gestured toward the young detective with the jar, and he grabbed it, slathered himself with the pungent goop. "Thanks, Chief."

"No trick, no trade." We studied the body for another few seconds. "Notice anything unusual about the money?" I said.

"You mean besides the fact that it's stuffed in his mouth?" I rubbed a palm over my forehead. "Besides that, yeah."

Charlie squinted down at Lomax. "Well, there's a lot of it."

"True. How about the denominations?"

"Nantucket sawbucks."

"Excuse me?"

"It's what the rich stingy Yankees around here call hundred dollar bills, Chief. I moved some furniture for one of these old ladies once. She pays me in cash. 'Take a Nantucket sawbuck,' she says. Like I was overcharging her, like the job was worth ten bucks anywhere else. Everyone's out to rip you off on Nantucket. That's the basic idea."

I studied the bulge of currency. "Nice way to get back at a cheapskate. There's probably close to a grand in there. Whoever did this wanted to make a statement. Twenties would have choked him just as well. No, they hated this guy."

"So you're saying—we should print the bills?"

"It's worth a try. Maybe they got careless."

We heard the front door open.

"That'll be Lonnie. Stay up here while I talk to him."

I left the room and trotted downstairs. Lonnie Fraker was standing in the foyer with two burly sergeants. The crew cuts and gun belts made them look like storm troopers. Lonnie himself was bulky and imposing, with a full head of black hair. It was too black; he probably colored it, not realizing that a little gray at the temples would add a note of wisdom and experience to his persona. He moved like had once been in good shape, but not recently, and he needed a new uniform. He bulged out of this one in all the wrong places. I thought irrationally of those chubby teenage girls wearing belly shirts and showing off their flab. Lonnie's face was wide and pointed. He didn't look quite real; more like a cartoon, some dark authority figure inked with a few clean lines in a Frank Miller graphic novel. He nodded at me.

"Chief Kennis. Glad you could be here."

The voice was startling. You expected a baritone rumble, but it was pitched much higher, with a Boston accent that flattened the vowels.

I nodded. "Captain."

He gave me a brisk salute." I see you've secured the scene. May I ask what you're doing with those red trash cans?"

"They're for police litter."

"The state police don't litter."

I met the steady gaze. "It's just a convenience."

"You can take them with you when you go."

"Fine. If the scene is compromised you'll know it wasn't us."

"Assuming your people actually used them."

"If that's an accusation, you should make it in writing."

"If I have to, I will."

Neither of us said a word for twenty seconds or so. It seemed like longer.

"All right," he said, finally. "The primary crime scene units will be getting here on the first plane. I'll need you to coordinate local police work so we don't step on each other's toes. For now, tape off the driveway and the front lawn. My men are taking casts of the foot prints and tire tracks down there."

I started to tell him I'd sent an officer back to the station for our own equipment, but just let the words out as a sigh. There was no way to get ahead of Lonnie on this one. I should have had the kit with me; he did. As he would have been delighted to point out. Anyway, he was still talking. "And you'll be doing the liaison work with the press. They'll be all over this story like black on beans. The networks, the cable channels, all the newspapers, NPR, you name it. Make 'em happy and keep 'em out of my hair."

"That's not my job. I have men canvassing the area right now, talking to the neighbors, running down names and checking the—"

"We'll handle all that."

"Not on my case."

"This isn't your case, Chief. Not anymore."

"It's my jurisdiction."

"Not for capital crimes. Listen, we appreciate your coopera-tion. You take care of the reporters and the lookie-loos, and work on the big bakeshop cookie heist. Leave murder to the professionals. That makes everybody look good." Lonnie's troops chuckled. The local cops were always good for a laugh.

I let out a long breath. "Lonnie, could we talk alone for a second?"

I walked to the big French doors at the other side of the room. They opened out onto the deck but there was almost a foot of untouched snow out there, luminous dark blue in the moonlight. The wind made the house shake. The storm door jittered in its frame.

"Hell of a winter," I said.

"I've seen worse. When I was a kid the harbor would freeze up for weeks at a time. That was wild."

"Yeah, well. I've still got that thin California blood. This is cold enough for me."

"You'll get used to it."

I turned to face him. "Let me tell you something the divorce lawyer told me when my marriage broke up. Miranda and I were arguing about custody. He said, two years from now you'll be fighting about who *doesn't* want the kids. 'I had them last weekend, you said you could take them for an extra week.' We were both offended. He said, 'This is your first divorce, right? Well, it's my four hundred and tenth.' Turned out he was right on the money."

"So what's the point?"

"Come on. It's the same thing here, Lonnie. I saw it in L.A. all the time when the FBI started big-footing an investigation. We can fence and mark our territory all we want, but this is a huge case. A week from now, you'll be wishing we had twice as many guys on the job and I'll be begging for more help, waiting for the forensics on the evidence I turned up—"

Lonnie raised his chin a little, glanced sideways at me with his thumbs tucked into his belt. "You found some evidence?

I had to give him credit—he had picked the one significant piece of information out of all that amiable chatter, as he might pluck a shell casing from a gravel driveway.

"Just this." I pulled the plastic evidence bag out of my pocket and handed it over. "We found a butt just like it at a robbery in 'Sconset last week. Camel Light, smoked down to the same point. I've been waiting for the DNA results. You guys could speed things up."

"Oh yeah, we could. Middle of the week at the latest. Anything stolen here?"

"A desk by the front door. Maybe some other stuff, too. The daughter can help with that."

Lonnie slipped the bag into his pocket. "Nice work. Thanks, Henry."

"Any time. Let's just catch these guys."

Lonnie shook his head, gazing out at the snow. "It doesn't seem like Nantucket, you know? Not the Nantucket where I grew up."

I shrugged. "Welcome to the real world."

"Easy for you to say, city boy. But if your real world keeps on coming, the big shots are gonna take off like rats in a DPW dump burn. And when that happens this place turns into a ghost town. That's why I want to turn these fuckers into a cautionary tale. Like an episode of *Cops*. 'These drunken joy-riders have learned a lesson tonight: they can run but they can't hide.' I like that guy on *Cops*. I like his attitude."

"Yeah, me too."

"No one gets away on *Cops*."

"Yeah."

We stood quietly contemplating a world of hapless scofflaws and relentless infallible peace officers. I broke the spell. "See you tomorrow, Lonnie. Get some sleep. You're going to need it."

We shook hands. I told my guys to stick around and be friendly and help. Then I walked out of the warm house into the night. The cold was dense and penetrating. It soaked through your clothes like ice water. Barnaby Toll was just pulling in to the driveway, stopped short at the yellow crime scene tape. I walked over, and he rolled down his window. "Oops," he said. "The job's getting done. That's what matters."

I opened the door, pulled the corrugated plastic equipment case from the seat and told Barnaby head back to the station. I stowed the equipment in the trunk of my Crown Vic: I was never going to get caught without it again. I climbed in behind the wheel chilled to the bone, but the heat came on fast and by the time I got back to Cliff Road the car was nice and toasty. That's part of the trifecta that make the big Fords perfect for police work: heat, A/C and acceleration. Our turbo charged models can go from zero to sixty in eight point seven seconds—I know because I tested them myself, drag-racing Haden Krakauer at midnight on Milestone Road. Hey, there has to be some fun in this job

I drove along now, just under the speed limit, thinking about Lonnie Fraker and *Cops*. Maybe this case would be like one of the TV chases he liked so much, the criminals overpowered and rounded up quickly. But I felt a superstitious dread in the pit of my stomach, where ulcers start. The longer this took, the worse it was going to get. And if it dragged on long enough, there wouldn't be anything left when it was over.

Chapter Three

Nantucket Nocturne

It all began two weeks before, on the night of December 2nd.

One more ordinary winter night on Nantucket, or so it seemed. Much later it would feel like the overture to a musical—a medley of tunes you scarcely noticed until you bought the cast album. Then you heard every theme and motif, every song played in advance. All the secrets and revelations, all the players and their plans were in the air that night, if I had known enough to listen. But of course I didn't. Only weeks later, after the last chord was played, would I realize how eerily prophetic the events of that night had been.

It started with a fight at a bar called the Chicken Box.

Normally the chief of police wouldn't get involved with some bar-fly altercation, but I was on the prowl, cruising the island, waiting for trouble. The town was empty at eleven o'clock. The wharf houses, standing on their pilings, marched out into the still, black water. There were only a handful of boats moored at this time of year. The tide was high. I slowed down to look at the little dory floating just beyond the sea wall. The Killen family put a Christmas tree in it every year. The lights strung in the branches seemed brave and sad to me. Bruce Killen had started the tradition, but his family had kept it up since his death.

Fiona had been obsessing about mortality lately, thinking about Bruce and all the others who had died young, mapping every new wrinkle on her own face. She was thirty-five. "That's middle-aged, Henry," she had told me sternly when I had foolishly insisted that she was still young. "There aren't many people that live past seventy."

I had just shrugged it off, but coming back to the island on the fast boat two days ago I had spent the whole trip staring at the ship's wake. The moving water had held a message. I realized what it was now and pulled the cruiser over in front of the Whaling Museum.

The poem came quickly:

Watching the foam
Churning white off the hull of the ferry,
Against the green dimpled water of the bay
Leaping wild, falling behind
Gone and replaced by the next.
A simple text
On the cycle of life:
You are going to die.
But on this day
For this moment, for now
You are glittering spray, flying upward
From the bow.

I'd give it to Fiona tomorrow.

I pulled back into the empty street. The radio crackled to life. Someone was starting a fight at the Chicken Box.

I hit the flashers but not the siren. It was late and I had always hated cops who abused their power that way, uselessly waking up half the town to demonstrate the importance and urgency of their mission, which was more often than not the need to buy a sandwich or go to the bathroom. The two cars I saw pulled over for me. I got to the Box in less than three minutes.

I stepped inside and absorbed the whole situation in a single flashbulb blink of perception: the two men struggling in front of the bar, the beautiful blond young woman with her shirt un-tucked, jacket half off her shoulders and an angry red welt on her neck. A crowd had formed around this tableau, isolating the players in a tight ring on the splintery wood floor. The bartender looked on, happy for a break in the monotony. Beyond the crowd, Ed Delavane was shooting pool, a schooner of beer on the polished wood lip of the table. He made a shot, ignoring the ruckus.

There was another schooner next to his. I had a split second to wonder who was drinking it as I moved into the big room. The bouncer was a burly bald guy refereeing a fight between the Lomax brothers, Danny and Eric. Living on trust funds, spoiled, smug and useless, they presented themselves as a classic cautionary tale about the toxic effects of unlimited money and privilege. Delusional yuppy puppies were common as seagulls in the summer but these boys were a year-round nuisance. They were going at it hard, Danny applying a brutal choke hold on his brother as I touched his shoulder.

"That's enough, Dan."

"Fuck you."

He released Eric, who reeled backward choking and gasping. Then he squared off against the new opponent. It took him a second to realize it was the chief of police.

"Shit," he said.

I lifted my hands in a pacifying gesture. "Don't make things worse with an assault charge against a police officer."

"Afraid to fight me, pig?"

He was obviously too drunk to care about my warning. He charged. I sidestepped, took his wrist and twisted his arm back into a simple hammer lock. Out of the corner of my eye, I noticed that I had caught Ed Delavane's attention. The big ex-Marine was watching the new turn in the action with a mean little smile. For people like Ed, it was all about who they could beat up and who they couldn't. Ed knew he could take the Lomax brothers, and the bouncer. I remained a question mark.

The girl on the barstool also looked amused by the proceedings. She had her shirt tucked in now, and her jacket back on. The bruise on her neck would be there for a while, though. I reached around, pulled Dan's other arm behind his back and cuffed him.

"Hey…come on, Chief!"

"You're under arrest, Dan. You have the right to remain silent. I suggest you use it." I turned to Eric. "You, too, son. Let's go." He followed us as we moved to the door. I turned back for a second, addressed the now restive crowd. "This is over. Drink responsibly."

I could only have meant that last comment ironically, but no one smiled. A young cop named Jesse Coleman came out of the bathroom, headed for the pool table, and corrected course toward the bar. He did it smoothly, but he wasn't even close to smooth enough.

I pushed Danny out into the bitter night, pulled Eric after us. The icy air sobered them up a little.

"Come on man, don't do this to me," Danny said.

"Dad'll be batshit," Eric added.

Too little, too late, I thought. I said, "I'm taking you in tonight for disorderly conduct. I'm sure your Dad will take care of it in the morning, Until then you can discuss your folly in jail. Maybe by morning you'll come up with some real solutions. I'd suggest AA and an anger management class. And try to avoid chasing the same women." I jammed them into the back seat of the cruiser. "I'll be right back. Fuck with my car in any way and I will personally kick both your asses and let Teddy take the credit."

I slammed the door and walked back inside. Jesse Coleman was at the bar, without his drink.

I crooked a finger at the bartender. "That kid was underage. I could close you down right now. Next time I will. Watch these people. Because I'm watching you."

"Sorry, Chief, you're right, I know, I should have, I will, I really will, thanks," he sputtered.

But I had already turned to the girl. Just looking at her, I knew why there'd been trouble. Girls like this were always trouble. Everything in her posture and her chilly smile seemed to say "I'm out of your league and we both know it."

She extended a hand. "Thanks, Chief. I'm Tanya Kriel. Good to meet you. You're a regular White Knight."

I took the strong dry hand and shook it once. "This can be a rough place, Tanya. You should be more careful."

"Don't worry. Danny was defending me from that terrible Eric." She smiled. "Or was it the other way around? It's so hard to keep track. Anyway I wasn't the victim, I was the prize. The the extra portion of pie a la mode. Everyone likes pie a la mode, right Chief?"

I glanced at her neck. "If you want to press charges you should come down to the station tomorrow."

She smiled as if we both knew that relying on the police was a joke. "I don't think so, Chief. But thanks anyway."

Finally I turned to Jesse, my voice sharp but quiet. I didn't want anyone to hear us over the music. Someone had cranked the jukebox and the Decembrists were blaring out of the speakers.

"You should have handled this."

"Hey, Chief, I was off-duty."

"You're never off-duty, Jesse. Figure that out or get another job."

I turned away, gave the bartender a last scary look, nodded at Tanya Kriel and walked back outside.

The Lomax boys didn't say a word on the way to the station. I handed them over to the watch officer and went back to my cruiser. I could organize the paperwork in the morning. I thought about going home. But I wasn't tired. I climbed into the warm car and continued on my rounds. I took Orange Street back, rolling past the sleeping hive of Marine Home Center, then down Washington Street into town. I turned up Main, bumping and undulating along the cobblestones toward the red brick Pacific National Bank building, I couldn't help smiling at the lines of small gaudy Christmas trees lit up on either side, decorated by school children.

There was something horrific about Christmas in Los Angeles, with the fake snow in the windows of Rodeo Drive stores air-conditioned against the eighty-degree heat. The season was boiled away to its mercenary bones, the grinning skeleton of commerce. Christmas was gentler here, or at least more picturesque.

The street seemed wider than usual since there were no cars slant-parked against the curbs. I noticed that Nathan Parrish, our local real estate mogul, was working late again. The light shone in his second floor office. Parrish had some big deal going on, but no one seemed to know what it was. He spent a lot of extra time in the office, though. I found it hard to believe that even the most elaborate piece of Nantucket business could require such long hours. I had slowed almost to a stop as Parrish's silhouette appeared in front of the shade. A second later another shadow joined him: a woman. They embraced and the shadows merged.

Well, that explained it.

I hit the gas and turned up Orange Street. Parrish was married, but the woman in the office was at least three inches taller than Carla. It shouldn't have shocked me. "Everyone will be dishonest," my assistant Chief Haden Krakauer had pointed out just this morning, adding, in a cruel mockery of earnest innocence, "You just have to give them a chance."

He had a way of turning platitudes inside out.

I drove out past the rotary and along Milestone Road toward 'Sconset. I was moving fast when I came up behind a Range Rover going sixty and weaving. I called it in, hit the flashers and pulled them over onto the grass between the road and the bike path.

A woman in her forties with a lot of red-tinted hair was driving, with a twenty-year old boy in the passenger side. They were both flushed. It looked like they'd been arguing. The fight had started in the middle of something else: the kid had lipstick smeared on his mouth, cheeks and neck, his fly was half-unzipped and several buttons were loose on the woman's blouse. There was no smell of alcohol or marijuana. The woman was lucid when she handed over her license and registration.

"This car is registered to Preston Lomax," I said, examining the registration with my flashlight. I glanced at the license. "You're his wife?"

"That's right. And this is Kevin Sloane. He's working on our house. He's a painter, he works for Mike Henderson. I'm just giving him a lift home."

I leaned in. "Working late?"

"Big deadline," Kevin deadpanned.

I addressed the woman. "I can see you're not drunk. But if you're stressed or upset—"

"I'm fine. We're fine," Mrs. Lomax said.

I took a breath. "I arrested your sons Eric and Daniel less than hour ago, charged with drunk and disorderly. I also have Danny for resisting arrest and assaulting a police officer. If the woman involved files charges, those boys could be looking at ten years for felony assault and sexual battery. I don't know what to tell you, Mrs. Lomax. There's a couple of twenty-somethings that still need your care and attention." I bent down to get a better look at Kevin Sloane. "And neither of them are this kid."

She studied the steering wheel. "I know that, Chief."

"All right. Take this boy home and get off the road. You have a big day tomorrow."

I walked back to my cruiser. I could feel the social claustrophobia of small town America—all the little scandals and drama rubbing up against each other. The real estate broker with his hanky-panky on Main Street, the troubled boys and their even more troubled mother, the bad marriages, the drinking and the bankruptcies, all over-lapping in piles like the clothes on a kid's floor. At least the city was anonymous. There was some separation between lives. No one knew what you were doing because no one cared.

I had met Preston Lomax the summer before, and watched on local TV when the tycoon was trying to get his house design approved by the Historical District Commission. Those hearings were often dull, but Lomax had brought them to the level of a cheesy reality TV show. They had initially refused his proposal. The structure was too tall, it had too many dormers, that kind of thing. Lomax said he was building it anyway and the town could sue him if they wanted to. "I have an entire law firm on retainer for the sole purpose of litigating small towns like this one into bankruptcy. I'm looking forward to it."

He had gotten his permits. The commissioners could see he wasn't kidding. And I had thought, when I read about it in the paper the next week, there were definite advantages to being crazy. You scared people and you got what you wanted. Of course Lomax was rich too, but that was probably how he got to be rich in the first place.

I watched his wife's car's taillights disappear around a bend, then climbed back into the cruiser and took Nobadeer Farm Road toward the airport, then back to the station by Old South Road—circuit complete.

The lights were on at the office of *The Nantucket Shoals,* and I decided to stop for a cup of coffee. The editor, David Trezize, always worked late. He seemed to put out the little newspaper single-handed, and he always had a pot of Jamaica Blue Mountain going. David covered police business in *The Shoals*. His writing was sharp-witted and he told the truth. His editorials were lucid, his tiny staff was dedicated but he could never seem to fill his ad pages and the paper was always on the brink of going under.

I found him lying on the floor under a desk, taking apart a hard-drive tower. "I can't fix this thing and I can't afford a new one. Time to fire someone I guess. What the hell, they're all useless anyway. I just made coffee. Grab yourself a cup."

I poured myself some and took a sip. Perfect as usual. "Congratulations on the prizes," I said. *The Shoals* had just won various awards from the New England Newspaper Association: best editorial content, best single editorial, best political coverage and a few others.

David shook his head. "Thanks anyway, but they don't mean much. My category is newspapers with circulation under five thousand. You can imagine what the competition at that level. It's not the Olympics, Chief. More like the Special Olympics."

I had to laugh. "Hey, it was still front page news in your paper last week."

David poured himself more coffee. "I'm shameless. What can I say?" He took a sip. "So you pulled Lomax over tonight."

"I ought to confiscate that scanner."

"It's legal, Chief."

"I know."

"So was it a DUI?"

"It was his wife. She was speeding." I put the mug down on a paper-strewn desk. "How did you know it was them? I never mentioned the name."

"You called in the license number."

I shook my head. "You're obsessed."

"And you arrested the two boys tonight, also. I heard you telling Barnaby Toll to get a pair of cells ready. Quite an evening for the Lomax clan."

"It's pathetic. All the money in the world ..."

"Money is like gout—or syphilis. The eating and the sex are fun, but too much of them make you sick and the disease is fatal if it goes untreated." He took another swallow. "Kathleen's all right though. The daughter? At least so far. She worked for me summers when she was at college. That's how her dad found out about Nantucket in the first place. Yeah. I guess it's my fault. She's a hard worker, smart and funny. She was cleaning up the mess around here one night—paper plates and takeout coffee cups and frozen burritos. She said, 'I don't want to come to work tomorrow in the middle of yesterday.' That stuck with me. I guess there's one kid in every fucked up family who turns out okay. Though with Preston Lomax for your father...I don't know. It seems like a miracle."

"You have to ease up on that guy, David. Seriously."

"Actually, no. It's just the opposite, Chief. I should be much tougher on him. Your problem is, you deal with stupid people and violent people and greedy people all the time and so that's all you ever look for. You don't expect to see evil and you don't recognize it when it's right in front of you. That's how Hitler came to power. No one could quite believe it."

"So Lomax is Hitler?"

"Give him an army and a political agenda and yeah. But all he cares about is money. Smart guys know taking over the world is more than trouble than it's worth. A leveraged buy-out is so much easier."

"Well, until he commits an actual crime, you'll have to settle for the occasional speeding ticket."

"Fully prosecute all minor infractions. Sounds like a philosophy of life."

"Well, until I can single-handedly correct the moral balance of the universe, it'll have to do."

He shrugged. "Fair enough."

We finished our coffee and I left. Driving home, I saw a car with its lights out. I flashed my high beams at them and their headlights came on. It reminded me of a trick the street gangs were playing for a while in Los Angeles, just before I left the city. They would drive dark, and if some helpful person flashed their lights, they'd shoot him.

It was good to be away from that madness, the constant expectation of random violence like a cut high tension wire, snaking along the street, vomiting sparks. I was finally starting to relax. When I got home I paused for a moment on the doorstep, listening to the breathing silence of the tiny island, thirty miles out at sea.

The overture was over.

The show was about to start.

Chapter Four
Poor Relations

Nathan Parrish was rich and he looked it. He was smart and he knew it. He was smug and he didn't care. He enjoyed annoying people. At the moment he was annoying his wife, who was sitting as far to the other side of the front seat as she possibly could. She had been lovely once, but after four kids she was starting to let her looks go. Nathan loved to needle her and she invariably provided him with opportunities. Today she seemed to be lobbing them his way.

"I think Sally Trusdale looks fabulous these days," she offered, as they turned off the Milestone Road onto a dirt track that twisted through dense brush toward the center of the island. "She's lost so much weight."

Nathan laughed. "You kill me, you really do. Women. You all rag on the beauties. You know: Kate Moss is too thin, Cristy Turlington is so *gangly,* Cindy Crawford is losing her looks—"

"Well, she is."

"Right. And she could lose more looks than most women ever had and still have plenty to spare. And both of us know it. But you talk about someone like Sally Trusdale who could have financed a Third World country with what she's spent on fad diets and plastic surgery, and she still looks like a pig eating pizza, and you say, 'Ohhh, she's looking so *good* these days.' And I've finally figured out why."

"I can't wait to hear."

"You don't like the setup. You hate the fact that the beautiful ones get it all and the dogs get dog food. You try to even it up with comments like that bullshit about Sally. As if your opinion could make everything more democratic and fair. So just stuff a sock in it, Honey. Because it doesn't work, all right? No matter what you say and how nice you are, ugly is ugly and doesn't make it. Gorgeous is gorgeous and everyone knows." He stamped on the brakes. "We're here."

Nathan climbed out into the frigid air. Carla stayed inside. He pulled the map out of his pocket, along with the antique deed and the Indian quitclaim, as he climbed to the top of the rise. He could see the car below him, its exhaust snapped away by the wind. He could see the ocean on all sides and the spires of town in the distance. The map rattled in the gusty wind. Just there, about fifty yards away southwest, that would be one border. No bogs, no wetlands, no problems. Just forty sweet acres of prime Nantucket real estate. Right now it was conservation land, purchased through the Land Bank. But he had the documents to prove that the old geezer who sold it to the conservation foundation hadn't really owned it. The title had been clouded even then, but old man Bradford was threatening to sell it to someone else, so everyone had moved fast and hoped no one would look too closely into the history of the parcel.

Unfortunately for them, that was what Nathan Parrish did for a living. He poked into things and he looked very closely at what he found. In this case he had found the last living relative of the original Indian owners, and documented the connections. Then he offered the man a hundred thousand dollars. The day before, the poor bastard hadn't even known he owned property. The guy had been contemplating bankruptcy. So he had taken the hundred thousand in cash and left Nathan with his notarized quitclaim and a deed that five lawyers had assured him would stand up to any attack in the Boston land court. It had taken two years and about ten times what he had paid for the actual property in time spent and legal fees and deals he had turned down to do it. But so what? He owned a piece of the rock. Forty acres of it, to be exact.

And he was going to bring a much-needed taste of the mainland here. As soon as jcpenney and K-Mart signed their leases he would be ready to start construction on his greatest project ever—the Moorlands Mall. Thirty great stores under one roof, with two acres of free parking. The idea of paving over all these deer-tick infested brambles and stunted pine trees made his heart light. They ought to pave this whole island. Why not? After all, Manhattan was just dirt and bushes once, too.

He knew what his sister would say. He was "raping the island."

Well, maybe that was the approach to use with the HDC and the Board of Selectmen, once he had them under his thumb completely, give them the advice they used to give women about actual rape. When it becomes inevitable, just lie back and enjoy it.

He barked a laugh into the wind. He couldn't wait to see their overstuffed, pink proper New England faces when he told them that! He was still laughing about it when he got back to the car. Carla asked why he was laughing and he told her, but she didn't think it was funny.

Typical woman, he thought. No sense of humor at all.

At that moment Nathan's sister, Cindy Henderson, was sitting behind the counter of the Adnan Mevlana boutique on Centre Street, listening to rich women in fur coats who complained about the prices, thinking all the time, *I hate my life, I hate my life, I hate my life*. It was a chant, a mantra, the focus of her meditation as she studied her mistakes.

Coming to Nantucket was the primary one. She had been a fool to imagine that her day-to-day life as an adult would relate in any way to the idyllic haven where she had spent her summers as a child. Her parents had been rich, so she had been rich. She had taken it for granted. But the big house on Cliff Road had been sold long ago. Her parents vacationed in Mexico now. And Cindy was in a different world. Her husband, Mike, liked to imagine they were middle-class, but it was hard to maintain that notion when the official poverty line income on the island was forty-two thousand dollars, and a painting contractor barely survived from customer to customer, never knowing where the next job was coming from.

They would have lost their house months ago if not for the Lomax job. She stepped away from the counter to straighten some sweaters left in disarray by the last group of ladies. She was sick of thinking about Mr. Lomax, sick of thinking about Mike's work, sick of her customers, sick of her job, sick of the wet cold weather and the northeast wind. Most of all, she was sick of thinking about what she had discovered this morning.

She felt as if there was no one on Earth she could bear to see right now—any human contact would chafe against her like wool on a rash.

Then Police Chief Henry Kennis walked in.

Chief Kennis was tall and good looking, too good looking for his small town job. He still wore some residue of his years in California on his face. It was attractively weather-beaten, as if he had done a lot of smiling into the desert wind. He had never adjusted to his height; he moved with the lingering awkwardness of an adolescent. Cindy could easily imagine every woman in life, from his mother to his ex-wife Miranda, constantly badgering him to stand up straight. But Cindy found his slouch endearing. She was glad to see him, even today.

"Hi, Cindy," he said. "Feeling all right?"

"Now I am. How are the kids?"

"Well, it's Christmas, so they're happy. They've finally figured out that I'm Santa. We're done with all that 'Hey, you use the same wrapping paper as Santa Claus' stuff. They busted me last year and now the pressure's off."

"Bruno Bettelheim says it's a huge part of growing up—solving that mystery."

"Yeah? Well, they're growing up fast, then."

"They take after their dad."

"There aren't too many mysteries to solve around here, Cindy. That's what I like about it."

Henry was a small town cop, a single dad, and an unpublished poet. It seemed like a bleak existence to Cindy, but the chief was happy. One day the winter before, when the flu had decimated the police force, Henry was directing traffic around some road construction. She was first in line as the traffic cleared in the other direction, fretting about her bills and a new cold sore on her lip. Henry was standing in the windy sleet, whistling a Scott Joplin piano rag. She had rolled down her window and called out to him, "My dad says people who whistle just got money."

"Not me."

"Why are you so happy, then?"

"Look up. Check out the sky," he said.

"The sky makes you happy?"

"Have you looked at it?"

"I don't understand."

"The sky, Cindy. It's right up there—you can't miss it."

So she had craned her neck out the car window, and stared up into a dramatic panorama of storm clouds rimmed with sun and pierced by great shafts of light in the east and those same clouds, torn to rags by the wind and revealing the blue sky behind them, in the west.

She realized that she never actually looked at the sky in the course of a normal day, not this way. She'd check for rain clouds if she were heading to the beach. But that was all.

"It's like…art," she said.

"And it's free. Grab a peek while you can. It'll be different in an hour."

"But…what about gray days? Or when it's just plain blue?"

There was a note of disappointment in the chief's voice: "It's never just plain blue, Cindy."

Then it was her turn to drive and he waved her through.

She had looked at the sky a lot since then, but she still didn't understand.

"I think I'd like some furry slippers for Fiona to wear around the house in the mornings," Chief Kennis was saying now. "She's always in her sock feet and those floors are cold."

Two more women came into the store while she was rummaging for the slippers. This was the busy season, but the Mevlana people would never let her hire an assistant. She glanced up at the new arrivals. "Hello," she said.

The taller one, with the knee length steel-gray down parka, the fake blonde hair, and the tight expensive face that must have been a cruel mockery of her original features, just stared at Cindy.

"Don't you mean—'Can I help you?'"

Cindy controlled the urge to slap the woman. "No, actually. You're on your own."

She bagged the slippers. Henry paid for them and left. The women started grazing through the bins of sweaters and the racks of dresses.

The chief was a comforting presence, but she always felt inadequate around him. There was some central current of life and he was drifting along with it. Cindy couldn't find it with infrared satellite photography and a navigational chart. He was content, but she needed things, the things she'd given up when she came here—her music, her painting, her master's thesis—all the things she didn't have the time or the energy for now. She had occasionally consoled herself thinking it can't get any worse, but things could always get worse. As her dad used to say, "You can't win them all. But you actually can lose them all."

◇◇◇

This morning's news had confirmed that. She had taken the test twice, two days in a row, first thing in the morning, according to the instructions. She had seen the double blue line both times. There was no doubt anymore. Between the condoms, the birth control pills, the IUD, and the spermicidal creams, it should have been physically impossible. But after years of discarded scratch tickets and losing lottery numbers, she and Mike had finally beat the odds.

"I'm pregnant," she said to herself for the twentieth time that day.

And then she started crying in front of two ladies from Short Hills with matching mink coats and American Express Gold Cards.

Chapter Five
Cop Shop Morning

It was a quiet autumn on Nantucket. The show was closed for the season and the audience had gone home. You could park downtown and the long lines of cars piling up at every stop sign had vanished like the beer cans on the beaches. The parties were finished for the winter along with the traffic jams. The Christmas trees were lined up along Main Street, and the Stroll had been a surprising success. The Chamber of Commerce was happy. House sales were up. Late autumn had always been the slow time on the island, with nothing on the docket but DUIs, domestic interventions, and disturbing the peace calls. We gave out warnings and calmed people down. The jail cells were empty and the court was taking Fridays off. The long weekends felt good. We were all grateful for the yearly respite. None of us expected it to end so soon.

Then one bright cold Monday in December, I found a critical piece of evidence in a real crime, which turned out to be one part of a much bigger investigation. All of a sudden, I was a cop again and I had to admit it felt good.

I spent the first part of the morning reviewing the night watch log. A loud party, some black ice fender-benders. The highlight was a carpenter pulled over for erratic driving twenty miles over the posted limit on the Milestone Road in an uninspected, unregistered F-150. He had an open bottle of peppermint schnapps wedged between his thighs, and a baggie full of marijuana in the glove compartment next to an illegal gun. He fled when Rory Burke hit the flashers and then took a swing at him when the kid tried to give him the Breathalyzer. Apparently the guy hadn't registered his car because he had twenty-five hundred dollars' worth of outstanding parking tickets. His license had been suspended for multiple DUIs.

I shook my head, amused in spite of myself. The only way this could be worse was if the guy had a dead body in the truck bed. And it turned out he did, in a way: a doe, shot out of season, bleeding out on a plastic tarp.

I shoved the log aside. I had noticed the guy in one of the holding cells this morning. Joe something; he'd been involved in a bar fight a few weeks before. The stale alcohol billowed off him like the reek of fertilizer from a ploughed field. I felt bad; the guy was in serious trouble. But there was nothing anyone could do to help. I shrugged. Maybe hitting rock bottom would do the trick, and this arrest would certainly drop him a little closer. I hadn't stopped smoking until I found myself coughing blood into a Kleenex.

The intercom buzzed. I picked it up.

"You got time to run out to 'Sconset? Donnelly and Boyce are out at the—hold on a second—the Lattimer house? On Main Street, I have the address. There was a burglary, no one knows when. The owners just showed up for the month like they always do and the stuff was gone. The guys didn't find much. The Lattimers are old Nantucket and they're not happy right now. They want to talk to you, nobody else."

I blew out a breath. What the hell—I had nothing else to do. "I'll swing by. Have Donnelly and Boyce stay there."

The Lattimer house was set back from the road behind a tall hedge, looming bulky and forbidding through the dense swirl of snow. It had been a whaling captain's mansion a hundred and fifty years ago. Four generations of crusty, ill-tempered Yankees had stubbornly refused to make the usual improvements. The place hadn't even been painted in more than a decade. There were no shiny new appliances, no ostentatious additions with white bookshelves full of framed family photographs and Steuben glass. The cramped rooms and dark narrow corridors remained intact. No walls had been knocked down. No steel I-beams had been installed to prevent the old pile from sagging on its foundation. It had been sagging since before the Civil War. It was a sharp uphill walk from the pantry to the stove in the kitchen.

I met Kyle Donnelly at the front door and followed him through the house, edging past the dark shelves full of bestsellers from the sixties (Bel Kaufman, Allen Drury, Louis Auchincloss) and dusty volumes of Nantucket history. Nicotine stained Cahoon mermaids and Jacobson ferry paintings crowded the lumpy plaster walls.

The Lattimers stood at the top of the kitchen, sipping tea and talking to Charlie Boyce. David Lattimer stood six-foot-three, with gangly disjointed arms and big hands, his posture bent slightly after a lifetime of stooping under doorway lintels. His eyes were deep set under bushy gray brows and his wide mouth curved up naturally as if he were perpetually amused by the follies of the people around him. He wore brown wide wale corduroy slacks and a J. Press Shetland pullover sweater. Philippa was almost as tall—six-foot-one maybe. She wore old blue jeans and a heather cable knit cardigan; no makeup, no jewelry. Thick gray hair fell to the line of her jaw, which was softening slightly without plastic surgery. She must have been a world-class beauty when she was young. Even in her late sixties she was striking. She and her husband were like emissaries from a race of giants. I felt small and poverty-stricken next to them, as if they were volunteering at a soup kitchen, ladling out my Christmas dinner.

"Thank you so much for coming," said Philippa. "Would you like some tea?"

"No thank you. If you could show me the room where the theft took place?"

David cleared his throat. "I was just telling this young man here, Detective Boyce? That these thieves were idiots. They took a Centennial Windsor chair. Those were made a century after the period. They're just Colonial Revival pieces, really. And they left a comb-back Windsor in the study with the original paint that's easily a hundred times more valuable. They take an Empire dresser…the shiny mahogany must have impressed them. And they leave a Queen Anne chest. Not that I'm complaining. It's just typical of the new people here."

"David…" Philippa began.

"No, I mean it, Darling. Even the thieves are ignorant and sloppy. And demanding. I'm sure they'll be very annoyed with us for not labeling the more valuable pieces! I'm so tired of these people and their demands. Everyone has to have a fancy truck and a little tract house. It's appalling. Anyone who can pick up a hammer thinks they deserve a home on Nantucket. And if they have to steal to pay for it, fine!"

"Do you know we never even locked our house," Philippa said, getting into the spirit of the conversation. "For years. All while the children were growing up. We never even had a key. I could leave my basket on the car seat downtown without a second thought. I'd never do that now."

David laughed. "You give them too much credit. We have Reyes lightship baskets all over this house. I'm sure they looked right at them and had absolutely no idea what they were seeing."

"If I could just take a look around," I began again.

"Of course," Philippa said. "I'm so sorry. Of course you're busy. Things were taken from the dining room and from David's study. Here, I'll show you."

Donnelly and Boyce had already been over the place. They were competent detectives. I didn't expect to find anything useful. I was there more for public relations than police work. I followed Philippa into David's study. David himself was just behind us. "I remember Chief McGrady," he was saying. "It was different Nantucket in those days. Bunny ran his Jeepster into a lighting pole right on Main Street one night, drunk as a hoot owl. He tottered down to the station to report it. McGrady was working late. He said, "You're a Lattimer, aren't you? Just go on home and let me take care of this." That was how things were in the old days. Chief McGrady would no more have arrested a Lattimer than sprouted wings and flown away."

"An extraordinary man," Philippa said.

"Big shoes to fill," I agreed.

They all hovered in the doorway for a moment.

"Well, we'll let you get to it," David said.

I walked into the cramped, book-lined study and turned on the desk light. There were two neat stacks of papers and an old IBM Selectric typewriter. A jar of pencils that needed sharpening, an ashtray that needed cleaning.

"Nothing to see, Chief," Donnelly said. "We dusted. No prints. So they were smart enough to wear gloves, at least. There's no sign of a break-in. Mr. Lattimer says they've been locking the place up for the last few years, but who knows? They don't have an alarm system. No neighbors around except at Thanksgiving. Could have happened any time since Labor Day."

Something caught my eye. I kneeled down next to desk. It was a cigarette butt, burned almost down to the filter. Two small amber cones were visible: the top of some insignia printed on the paper. I recognized it instantly: a Camel. I picked it up with a pair of tweezers from my coat pocket and held it up to the two detectives. They weren't impressed.

"We saw it, Chief," Boyce said.

"Mr. Lattimer smokes Camels," Donnelly added.

"But he doesn't usually leave them on the floor. Look at the ashtray on his desk."

There were two butts stumped out in the square cut-crystal.

"So he dropped one and forgot about it. He's old. Lucky the house didn't burn down."

I nodded. "Sure. Makes sense. But look at the cigarette. Check it out." I extended the tweezers under the desk lamp. The two detectives made a show of looking it over.

"Nothing?"

"Not that I can see," said Donnelly.

Boyce just shrugged.

I smiled. "I have the advantage here. This used to be my brand. See the little gold band just above the filter? Camel Lights."

"So?"

"So Lattimer smokes regulars." I plucked a butt from the ashtray. "See? No gold band. These guys were dumb enough to leave a cigarette butt here. And now we know what brand they smoke."

"Yeah but…I mean, what do we do with that piece of information, Chief?"

"Remember it."

I set the cigarette down on the floor again. "Bag this. Finish up with the Lattimers. And get me the paperwork by this afternoon."

I checked the dining room, but didn't see anything useful. I looked into the kitchen one more time on the way out.

"Mr. Lattimer?"

David and Philippa were sitting at the round table by the window, finishing their tea. David looked up.

"Who's your caretaker out here? I'd like to talk to him."

"Pat Folger. But he's not posted on guard duty. He saved the pipes from freezing twice last winter. That's what we pay him for."

"Of course. I'm not blaming him for this. But I'd like to get his thoughts."

"I'll tell you his thoughts! We should get electronic locks and surveillance cameras and alarm systems tied into the state police headquarters. We should barricade ourselves in here and live like fugitives! Those are his thoughts. But I won't do it. That's not the Nantucket I love. If it comes to that I'll sell this house and move away and never look back. I'll live in the city and enjoy my memories."

I had nothing to add. "Thanks for your time, Mr. Lattimer, Mrs. Lattimer. I'll keep you informed on the progress of the investigation."

I took the long Polpis Road loop back to town, through 'Sconset and then out past Sankaty Light, through the old golf course and then skirting Sesacecha Pond, which was now open to the ocean again. It was the tourists' route, with the cranberry bogs and the moors opening up on my left and the glimpses of Polpis Harbor past the big houses on the right. It took longer than Milestone Road and the sharp curves meant you had to pay attention to your driving. But I was in no rush and the big Ford took the turns with easy precision.

I was headed around the rotary when I got the call.

It was one of my best patrol officers, Sam Dixon, on the line. Chief Selectman Dan Taylor's kid, Mason, had barricaded himself inside his room with one of his father's guns, and he was threatening to commit suicide. At least he hadn't done it yet.

The big problem was Dan Taylor himself. That was why Sam called me. Dan had run the Board of Selectmen since long before I arrived on the island and he acted like he was the mayor and Nantucket was Chicago and the year was 1893. Well, with the island caught up in the new Gilded Age, at least that part made sense. In addition to authorizing new stop signs and illegal parking zones, Dan spent most of his time ingratiating himself with people like Preston Lomax. Dan did caretaking for half of them and he was working on the rest. Like most professional suck-ups, Dan turned into an insufferable bully with anyone ranking lower in the social pecking order. That included most of my officers, the other town employees, and his own son. I had always pitied Mason, being raised by that petty tyrant.

But it turned out the suicide standoff had nothing to do with Dan.

Mason Taylor was killing himself over a girl.

It wasn't so strange; I'd researched the phenomenon after a couple of teen suicides the winter I first got to Nantucket. The synapse in the brain that helps us understand our own mortality is still under construction with teenagers. They don't get it that impressing the girl you love with the seriousness of your passion by killing yourself ultimately won't do you much good, since you'll be dead afterward.

The Taylors lived in Nashaquisset, a subdivision off Surfside Road, walking distance from the high school.

On the second floor, Dan was trying to break down Mason's door. I took the stairs two at a time, bounded half the length of the hall and caught Dan's shoulder just as he started another charge. Randy Ray stood by, haplessly looking on, side by side with Sam Dixon, who should have known better. He'd been smart enough to call me, but "call the chief" shouldn't be the default response to a crisis. What if there were two crises going on at once?

I took the Head Selectman off balance and spun him around. He staggered a few steps as he turned to face me.

"Stay out of this, Chief," he snarled. "This is none of your goddamn business."

I watched him, waiting for a movement. "Your boy has a loaded firearm in that room, Dan. That makes it my business."

"The hell it does."

"Step away. Let us handle this."

I put my hand on his shoulder. He shrugged it off

"I'm going to have to ask you to vacate the premises," I hoped the official-sounding jargon would calm him down. Nice try. He launched himself at me, throwing a big sloppy roundhouse punch at my head. I stepped outside of it and gathered his arms together from behind in a tight bear hug.

"Stop it," I said. "Don't make this worse than it is."

He relaxed a little and I let him go. Then he was charging the door again. I tackled him at the waist and we both went down on the hardwood floor, as my two officers stumbled back to stay out of our way.

I landed on top. Dan's breath exploded out of him. I yanked his arms behind his back, cuffed him, pushed myself up, stepped away and turned to Sam. "Get him out of here. Take him to the station. Lock him up but don't book him."

I helped Dan to his feet. "I have you right now for felony battery, assaulting a police officer, and resisting arrest, Dan. But I understand the extenuating circumstances. I feel bad for you, okay? This sucks. So shut up and behave and you'll be back on the street, no charges filed by this afternoon. Sound fair?"

He nodded, sullen but defeated.

I jerked my thumb over my shoulder and the boys got the message. They hustled Dan downstairs and out of the house. I was alone with Mason Taylor.

I knocked on the door. "Mason?"

"Go away!" The voice was high-pitched, muffled through the door, clotted with tears.

"It's Chief Kennis, Mason. Remember me? You stood up during the Q&A at my drug lecture last year and said, 'When I say no, the drugs think I'm playing hard to get.' You made me laugh."

"I got in trouble."

"Well, yeah. Smart-mouthing the chief of police in front of the whole school. But I remembered it."

"I got suspended."

I played a hunch. "Did you impress the girl, though?"

"How do you know about Alana?"

So: Alana Trikilis, daughter of a local garbage man. Sam Trikilis was a good guy, one of the few authentically happy people I had ever met. He enjoyed his customers and the drive to the dump and even the dump itself. The trash pile was his archaeological dig site.

I had seen his daughter's drawings in *Veritas*, the NHS student paper. The most recent one, which showed the members of the Conservation Commission and the town Selectmen dressed as clowns, clambering out of a tiny circus car, featured an especially cruel and accurate caricature of Mason's dad. Alana probably got in a fair amount of trouble herself. Maybe she and Mason were kindred spirits.

"Hey," I said. "I read *Veritas* for Alana's cartoons. She's brilliant." Silence from the other side of the door. "Mason?"

"She doesn't even know who I am. But now she will."

"What? She'll come to your funeral?"

"She'll be crying at my funeral. Then she'll realize. Then she'll know."

I took a breath. "There has to be a better way."

Another silence. I waited, heard the front door open and close; footsteps on the stairs. Haden Krakauer appeared in the hallway. I put a finger to my lips. Haden crept forward, cocked his head in a question. I shrugged. Not much progress yet—the kid was still in there and he still had the gun.

"I wrote her a poem," the kid said. "She likes poetry. Yeats and Eliot and Billy Collins." I smiled. The ex-poet laureate would be flattered to be placed in that company.

"Was your poem any good?"

"It sucked. I couldn't even finish it."

"So you don't know what Alana would have thought about it."

"She would have hated it,"

"Not if it was any good."

"Whatever."

That might be the worst possible word to hear from a suicidal kid—the essence of giving up, in three descending syllables.

"I write poetry," I said. "We could work on yours together."

"I don't think so."

"Give it a try. Girls love a good poem, written just for them. It could turn things around."

"I don't know."

He was wavering. "Put the gun down. Pick up a pen. Actually, that's a pretty good philosophy of life."

"Is that what you do?"

"It's what I'm doing right now. Come on, let's see what you've got."

"It's bad."

"That's why we're working on it. Writing is re-writing." Another silence. "Mason? You still with me in there?"

"Okay I have it. But—it's just…I can't—the idea is I don't know what to say, or that, I don't know…I want words to do more, you know? More than they really can. Like if I had the right words…like a spell, like Harry Potter or something."

"That's good, that's a start. Like what?"

"I don't know—massage her neck or put cold towels on her eyes? She gets really bad headaches."

"There you go—that's a beginning. Start a list. It can be a list poem. Use all the senses. What do you want—words to make her taste? Just wing it, whatever comes to mind."

"Raspberries? And chocolate? The first sip of coffee in the morning."

"That's great! The first sip of coffee. That's definitely the best one. How about smell? What do you want words to make her smell?"

He was getting into it now. "Old books? Cut grass? Roses? Not the ones you buy in the store, they don't even have any smell. I mean the ones that grow here in the summer. Real roses."

"Fantastic, that's a cool distinction. And it's kind of a metaphor, too—she's the real thing. The Nantucket rose."

Another long silence. "This won't work. Words can't do anything and this stupid poem won't do anything either. It's just a stupid waste of time."

I could feel him reaching for the gun.

"But that's the whole point," I blurted. "That's what the poem's about and that's your ending, that's how you wrap it up." I was already writing it in my head. "I'll tell you what. I have an idea for the last quatrain. If you like it you can have it, you can write up to it, and know you have a strong finish. What do you say?"

"What is it?"

"Okay …. Something like—this is tragic, this is why I rant. I want words to do magic. And they can't."

A pause. Haden stared at me. I knew he wanted to break down the door, just like Dan did.

Then, from Mason: "That's pretty good, Chief."

I let out a breath. "Then use it, go for it, write the hell out of it. It sure beats a suicide note. Can you do that?"

"I think so."

"Then let us in and give me the gun. You've got a lot of work to do."

Walking away from the house a few minutes later, Haden said, "Nice work, Cyrano. You're going to be ghostwriting poems for that kid forever."

"I think he'll do okay on his own. The first sip of coffee? That was a nice line."

We paused at my cruiser. Randy and Sam Dixon had cleared off the lookie-lous. "Who'd ever think a cop could use poetry on the job," Haden said.

"It's happened before. Back in L.A we had some gangbanger in a hostage situation in Compton. I knew the kid, I knew he was a rap battler. So I got into a rap battle with him."

"Come on."

"I'm serious."

"Okay, Eminem, what did you say to him?"

"I don't exactly remember…a lot of black-white trash talk."

Haden grinned. "I have to hear this. Come on, you must remember a little of it."

"Well…let's see—the last part went, 'Yeah I'm cool, I went to high school, and I graduated, fool, that's why I rule your black ass now, check it out how, Mr. Fish Belly, Mr. Ofay, Mr. Pig, and you're the jig, bingo nigger I know the lingo, too, and I'm bigger than you, I'm not frontin while you hunting for a word, drop back and punt runt, them drugs is stunting your ass, you flunk this class you been tested and bested now your ass is arrested.' Something like that."

Haden was laughing.

"Hey, it worked. Like my old captain used to say: bullshit baffles brains. The kid was working on his response, you know? Figuring out what he was going to say against me. And before he knew what was happening someone had a gun at his temple and they were taking the nine out of his hands. On the way out he said. "I would have whipped your ass you wigger motherfucker." Wigger—that's a white boy trying to be black. Hey, whatever works."

Haden patted my shoulder. "No wonder you were a legend in the department."

"Yeah, right—a legendary fuck up. But not that day."

We got into our separate cars and drove back to the cop shop. I was hoping Mason would get the girl, and thinking about poetry in general. Of course, I hardly ever used it directly in my police work, but the type of thinking poetry requires, that willingness to follow an idea when you don't get where it's going, or trust a connection that occurs to you out of nowhere, that odd giddy sense of being not quite in control of your own thoughts, had always been essential for me when I confronted the aftermath of unexplained violence or the mystery of a crime scene. Haden would demand examples and I couldn't think of any offhand. It didn't matter, though. The most sensational murder in Nantucket's history was about to make my case for me—if I could find some way to solve it.

Chapter Six
Tanya Kriel

Tanya Kriel hated Nantucket. She had sworn never to come back, but here she was, struggling through another winter on the rock. Well, at least she had a good reason, the best possible reason: revenge.

She wasn't one of those people with an "It used to be nice on Nantucket" bumper sticker. It was easy to imagine Nantucket with fewer SUVs, more open land, no ugly trophy houses, all of that. It was easy to imagine it with no electricity, too, but so what? It was probably worse in the old days, before the Irish and the Jamaicans and the eastern Europeans arrived: all white bread old money wasps, adding up their stock portfolios and drinking martinis in those hideous pink pants. The island had obviously been a haven for rich people at least since the twenties. They might have changed, but they didn't change much. Tanya actually preferred the ostentatious new millionaires. She found the moneyed biddies who insisted on driving rusty Hondas and getting their clothes at the dump even more pretentious, more insidiously smug, than the red-cheeked dot com scavengers in their Humvees.

Her own '92 Ford Ranger had a homemade bumper sticker. It said:

Consider Privilege.

Checking her rearview mirror, she was pleased to note that it made the occasional tiny woman in a massive gas-guzzling truck suitable for industrial towing or wartime troop transport, wince uncomfortably. Maybe she was making them think, but probably not.

She was happy to make them nervous for a few seconds. She picked her battles carefully.

She had returned to the island with a mission and it was easier to concentrate on that mission in the winter. Apart from a brief flurry of conspicuous consumption in December, the place was fairly quiet from November to May: just the slaves driving from the barracks to the job-sites, making everything perfect for the perfectionist housewives who had nothing to do but redecorate. She knew the word "slaves" was highly charged. She had gotten into arguments about it. Plasterers and housepainters had gotten furious with her at the Box or the Muse when she described them that way. They felt free. She understood that, but it was an illusion. They made just enough money to pay for the necessities of their lives. It was a lot of money, but Nantucket's economy was precisely calibrated to leave them with nothing at the end of the month. No health insurance, no savings, no prospects—just a rented room, a leased truck, and an ever-increasing debt load.

Tanya didn't have any debt. She didn't have any credit cards. She didn't have a credit rating. She owned her battered old pickup outright, stayed with friends or took house-sitting jobs and tried her best to stay under the government radar. She had never been arrested or fingerprinted. She didn't own a computer, and had never been on the Internet. No "cookies" defined her tastes and predilections for the benefit of large corporations. She paid cash at Stop & Shop; she didn't have a Stop & Shop card. She wasn't on their database. People thought she was paranoid. That was fine with her.

She was standing in front of a wooden stepladder, not painting the window sash set up on two nails driven into the ladder's legs to make a crude easel. Her mind was wandering. Slaves. Yes, she had re-entered the slave economy, but there was no other way to do what needed to be done. She needed access, and housepainters got it. They were supposed to be inside people's houses when no one was home; trespassing was part of their job description.

So she had driven by the Lomax job site on Eel Point road last June, hoping to find out who the painting contractor was. It had all happened faster than she expected. She'd met Mike Henderson that afternoon and he had hired her on the spot. He was short-handed and she was experienced. He was attractive and she was beautiful—that had something to do with it. The difference between them was, she knew the effect her looks had on people, and he had no idea about his own. She could tell he saw himself as an awkward lug in need of a shower, with a big head and a small bald spot, shy despite his size, hen-pecked and stinking of thinner. But she loved his looks instantly. She loved the lack of vanity in his disarrayed hair and paint-spattered Nantucket Whalers sweatshirt. She loved the natural authority with which he ran his crew, showing a new kid how to smooth the paint with the flat of the brush, doing it gently, saying "Here's a little trick—it'll make your life easier," helping another kid who had spilled some paint onto a drop cloth on the new deck. The kid had no idea how fast the paint would penetrate that thin cotton, but Mike did. He bundled it up and was rubbing the cedar planks with dirt a few seconds later. Tanya had grabbed a handful of garden soil and joined him. He grinned up at her.

"Painting is the perfect job if you never grew up," he said. "Where else can you clean things with dirt?"

The main thing was, he didn't yell.

Tanya was used to men who yelled. Her sister Anna had been, too. Maybe that was why Anna got involved with Lomax in the first place.

She knew Mike was attracted to her, but she soon found out that he was married and she kept the flirting low-key. She didn't want any complications or distractions; she didn't want to get sidetracked. She had a job to do and she was making progress. She was getting to know the two brothers, Danny and Eric, flirting with them, playing them off against each other, chipping at them for information, digging and brushing off each find like an archaeologist reconstructing an ancient city in the desert. She was making good progress. It would be criminally stupid to slow herself down with some useless infatuation.

But that was exactly what had happened.

She set her brush in the paint can and stepped back from the ladder with a sigh. She couldn't concentrate this morning, and she wasn't here to paint anyway. She was thinking about Mike Henderson all the time now. Any time when she wasn't thinking of something specific—what to paint next, what to buy at the grocery store, what Diane Reem was saying to the author of the latest "extraordinary book" on NPR—she was thinking about Mike. Her mind was pulled there. His smile had its own gravity. She liked the tug of it, like the soft pressure on your knees and your thighs when you're lying in bed on Sunday morning. The whole mass and rotation of the planet seems determined to keep you horizontal. She never really wanted to get out of bed and she didn't want to stop thinking about Mike Henderson, either. It was a form of laziness. She didn't have the energy to turn away.

So instead she was doing this. She had gotten out of bed on Sunday morning to come here. Mike was meeting her. They were going to prime the spindles on the sweeping grand staircase. It was a two-person job, so it made sense to do it together. It also made sense to do it on Sunday when there would be no carpenters, Corian guys, electricians, plasterers, and plumbers crowding them and kicking up dust. In fact the site was deserted, just as Tanya had hoped it would be. She glanced at her watch. Mike was due any second. She bent down and untied her sneakers, toed out of them and pulled her socks off. The house was warm but the wood floor was cool. She unbuttoned her pants. Mike had been undressing her with his eyes for weeks, especially since she stopped wearing a bra under her T-shirt. Now it was time for the real thing. She wasn't sure what she was hoping for. Did she want him to leave his wife? The morals of home-wrecking didn't trouble her. Mike didn't have kids and Tanya was Darwinian about marriage. Weak animals got predated by stronger ones; if his marriage was flimsy enough to be killed off by some stray girl and her ten-ounce Kegel weight exercises, it deserved to die—just like the slowest eland in the herd.

Besides, if Tanya were doing the venal marriage hunt there was much better prey than Mike available. That was the last thing she wanted. She didn't want to marry Mike; she could imagine him stumbling around some tiny apartment, reeling from his divorce, displaying all his bad habits and sanitary lapses at close quarters. He probably snored and left wet towels on the bed. No, it was nothing like that. It was much simpler than that.

She pulled her T-shirt over her head.

Maybe this would be bad and the disappointment would break the circuit in her head; maybe it would be so good that Lomax wouldn't seem important anymore. Maybe it was just an itch and scratching it would allow her to concentrate. She didn't know and it didn't matter. The speculation would be over soon. She pulled down her panties and kicked them aside. She was naked in the big unfinished foyer of the Devil's trophy house.

After today she'd know.

Chapter Seven
Propositions

Driving out to Eel Point on Sunday morning, Mike Henderson found himself thinking about the old Downyflake restaurant on South Water Street, near Hardy's hardware, which was gone now, too, making room for clothing stores and antique stores and even a luggage store. He had never understood that one. What does a tourist on Nantucket need with luggage? Something to stuff all the hideous Lily Pulitzer clothes and Nantucket University sweatshirts into? The Nobby shop across the street had changed, too.

It was all for different reasons, Mike understood that. The Hardy's people had just retired and cashed out. The Nobby shop had been forced to bring the building up to code after a fire. And an explosion in the kitchen had wiped out the old Downyflake. But they were all gone, along with Robinson's Five & Ten and Cy's Green Coffee Pot. Cindy complained that there was nowhere to buy a thimble on the island anymore. It wasn't just stores either; the airport had been given a makeover. It was bleak and sterile now, like the new Steamship Authority building. All the charm of the island was being scrubbed away or demolished. The Historical District Commission tried to protect the outsides of houses, but there was no law about the interiors. Why did rich people feel the need to ruin the things they loved? Maybe they couldn't feel it was truly theirs until they had marked it somehow. Mike had been part of that process for a long time. He was part of the problem. All that new trim needed to be painted, all those new floors needed to be refinished. Mike had made a pretty good living from the rape of the island.

He knew that his brother-in-law, Nathan Parrish, was planning to build a mall out in the moors near the Pout Ponds. He had sworn Mike to secrecy, but of course everyone knew about it. The island was too small and the news was too big. Mike had thought of begging Parrish for the painting contract, but the job was out of his league, and asking Nathan for favors would just brand him as a loser. You only got special treatment when you didn't need it. He hated the idea of the mall, anyway. He knew that the Nantucket he loved was fading but fast, but a Kmart in the shadow of Altar Rock felt like a death blow.

He didn't want to be part of that. And he didn't need Parrish—he had the Lomax job. Of course that was moral sleight-of-hand, too. Nathan had told him, extracting melodramatic vows of secrecy, that LoGran, Preston Lomax's company, was one of the major investors in the Moorlands Mall. Everything was connected. Pretending to be above it was arrogant and silly. He could scarcely set himself up as a moral paragon. Here he was, driving to a deserted construction site to ogle some girl in her twenties. Of course he wouldn't put a move on Tanya Kriel. She was almost half his age. It would be disgusting. It would be reprehensible. But he didn't fool himself that way either. He had stayed true to Cindy during the worst times of their marriage, but it was a circumstantial fidelity. No woman had tried to seduce him; there had been quite a few he would have gladly gone to bed with if they had made the first move. But they hadn't. So nothing had happened. Hardly something to brag about.

The thought of Tanya Kriel putting his flimsy morals to the test made him queasy. She was so beautiful: austere Nordic features and a firm athletic body that approached human perfection. Of course Cindy couldn't compete with that; Tanya was young, her presence radiated health and hormones and fertility, energy and eagerness and grace. He had never seen her make an awkward movement. She had worn absurdly short cutoff shorts all summer. She had dancer's legs, supple and strong. He would catch a glimpse of the tendons in her thighs flexing as she climbed a ladder. It felt like sunstroke. She had caught him watching her, fighting to keep his eyes on hers as she pulled her shoulders back and stretched as they talked. Now it was winter, she was bundled up and the tension had slacked off a little.

But she still stalked through his fantasies and speculations: what would he do if she did this, or that, if she touched him, if she said something unmistakable. Which of course she wouldn't. It was all pathetic and sad. Even thinking about it was asinine.

But the fact remained: He couldn't turn down an opportunity to be alone with her for a few hours. He shrugged as he turned onto Eel Point Road. Was that really so bad? He had made love once with his wife in the last three weeks, and just twice in the three months before that. He knew it for certain; he had started marking the dates on his calendar. He was horny and lonely, but daydreams kept him going. He was in jail and Tanya was the pinup on his jail-cell wall. Nothing wrong with that.

He parked in the wide circle in front of the house. Tanya's Ranger was parked at the other side of the driveway. He killed the engine and stepped out into the sharp northeast wind. He looked around. In the spring there would be about eighty thousand dollars worth of new plantings here, saplings and hedges and flowers. Now it looked raw and unfinished. He could smell the ocean. The harbor was a dark iron blue; the exact color of Tanya's eyes.

He braced himself and opened the front door.

She was standing just inside, naked, and after the first shock of seeing her he could feel reality filling the gaps of his ardent but inadequate imagination: This is what she really looked like. Her nipples were darker, her stomach softer than he had guessed. There were no tan lines. She must have sunbathed nude all summer. She was absorbing the force of his undivided attention nervously. She was actually blushing.

"Did I make a mistake?" she asked him.

"No," Mike said, "but I'm about to."

He stepped up to her, ran his hand across her ribs and up to cup her breast. At the first touch he could feel the combustion inside him, chemical fire, instantly out of control. He couldn't remember the last time he had felt this way. Maybe he never had.

She took a step toward him and they were kissing.

His clothes came off and they found their way to a pile of drop cloths. The thought scampered across the dark road of his mind that she had planned this carefully; but he was glad. It was good to lie down with her, on her. Her hands were moving over his stomach and his chest. He knew the concept of skin hunger but he was beyond that. He was ravenous. He was starving.

So was she. So they devoured each other.

After the first time, Tanya said "They delivered the beds yesterday. Let's get comfortable."

They slipped upstairs to the king-sized mattress in the master bedroom. There was a drop cloth draped over it, but it slipped out from under them somehow as Mike grabbed the big oak headboard for leverage.

It would have been perfect, except for a small catastrophic detail: Kevin Sloane, the youngest member of Mike's paint crew, had left his iPod on the job, and he chose ten-thirty on Sunday morning to retrieve it. He recognized both of their trucks and when he slipped into the house, he heard them going at it upstairs. He found them easily and snapped picture after picture on his smartphone. Finally they noticed him. Mike jerked stiff, paralyzed. Tanya just stared. The moment had outdistanced their ability to react. There was nothing to do anyway.

They were busted.

Finally Kevin spoke into the shrieking silence. "Looks like I'm getting a big raise,"

Then he turned and walked out of the house. It was going to be a really big raise.

And that was only the beginning.

Chapter Eight
Fiona Donovan

I'd been saving Fiona Donovan since the first day I met her.

Today I was going to have to save her from herself.

When I pulled into the parking lot of the Faregrounds Restaurant, she had a man's head caught by the edge of her passenger-side window, the glass up to just under his chin, immobilizing him against the frame. Another eighth of an inch and he'd be strangling. She could probably decapitate him if she closed the window all the way, but I wasn't going to wait around to find out. I trotted over to her old Jeep Wagoneer.

I heard her voice first, that lilting Irish accent. "Now do you understand your attentions aren't welcome?"

"I urgh—" was all he could get out.

"Roll the window down, Fiona," I said.

She spoke to her victim. "I need a better answer than that. Try to speak clearly."

"Yes," He gagged. "Yes!"

She released him as I walked around to the driver's side. The man stumbled backward and fled.

"Was that the man from Ram's Pasture?"

"One of his friends. Acting on the lad's behalf."

I had met Fiona in October, hiking at Sanford Farm. Some drunken carpenter had been stalking her and they were in the middle of a shoving match when I came around a bend in the path. I grabbed him and shoved my badge in his face.

"This is a public park," he said. "I got a right to be here."

"Sure, you can be here. You just can't talk to this woman."

"You can't stop me."

"Yes I can. Consider this a restraining order."

He stared at me for a long moment. Then he started trudging back toward Madaket Road.

She stuck out her hand. "Fiona Donovan."

"Henry Kennis. Chief of Police."

We shook. Her grip was strong. "And they say you can never find a policeman when you need one," she said.

"Well, on Nantucket we don't have that problem. We're working toward a one-to-one ratio, cops to citizens."

"That will be cozy."

"I hope so,"

"Well I can do my part. Let me buy you a beer."

That's how it began, and it had been moving along that easily ever since. Women were usually a lot more difficult—from my ex-wife Miranda to my old flame Franny Tate, who had told me flat out that she wouldn't waste the airfare flying to the "outskirts of nowhere" to visit someone who had given up and chosen the life of a small-town loser. I don't mind the label. Everyone on Nantucket except the few remaining natives had failed somewhere else before they wound up here. The place is like a bird sanctuary for dreamers and eccentrics.

I walked Fiona into Faregrounds, now—the site of our first drink and our primary hangout ever since. Patriots football was super-charging the atmosphere of rowdy boosterism.

She caught the bartender's eye. "A Guinness and a Bud Light," she said, just before Tom Brady threw a forty-nine-yard bomb to Rob Gronkowski, who caught it in double coverage and ran it in for a touchdown. The bar went wild. The Pats were playing Detroit and the game was a rout. That didn't bother the half-drunk Nantucketers around us, but I knew Fiona preferred to watch a real contest.

Half an hour later we were walking out into the snapping cold air. The wind had picked up. There was more snow coming.

"I'm terrified of turning into an American," she took my arm. "Some sort of fake attempted American, like the girls who live with me. Wearing Old Navy jeans. Reading idiotic magazines about celebrities. Using outdated surfer slang and pining for a Big Mac."

"I don't think you have to worry about it," I said.

"I don't even watch actual football anymore. Except the World Cup. And I'm losing my accent."

"No you're not."

"I didn't even know I had an accent until I came here."

"And all the men found it so devastatingly attractive?"

"They do, don't they?"

"Well, I can't speak for all of them."

We walked through the parking lot in silence. We passed her car and headed for mine. The wind was thrashing the trees, straight out of the northeast. We could hear the faint dark rumble of the ocean between the gusts.

"So, did you like the poem?"

"It was lovely. But I wouldn't say it was particularly encouraging."

"No?"

"I tell you life is too short. You try to cheer me up by saying it's shorter than I think and I'm a bit of foam falling behind a ferry. For some reason that fails to brighten my mood."

"But it's true."

"That's not enough, Henry."

"It is for me."

She took my hand and gave me a rueful smile. "Lucky man."

We walked along in silence for a while.

"Come home with me?" I asked finally.

"It's your Sunday night with Tim and Caroline."

"They like you."

"They like having you to themselves. As you very well know."

"We could drive around for a while and make out."

"In a police car?"

"Why not? We can park at Surfside, scare all the kids away."

"Not tonight. I have things to do and you need to get home. Doesn't Miranda drop the kids off at five?"

I shrugged. "Checkmate."

"Next week, I promise. Take me to dinner and ply me with liquor."

I laughed. "That should work."

"All right. I'll ply *you* with liquor."

"Now you're talking. Two glasses of wine and you can pretty much have your way with me."

I had tried getting her drunk on one of our first dates. I bought Irish whiskey and matched her shot for shot. She was very maternal and business-like, giving me a glass of water and wiping my face with a warm towel when I puked, and then putting me to bed. Her note the next morning had said simply, "Nice try."

"Wednesday night?" I asked her.

"I'll pick you up at seven. Dinner at the Boarding House. I'll buy you a split of pinot grigio, and pounce."

We were at my truck. She stood on her tiptoes to kiss me. "Don't be late."

I took off. As usual I felt she was keeping things from me—her true feelings, her plans and ambitions, the way she spent her time when were apart. But that was all right. In this gossip-ridden little town, the capital city of Too Much Information, Fiona's secrets were a relief. What you don't know, you can't judge. I was happy to leave it that way.

Chapter Nine

Stray Humans

"They're coming," said Pat Folger.

It was the most dreaded phrase on Nantucket, worse than "You are called for jury duty," "You're number sixty-five on the stand-by list" or even "The airport will be closed indefinitely due to fog."

It contained all the frustration, anxiety, and despair of working in the trades in what Elaine Bailey like to call a "Premiere destination resort community." You were at the mercy of spoiled petty demanding people, pampered into a new infancy—adult toddlers, pointing and screaming at the baubles and treats they craved, stamping their Manolo Blahniks and jamming their perfectly manicured thumbs into their collagen puffed mouths at the slightest delay. Dealing with these new millionaires was like working in the king's nursery, where the young prince could have you beheaded if you denied him an extra cookie.

Most of the time it didn't matter. These owners were working in New York, or traveling in Europe. The only evidence of them was the occasional whining phone call or fax. But they always showed up eventually, generally when the final payments were due, and the richer they were the more reluctant they were to part with their money. A few years before, Pat Folger had built an eighty-thousand-dollar custom kitchen for a fast food franchise tycoon. He arrived on the island owing Pat sixty-thousand dollars. He was happy to write the check if the kitchen "passed the test." Pat had no idea what he was talking about, but it became horribly clear when he dumped a bag of marbles onto the counter. If they didn't roll, he would consider the counter sufficiently level. But of course they did. Not even NASA built things to that tolerance, but Pat had to spend three weeks tweaking and shimming the kitchen, which everyone knew was never going to be used anyway.

That goblin was a Woody Guthrie-like friend of the working man compared to Preston Lomax, whose perfectionism and malignant eye for detail had resulted in numerous lawsuits, and occasional fistfights, as he accumulated houses all over the East Coast, from Hilton Head Island to Woodstock, Vermont. Everyone knew he would be stalking through the house, looking for reasons not to pay. And everyone was pretty sure he'd find some. Perfection was hard to come by in the building trades.

Especially in the painting trade; and most especially, on Mike Henderson's paint crew.

They were an odd bunch, castaways and drifters, losers who really couldn't make a living anywhere else. "Stray humans," Cindy called them. She said Mike collected them like stray dogs, but Mike knew he was one of them himself. So were all his friends. The island was a forgiving place. The people who actually lived there, the year-round residents who had come from somewhere else, had generally come to hide out and regroup and start over.

Bob Haffner, for instance. He was Mike's foreman. Bob was a skilled painter. He was highly organized and he knew where all the putty knives and nail sets and pot hooks were on any job site; he knew how to get things done and how to get people to do them. He could get a Sunday's work out of Derek Briley during World Cup finals weekend or an extra hour's work on a Friday afternoon out of a jaded slacker like Kevin Sloane. He was good with people, because they knew he had made every mistake they would ever consider and possessed every flaw and weakness they could ever imagine. All he really cared about was finding new and ever more elaborate ways to avoid working and get stuff free. Painting was a temporary expedient that had somehow become the major part of his life for the last fifteen years. Most painters as good as Haffner would have started their own company long ago. But Bob didn't want to commit to the business. He was sure one of his schemes would pay off any day now. This was a man who saved everyone else's receipts so he could go head to head with the tax auditors after he had written himself off as a loss for the third year in a row. This was a man who got his clothes at the dump and stocked his larder out of the church food pantry. This was a man who would convince cancer homecare workers that he was dying just so he could get hot meals delivered to his house for free.

At least he wasn't drinking anymore. But he couldn't stay away from the twelve-step programs. It wasn't just AA or Overeaters Anonymous or the Gulf War syndrome groups. He was in several combined groups, too: co-dependent phobic liars with obsessive compulsive Gulf War syndrome and adult children of overeating masturbation addicts with recovered memories of same-sex child abuse. There were times when he couldn't remember what meeting he was at and what kind of insane shaggy dog story he was going to have to invent to maintain his good standing with the other victims.

That was when he realized he was addicted to twelve-step groups.

"Is there a group for that?" he asked Mike. "It would be so perfect."

He was cutting in the big living room ceiling and Mike was rolling it when Pat Folger walked in. They ignored him. He turned off their radio and said it again.

"You hear me? They're coming. Next Tuesday. With three moving vans full of furniture."

"Just three?"

"Are you gonna be ready?"

Mike set the roller in the pan and turned to face the squat red-headed contractor. "How about you, Pat? I can't paint stuff that isn't built yet."

"There's plenty for you to paint."

"How about the mantel? Or the cove molding upstairs? Or the loft baseboards? Half your guys are at the Chicken Box, Billy Delavane is out surfing, your son quit last week. Costigan is the only guy you have working. My whole crew is here and we're painting ourselves out of a job."

"No. You're *talking* yourself out of a job."

"Then fire me. And good luck finishing this place by Tuesday."

"Don't tempt me."

Folger stumped out of the room.

"He's always complaining that he gets no loyalty," Haffner said, going back to work. "I feel like telling him, Pat—that's because you're a toad and everyone hates you."

"That would go over well."

"Shall I do it? I could do it right now."

"Actually, I'd prefer it if you waited until we all got paid."

A few minutes later, Billy Delavane poked his head in the door. "Stop painting and do something you're good at," he said, "like drinking coffee."

He extended the paper tray from Fast Forward. "Black for Mike. Cream and sugar for Bob."

"It's more than that," Haffner corrected him. "Fuck the coffee. It's just a *vehicle* for my cream and sugar." He took his cup.

"Don't worry about Pat," Billy said, taking a first sip. "The last few weeks on a job, Pat goes insane. Just like your dad used to. He fired his own son yesterday."

"Hey, Dad never fired me."

"He came close. Like at Butler's, when he said 'take down the ceiling'—he meant scrape it, but you ripped the whole thing out, right down to the strapping. Or when your dog walked all over the stenciled floor? That was a good one. I thought he was gonna have a seizure that time."

"Okay, okay. He should have fired me but he didn't."

"Pat's even worse, though. He'll scream at anyone. He threw the Lomax kid off the site yesterday, just because he asked you a question."

"He wanted to know if we were using eggshell paint on the walls. So what?"

Billy hiked his shoulders. "Hey, I have no idea. Avoid Pat this week. That's my advice. And if you can't avoid him, just say 'yes.' He likes it when people say 'yes.'" Billy glanced at his watch. It was a gold Patek-Phillipe, out of place on a job site, but he wore it everywhere. "My break's over," he said. "See you guys later."

On the second floor of the house, Tanya Kriel was painting trim with Lu-Anne Dowling. Lu-Anne was a lesbian, so feminine and charming that Haffner had flirted with her for weeks when she was first hired, until he caught her with the tile girl in the upstairs bathroom. Lu-Anne had no political or philosophical mission; she just liked women. She had a little crush on Tanya but she knew it was hopeless. She was talking about a party she'd been to the week before. She didn't know who was straight and who was gay, which had resulted in a few drunken embarrassments. Tanya was nodding, but she was thinking about other things.

Primarily, she was thinking about murder.

She had come up with some good ideas for dealing with Preston Lomax recently. The best one involved using his own vices to cover her tracks. He was a smoker, Eric had told her that. During her sister's time he had quit—no patch, no gum, just cold turkey—he had been insufferable on the subject of his peerless self-discipline. But apparently he was back to three packs a day now. So much for the captain of industry and his iron will. Tanya smiled: this was an opportunity. Nicotine in pure form was one of the most poisonous substances on Earth. All she had to do was drop a crumb of the stuff into his drink and he'd be dead in less than a minute from cardiac arrest brought on by the overdose. She could just hear the doctor saying, "Extraordinary, Mrs. Lomax. Your husband smoked himself to death in the most blatant way I've ever come across in thirty years of practicing medicine."

Which begged several questions: how to get the stuff into his drink, for one thing. Also she had no idea what it tasted like. Would he notice it? If it acted fast enough, that wouldn't matter.

She was starting to catalogue other poisons—she had been reading on the Internet about some stuff called brucine—when the clamor of an argument broke her concentration.

Haffner had come upstairs and he was yelling at Kevin Sloane. Tanya hadn't said a word to Kevin all day; she could hardly bear to look at him after what he'd done. The idea of him just standing there, watching her with Mike, seeing everything and just sort of soaking it up into his gonads like some hideous carnal leech made her literally sick to her stomach.

Mike had avoided Kevin, also, she'd noticed. They'd barely spoken all day.

"You call this sanded?" Haffner was shouting. "This isn't sanded!"

"Hey, bite me, man. I sanded it."

"No! You moved a piece of sandpaper over it. But that doesn't matter because *it's not smooth* and it can't be painted until it's smooth. Get it? That's why we sand things. Not so we can say we sanded them. Not for fun. Not for the exercise. We sand things to *make them smooth.* So we can paint them. Is that really too much for you to grasp? Is that too tough for you? Do you need a little chart with stick figures?"

Mike had climbed the stairs and Kevin turned to him.

"Did you hear the way he's talking to me, Mike?"

"I heard him."

"He's being a dick, man."

"This kid isn't a painter, Mike," Haffner said. "I can't talk to him. You give it a try."

Kevin looked calmly at Mike.

"I don't think he should be allowed to talk to me that way."

"I tried being polite. That didn't work," Haffner said.

Kevin's eyes were steady. He wouldn't look away.

"I think he should apologize."

"The hell I will!"

"I think you should exert your authority, Mike. Things can get way out of control when the boss is afraid to exert his authority."

"What the fuck is going on?"

"Shall I tell him?" Kevin asked. "I'll be glad to tell him."

Mike turned to Haffner. "Apologize, Bob. You were out of line."

"Out of line? You're paying this little turd eighteen bucks an hour to get in everyone's way, he's acting like he owns the place and I'm out of line. This is bullshit."

"So let's patch it up and put it behind us."

"You patch it up, boss man. I'm outta here."

He stalked down the stairs. They heard the door slam. Kevin smiled at Mike.

"*You* could apologize. That would be okay."

Mike fought down the urge to punch that smug grin into bloody pieces. Kevin had the power and he knew it. Pretending things were different wouldn't change them. He looked at Tanya. She looked away.

"Sorry," he said.

"That's it?"

"I'm very sorry Bob was rude to you. All right?"

"I don't know. I detected a little sarcasm there. Am I right? Was there a little irony in your tone?"

There was a gagging silence. Mike couldn't bring the word up his throat.

"Mike?" Kevin prompted him.

"No."

"Well, good then. I guess we can all get back to work."

He walked to the next door casing and started sanding it in the most cursory way possible. Tanya looked at Mike. Her look said *Is this how it's going to be?*

Mike looked down. He had no answer for her.

Which meant *yes.* Mike's future was firmly in Kevin's hands. He was holding Mike's marriage hostage and that gave him power and power felt good; better than good. It was like snorting amyl nitrate. It obviously gave the little creep a major head rush.

Mike started back down the stairs. He had created a monster, and the monster was having the time of his life.

◇◇◇

Across the raw mud of the Lomax compound, on the second floor of the main house, the remaining member of Mike's crew, Derek Briley, was finish-painting window casings, eavesdropping on another local monster. Lomax and his friend Nathan Parrish were chatting away, not ten feet from him, exchanging confidences of various kinds, primarily business related, and Derek was soaking up every word. All he had to do was keep on working. He was nothing to them. He might as well be a dog lying in the sun with his head on his paws, tame and witless.

Derek was anything but. He had a mean streak and he was clever, with a cockney shrewdness that was far more useful than the educated intellectual clog dance his boss went through before every decision. Derek had most things decided in advance. One good example: he'd never diddle the help, no matter how cute they were. He'd warned Mike about it jokingly one day when he'd seen the boss making goo-goo eyes at Tanya Kriel. "This for thinking, that for dancing," he'd said, pointing to his head and his crotch. But Mike didn't listen. Scratch that. He listened all right; and he thought about it long and hard. Oh, yeah, he did the full clog dance, then he went ahead and did whatever stupid thing he was going to do in the first place. Mike's thinking was like the Circle Line tube. A lot of noise and jumble to get back to where you started from. It was different with Derek. When he was thinking he was working things out, figuring the angles. His kind would always get the better of a Mike Henderson. End of the day, bullshit baffles brains. That was Derek's philosophy.

So Derek knew exactly what to do with the information he'd picked up this morning. These men were talking secrets, and the best way to kill a secret was to let it out. That meant the newspaper, and that meant *The Shoals,* because Derek seriously doubted the other paper would even run the story. Derek liked *The Shoals.* He liked its attitude; the editorials gave him a laugh. So that was that; he'd swing by the newspaper office after work, stir things up a bit. Derek wasn't particularly soft-hearted, but he loved Nantucket.

And he wasn't going to let these fat cats wreck it without a fight.

Chapter Ten
High School Confidential

The intercom buzzed as I walked into my office Tuesday morning.

"They're bringing in the Snoopy kid, Chief. He's got his lawyer and they want to talk to you. Apparently your drug speech at the high school got him thinking. Not cleaning up or going straight. Just thinking."

"Hey, he's innocent until proved guilty, Jesse. Remember?"

"Snoopy tells no lies, Chief."

Snoopy was the drug-sniffing dog the Nantucket police had purchased three years earlier for seven thousand dollars. His actual name was Westcott, but Snoopy stuck. He was a perfectly friendly pure-bred beagle, but was supernaturally good at his job. I didn't really approve of using drug dogs, but as Haden Krakauer had pointed out when he first brought up the subject, "Snoopy has seniority on you, Chief."

Of course, the individual who really had seniority over me was Haden himself. He'd been up for the job when I was hired. He should have had a built-in grudge, but he had decided to like his new boss anyway. "Maybe I'm not as ambitious as I thought I was," he had explained. "Or maybe I'd rather deal with criminals than the Board of Selectmen." He was handling the drug bust. I could leave him alone for awhile. He was good with kids.

I was going to have to check in with Simon Bissell, the superintendent of the school, before I inspected the car where

Snoopy had found the drugs. It wouldn't take long, but I would have preferred to avoid Bissell. As an authority figure who went out of my way not to abuse my position, I detested Bissell's tyrannical posturing; as a parent with two children in the school system, I dreaded it.

This was the man who wanted to paint traffic lines in the hallways to make sure the students walked from class to class in an orderly manner. He had suspended one of the editors of *Veritas* because the student wrote a story trying to find out why the school pool had been built a foot short of regulation length. Exactly how that had happened was still a mystery, but the kid had managed to dig up the fact that the contractor was Bissell's brother-in-law.

The teachers all hated Bissell because he had completely restructured the high school curriculum into an elaborate MCAS prep session. Snoopy had been his idea. He had bullied the drug dog concept through Town Meeting with great fanfare. But there had been no results yet. Maybe this was the first one, but somehow I doubted it.

Bissell was sitting stiffly behind his desk when I arrived. The tightly combed hat of hair was obviously a wig. The blue blazer and red bow tie was his standard uniform. His face was all thin sharp lines, pulled down into a disapproving scowl. He looked like someone had just offered him a big plate of something messy—crabs in the shell and a wooden hammer.

"I want to make an example of this Jared Bromley boy," Bissell said. No greetings or preliminaries. "He hid ten ounces of cocaine in the engine compartment of his car. Clearly he was planning to sell it on the schoolyard to other children. Unfortunately for him, he chose to do that on a day when the school system's illegal substances canine task force was conducting a surprise inspection."

"I understand," I said. "But right now I'd just like to get all the facts straight. See the car, talk to the boy and…"

"The facts are not in dispute, Chief Kennis. The question is, what are you going to do about them? This boy must be punished to the full extent of the law. This is not the moment for leniency. We must send a strong, clear message to the deviant element in our school community. This behavior will not be tolerated."

I let the words jostle past me like a crowd of commuters pushing out of a subway car. When they were gone, I took a breath and stepped inside. "The case is a priority for us, Mr. Bissell. That's why I'd like to see the car as soon as possible."

Bissell sighed dismissively: this incompetent policeman didn't understand the gravity of the situation and he never would. Bissell flicked his wrist at the door. "It's at the side of the building, next to the maintenance shack. A bright red pickup truck. One of your men is there. I'm sure you'll have no trouble finding it."

Bob Coffin was leaning on the fender, arms crossed against the cold. A heavyset ex-high school linebacker, Coffin looked stoical standing in the snow. This was his life. At least he wasn't a crossing guard.

"Hey, Chief," he straightened up.

I nodded. "Coffin."

Coffin popped the hood and braced it. We leaned in toward the engine. "It was all right there, Chief. Two eight balls, tucked right behind the battery."

"Was the car locked?"

"No one locks their car on Nantucket. You know that."

"Even the drug dealers?"

"I guess not."

"That doesn't strike you as odd?"

Coffin shrugged. "This ain't L.A., Chief."

"Has the car been printed?"

"About half an hour ago."

"OK. Close it up and get back to the station. We're finished here." I stepped away from the car as Coffin slammed the trunk and paused a moment. "Thanks Bob," I said. "See you later."

Coffin nodded and trudged off toward the slant-parking in front of the school. I watched him go, looking past the beige, ground-hugging building to the cars passing on Atlantic Avenue, almost invisible through the screen of snow. The cold air was tight on my face. I stuck my hands in my coat pockets. How many years it was going to take before I got used to winter? I might never get used to small-town life. It was a miniature world. Superintendent Bissell behaved with an arrogance comically disproportionate to his job. But maybe he was right. In this isolated, painfully inter-connected island world, you didn't need much real authority to do a lot of damage, and that was how true tyrants measured their power.

Still, maybe you could do some good in a place like this. That was the flip side. Maybe you could apply some big city experience to a questionable drug bust. Maybe you could stop bureaucratic preening and lazy police work from wrecking a kid's life. Maybe. I was way ahead of myself. Guesses were useful, until you refused to part with them. First I had to talk to the kid, check the forensics on the car. It was getting late. I started for the front lot, following Bob Coffin's tracks in the new snow.

Driving back out to the station, I saw that the snow had abolished the ordinary civic landscape. Sidewalks, back yards, even the normal boundaries of the streets themselves, vanished. You crept along, exploring the new wilderness. It was like the roads had never been built, or had fallen to ruin under the packed white powder. The mounting blizzard meant that school would be closed tomorrow. Miranda was off-island at some business guru's real estate seminar (called, all too appropriately, "Love What You Sell, Sell What You Love"), which meant I'd be taking the day off with the kids. The long-promised sledding at Windmill Park, slightly marred by the pager at my waist, but still fun. Hot chocolate at The Bean, and then lunch together, and leisurely homework in the afternoon. The fist of tension behind my chest from the long morning started to unclench.

I always felt better when Miranda was gone. It had taken me a long time to understand her, in part because I was reluctant to accept the truth. It had been dormant during our years in Los Angeles. A slim shy girl with the face of a Titian Madonna, she had called herself a "seeker" in those days. When people like that actually find what they're seeking, the results can be dispiriting.

I had watched Miranda's odyssey of self-discovery move through Sufi-ism, Scientology, Torah class and even a very expensive set of Tony Robbins Personal Power tapes. Those tapes should have been a clue, but I couldn't help being startled when the self that Miranda finally discovered turned out to be a Nantucket real estate agent. There had been clues, I realized. She had never been interested in the movies I loved, but she always kept track of the grosses. She knew how exactly much each star made, and how much they received in their divorce settlements.

After the move to Nantucket, money and all the details of its loss, transfer, and acquisition took her over completely. She was working for Elaine Bailey, the ultimate land shark.

Miranda had known Elaine most of her life—Elaine had sold Miranda's parents their first house on the island—but their affinity ran deeper. Miranda had lost her groping connection to the poetry of things; Elaine had never had one to begin with. Neither of them could appreciate the evening light on the moors or the sight of a redwing hawk gliding on the thermals above Madaket Road. They didn't read, not even the newspaper (except the real estate section). They didn't go to plays or movies. They didn't watch television, except sports channels and CNN. They didn't fish or sail or even walk the beaches. They drove around in giant SUVs, showed houses, closed deals, gossiped, drank white wine, and went out to dinner. That was it. That was life.

That was the life my ex-wife had been seeking.

Miranda was in her element at last, and it made her supremely boring. No matter what subject she was talking about, she wound up talking about real estate. Deforestation of the Brazilian Rain Forest? That makes it the perfect spot for a gated community! Jungle View homes, a perfect real estate broker's idea of a name, since there was no jungle to look at anymore.

I feared it was all rubbing off on the kids. Both of them were pushing me to buy a place, which was an economic impossibility. They didn't care about that. They were relentless. Tim had used the phrase "investment opportunity" the other day. Caroline was alarmingly knowledgeable about which parcels of land were subdividable and which houses had deed restrictions. A day of non-commercial play on stubbornly public land would do both of them a world of good.

David Trezize was waiting outside the police station when I pulled up. Stumpy and forlorn, standing bundled in the snow, David looked like the public defenders I had dealt with in Los Angeles. He had the same slouch. It came from delivering bad news to an ungrateful world for not enough money. That was actually a pretty good description of police work, too. I stood up a little straighter as I approached the editor. I hadn't dropped by the newspaper office in a while.

"Chief Kennis," David called out. "Do you have a second?"

"Just about. I'm running late."

"I wonder if you have any comment on a story I'm going to be running this week," David was saying. "It reveals that hard drugs are being sold in the Nantucket schools. And the police are involved."

I felt the first sizzle of anger behind my eyes. "Which police-men are you talking about?"

David smiled. "Well, that's the question, isn't it?"

"Who's your source on this?"

"Come on, Chief. You know I can't tell you that."

"So some anonymous person says cops are selling drugs. And you print it. I have an anonymous source that says newspaper edi-tors are having sex with farm animals. Will you print that, too?"

"Absolutely, Chief. If I trusted the source. And I do trust this source. Actually, I was almost scooped on this one. *Veritas* was going to run the story, but Bissell spiked it. He doesn't believe a student newspaper should report a story like this. Which leaves it up to me. Apparently the *Inky Mirror* wasn't interested."

I squinted down at the little editor. "Who wrote that story?"

"Jared Bromley. The only one there who can write."

"It's a lost art, David. I have to read crime reports every day. But if you want my comment…I believe the story is false. And I know there has to be a better way to sell newspapers than libeling the police force."

"Are you going to sue me, Chief?"

"Don't worry, David. I have real work to do."

I turned and walked around the corner to the front door of the station. Maybe it was impossible to be friends with a reporter. We were natural adversaries, and neither of us could afford a conflict of interest. I knew I had offended David, but there was no way around it.

In the interview room downstairs, Jared Bromley sat at the Formica-topped deal table with his lawyer, Charlie Hastings. They could have been brothers: two tall, thin, pasty, disheveled guys. Their heads were too big for their bodies; their noses were too big for their heads. Jared had his dirty hair in a pony tail; Charlie needed a haircut.

Charlie didn't even look that much older than Jared, but he was a good lawyer. I had seen him in court. He was quick and funny. One of the judges had teased him about his youth during a court date last Halloween, asking him what costume he would be wearing this year.

"I'm going to really scare people," he had responded easily. "I'm going as a lawyer. What do you think?" He did a quick turn to show off his pinstripe suit. The judge laughed, and Charlie got his client's sentence reduced to time served and a year's probation. He was wearing the same suit today, and he looked just as uncomfortable in it, as if he'd been dressed up for a family photograph.

Jared was wearing jeans and a torn Whalers T-shirt. Their coats and gloves were in a dripping pile on the table. They stopped talking when I walked in.

"Hi, fellas," I said. "Thanks for waiting."

"This is ridiculous, Chief," Charlie said. "I've got appointments backed up and Jared's missing his AP English class. Come up with a charge or let us out of here. And how about a few pictures on the wall? This place is depressing."

I took a breath. "I'm not charging anyone with anything, Charlie. I want to clear a few things up. It won't take long."

"All right, here's the first thing: My client will gladly take any drug test you care to administer. He doesn't even eat poppy seed bagels."

"Jared, what I wanted to know was—"

"There's nothing he can tell you, Chief. That's the point."

"Still, I'd like to talk to him directly. If that's okay with you, Charlie. I know he can speak for himself. I log onto Sharkpool a couple of times a week."

Jared perked up. "You read my blog?"

I smiled. "I liked what you said last week about the superintendent's hiring practices. Let me get this right. Oh yeah. 'No wonder they're flat on their faces. They set the bar so low they tripped over it.' In September you said Bissell's assurances about curriculum changes were 'as meaningless as the nutrition facts on a candy bar wrapper.' Good one."

Jared shook his head, looking down. Was he blushing a little? "You sure know how to get on writer's good side, Chief Kennis," he said. "Direct quotations."

I hooked a chair and sat down. "The last time our paths crossed, you called in a complaint about a beach party that was going on in front of your family's house. Nonantum Avenue, right?"

"Why would you remember that?" Charlie asked.

"I was driving around that night. I took the call. I wound up doing a little bullfight number with one of those kids. Toby Grimes, that's his name. Jack Grimes' boy. He wound up face first in the ocean. I never had to touch him. Funny thing is, he wasn't mad at me."

"Even Toby's not dumb enough to go off on the police chief," Jared pointed out.

"My point is, Toby was mad at you, not me. That's all he talked about on the way in to the station."

"Well, he's even madder at me now."

"Care to discuss that?"

"Not really."

"It's common knowledge around the school that Toby is selling drugs, Chief," Charlie put in. "He should be sitting in here with you now, not Jared."

"Is that true, Jared?"

The boy shrugged.

"Did you write a *Veritas* article about this?"

"Why would you say that?"

"Because the other editor is Heather Logan and her last couple of editorials were about the poor showing at the last pep rally and a passionate defense of dress codes."

Jared laughed. "'We're being pressured painfully into a predatory pressure cooker of peer group pressure.' She's so right. Not to mention…alarmingly alliterative. I wish she could have used the word 'pressure' one more time in that sentence."

"Can I see a copy of your editorial?"

"Sure. I'll bring it by the station tomorrow."

I let a little silence settle between us.

"So. You leave your car unlocked?"

"Like everyone else."

"Which means anyone could reach in and pop the trunk."

"But that's not the interesting question, Chief. Anyone could… and we both know who did. The motivation's obvious. That covers who, what, where, and why. The interesting question is when. Because on any other day, it wouldn't have really mattered."

"What are you trying to say?"

"It's like the Spanish General, Golz, tells Robert Jordan in *For Whom the Bell Tolls:* To blow the bridge is nothing.'"

We all looked at each other. The only sound was the big electric clock on the wall ticking. I stood up. Jared Bromley had gotten my mind working. I looked down at the boy. "So you're not selling crack."

"No."

"Well, that's good. Keep walking that straight and narrow, Jared. And get out of here. You're late for AP English."

I walked them out of the station and watched them drive away. Something was bothering me.

Jared had picked one of my favorite books to quote from, and the rest of Golz's speech was banging around in my head. *Merely to blow the bridge is a failure. To blow the bridge at the stated hour, on the time set for the attack is how it should be done.*

What had Bissell said? "He chose to do that on a day when the school system's drug illegal substances canine force was conducting a surprise inspection."

To blow the bridge is nothing.

For Toby Grimes' plan to work, he had to know the exact time of the task force inspection. And no one had that information except the police. Which meant that David Trezize was right—cops were involved. Even Jared Bromley knew it, if his article was as sensational as Bissell seemed to think. Once again, everybody on the island knew more about what was going on than I did. Maybe I hadn't been looking closely enough. Well that time was over. No more secrets in the locker room, no more small-time criminals in the blue uniform I loved.

Things were about to get nasty. That was fine with me.

Chapter Eleven
The Editorial

David Trezize wrote:

> "Last week, Preston Lomax, one of the new owners of our island, choked a waiter at Topper's in front of almost a dozen witnesses."

He paused. The cursor blinked at him. He was right on the brink of something uncontrollably bad. He knew he should delete Lomax's name. People would know who he was talking about, anyway. Did he really want to declare war so openly? Yes…he did. Besides, the incident had happened. That much of the piece was news. It was the least he could do for the devoted readers of *The Nantucket Shoals.* David grinned and went on.

> "Apparently there wasn't enough ice in the master's ice water. No one in the restaurant came to the young man's aid, and he knew better than to expect them to. A few days later he did what a peasant would have done in Europe four hundred years ago, to protect his family from a rogue prince's *droit de seigneur*: he fled.
>
>   He wasn't the only one. People are leaving every day.

My friend Richard came to Nantucket in 1983, intending to stay for the weekend. He's been here ever since. He's leaving now, too. He can't afford to stay, but he's no longer even sure that he wants to.

He's been complaining for years, summer complaints mostly. The old familiar litany: the mopeds, the crowds, the fleas, the ticks and the parking tickets; the traffic, the prices, the noise. But in the last few years a new gripe has started to overshadow all the others, the sum of all his other complaints.

The rich people.

They've been driving him crazy. "Leather pants!" he'll say out of nowhere one day. "Why are they wearing leather pants in July?"

"They just wander around…eating ice cream," he told me last summer, so comically aghast that I had to laugh. But I know how he felt. I've felt the same way. Part of it is simple envy. I'm no Marxist. I want their stuff, their Mercedes and their house and most of all their leisure, their free time—their freedom. They flaunt the things I may never have, so I'd be nuts not to resent them.

But there's more to it than that. I look at developments where ugly houses have been plunked down on every little rise in the moors, spoiling land that should have been wild forever. I look at the boutiques and specialty shops that are opening on every corner, I look at the lunatic real estate prices, and it seems to me to be entirely the fault of the rich people. They decided they liked Nantucket. They made it into their new toy. The force of their money rolled across the island very much the way it does on their own properties when bulldozers and backhoes and fifty trucks of dirt and dozens of landscapers sweep into the beach plum and scrub oak and obliterate it, burying it under five acres of perfect lawn, hot house trees and flower beds, a state-of-the-art sprinkler system and a couple of tons of raked crushed shell driveway. The lawns are beautiful, but the plant food and weed killers are contaminating our harbor and our aquifer.

Perhaps Richard is lucky in a way. He's moving back to the land of highways and fast food and shopping malls. There will be no dissonance between what he sees around him and the way he lives, no constant sense of loss and disillusion. It may be easier, after all, living in a place that never had a chance to be paradise, a place that will never be paradise lost."

David pushed his chair back. It was done. Now, if he only had the guts to run it. He recalled once again the conversation he'd had with Lomax at a fundraiser a few days after the shoving incident at Topper's. Although the waiter had threatened to press charges, when David went to interview him for a story the following day, he discovered that the kid had already left the island. David asked Lomax straight out what he knew about the boy's sudden departure.

Sucking an oyster from the raw bar into his mouth, Lomax said simply, "He was afraid of my money." Swallowing, he added with a grin, "If you write about this, you'll find out why."

David hit the save button and stood up.

What the hell. For once he was happy about his little paper's small circulation. Lomax might never even see the editorial. He probably sneered at the local newspapers. He was a *Wall Street Journal* kind of guy.

David took a last look around, turned out the lights and went home.

Unfortunately for David Trezize, Preston Lomax read the *Nantucket Shoals* every week, from cover to cover. He subscribed to it so that he never missed an issue, even when he was in the city.

And he especially enjoyed the editorial page.

Chapter Twelve
Betrayals

I spent the morning interviewing everyone on the police force about a drug connection. No one knew anything; most of them seemed offended that I'd even ask. I had begun to think that Jared Bromley had been making trouble in his *Veritas* article. Maybe Bissell was right to spike it. Jared wouldn't name names and, short of my actually arresting him for a crime he obviously hadn't committed, there was no way I could put any real pressure on the boy. It was absurd. Was there some shadowy drug cartel operating out of this small town police station? It seemed more and more dubious. But Jared had been scared. That stuck with me.

Driving by the VFW Hall on my way out of town an hour later, waiting for a crowd of pedestrians outside the auction to push back onto the sidewalk, it occurred to me that I didn't need to be accepted by the community. Perhaps I shouldn't be. Maybe I could see more clearly from the outside.

Fiona Donovan understood that. She was well-versed in the small advantages and dry comforts of exile. She would be amused by my dogged, stumbling progress. We were both relentless. That was part of what drew us together.

I had grabbed an impromptu picnic from Fast Forward on my way out of town. Fiona had told me we couldn't see each other for our usual Saturday lunch because she had to finish a big cleaning job in Madaket. Her sandwich was on the seat beside me—curried chicken salad, wrapped in plastic on a paper plate. This would be a nice surprise.

When I got to the house, a big rambling Victorian set in the dune grass only a few yards from the high tide line, Fiona's Opel wasn't in the driveway. I pulled up between a black Ranger and an old white Honda Civic filled with milk crates jammed with cleaning supplies, cut the engine, and climbed out of the cruiser. The driveway had been shoveled, snow piled up on either side. Even more was piled above me in the leaden clouds.

The house was open and Fiona's Irish girls were working downstairs. They didn't know where she was. She hadn't been in all day. I tried her cell phone but it was turned off. I got her voicemail without a ring.

I thanked the girls, stepped outside again to Madaket Road, looked past the Westender to the first curve. It was empty and silent. Where was she? Well, where would she be on a Saturday morning?

I walked back, the wind snapping at my coat. I climbed into the car, keyed the engine and put the heater on high. Something had touched my mind on the way out here, like a gnat on the surface of a pond, too light to break the surface tension. I rewound the drive, back past the dump, the Cliff Road intersection, the horse farms, the fresh white trim and raw shingles that marked Bruce Poor's new development near the Monument. Nothing came to mind.

I moved on, down Quaker across Milk Street where it turned into Prospect Street, past the old Mill, a left on York Street, a jig to the left on Orange then down West Dover. Then Union to Washington Street, running parallel to the harbor, back into town. I drummed my fingers on the steering wheel, listening to the wheezing gale and the rumble of the surf.

Then I got it. It was obvious when I finally made the connection—the Osona auction at the VFW. Ten minutes later I parked illegally at the new bus depot across the street, shamelessly abusing the perks of authority, and slipped inside the overheated building.

It was the last auction of the year, and much later in the season than normal. But a combination of a huge estate liquidation and the unusual crowds on the island in mid-December (parking on Main Street was scarce as August), had convinced Raphael Osona to try a late season event. The gamble had obviously paid off. The hall was packed.

On the block was an Elizabeth Saltonstall still life: driftwood and scallop boxes. The bidding was moving briskly at two hundred dollars. I eased up behind Rick Folger. He was standing with Alana Trikilis and Mason Taylor. The two younger kids were holding hands.

The bidding went up to three hundred and stayed there. Then it was going, going, gone.

Rick slumped a little, shaking his head.

Alana cocked her head at him. "I don't get it."

"That picture was worth at least twelve hundred bucks. What a steal."

"Wow," Mason said "You really know about this stuff."

"For all the good it does me."

"Well, it could do you a lot of good, Rick," Alana said. "If you had bought that picture you could have tripled your money tomorrow morning."

Mason poked her. "I thought you hated materialism."

"Yeah, but I love…material."

I quartered the room, studying the sea of faces. It didn't take long to find Fiona. With her thick red hair and a green dress that picked up the color of her eyes. She had a paddle in her hand but she wasn't using it. A set of dining room chairs, some Tiffany silver, and a set of nesting lightship baskets all sold while I stood against the wall watching.

I controlled the desire to approach her. *What was going on?* Better to hang back and observe. She seemed to be alone, at least. When the bidding started on a piece of 19th century silver, she sat forward a little. I shifted position for a better view. Fiona had told me all about this.

Her great-great uncle, Thomas Donovan, had left Ireland in the 1830s and wound up as a silversmith on Nantucket. Silver was an approved form of ostentation in those days, when the Quakers who lived on the island did little to show off their wealth. No nice clothes, few jewels; but the competition was fierce when the dinner dishes came out of the cupboard. Quakers liked silver, whale ship captains could afford it; and their wives had a lot of time on their hands.

Thomas Donovan had apprenticed to Benjamin Bunker and later opened a shop of his own, which was destroyed in the great fire of 1846. Fiona had found a number of fine Donovan pieces over the years (he always put his TD mark on them somewhere), mostly commemorative spoons, plates, and tankards. Most of them were priced out of her range, but she had found several excellent spoons (one with a bluefish coiled around the handle) in a bread pan full of mismatched place settings at a yard sale in Polpis last summer. The whole pile of junk flatware was selling for a dollar. The spoon alone was worth at least five hundred. Fiona had argued the lady down to fifty cents with a cool poker face. A little bargaining was expected at a yard sale.

Porringers—the little bowls with wide flat reticulated handles—had been a specialty of Thomas Donovan, and Fiona's father had collected more than a dozen before the prices spiked in the eighties. He used them, too: there were always coins in one and little hard lemon candies in another. Fiona and her mother kept the porringers polished and gleaming. Along with a lovely painting of Lough Inagh in Connemara County, Galway, by Fiona's grandfather, they were the only family heirlooms her parents had managed to preserve. That explained part of her interest. But Fiona also loved the silver itself, the gleam and density of it, the heft and texture of the beaten metal. She had always understood that trite image of misers gleefully running coins through their fingers.

They had started bidding on a porringer now. Several people showed interested. Every time the price hit a plateau, the same thing happened. Fiona brushed her hair off her forehead, and someone made another bid. I could feel a rhythm in it. I moved forward a little to get a better view of the room. One of the bidders was Preston Lomax, and I saw David Trezize against the far wall, studying the tycoon intently.

The bidding had come down to Lomax and one other man, Nathan Parrish. I recalled an erratic driving traffic stop on Polpis Road in October. Parrish had passed the Breathalyzer and promised to pay his overdue parking tickets. I remembered him as perfectly polite but insufferable. The incident had irritated him, the way you'd be irked if you got home and found you'd forgotten something at the grocery. A policeman he'd forgotten to purchase! He'd correct the oversight in the morning, put a check in the mail.

But no check had ever arrived; not even a donation to the Policemen's Benevolent Association. Maybe Nantucket cops weren't worth buying outright. You were better off with a time-share.

I knew much more than I ought to about Parrish. For instance, I knew what the developer was really doing when he told his wife he was working late. He was a cheater, in business and at home.

Fiona brushed her hair off her forehead again.

Parrish raised his paddle, just like a puppet.

"Twenty-five hundred," Osona said. "Do I hear—thank you. Three thousand, from the gentleman on the right."

The same ritual of swept hair and raised paddle: the price crept up again. And again. Lomax was determined to have the little silver bowl. Or maybe he just wanted to beat Parrish. I could understand that. At five thousand dollars, Fiona made her move, but Parrish didn't respond. She leaned forward, staring across the room. Even the back of her head looked angry.

Parrish shook his head.

"Five thousand dollars. Thank you, sir. Sold to the gentleman on the right."

Fiona was still staring at Parrish. He shrugged.

The auction moved on. Fiona rocked back in her chair and I eased myself away toward the doors at the rear of the room. Other people were standing; I wanted bodies between me and Fiona.

People greeted me but I didn't want her to hear them. I didn't want any contact with anyone until I had time to figure out what I'd just seen. Was Parrish her sponsor? Her patron? Her partner? Did they work the auctions together? It would make sense: She had the knowledge and he had the money. There must be any number of similar arrangements in the world of estate sales. How much did Fiona understand about Parrish? Was he cheating her, too?

I put my palm to my forehead and pressed my temple hard. It felt like the pressure of my thumb and pinky were the only force keeping my head from bursting. The explanation was no good. It didn't explain why Fiona had lied to me. It didn't explain why a prominent local businessman was willing to spend—what was his last bid? Forty eight hundred dollars?—on some trinket for a woman who wasn't his wife. It looked like Fiona wasn't worth five thousand. No wonder she was pissed off.

Was I imagining all this? No—the intensity of that last silent exchange was unmistakable. They thought they were safe, unobserved in a crowded place with everyone looking elsewhere, absorbed with the always entertaining Raphael Osona show. But I had been watching them. And a man like Parrish doesn't drop four grand in afternoon for a friend, or even a partner. Fiona was tough. You'd have to put your money where your mouth was with her.

And just where had Nathan Parrish's mouth been, exactly? That was the question.

I knew how to get the answers I wanted from a stranger, in that little blank-walled interrogation room at police headquarters. How you did it in a quiet bedroom, in your own house with a woman you loved, I had no idea. But I would figure it out, because I had to know, and it had to be soon.

Chapter Thirteen
Goliath Wins

For David Trezize, the day of personal catastrophes that he called Black Friday actually started on Thursday night. Or was it the Monday before that, when he decided to run Jared Bromley's *Veritas* article? Or the week before, when he'd run his own editorial? Trying to pinpoint the origins of things gave him a headache. He had been angry about the way Nantucket was changing for a long time. His editorial had been an open declaration of war after years of private griping and sniping. Jared's article had focused everything and brought it into the present. The boy's eagerness to see the piece printed in *The Shoals* was exhilarating. David had thought the boy might be afraid of the repercussions. He wasn't, though. He'd already been censored and framed. He was enjoying the battle. Which made sense: Jared was a kid, he had nothing to lose. He wasn't trying to run a newspaper on the edge of bankruptcy, raise a family, and maintain a reputation as a solid citizen. But David was. And David should have been afraid. Things were moving too fast, deadlines were too close, and the excitement of the chase was overpowering. If there had ever been a chance for a moment's sober reflection, it was gone the moment Derek Briley walked into his office, at forty minutes before deadline on Monday.

There were reporters at every desk. The place smelled like toner ink and burned coffee. Sandra and Bea in the business office were typing in the last classifieds. Byron Chadwick was pecking away at his Board of Selectmen report, which David knew in advance he would rewrite from scratch. He hoped there'd be time this week. He touched the big man's shoulder.

"Finish up," he said.

"Almost there."

"Good."

He let himself into his office and shut the door. It was a cramped ten-by-ten cubicle with just enough room for his desk. The window looked out into a tiny graveled strip in front of a retaining wall, five feet below street level. The one decoration was a blown-up still of Steve McQueen in *The Great Escape,* skidding to a pause on his stolen Nazi motorcycle, assessing the line of barbed-wire fences. Patty had always laughed at that. David wasn't Steve McQueen's Hilts; he was more like the Donald Pleasance character, Blythe—mild mannered and ineffectual. But determined, at least.

And handy with a pen.

Derek Briley appeared at his office door a few minutes later. The wiry Englishman strolled in without knocking, sat down, and lit up a forbidden cigarette.

"Thought you might like to know where the money's coming from for that Moorlands Mall you've got your knickers in a twist about," he said. "It's your old friend Preston Lomax."

"What?"

"Preston Lomax. He's the one behind it."

"Excuse me. Who are you?"

"Name's Derek Briley. Housepainter. Steadiest hands on the island, and sharp ears, too."

"All right…so, you're saying that Preston Lomax—"

"Right. You thought he was just another rich bloke mucking things up small time. Having his tantrums and whatnot. No such luck. He's taking over, mate. Talking to Kmart and Marshalls. Bidding out the parking lot grading job. Putting real roads in the moors, civilizing it, like. You can't stop him, his boys have the Planning Board in their pockets. He said for once someone's going to pave a street on this stinking rock that doesn't flood when you get a drizzle. It's a whole off-island professional attitude. He's going to shape us up proper. Thought you might like to know, after that bit you wrote last week."

David stared at him. Someone poked their head in the door, thought better of it, disappeared.

"How do you know this?"

"Overheard it, mate. The big shots don't mind talking in front of the sub-humans. You're invisible, aren't you? Far as they're concerned. So I say, take advantage. I mean, if it's there to be taken, right? It's how you get ahead in the world."

"Yeah, I guess it is." David stood. Briley got up also and they shook hands across his desk. "Well—thanks for coming in. I'll be following up on this over the next few weeks."

"The next few weeks? Do it now, mate. You've got the story in your hand. Start as you mean to finish, that's what I always say."

David sat down and rolled his chair back from the desk. He believed Briley. The story made sense; he probably should have put the pieces of it together for himself. And it revealed Preston Lomax for what he was: an enemy, not just to the occasional waiter who happened to cross his path, or a kid who wanted to blow the whistle on his cocaine habit. No, he was an enemy to the whole island and everyone who lived here. He was a profiteer, an amoral mercenary who was well on the way to desecrating one of the last wild and beautiful places on the Eastern seaboard, just for a chunk of money he didn't even need.

David opened a file and started typing. Briley was right. The story was running this week. He could follow it up later. He had what he needed right now. He finished the piece, unnamed source and all (Briley didn't have his green card yet), and slotted it on the bottom of the front page, bumping the sewer-bed improvement project to the back of the paper. It was three minutes before deadline.

He was scared, but you were supposed to be scared. Steve McQueen smiled down from his motorcycle. Hilts understood—you had to jump the fences, even if you wound up tangled in the barbed wire afterward. It was the effort that mattered. You kept going until they stopped you.

David glanced at the clock. Two minutes. He hit the save button and sent that week's *Shoals* to the printer.

He felt pleased with himself throughout the next day, watching the renewed interest in his newspaper, happy to breathe for a moment the recycled air, or perhaps the secondhand smoke, of Woodward and Bernstein and Seymour Hersh. Everything was fine until that evening, when he stopped on his way into the Languedoc restaurant and spoke to Preston Lomax.

He should have paused with Sasha. They were an official couple now, and her ex-husband had designed the Lomax mansion. But he wasn't sure how to present her. "My friend, Sasha" would sound evasive. "My girlfriend, Sasha," grotesquely ironic, given the purpose of this dinner. "My partner, Sasha" was an outright lie, and a mealy-mouthed euphemism, even if it was true. "My soon to be ex-girlfriend, Sasha" was the most accurate, but no one was giving points for accuracy. In the end he just pushed her forward gently. She nodded at Lomax and followed the hostess to their table.

"Mr. Trezize," Lomax called out. David turned and walked the few steps to his table. Lomax was eating with his wife, who seemed to be adding up the thread count in the tablecloth.

"Yes?"

"Interesting issue of the paper this week."

David shrugged. "I don't read the *Inquirer and Mirror.*"

Lomax smiled. Or at least it looked like a smile. Dobermans seemed to be smiling, too, just before they struck. "Mendacious and evasive," Lomax said. "Like your editorials. Of course you read the *Inky Mirror.* And you know exactly what I'm talking about." The force of the man's personality was overpowering, like the heat from a roasting oven. You pulled back from it automatically. "So? You have nothing to say for yourself? Then I suggest you hire a lawyer. Because I'm suing you for libel."

David cleared his throat. His voice was somewhere at the bottom of that cough. He hauled it up.

"Truth is full vindication."

"What?"

"In libel law. Truth is full vindication. At least ten people saw what you did at Topper's. And your company's funding the Moorlands Mall will be common knowledge soon. I just ran it first."

"You also suggested that I buy drugs from policemen."

"No. We said it happens. No names were mentioned."

"And how many other Eel Point homeowners used a local contractor? That narrows the field a little, Mr. Trezize."

"Mr. Lomax, if you don't use cocaine you have nothing to worry about. And neither do I."

"Save it for the courtroom. You'll be spending a lot of time there. With your divorce not final, you could be there fighting for custody over this little...dalliance." He nodded toward the back of the restaurant, where David's soon-to-be-ex-girlfriend was studying the wine menu. "The Commonwealth of Massachusetts frowns on adultery. Being 'separated' has no meaning in the eyes of the law, as I'm sure you're aware, with the breadth of your legal knowledge. You're married, you're cheating and you've been caught."

"Hold on a second. How can you—"

"A single father is so vulnerable in this state. Why, if someone should call in a report of you engaging in child abuse, for instance, you'd automatically be put on probation by the Department of Social Services, whether you did anything or not. Isn't that appalling?"

"What the hell are you trying to...?"

"But it gets worse. If the police receive one more anonymous call, the DSS removes Jan and Jenny from the danger and hardship of your home. It makes sense. We have to protect the children, don't we?"

Lomax knew his children's names. How did he know their names? "Wait a second! You can't just—"

"Of course I can. Anyone can. But don't worry. You'd be able to clear yourself eventually. After the caseworkers have interrogated your children and your visitation rights have been suspended and your reputation's been wrecked. People would never look at you the same way again. They just love to believe the worst about their neighbors, don't they? It's a terrible thing."

Lomax laughed, a big, guttural guffaw, like a James Bond villain. All he needed was a Nehru jacket and a Siamese cat. David felt a geyser of sheer hate rising from his toes to the base of his spine. His fingers were tingling with the urge to grab that wattled throat and squeeze until the eyes bulged and the grinning red face went blue.

"You make me sick," he said. "You're not a businessman. You're a thug. You scare people for a living. You're an overfed bully and it's time someone stood up to you. I'm happy be the one to do it."

"Oh really? And where will you do that? In the pages of your gossip sheet?"

"You're damn right I will, and nothing you can do—"

"Nothing I can do? I've already done it. It's *done.*"

David felt a sudden twist in his stomach. "What are you talking about?"

"I want to go back to my dinner, so I'll just say this. Men who work at newspapers teetering *one advertiser away* from going under shouldn't throw slanders. It's like the glass houses and the stones. Just as messy, but much harder to clean up. Have a pleasant evening, Mr. Trezize."

Lomax cut into his steak. David was dismissed.

Who had Lomax talked to? What had he said? What was going on? What had he done? Could it be stopped? Could it be fixed, somehow? David turned away and stumbled to his table. Sasha smiled up at him.

"I ordered champagne. Is that all right?"

"What?"

"I thought it would be festive."

He stared at her in frozen panic. Who was she? What was she talking about? What world did she come from? Apparently things were festive enough there to justify sitting around in fancy restaurants, ordering champagne. But that was absurd, there was nothing wrong with Sasha, she had no idea what was happening, she was just trying to have a pleasant night. Which was funny enough since he had come here to break up with her. She was about to be dumped, and she hadn't figured that one out either. So sure, why not? Bring on the champagne! Let's celebrate! I'm being framed for child abuse and my newspaper is being destroyed! You're annoying and unattractive and I can't stand to be with you! Merry Christmas and Happy New Year! Let's all get drunk and puke on ourselves.

She was watching him. He had to say something. He needed an exit line. He had to get out of here, check his messages, start making phone calls.

"I have to go," he said. "I don't want any champagne. I took you here to break up with you. Sorry, I should have said something, but I was going to tell you and let you yell at me or cry or whatever, make a scene—but I don't have time now."

Sasha reared back a little in her chair as he babbled on, her face pulled tight. "David, what are you—?"

"It's over!" He was shouting. He got his voice under control. "We're finished and I have *real problems* to deal with. So... goodbye. I have to go now."

"Are you okay...?"

"Sure, I'm okay. I'm fine, Everything's great. Can't you tell?"

He fled the restaurant.

He couldn't remember where he had parked his car. *India Street! That was it.* He scrambled into the Escape, gunned the motor and peeled out. He barely managed to stop at the stop sign on Federal Street. A couple with two kids stared at him balefully as they crossed the street. Parents always looked at you that way when you pulled up to intersections, as if they knew you were planning to run down their children and only the force of their will was stopping you.

He glanced in the rearview mirror. There was a cop behind him, probably running his license plate, trolling for violations and infractions, checking to see if his registration sticker was up to date. Well, it was, he had nothing to worry about. Maybe a parking ticket or two, left over from the summer. Would that be enough to pull him over? Sure, if they felt like pushing someone around. They didn't really need an excuse, just a mood. They could do pretty much whatever they wanted, they could mess with anybody.

"Not me," David heard himself say aloud. "Not tonight."

The cop kept going on Orange Street when David turned right on Cherry. But he still had to deal with that bitter spike of adrenaline. He had read somewhere it was the "fight or flight" hormone. Which was great for cavemen being chased by saber-toothed tigers. What he supposed to do with it? He had no way to fight against Preston Lomax. And flight was impossible. He lived here. In some ways, he would have preferred the saber-tooth tiger. At least it would be quick. All the adrenaline had done was make his hands shake. That was useful. Modern man needed a better drug than these homemade glandular potions. Maybe that's why they invented alcohol.

When he got home, he poured himself a little vodka over ice, squeezed some lemon into it, and took a sip. The effect was instantaneous. He shoots, he scores. He took one more swallow, set the glass aside and picked up the telephone.

It didn't take long to find out what had happened. His third call was to Elaine Bailey. He could tell from the tentative way she said, "Hi, David," that he had guessed right.

"What's going on, Elaine?"

"I was going to call you. But it's just been so frantic at the office. We had to let Teddy go and Doris is out on maternity leave, so…well, it's been a madhouse down there."

"You probably made a million dollars this month. So don't complain. It's unseemly."

"I'm not complaining, I'm just saying. We're way behind with everything right now."

"Are you pulling your ads?"

"David—" The apologetic whine told him everything.

"The insert, too?"

"I don't really have a choice. We do a lot of business with the LoGran corporation. A lot of business. And not just sales, though the sales have been huge. They refurbish these houses and rent them out to corporate customers at premium rates and we have the leasing contract also. We're the sole agent for an enormous project I really can't talk about right now."

"The Moorlands Mall."

That stopped her. "No one knows about the mall."

"Now they do. Didn't you see the paper today?"

"No, I didn't, I haven't had time to do any—this was in your newspaper, David?"

"It's news."

"It's a secret."

"How long have you lived here? Thirty years? And you expected to keep a secret?"

"Who told you?"

"I don't reveal my sources."

"I could force you to tell me. I could sue you. It's a new era. You can't cover up for people anymore. People get arrested for that now. And they get convicted. That WikiLeaks soldier is cowering naked in solitary confinement *as we speak.*"

David took a deep breath and another swallow of vodka. The last thing he needed to do was antagonize Elaine Bailey.

"Listen, Elaine. I'm sorry. I shouldn't have mentioned the Moorlands Mall project. I'm certainly not going to write anymore about it in the paper." He was lying and he knew it, but the lie just squirted out. He didn't care, he wasn't thinking about ethics. He just hoped she'd believe him.

"Not good enough" she said.

"It's the best I can do."

"People always say that when they know they've done badly."

David took a breath. "I'll be honest with you, Elaine. The paper is hanging on by a very thin thread right now. We don't have the classified ad revenue because our circulation is too low, so we need every advertiser, every member of the business community who thinks it's important to have an alternative voice on the island that isn't afraid to—"

"David. Please. I don't need to hear your stump speech. If an 'alternative voice' really was so important, people would be *buying your paper.* And you wouldn't have any circulation problems. Frankly I'd been questioning the value of our financial commitment to the paper long before Preston spoke with me. It's simply not a cost-effective way to position ourselves."

"Maybe not now. But the paper is growing, and the idea was, we'd grow together so that we could—"

"I run the largest independent real estate firm in southeastern Massachusetts, David. I don't need to grow with you. Perhaps you need to find some struggling new firm who can share your adventuring spirit. You'll have plenty of room in the paper from now on."

"I won't have a paper from now on if you pull out!"

The sentence was a high-pitched shriek.

Elaine waited a moment, as if to let the reverberations of his hysteria die down. "Well, perhaps that's for the best."

"Elaine—"

"It's late, David. I have to go. Good luck. And take care of yourself."

"You've already done that, bitch," he said to a dial tone. Why did people always say "Take care of yourself" when it was painfully obvious that they didn't give a shit?

He hung up the phone, and leaned back into the frayed sleeper sofa. It smelled like the inside of a laundry hamper. The little apartment was a mess. He closed his eyes. There had to be some way out of this. Bailey Real Estate was his biggest single advertiser. He'd need at least three new accounts to fill the gap. But he'd already been everywhere and tried everyone. They were all very encouraging and supportive. But he didn't need them to be supportive, whatever that meant. He needed their support. He needed their ad revenues. He needed their money. And he wasn't getting it.

Bailey Real Estate's monthly check was due in the next few days. Without it he wouldn't be able to meet payroll. He could dip into his savings to keep things going, but eventually he'd be broke and in the same situation he was in now. He thought of Orson Welles in *Citizen Kane,* responding to the fact that his newspaper was running at a deficit, costing him a million dollars a year. "Hmmm," he said, "At that rate I'll have to close in just…sixty years." David could go two months, that was the difference. After that, he'd be bankrupt. He didn't know what to do. There was nothing to do. He poured himself a second drink. After the third one he managed to shut his mind off and go to sleep.

Patty's phone call woke him at eight thirty the next morning. He would normally have been up for hours. The vodka must have gotten to him. He felt sluggish. His head ached. He hadn't woken up with a hangover in years. He reached for the clock, but he couldn't turn the alarm off. He finally realized it was the phone, and picked it up on the fourth ring, just as his answering machine activated. The call would be recorded, for what that was worth.

"That's it. I've had it," Patty said into his ear: no greeting, no pretense of civility. "You can flaunt your sex life all over town if you feel you have to, but not in front of my children."

He sat up in bed. "What?"

"There are laws against this shit, David. We're still married, technically. You're traumatizing my children and I won't stand for it."

David was waking up. "Your children? You have kids you haven't told me about?"

"You can turn your life into a porn movie, you can do whatever you like now, but I won't have them exposed to it."

"But exposing them to you and Grady is fine."

"Oh, so that's what this is about. If you're just trying to get revenge on me for Grady, you're deluded. I couldn't care less what you do with that disgusting pig. Just don't tell me she's the love of your life because we both know that's ridiculous."

"I don't do that 'love of my life' stuff anymore, Patty."

"You should take a good long look at yourself. Grady and I have a real relationship. We have mutual respect and common interests and passion and—"

"And I'm sure the kids find it very uplifting when they catch you smooching in the kitchen."

"How did you—?"

"Just a guess. But clearly a good one." He was waking up now. "You know, Patty, you really are the queen of the double standard. Nothing applies to you, nothing sticks to you. Nothing counts when you do it. You make the rules and you're above the rules. Well, not anymore. You don't scare me anymore. There's nothing you can do to me, so stop dancing around making scary faces. You just look like an idiot."

"I certainly can do something to you, David. I can take the kids away from you. And that's exactly what I'm going to do. I'm suing for full custody and no visitation rights."

"Good luck then, because you won't get it and you don't even want it. You're the one who calls me up screaming when you have to have them for *an extra night,* or I screw up your love nest by having to work through the weekend. In case you've forgotten that was *three weeks ago,* when I was getting out the Christmas Stroll supplement."

"Fine. I admit it will make things harder for me. There'll be some sacrifices, but I don't care."

"Oh really? When was the last time you made a sacrifice? When you had to settle for just one pair of shoes on sale?"

"At least I dress appropriately. I don't wear blue jeans to work"

"I have to go."

"Fine. You'll be hearing from my lawyer."

David hung up the phone, climbed out of bed and went into the bathroom. The headache got worse when he stood up. His stomach was upset, too, but it wasn't from the booze. He knew this feeling: anger as acid indigestion. Patty's accusatory whine was in his blood like two cups of bad coffee. He drank a full glass of water at the sink. As he turned to lift the toilet seat, there was a knock on the door. He took a few steps and stuck his head out of the bathroom. The top half of the front door was glass.

There was a cop standing there, squinting, his hand to the dirty pane, trying to see inside.

A cop. Just as Lomax had predicted. No, no, not predicted. Arranged.

He stood up straight and took a breath. It didn't matter. He had nothing to hide. He walked to the front door and opened it A gust of cold air cut through his robe and his pajamas. Accumulated snow that had been piled against the door fell in on his feet.

"Can I help you?"

"David Trezize?"

"Yes."

"We've had some calls—can I come in?"

"Of course."

The cop stepped inside and unbuttoned his coat. David had forgotten to turn the heat down last night.

"Mr. Trezize, I'm here this morning because we've had reports about physical abuse. Apparently, you struck one of your children and pushed the other one down during an altercation in the Stop & Shop parking lot two days ago. When the children started crying you told them forcibly to be quiet and continued to—"

"That's absurd. I'm sorry, Officer, but I mean really—I would never do something like that."

"The report goes on to say—"

"I don't care what the report says. Who made this report? Who told you this shit?"

"I'm going to have to ask you to watch your language, sir. The report was anonymous."

"One report?"

"That's right sir. Now we have to make a full investigation of—"

"I beat up my kids in the most crowded parking lot on Nantucket and *one person* called in a report. Just one. Doesn't that strike you as a little weird?"

"Not at all, Sir. We generally figure that for every call we get, there are ten people who choose not to get involved for whatever reason."

"So now there are eleven 'witnesses' to something that didn't happen because you automatically multiply any crank call by ten? I can't believe this. Listen to me: I could never hit my kids. I don't even yell at my kids. I'm a New Age pussy who doesn't believe in discipline. Ask my ex-wife."

"We fully intend to interview your ex-wife, Mr. Trezize. And your children. But from what I can see just talking to you, you clearly have some serious anger issues. And you've been drinking."

"I had some vodka last night," David said, slowing his voice down, speaking softly. "There's nothing illegal about that. Come on. My children weren't even with me."

The cop seemed to physically ease off, leaning back a little. "All right, Mr. Trezize, I'll tell you what I'm going to do. After we talk with your family, if they confirm your story, we'll let it go. But I still have to file a report, and if there's even one more complaint against you, the DSS will have to open a full investigation. This is very serious. You could lose your kids and wind up in jail."

"With no proof? What happened to 'innocent until proven guilty'?"

"Well, that's a luxury the state can't afford, Sir. When the health and well being of the children are involved."

David stared at him. "What if you're wrong? What if you made a mistake?"

"The Department of Social Services would institute full restitution at that time. But it rarely happens. Where there's smoke, there's fire, Mr. Trezize. That's been my experience. You be careful now. Have a good day."

He turned and walked back to his blue and white cruiser. It criminalized David's yard, just sitting there. David watched the cop pull out and drive away. The day was still and bitterly cold. For some reason he didn't move. He felt as if he could stop time by standing here. As long as he didn't think about anything or feel anything he could maintain the stasis. He was a figure in a diorama, a member of some extinct tribe, posed stiffly, going about his ancient daily business, everything beyond his driveway artfully painted to give the illusion of three dimensions: "The Lost Middle Class of Nantucket" exhibit in the Natural History Museum.

David shut the front door and leaned against it. His feet were frozen and his head was on fire. He had to do something, some action was necessary now, but all he could think of was socks. He needed to put on some socks.

He climbed the narrow stairs and rummaged in the top drawer of his dresser for the thick pair of woolen socks Patty had given him for Christmas two years ago. He grabbed it and sat down carefully on the bed. He tried to put the right one on with his legs crossed, but in that position his foot was sideways and he couldn't line up the heel properly. He tried twice. Finally he gave up and propped his foot on the edge of mattress. It slid off the sheet. He was going to have to lean all the way over. It wasn't worth it. Everything was impossible.

Part of him wanted to find Lomax, grab him, scold him, shame him.

He sat up suddenly, rubbing his palms along flannel of his pajama pants. He could do it. Lomax was throwing the traditional Nantucket end-of-the-job celebration party for the tradesmen, where the worker bees got to dress up and mingle with the one percent. David hadn't been invited, but so what? It would be the perfect place to confront the troll: under his own bridge, with all his cronies around him.

The idea spread inside David like spilled wine through a silk tablecloth. He had to do it. It would be a mistake, but he didn't care anymore. Things couldn't get any worse.

As usual, it was David's optimism that was his undoing. Because things can always get worse, much worse; and you never know exactly where the bottom is, until you hit it.

Chapter Fourteen

Secrets

Cindy Henderson didn't want to go to the Lomax party. She hated parties in general, with their pointless social requirements. You had to smile at people you disliked and make conversation with bores. Invariably you would run into someone whom you'd been successfully avoiding for weeks. And of course, after fifteen minutes of small talk, you'd wind up inviting them over for dinner, or planning a two-family vacation, backpacking in Zion National Park—anything to end the conversation. It would be funny, if it were happening to someone else.

Mike had suggested she stay near, to use him as a human shield. It sounded good, but then she would be exposed to the supernaturally tedious conversation of his tradesmen friends. Who bid what on which job, how many board feet of lumber someone got how much cheaper in Vermont, which builder was struggling with the HDC over the pitch of his roof; which plumbers cleaned up after themselves. It was better to just stay home.

For once, Mike didn't seem to mind. "Don't bother," he'd said that morning at breakfast. "I'm not going to stay long. The last thing I want to do is spend more time in that mausoleum."

"Are you sure?"

"Don't worry about it. Take the night off."

He was so accommodating and thoughtful, she became instantly suspicious. Did he not want her there for some reason?

Was there someone he was afraid to have her meet? He had spoken so quickly, jumping right in after her comment, as if it was rehearsed. Over-rehearsed, actually: he needed to take a beat, relax and at least appear to consider what Cindy had said, before starting his prepared remarks.

"I think I will go after all." She carried her coffee cup to the sink. "I got a new dress from the J. Jill catalogue and I've been wanting to wear it someplace."

"Are you sure? Because it's really—"

"I'm positive, Mike. This will be fun."

He shrugged. "Great. Just let me know when you want to leave and we're out of there."

She kissed him on his way out the door, and held him for an extra second or two, to show that everything was fine between them, precisely because it wasn't. He sensed something off-kilter in the gesture.

"You okay?" he asked.

"Fine," she said. "Go to work."

She kissed him again and pushed him out the door. She was sure he had secrets; but she had her secrets, too. She wondered if there were any marriages without them, where everyone told the truth and had nothing to hide. Maybe that was what the storybooks meant by "happily ever after." Or maybe happy was just an average, drawn between the rages and the joy, the sum of the constant struggle to stay close when everything inside and outside you seemed to be pulling you apart.

It was so much easier to lie.

It was comfortable to have a little private place for yourself, like a daybed where you could snuggle under a quilt for an afternoon nap. Like the fact of her pregnancy. Until she told Mike about it, or started to show, the baby was hers and hers alone. She could feel and do about it precisely what she wanted, without having to consult anyone, without taking anyone else's feelings or advice or demands into account. It was none of anyone else's business right now, not even Mike's.

But there were other things she was happy to keep private. The principal one was named Mark Toland.

When they were seniors in high school, he had swept her up into a brief affair and then casually dumped her. Two years later, he had come to visit her at college, to apologize and win her back. But she had been seeing someone else. The other boy had walked in on them. He'd heard all her one-sided stories about Mark, and instantly recognized the gloating sexual predator she had described in her acid post-coital monologues. There had been a brief shoving match, but Mark was no fighter. His parting words were "Keep your alpha dog on the leash. Before he bites someone and they put him to sleep."

She had written to Mark occasionally, after that. She felt bad about the way she had described him to the now-defunct boyfriend. She had left out a few essential items: his brilliance and talent, his wit, and energy. And his heavy-lidded, dark-haired good looks. He was tall, with the lean muscles of the Olympic swimmer he had almost become. Of course, the boyfriend had noticed that part. And Mark was rich. He came from six generations of family money; they had begun as cotton and lumber brokers for paper companies. Now they were the single largest manufacturer of notebooks and loose-leaf paper in the world. Mark's older brother Alex was doing most of the grunt work running the business and Mark was free to take his huge trust fund and do whatever he pleased.

As it turned out, what pleased him was making movies. After putting in five years of work and hustle in Los Angeles, he was finally doing it. His family frowned on the business from a distance, but didn't interfere. As they saw it, if he chose to do contemptible cheesy things like flattering scoundrels, compromising his integrity, and—worst of all—*spending his capital* pursuing an odious fantasy, it was all right with them. As long as he didn't come back after he had burned through his inheritance, looking for handouts.

It was a workable truce.

And now he was going to have the satisfaction of rubbing their aristocratic noses in his implausible success. He had been gloating about that on the phone a few days ago. They had been chatting for several weeks, since he was back East scouting locations for his first feature film, and a mutual friend had given him Cindy's number. He always called her at the store now, so the only interruptions were from customers—rich ladies with rich husbands, buying party dresses with corporate credit cards, comparing Mevlana handbags from the sale rack, laughing together. Maybe money did buy happiness. Maybe it really was that simple. You could certainly lease something pretty close to it. These women were certainly enjoying themselves. They didn't need to flirt with old boyfriends on the telephone

Still, the only thing Cindy enjoyed now was a phone call from Mark Toland. The mornings when she didn't hear from him seemed poisonously drab; grim stretches of time like Selectmen's meetings or the eight-hour childhood ferry trips when the harbor was frozen.

"Listen, I'm in New York for two weeks," he had said suddenly, the other day. "Come down here. We can see each other and neither of us will have to say a word."

The boldness of the invitation shocked her. "I couldn't."

"Sure you could. It's easy. You show your ID at the ticket counter and they look up the round-trip ticket I'm going to buy you. Then you get on the plane, eat peanuts, and read. Next thing you know, you're here."

"No, Mike would never…I mean, I don't know what I could possibly tell him, that would—"

"You have family in the city. Say you're visiting them. Hell—visit them. It won't even be a lie."

"I have to think about it."

"Okay, but you can always think of fifty good reasons not to do anything if you think about it long enough."

Then they had hung up and she hadn't heard from him since.

The conversation seemed a little crazy to her now. She hadn't actually seen Mark since the afternoon he had shown up at her dorm room, all those years ago. She had no business flirting with him over the telephone at this late date. Even daydreaming about meeting him in New York made her feel sleazy and cheap. She had really only let it start because she felt Mike was hiding something from her, which probably wasn't even true in the first place.

She was married, she was six weeks pregnant, and she was going to a fabulous party with her handsome husband in a killer backless silk dress that would get everyone talking about her the way she wanted them to. She crumpled up the slip of paper with Mark Toland's numbers, threw it away and started running herself a bath.

It was like her mother always said: "Life is good if you let it be."

Chapter Fifteen

The Pen

The Lomax house, surrounded by miles of winter darkness and standing alone on its snow-smothered acres, light blazing from every one of its one hundred and twenty-six windows, looked like a luxury ocean liner icebound in the Bering Strait. I had a brief vision of it tilting up vertical and sinking without a trace—then we were pulling into the crumbled snow piled in the wake of the plow. There were cars parked on both sides of Eel Point Road.

We trudged to the house, me steadying Fiona by the elbow, climbed the frost-slick front stairs pushed inside. I was irritated, my feet were soaked through, I had skidded my car into two walls of banked filthy snow on the way to the house. As far as I was concerned, people who talked about a "winter wonderland of white" had to be doing it from a bungalow in the Florida Keys. They never discussed the sheer bulk of the stuff, or the malign stamina with which it kept coming, burying your car over and over again and shrinking the world. Everything bulged white, every tree branch and fencepost and mailbox; and the world crowded in on you. It was like living in a one of those gift shop paperweights, trapped in a little glass bubble, waiting for someone to shake up the next blizzard.

Fiona had little patience for my complaints. She loved the winter, especially a night like this one when the cold was so pure. No wind, no snow falling, no distractions; just the dense, intoxicating icy air, like Vodka straight out of the freezer.

The party was already busy and the music was loud. I immediately caught sight of my ex-wife Miranda, on the arm of a real estate broker, Joe Arbogast. I left Fiona admiring the Lomax silver collection and eased my way through the chattering crowd to Miranda.

We all said hello and Joe went off looking for another round of champagne.

"Henry, hi," Miranda said. "We were just saying, if you come over Christmas morning, you can take the kids for lunch. Joe wants to come over and—you know."

I shrugged. "Sounds good. They're looking forward to Tortola."

"I got the beach house again. Everyone at school's going to hate them. They'll be brown as berries."

We stood quietly, listening to snippets of other people's conversations. Nathan Parrish's wife saying "You can't buy people," and Nathan answering: "On the contrary, Darling. It's easy to buy people. Selling them is the hard part. They depreciate faster than a Ford Explorer."

I could hear Lomax from across the room: "People come here because they can't make it anywhere else. It's been that way for a thousand years. The Indians who came here couldn't string their wampum straight. I went into one of these bookstores the other day, during Christmas Stroll. And I wanted to buy the big book of the season, the new Grisham. They told me it was in—they had it in the basement. But they hadn't brought it upstairs yet. Our biggest retail day of the year, and they keep *the new John Grisham novel* in the basement because they're too lazy to unpack it. Try getting away with that at Barnes & Noble. You'd be out on your ass in a heartbeat. But that's Nantucket for you. That says it all."

I turned back to Miranda. "So you're still with Joe."

"He wants to marry me."

"That was quick."

"Quick is good. Even in police work. You told me that. Most crimes are solved in the first week, or they don't get solved at all."

"I don't know, Miranda. You're in the first blush of a love affair and you're already comparing it to a murder investigation."

Fiona drifted over as Joe returned with two flutes of champagne.

Miranda took her glass and nodded. "Hello, Fiona."

"I like your hair."

"I just had it cut. For the benefit of my women friends. Men never notice anything."

I put up my hands. "Not my job anymore."

"I was going to say something," Joe added.

"I'm sure you were." Miranda leaned over and kissed his cheek. Then she glanced around. "Beautiful house."

"It should be,' Fiona said, "My girls have been cleaning it for two days."

"He has such beautiful things."

Fiona shrugged. "He can afford them."

The music stopped and at that moment someone near the fireplace laughed. Fiona looked over and looked away, but not quickly enough.

"Got to mingle," Miranda said, and she pulled Joe toward the French doors.

I stared at the fireplace through the shifting jumble of heads and shoulders. I heard the laugh again. It was Nathan Parrish, talking to Lomax. Fiona put her hand on my arm.

It had been more than a week since the auction, but I hadn't been able to bring it up. I'd only seen Fiona twice, and she had been in such a fine lively mood both times that the whole subject seemed absurd. I knew she'd put me on the defensive, trying to explain what I'd been doing at the VFW Hall in the first place. There could be any number of explanations for the furtive collusion I had glimpsed that afternoon. But more and more, I wanted to hear one of them—preferably one I hadn't thought of myself. Ideally, one that was true.

The lying bothered me the most. If she had a bidding partner, if that was all it was, why be so devious? The uneasy suspicions kept pouring in and with no way to drain them, they were overflowing like a bathtub, gradually flooding the house. Water damage. You couldn't fix it, that was what the contractors always said. You had to tear things out and rebuild from scratch.

"I have to talk to you," I said now.

"Henry, it's a little crowded in here for—"

"You like the cold. Let's go outside."

The music had started up again. I read her lips: "All right."

We got our coats and stepped out into the bitter night air. There were no other lighted houses visible. It was so isolated, so remote: this patch of gaudy illumination in the middle of the dark Atlantic. I helped her over the low stone wall and we walked to the side of the house. We could still hear the muffled bluegrass music and the rustle of conversation.

"I saw you at Osona's auction last week," I said.

"You—? But, how did you—?"

"I drove out to Madaket for lunch. You weren't there so I tried the next likely place."

She looked down. "Detective."

"I saw you...working, with Nathan Parrish."

"Well, that's what we do. We work together. He likes collecting and he doesn't want to be taken advantage of. I love things and I can't afford to buy them. I was cleaning his house and he came in, very highfalutin and snobbish, so I couldn't resist telling him that his precious Andrew Sandsbury lightship basket was a fake. I ran into him at an auction a few weeks later, kept him from making a bad mistake over a Colonial hutch. We've been working together ever since."

"So...nothing else is going on? Because it seemed like something else was going on."

"Henry, he's married."

"So was I. So are half the men at this party. It wouldn't stop most of them. And you happen to look like the younger version of Carla Parrish. The perfect trade-in."

"He loves his wife."

"Well, he's cheating on her with someone. I saw them together."

"Really? And how did that come to pass?"

"I was driving a late shift on Main Street a few weeks ago. I saw two silhouettes behind the shades in his office. Then they … merged. He had a girl up there and she wasn't taking dictation."

"Well, she couldn't have been too picky."

"No?"

"He's a bit old for me, frankly. Besides, he's fat and he drinks too much."

"But he's rich."

"Well, that might explain it. If you're that sort of person. I wouldn't touch him with the wet end of a floor mop, and there's nothing more to say about it." Yet she started anyway. "I, I want to—"

"What?"

"I want…I don't know."

"Come on, tell me."

She got hold of herself, and looked me in the eye. "I want to have a nice time tonight. I'll tell you why I lied. I was buying you a present."

"I thought you didn't approve of Christmas. You told me that—"

"We should have it every other year. I know. But anyway…it wasn't for Christmas. It was just for you. I hate to see you with those awful Bic pens you use. I heard there were going to be some nice fountain pens at the sale, so I made sure to get you one."

She reached into her pocket and handed me a small, oblong box, wrapped in dark paper.

"Fiona—"

"Open it."

It was a Montblanc with a gold nib, maybe forty years old.

I tilted it toward the light from the windows. The inlaid nib flashed. "It's beautiful."

"You're a beautiful writer and you should have a nice tool for your work. Poetry's a gift from God. Which I do appreciate, whatever you may think."

I laughed. "But unlike you, God leaves the price tags on. Not to mention that 'some assembly required' stuff. Thanks a lot, buddy."

She stared me down, refusing even to smile at my little joke. "You should be thankful for the good things in your life."

"I know." I pulled her toward me and kissed her. Cold lips, warm tongues. When we separated I said. "Very thankful."

"Come on, you great beast, let's get inside before we freeze to death."

Chapter Sixteen

Intrigues

Cindy opened the car door and unfolded herself into the bitter wind, grateful that she had decided not to wear heels. Crunching up the driveway they saw Bob Haffner smoking a quick cigarette before going inside

"You never go to parties," Cindy said.

"Yeah, but this guy is serving food. Real food and lots of it. I talked to the caterer. That's why I haven't eaten in two days." He grinned. "I'm ready. And for whatever I can't finish…pockets!" He bowed out the big cargo pockets on his overcoat. "You'd be amazed how much I can stuff in these. I'll be set for a week."

He stumped on ahead of them and Mike said, "At least he has a plan."

Inside, they saw Tanya Kriel at the same moment.

She was wearing a low-cut maroon dress, ankle length, slit halfway up the thigh. Her hair was piled up, with tendrils of it brushing her cheekbones. A black velvet choker around her neck gave her the provocative look of a concubine. With a small jolt, Mike realized that he had actually never seen her dressed in anything but her painting clothes. Even in caulk-crusted work pants and an old sweatshirt she set off all the alarms in his limbic system. This was much worse. He had seen her naked and it didn't matter. He had made love with her and it didn't matter. He wanted her here and now, in some deserted guest room upstairs, or else in front of everyone, like hormone-deranged high-school kid.

He knew the lust and longing would be all over his face, like barbecue sauce and pork grease after eating a rack of ribs with no napkins. The thought of these two women standing next to each other was unbearable, impossible. It was matter and anti-matter: something would explode. Probably him.

"I have to find a bathroom," he bleated. Cindy stared at him.

"Hi Mike," Tanya said. "Is this Cindy? Show off those world-famous social graces and introduce us."

"I'll be right back," He pushed his way into the crowd. Cindy watched him go, and then turned to shake Tanya Kriel's hand.

"I'm on Mike's crew," Tanya said.

Cindy smiled at her. "I know."

And she did. She knew everything now. It was obvious. All the nightmares were real. All the gossip was true. It all matched: the long hours at work, the weird new distances at home. And that pile of drop cloths, somewhere in this house, somewhere near where she was standing right now. Tanya was watching her as if she was about to faint. Good call. Would you put a damp washcloth on my forehead, you bitch? Would that make you feel better?

"Excuse me," she said. "I need a drink."

As Mike stumbled across the Lomax house Great Room, fleeing from his wife and Tanya Kriel, he side-stepped a waiter with a platter of crab eggrolls, slipped on a slick patch of floor where someone had spilled a drink, and pitched headlong into Preston Lomax himself—host, employer, lifeline.

The older man caught Mike under the armpits, and pushed him upright. "Michael Henderson, the Cutting Edge painter. Just the man I wanted to see."

Mike stood up straight, intensely relieved that he wasn't drunk. Utterly insane, yes …but that was easier to hide. He looked up into the man's eyes, a pale whitish blue like a winter sky with snow massing below the horizon. "Mr. Lomax."

"One of your people was rude to my son last week."

"Really?" he asked. "I had no idea."

"You know nothing about it?"

"No one said anything to me."

Pat Folger appeared from the general direction of the bar and stepped in between them. Both Mike and Lomax moved back to accommodate him. Folger was as dressed up as he was ever going to get, in a plaid jacket and brown turtleneck sweater. He brandished a highball glass of scotch at Lomax. "Didn't your son give you the message? I'll repeat it, then. My painters don't work for you. They work for me. I'm the general contractor on this job. I don't go into your office and tell your employees how to comport themselves. So don't send your son to do it to me."

"Listen, Folger—"

"No, you listen for a change. You think I need you? Guess again. I have six jobs going on right now and five more lined up on top of them. I barely managed to fit you in. And I'm starting to wonder if it's worth the trouble."

"How dare you—?"

"I'll tell you how. I have as much education as you. I have an MBA from Wharton, buddy. I can speak more languages than you. I've read more books than you. And I probably have almost as much money as you do. I could learn your job in six months and do it better than you can. Could learn to be a master carpenter in six months? You think you're better than me but you're not. So behave, or you can find someone else for your next project. Because I've had it with you, Lomax. You've been pissing me off since before we met."

A small group had gathered to listen, including Nathan and Carla Parrish.

Lomax was too stunned to respond and Mike pushed past the crowd, jaywalking through that brief cognitive gap as if it were a break in the traffic. He made his escape as Folger grunted in disgust and stalked off in the other direction.

Mike started laughing as he ran upstairs. Pat Folger might be a scary guy when he was in your face. But there was nobody better when he was at your back. Mike made it to the second floor and stood still, panting. The party noise was muted here. The band had taken a break. He headed for the guest bathroom. He needed to splash some cold water on his face. Halfway down the hall he heard sounds coming from one of the two master suites: little cries and moans floating like tuneless modern music over the rhythmic thump of the headboard against the wall.

Someone was making love in Lomax's bed, in the room that was so sacrosanct that only Mike himself was allowed inside to do touch-ups, with surgical gloves on his hands and freshly laundered socks on his feet. The bed was decked with lace-trimmed pillows, and the idea that someone had just scattered them all over the floor he found oddly gratifying. There might even be some stains on those eight hundred dollar Pratesi sheets before the night was over.

He moved closer to the door to hear the high thin nasal voice coming from inside. He knew it from the endless punch lists ("This is appalling! Look at this! There's paint all *over* this doorknob, Mike! That's an *antique solid brass* doorknob! Don't just *nod* at me! Tell me how you're going to fix this! Show me I was right to trust you with my *home*."). Now that voice was saying, "Yes, yes, yes. Yes! *Yes!*"

He was sure it was her, though "Yes" was one word she had never spoken in his presence. She was in the bedroom and her husband was downstairs. So who—?

"Kevin! Yes, Kevin! Oh, God, Kevin! That's so good! Yes! Harder!"

Mike stepped closer. Was it possible? The poetic justice of catching Kevin Sloane exactly as Kevin had caught him was too good to be true. It was also appalling, as Diana might say herself. And hilarious.

Leaning into the door casing, straining to catch a sound that would identify his nemesis, he didn't hear the footsteps behind him. The gentle hand on his shoulder banged through his nervous system like a blow. He spun around, sure it was Lomax. He had no excuse or explanation for his presence here, eavesdropping on this grotesque infidelity. His mind was a blank.

But it wasn't Preston Lomax. It was the daughter, Kathleen.

"Kevin is in there with someone, isn't he?"

"What?"

"He thinks I'm still off-island."

"I don't know—he—you…it's not—you can't—" Mike pulled himself together. "Listen, come with me, we have to get out of here."

He took her arm but she shook it off.

"He's with someone." Before he could stop her she side-stepped him and lunged through the door.

"Kevin? Kevin, Jesus, what are you—"

She gasped like she was choking on food.

"Oh, my God. Mom. Oh my God. I can't—Oh God. Oh God."

She bolted past Mike, almost knocking him over and ran down the corridor for the stairs. Mike stepped into the room, a flash like the first few moments after a car crash: everyone checking to make sure they were intact, ears ringing and nervous systems jangling. The silence was a vacuum. It sucked everything into it. Kevin and Mrs. Lomax sat upright in bed, the covers pulled to their necks. They had the same wild-eyed animal still-ness. Terror twins, identical despite the age difference.

Mike knew exactly how they felt.

Mrs. Lomax spoke first, with the calm and perfect diction of catastrophe.

"I don't think any of us should talk about this. To anyone. Ever."

"Good idea," said Kevin.

"That's fine with me," Mike said to her. Then he turned to Kevin. "You're fired. Don't let me catch you on the job again. I'll mail you your last check."

"Hey, wait a second! You can't—"

"Kevin. Think about your situation. Then decide."

He left the room and shut the door behind him.

Chapter Seventeen
Tactical Delay

In the great room downstairs, Nathan Parrish and his wife Carla had joined Preston Lomax amid a group of captivated women at the foot of the stairs. Lomax had recovered nicely from his brief contretemps with Pat Folger. He was as resilient as a rubber ball. Carla looked him over now. She was amused at that his efforts to look like an old time Nantucketer, falling short in ways only an old time Nantucketer would notice. His loafers weren't topsiders, his blue blazer was too light a shade of blue, and his "Nantucket Red" pants were too red. The dusty pink faded with repeated washings. His were obviously just off the shelf. Lomax was a shade off, and he always would be.

But she had to admit he sounded impressive, telling his guests the story of his most recent indulgence: an indoor red-clay tennis court.

"It takes up most of the basement in the Virginia house," he was saying. "I thought there'd be drainage problems. You have to water that surface daily. But the engineers did a great job. I wish they'd consulted with the idiots who built the roads in this town! Every time it drizzles half the island gets flooded."

The women laughed nervously.

Carla was standing next to the newel post. "Preston," she said, "what happened to your mortgage button?"

Mortgage buttons were small ivory medallions that Nantucket homeowners traditionally placed at the top of the ground floor newel post when the mortgage was paid off and they finally owned their house. Nathan and Carla had been at the auction where Lomax overpaid for a set of antique buttons. He made quite a fuss about the little ivory coin he chose to display, which was ironic since he had built the house and never had to struggle with monthly payments. The button didn't represent a hard-won victory over penury and foreclosure; it was merely another bogus token of insider status, like the professionally rebuilt 1955 Chevrolet Bel Air convertible with two-tone coral-and-gray exterior and powerglide transmission that he had bought off the Internet so he could drive an antique car in the island's Daffodil Day parade.

"I'll tell you what I did with that button, Carla," he was saying now. "I gave it to David Lazarus to scrimshaw. He's etching my family crest onto it. Then it really makes a statement. It will be my flag in the dirt here."

Parrish laughed. "Of all the things in the world to get corny about—you chose your ancestors and real estate. This may be the place for you after all."

"There's only one small problem," Carla said. "The scrimshaw will ruin the button's authenticity. You'll be branding it like a cow. This belongs to Preston Lomax. It's unbearably gauche. But it's kind of perfect, too. It could be the dust jacket illustration for a book about everything that's gone wrong with Nantucket."

Lomax laughed. "Feel free to borrow the button if you ever write the book."

Parrish stepped between Lomax and his wife, as if to physically cut the current of jocular animosity running between them. He patted the bigger man's shoulder. "I like the sense I get from it. I like the idea of you sticking around for a while. We have a lot of branding and ruining to do together and I'm looking forward to every minute of it." He lifted his glass of wine in a toast. Carla sneered and drifted away.

Lomax touched his glass to Nathan's. "It's going to be quite a project, Nathan."

"The town is going to fight me."

"Of course they will. But money always wins. It's that simple. We could save millions on court costs and lawyers' fees by simply comparing their tax returns of the litigants, and then settling things on that basis. It would be honest at least. But people don't like the truth. That's why it's so easy to lie to them. And so profitable."

"Speaking of profits…any word on that first check? I'm eager to break ground."

"Great news. The money's in place. But you know…it's coming from Dubai, and the government is worried about terrorist connections. Ridiculous—they're the good Arabs. Their Royal Family has done more to bring that country into the modern world in one decade than…well, in any case. There's nothing to be done. The State Department due diligence on this money has been very intense, very detailed. But cash should be flowing by the first of the year."

He set his empty glass on an end table. "Now, if you'll excuse me, I have to rescue my wife from the Board of Selectmen."

Parrish watched him slip away into the packed living room. All this talk of Homeland Security and the Emirates soured his stomach. He knew that line of talk. This was his own trick, being used against him. Nathan never said, "I won't have your money for eight months, if ever." A jolt of reality like that could lead to lawsuits or even physical violence. More importantly, it violated the "Urge to Hope" which he otherwise exploited. Instead, he hedged: "The money will be in place by next Tuesday." And next Tuesday he said, "The papers should be filed by the end of next week, and money flowing the week after that."

And the week after that?

"One of the signatories has been in Europe, but he's due back at the beginning of the month." He just kept doing it: Things should be in order by the start of the new fiscal year, after the holidays, when the Chinese government signs off on the new loan restructuring…when the bubble payment rider is approved at the board meeting on the tenth…he kept people going for years this way, gradually *Degrading Expectations* until the interested parties actually lost interest and gave up, without ever forcing a confrontation.

Lomax was another master of what Parrish called "Tactical Delay"—maybe better than Parrish, himself. But that made sense. Lomax was a lot richer, too. Parrish let out a long tired breath. Then he drained his wine and went looking for a refill.

Chapter Eighteen
Full Disclosure

David Trezize arrived at the party just before ten. He had been drinking, which was a bad idea, and he'd been driving, which was worse, skidding on the icy roads and rehearsing what he was going to say. Words were his weapon. He had to use them for maximum effect.

He had approached the intersection of Vesper Lane and Joy Street too fast and slid right across it, brakes stuttering uselessly. He was stuttering himself by then, losing his nerve.

At the Eel Point house, cars were parked up and down the side of the road. It was a long walk in the cold, and the frigid air sobered him up. He slipped on the deck and landed on his elbow. He sat down in the snow, fighting tears of pain and frustration. But the fall turned out to be a good thing. It made him angrier. It got him moving.

He pushed into the warmth and the noise of the Great Room. He saw Lomax, squat and dissipated like some diseased Roman emperor just before the fall of the empire, standing by the French doors to the back deck. He was talking to Patty and Grady Malone. So he was going to have to confront Lomax in front of his ex-wife? Fine, fine, what did it matter? This concerned her anyway. David launched as soon as he and the tycoon were face to face.

"I hope you're proud of yourself, you miserable shit."

Lomax smiled. "Excuse me?"

"I read that piece about you in the *Wall Street Journal.* They called you a 'far-sighted financial strategist.' You're not a far-sighted financial strategist! Unless you call destroying helpless people a strategy. You find companies in trouble, you buy them out cheap, fire everyone, sell everything, and move on to the next victim. You're a scavenger. A repo man! You're a vulture. You think you're larger than life? You're smaller than life! You've got no style—what are those fucking plaster mermaid sculptures holding up the mantelpiece? You've gotta be kidding."

"Are you finished?"

"No! You want to wreck my newspaper, fine. But you leave my family alone. Fuck with them again and I'll kill you. And I'll get off because every member of the jury will be so happy to see you dead."

"Sad, bitter little people keep saying that to me. But I remain happily alive, and immensely popular. This isn't funny anymore, David. I want you off my property."

"Yeah, it's all about the property, isn't it? This territory is sacred because it's been sprayed with your money. Well fuck you. Fuck all of you. I wouldn't give a Nantucket sawbuck for the whole useless bunch of you."

He pushed someone aside, knocking their glass, and walked out the door, slamming it behind him. Gradually two dozen conversations began to fill the reverberating silence. Lomax handed a napkin to a guest whose drink had spilled.

Across the room, Bob Haffner was stealing caviar when Mike and Cindy started to argue. The caterer, Annette Sprague, was an old girlfriend of Bob's. She had come full circle, from pushing him away and saying "I love you…but like a *brother*," through a tumultuous love affair, a screaming, plate-smashing break-up and then the slowly accumulating affection growing back like wildflowers in a burned forest. At this moment she actually felt like Bob's big sister, attached to him for life whether she liked it or not. So she gave him quick hug when he came into the Lomax kitchen and turned away while he shoveled the Sevruga into a plastic bag. She had to smile: the combination seemed to sum up her old boyfriend perfectly.

Just beyond the kitchen, Mike and Cindy Henderson were facing off, and Bob stepped to the door to listen.

"No wonder you didn't want me to come to the party," Cindy said. "You knew she'd be here. I mean, my God! It's so trite. She's a home-wrecker straight out of Central Casting."

"She's a pretty girl, Cindy. Should she wear a burka so you won't feel threatened? Because that's going to be a tough dress code to enforce six months from now, when half the pretty girls between Coral Gables and Prince Edward Island show up here for the summer."

"They're not working for you every day."

"Some of them will be. I hope. And my dress code is shorts and a T-shirt. What do you want me to say? That I have eyes only for you?"

"So what's the truth?"

"The truth? The truth is that I want every good-looking woman I see every day—the girls at the coffee shops and the landscaper girls and the rich women driving Range Rovers. So does every other man you've ever known, including the sainted Mark Toland, who's living in Hollywood making movies with his own casting couch, that is, his *bed*—where he and today's special wind up after a few drinks for a 'private read-through' of whatever script he's flogging that week."

"You don't know anything about Mark Toland."

"But I'm supposed to believe he's the big exception. Well, we have one piece of evidence. He wasn't interested in you."

"I don't want to talk about Mark."

"Great, because I don't want to talk about Tanya Kriel. If there's anything else on your mind I'd be glad to hear it."

Cindy looked away.

"I'm pregnant," she said.

"What?"

"I'm pregnant, Mike. I took the test three times."

"Cindy—"

"I think it happened the night we had to stay over in Hyannis, just before Halloween. Remember that night? We had dinner at Bangkok Kitchen and we missed the eight-thirty boat."

"I remember."

They stood silently for a long moment. The band started up again—raucous bluegrass with a badgering banjo solo. Mike felt like they were using his nerves for the strings.

"How do you feel about this, Mike? Are you happy? Nervous? Pissed off or freaked out or all of the above or...what? Just tell me what's going on in your head because I feel really horrible right now."

"I don't know."

"Not good enough. Not even close."

"So what am I supposed to say?"

"You're not supposed to say anything! You're supposed to grab me and hug me and howl with joy because we're finally going to have a baby together."

"It's a shock, Cindy. I don't know if I'm ready for this. I mean, it's—how long have you known?"

"A couple of weeks. I didn't want to say anything because... frankly? I was afraid we'd have a conversation like this one. Which I wasn't ready for."

"Do you want the baby?"

"Of course I want the baby! What kind of a question is that?"

"It's practical. We're on the edge financially, we're fighting constantly, I'm not sure this is the right time."

"There's no such thing as the right time."

"Yeah, that's what everyone says."

"You wish this hadn't happened."

"Well, I—"

"If I have this baby, you'll have to really settle down. You'll have to really make a commitment. We'll be a family then. You can't walk away from a child, not the way you can from another person. You're stuck. It's not a vow or a promise or some abstraction. It's a *whole other human being* and you're its world and you have to make that world a safe place. So screwing the cute girls on your crew really isn't an option anymore."

"Wait a second! I didn't—"

"Don't lie and make it worse, Mike. I heard her bragging to her friends while you were upstairs. Apparently you two invented a whole new use for drop cloths."

"Cindy—"

She was watching his face the way a fox watches a bush, waiting for any tiny movement that will reveal its prey. She saw it and pounced. "So it's true."

"Listen, it was only one time and we—"

I don't want to hear about it Mike."

They stared at each other. The music jittered on. Mike shook his head. "I don't understand how she could have said that."

"She didn't."

"What?"

Cindy allowed herself a cold, thin little smile. "She didn't say anything, Mike. You fell for the oldest trick in the book: tell one conspirator that the other one confessed."

"But the drop cloths—"

"There's been a rumor going around about those drop cloths for weeks, but no one knew who was using them as a love nest. Until now."

"Christ. Cindy, you have to—"

"I don't have to do anything! I certainly don't have to have your baby and I really, really don't want to at this moment. In fact just the thought of it makes me sick." She eyed the room. "I'm taking the car and going home. Call yourself a taxi if you want. Or get a ride with your girlfriend."

She pushed past a little clot of people who were actually clapping their hands to the relentless, machine-like bluegrass, and she was gone. He stood there until the song ended. Bob Haffner dodged out of the kitchen behind a waiter. Mike saw him and he held up his bag of caviar for an explanation.

"I didn't hear a thing," he said edging himself through the crowd in the slip stream of the waiter. "I got stood up and I'm outta here."

Mike stepped back and leaned against the wall, crossing his arms over his chest. He didn't want to run into anyone else, or make conversation. He certainly didn't want to go home. Maybe this could be his new home. On Nantucket, painters often lived in the houses they were painting, at least until the caretaker found them or the owners came up for an unplanned weekend. He glanced at the kitchen door casing. The thin edge against the wall needed another coat. He resented his mind for noticing crap like that at a time like this. When he was standing in front of the judge for his divorce hearing he'd probably be critiquing the finish on the bench. He closed his eyes. There was a rustle of movement near him and the nerve-sharpening smell of a familiar perfume. He could feel the little hairs stiffening on the back of his neck.

"Hi, Mike," Tanya said softly.

He couldn't speak; he couldn't even look at her. Two out of five senses were more than enough. And then there was taste, you can't leave out the information transmitted on the tongue.

She stroked his arm. "It looks like we're busted."

"Yeah."

"But the good part about that is, we don't have to worry about getting caught anymore. And I counted, Mike. There are at least six available beds in this house. Getting naked will be easy because I'm not wearing anything under my dress."

She took his hand and placed it on the thin silk at her side. She led it down to where he could feel for himself that she was telling the truth.

The touch was like a drug that changed his body chemistry so all his desires were condensed into one and he craved nothing but the needle. Every cell in his body was raging for the next fix. How could you possibly fight that? He pushed the words up his throat: "This is wrong."

"I don't care. And neither do you."

She led him upstairs as the band started their next set. They avoided the master bedroom this time. It was jinxed. Everyone got caught there. In the guest bedroom on the third floor they could barely hear the music. Tanya's dress came off in a single gesture and she stripped him slowly, kissing him all the time. She pulled him down on the narrow bed. Once again Mike had the astonishing sensation of every sexual fantasy he'd ever imagined coming true.

And it proved to him, once again, just how puny and pedestrian his imagination really was.

Chapter Nineteen
Conspiracies

Mike and Tanya lost track of time. They even fell asleep briefly, before waking up and making love again. When they finally started to pull their clothes on, the party was over. They opened the door softly, listening. Even the caterers had left. The house was silent. They straightened the room up and started to creep downstairs.

On the first landing they heard Lomax talking. They couldn't make out the words, but his nasal growl was unmistakable. They glanced at each other and tiptoed down a few steps.

He was with his wife in the living room. The high ceiling caught and amplified his voice.

"I don't suspect anything, Diana. I don't make guesses. I had you followed and I had you photographed. You still have enough residual notoriety from your modeling days to make those pictures very interesting to a lot of unpleasant people. I ran into Larry Flynt at LAX a couple of years ago. He told me that a good shot of you would double his newsstand sales. You should be flattered."

"You don't have to threaten me, Preston. I just want to know where I stand."

"Where you stand? I would say…on the edge of a cliff, Darling. So step back, before you fall. Since you seem so fascinated with my will, I should tell you I've rewritten it. In the new version everything goes to charity. You get a small allowance, just enough to live on. Not enough to peel off a Nantucket sawbuck every time you want someone to help carry the groceries; sorry. And you're cut off if you're ever seen with another man. Which doesn't mean you can't carry on your little romance. But it will have to be furtive and tawdry, just like your late night phone calls. It's ironic: there's actually more money in the will for your surveillance than for your support. I'm sending the new will to the estate lawyers on the first of the year. That gives you less than three weeks to kill me, if you think you can get away with it."

"Preston—"

"In any case, I suggest you recruit a new accomplice. That little house-painter doesn't have the balls. Not that I think you're really capable of murder No, I just want you to count down the time until I legally foreclose on your future. Happy holidays."

Mike looked over at Tanya. She tugged his arm, but he shook his head. He wanted to stay.

"Preston, please…what will I do now? Where will I go?"

"Read your pre-nup. You get nothing if you commit adultery. But I wouldn't put you out in the cold. When I got rid of the Hilton Head estate, I made sure you had life residency rights to the guest cottage."

"But that's just two bedrooms! And that tiny kitchen! I can't cook in that tiny kitchen!"

"You've never cooked in any kitchen! I bought you a thirty-thousand-dollar six-burner Aga stove, and you never used it for anything but the teakettle. The kitchen on Hilton Head has a micro-wave. You can heat up whatever you want. You can get mail under the name of Hodgson, and the phone in the cottage is in their name, too. It's an excellent hideout and you're going to want one, believe me."

"But what about all the people here, the designers and architects and decorators and tradespeople? The plumbers and painters and electricians? Are you just going to run out on all those bills? Just—leave all those people high and dry?"

"I wouldn't say 'high and dry.' There's something obscurely comforting about that phrase, don't you think? I prefer soaked and buried."

"And then what? You vanish without a trace?"

"A trace would spoil everything."

Mike and Tanya stared at each other. He grabbed her wrist like a lamppost in a hurricane. But this wind was too strong. Mike needed that final check. His mortgage, the IRS payments, his truck loan, the workman's comp money, the overdue credit card bills…the whole preposterous balancing act was anchored by one thing, now, the twenty-three thousand, six hundred and forty one dollars from the Lomax job. He had assumed it was already in the mail. He'd been checking his post box with increasing nervousness for the last few days.

Without that money he was finished.

He felt a wash of animal panic. They'd foreclose his house, repo his truck. He had written a big check to the Mass Department of Revenue, gambling that the Lomax money would arrive in time. That one was going to bounce, and up into five figures which is felony fraud in this state.

Could he leap downstairs and grab Lomax, put a kitchen knife to his throat until he wrote the check? No, no, no, it would have to be cash. With this guy even cash was suspect. He probably had counterfeit bills stashed away. And he knew what came next. Lomax would charge him with assault-and-battery not to mention grand theft and trespassing.

It didn't matter. Lomax had hollowed him out. He was weak and nauseous. He had no strength to attack anyone.

At the far side of the giant living room, at the door to the little study Mike had repainted so many times, he noticed a flicker of movement. Someone else was eavesdropping. He recognized the tangle of red hair, the pale white face: Kathleen, the daughter. Their eyes met across the sixty feet of tainted air. For a second, Mike was sure she was going to bust them, jump out, point a finger, start yelling. She moved her hand, but it was only to cross her lips with a conspiratorial finger. She was scared, too. She had no more business being here than Mike and Tanya did.

The difference was, they could escape.

Tanya's voice was a harsh whisper. "Let's get the hell out of here."

They crept down the stairs, darted past the wide entry to the living room, in plain sight for a second or two. But no one was looking. They found their coats in the foyer and a minute later they were closing the massive front door behind them. They stood in the deep breathless cold of the winter night.

"I came here to kill him," Tanya said.

He could barely hear her over the roaring panic in his head, like the snarl of a job site air-compressor, building pressure. When it finally shut down, the silence meant the carpenters could use their nailguns again. They could get to work. Until then they were stalled. He faced Tanya, with nothing to say.

"He killed my sister," she added. She could see he couldn't grasp her words. She shrugged. "It's a long story."

They stood silently, haunting the night with their breath.

"You want a ride home?," she asked.

He pulled his social self around him, buttoned it like a coat. "Yeah," he managed. "If that's okay. I'm sorry."

"Don't be. You've got a lot of thinking to do. Lomax put you in a bad spot. But you're smart. You'll get out of this. People do."

Yeah, he thought. Except the ones who don't. They're called homeless people. He might have been able to handle living in a box and eating out of soup kitchens. But he had a wife and she was pregnant.

They didn't talk at all on the drive home. Or maybe Tanya said something. He didn't notice. He was pawing through his circumstances, his jobs and customers, his family and friends, debts he could cash in, obligations he could stall, looking for a solution. It was like rummaging through the kitchen junk drawer for his car keys. The only real question was, how many times would you dump it out and sort through stamps and corkscrews and defunct cell-phone chargers before you accepted that the keys weren't there?

So he kept searching. An advance on the Keller job? But that wasn't supposed to start until Spring. Or the Silverstein job? But they were living here and they'd expect him there every day. That was fine—he wouldn't be working for Lomax anymore. But the money wasn't enough. He'd have to start at least three jobs and lay off people at the same time. He couldn't afford to pay anyone anything. He could conceivably get first checks from Foley and Landau but the Foleys were here all winter, too—and the Landau's caretaker was Pat Folger. Pat would be checking up daily, and he'd be delighted to bust Mike with the owners if he wasn't on the job.

Mike stared out at the dark trees streaming past the passenger side window. He couldn't make this work. He couldn't be on all those jobs simultaneously, with just him and Haffner. Maybe he could keep Briley, but everyone else had to go. He added it up: if he got all the checks this week, or next week at the latest, if he could convince the Kellers to let him start early, that would just cover his outstanding obligations. No, he'd still be about twenty-five hundred shy. And that was only until the first week's wages were due; and he'd have no more money from anyone until he got to the halfway mark. He was up to the limit on his charge at Marine; how was he supposed to buy the materials for three new jobs at once? That was around fifteen hundred bucks right there. He added it up. He needed six thousand dollars to survive this siege. Not even to survive it, just to get to the next onslaught. But if Bob and Derek would agree to wait for their checks until Mike got the next checks from the owners, and everyone agreed to let him start, and paid him quickly…no, no good, with the materials and the mortgage, he was still four thousand dollars in the red. And he needed some money to live on—food and gas. A grand? Would that do it? Say it would: that meant he had to find five thousand dollars by tomorrow.

Tanya pulled into his driveway. Lights were on in the little house. Cindy was up. He glanced at the dashboard clock: 11:45. It wasn't even that late.

"You're home."

"Thanks." He unfolded himself into the cold night air. He stood in his driveway, watching Tanya's truck back out into the deserted street and the answer came to him, discovered like those keys in the junk drawer. There was only one place to go, only one person he could turn to at this moment.

He climbed into his own truck and started the long drive to Billy Delavane's house in Madaket.

Mike had known Billy Delavane all his life. They had grown up together, building forts in the national forest with Strong Wings, sledding Dead Horse Valley on snow days. They had combed the prized sections of Madaket harbor together, with push rakes and dip nets, when family scallop season began in October, opening their one bushel a week at the Delavane shanty on North Wharf, cooking them at big family dinners on autumn nights.

They had learned to drive battered, family pickups on the rutted grass at Tom Nevers, done the parties at 30th Pole, and the Madequecham Jam every year, before the cops started breaking it up; chased the same girls, drank the same cheap beer, bought the same weed from the same sleazy high school entrepreneurs.

Both of their parents were in the trades; Mike's Dad had painted behind Danny "Duke" Delavane since the mid-seventies. They had each learned their skills on a thousand job sites; they had eventually inherited their family's companies, customers, and crew. But Billy had hated being a general contractor, sucking up to imperious customers, arguing with crazy subs and chasing money. Working for Pat Folger was easier.

After his parents died, Billy didn't have to work anymore, but he liked it. He could hold all the calculations for a seven-foot bar or a three-story staircase in his head, and rout a newel post by hand while he watched a Red Sox game. So Pat Folger kept him around. Pat had a ruthless knack for making the most out of his employees. He said if you want to survive on Nantucket you have to know how to get limited use out of limited people. Some of his guys were drunks; he didn't expect them at work

until ten in the morning. Some of them were only happy banging shingles or running baseboard; he made sure he had enough
shingles and baseboard going to keep them busy. Billy surfed
and Pat didn't expect him at work when there was a south swell
running and an offshore breeze to smooth it out.

Billy's family had lived on the island much longer than
Mike's—six generations. They had held onto their property not
out of some shrewd investment strategy but simply because they
loved it. Now Billy and his brother probably owned twenty-
million dollars' worth of undeveloped land and crumbling
nineteenth-century houses around the island. Occasionally they
sold off a one-acre tract or a beach cottage to pay the taxes.

Mike had helped Billy clear out his parents' house after they
died. It was packed with thirty years' accumulation of pack-rat
trash: collections of animal skulls and fishing lures, mold-rotted
books and antique jam jars, bales of twine and barbed wire,
lobster pots and scallop boxes, checkbooks and unopened bills
from the 1960s, lampshades and chair cushions, broken radios,
and unraveling wicker. After a week of ten-hour days they were
able to see the floor. When the Thomas Tompion grandfather
clock and the Tony Sarg puzzles had been taken to the auction
house and everything else had been carted to the dump, the
cleaning had begun. The once-white walls were stained a toxic
amber from decades of cigarette smoke; they were black from
mold where the roof leaked. Mike and Billy wore vapor masks
and rubber gloves and scrubbed the place for another week. Ed
never volunteered to help; neither did anyone else.

It made sense: Mike and Billy had always been the real brothers. There was a ten-year gap between Mike and his big sister,
so it was natural for him to invent his own siblings. There was
rivalry, mostly over women. But when Billy got a local jock's
girlfriend pregnant, when he was broke and desperate, Mike had
pulled six hundred dollars out of his college savings, along with
another four hundred for travel expenses (it was already pretty
clear that he wasn't going to college), so Joyce Thayer could go
to Boston and get an abortion.

Joyce had stayed in Boston. Apparently she met someone that year at BC and wound up having the baby. She never said anything to Billy and she never came back to the island. Billy tried to reach her. He wrote several long letters, but never got an answer. As Mike reluctantly pointed out at the end of a long drunken night, that itself was an answer—an emphatic one.

Billy had eventually paid Mike back the money, and he was a rich man now, generous, always glad to help Mike with short term loans—a thousand here or there until a check cleared or a job started. But this was different. He had never borrowed this much money from Billy before. More importantly, he had never asked for a loan without knowing when he'd be able to pay it back. And he'd never been this desperate, driving too fast with rage and dread self-loathing climbing his throat as he took a turn too wide and the wheels shuddered against the jumbled dirty snow on the shoulder. These curves were deceptive. He eased back to forty miles an hour. Soon he was crossing Millie's bridge, turning onto the ruts and craters of Maine Avenue.

The lights glowed from Billy's beach shack. Mike parked and sat in the car, listening to the surf and the faint sound of Van Morrison from Billy's house, carried on the wind. "Blue Money." How appropriate. He had no idea what he was going to say, or how he was going to begin.

As it turned out, he didn't have to say anything.

Billy came to the door in sweatpants and an old Delavane Construction T-shirt. The wood stove was going and the little house was warm. There was a faint smell of varnish. Van was singing "Cleaning Windows" now. Maybe it was a message; people always needed their windows cleaned. Billy's pug, Dervish, jumped up, front paws on Mike's knees, curlicue tail twitching. Mike leaned over to rub behind the little dog's ears. Dervish had a nice little set-up here. A warm house, constant attention, and all the food he could eat. "Hey, Dervish," he said. "Good boy." Dervish stretched to lick his nose. Some people would have been disgusted by that; Mike took it as a compliment.

He straightened up and Billy said, "Come in. Have a drink. Tell me how much you need."

"No, look, I didn't—"

Billy took his shoulder and pulled him inside. "Hey, relax, check yourself out. It has to be money, unless Cindy's leaving you. Or you have something incurable, and I can't help with that." He kicked the door closed with his foot and stared at Mike. "Wait a second. Is Cindy leaving you?"

"No, not yet...at least, I hope not."

"Then, let's get out of here. I've been working this bird feeder all night. I was just getting some sealer on it."

"You missed the party."

"No, I showed up early, had a few drinks, and split. Pat was trying to corner me. The McKittricks' basement is leaking and they're suing him. He wants me to testify if it goes to court." He grabbed his coat off the rack near the door, and pulled it on. "I built the kids' bunk bed and installed the cabinets. What the hell do I know about the basement? Anyway, if he wants to talk about, it he can do it on his own time, on the job. It's not cocktail party talk. Except, Pat doesn't have anything else to talk about. Come on, let's get to the Box before it closes."

Mike explained the situation as they rode back to town. He was finishing as they turned away from the Stop& Shop into the Chicken Box parking lot: "So I need five thousand dollars and I have no idea when I'll be able to pay it back."

Billy laughed. "Don't stop there—really sell me. Say you'll gamble it all away at Mohegan Sun and then avoid me like I was contagious for the next five years."

"No man, come on, you know there's no way—"

Billy punched him on the arm, "I'm kidding. Relax. Gentleman's rule: retain your sense of humor under duress."

Mike let out a long breath. "Oh yeah—I remember those rules. Your dad was great. Borderline psychotic, but great."

"And he really was a gentleman, in his own way. He never broke his own rules. Don't argue about politics. Pick up the tab.

Notice small improvements. Remember birthdays. Call home. Walk the dog."

"Help your friends."

Billy nodded. "Treat them like family. Because they are."

He leaned over and pulled his checkbook out of his pocket, pulled a pen from the ashtray, scribbled a check, tore it off, handed it over.

Mike was confused. "This is for seventy-five hundred dollars."

"That was one of my dad's best rules: a gentleman never asks for as much as he needs."

"Thank you."

Billy cuffed him lightly on the head, "Come on. Let's shoot some pool and have a beer. You're buying."

Chapter Twenty
Romance and Retribution

"I just wish there was something I could do to him," Mike said.

They were still at the Chicken Box, drinking draft Guinness. Billy Delavane was running the pool table. With Billy's check in his pocket Mike's frenzy had subsided, but he could still feel the noise of it resonating in the silence, like a football stadium after a playoff game.

"There's things you can do. Four ball in the corner." Billy had an expert ease with the pool cue, leaning over the table, giving a couple of smooth piston warmups and a single sure strike that sent the cue ball rocketing at the corner. It knocked in the four ball and floated back to the middle of the table. "Six in the side."

Mike took a long swallow. "Like what?"

"You're a Nantucketer. You have to use the classic Nantucket weapons."

"Mildew? Red tide? Powder Post beetles?"

Billy looked up, grinning. "Gossip," he said.

"Excuse me?"

"That's your weapon. Good old-fashioned small-town back-stabbing gossip. Three in the side." He walked around the table for the shot. The white ball brushed past its target, tipping it down and gone. Another rumble; then silence, or as close to silence as you could get, with U2 howling about a street with no name from the other side of the room. The Irish lads had control of the jukebox tonight.

Mike finished his beer. "How would that work?"

"Look around you. There are some crazy people on this island. Some of them are so crazy they can't live anywhere else. A lot of them have guns. And most of them have been working on the Lomax job for the last eight months. I see four carpenters, three floor guys, two electricians, and a partridge in a pear tree. No, that's Pat Folger getting a rash in his dress up wool turtleneck. He must like to suffer."

Mike took in the crowd at the bar: Tom Danziger, Lomax's electrician; Arturo Maturo, his plumber. Both of them were capable of murder. And the landscaper—Jane something… Stiles, that was it—was shooting pool at the next table with the big blonde who ran her crew. Those girls were scary. Pushing a lawnmower all day made you strong, and Jane had a temper. Mike had watched her fire a customer last summer, one day before a giant wedding reception was scheduled at the lady's house. "You don't treat me like a human being, and I'm sick of it," she had said, and stalked off across the uncut lawn, past the un-pruned hydrangeas, over the un-weeded driveway, while the lady sobbed, "What'll I do, what'll I do?" Jane turned back. Her Parthian shot: "Treat people better."

That girl was one tough customer. Was she a killer? Who knew? Mike was warming to Billy's plan. His dad always said. "Kill 'em with the truth." This crowd might just take the phrase literally.

Why not? This was definitely a truth worth killing for.

Billy checked his watch. "We have time. Let's get another round."

"It's a good thing I don't own that watch," Mike said. Tilting his head down an inch, toward the Patek Phillipe on Billy's wrist. "I'd have sold it a long time ago."

"I don't think so. Not if you knew the history. Not if you'd lived it."

"And you're never going to tell me, so fuck it."

"Sounds like you're finally giving up. Quit when you know it's futile."

"Dad's rule?"

"One of the best. Okay, here we go."

He nodded as they approached the crush of bodies at the bar, giving Mike his cue.

Mike started talking in mid-sentence. "—that's what I'm trying to tell you. I heard Lomax talking. I was right there. He's going to stiff everyone. He doesn't care. Fuck, man, he was bragging about it! He's like some creepy kid pouring gasoline into an ant hill. He likes killing the bugs. That's us, by the way. We're just a bunch or worker ants to that piece of shit."

Everyone was listening now, and pretending not to.

"Jesus. What are you going to do?" asked Billy.

"I don't know. But I know what somebody should do. If he's dead the estate sells the house and everybody gets paid. Fuck, man, I'd kill him for free. If I had the guts. I'll tell you something, though. If someone's gonna do it, they better do it soon. His bags are packed. He's splitting. I'm serious, man. He's outta here. And once he's gone, forget about it. We're all screwed."

Mike turned to the bartender. "Two more, Larry. We really need 'em right now."

Mike put a ten on the bar, grabbed the mugs of stout and gave one to Billy. They threaded their way back to the pool table, angry conversation igniting behind them.

"Sounds like a lynch mob," Mike said.

Billy took a long swig and set his glass down listening appreciatively. "Yes sir," he said after a moment or two. "Our work here is done."

An hour later, Mike Henderson stood in his living room, staring down at his wife's note. It had been scrawled in a hurry. It was terse and uninformative. Cindy was in New York. She had to "get away." She had "a lot to think about" and "decisions to make alone."

He had a pretty good idea what those decisions were—keep her life with Mike or discard it, baby and all. He knew Cindy would be at her parents' apartment. They hated him. When she had asked them to pay for the wedding her mother had said, "We'll pay for the divorce." That was probably what they were discussing today—the most cost-effective way to rid themselves of the loser they had warned her against, in vain.

Conrad Parrish, Cindy's father, was a brain surgeon with an unabashed God complex: "I hold fate in my hands, Mike," he had announced one night after too many sea breezes. "I reach into the pulsing heart of creation and confront the mystery of life and death, every day. I'm God's good right hand: his mechanic. I correct his mistakes. That's quite a feeling. Savages would build shrines to me: the white man with the knife who slices their flesh apart and heals their sickness. And I'll tell you something. Those pygmies wouldn't be far off."

"You're insane," Mike had muttered.

The night had gone downhill from there.

Mike had no desire to call Conrad Parrish at this hour, frantically searching for Cindy, begging him for a clue to his daughter's whereabouts.

So he sat in his bathrobe, watching The Weather Channel. The forecasts were inaccurate, sometimes ludicrously so, but he enjoyed them anyway. He liked the radar graphics; he liked watching the great green masses closing in on the island, while the self-important anchors made high drama out of scattered showers or a dusting of snow. They were naming ordinary storms now—"Winter Storm Iago." What was next? "Summer Drizzle Amelia"? It was insulting to hurricanes—and their victims. Mike especially loathed the brazen way the forecasts changed: a week of rain became a week of sunshine with no acknowledgement or apology. Not even an "oops" or a blush. Just a radically different forecast as if they'd been saying it all along.

They needed their illusions, just like he did. His happy marriage, his growing business, they were as bogus as the weather maps.

He heard his back door open, and Tanya Kriel walked into the room. She was unzipping a bulky parka, pulling off a knitted watch cap that glittered with snow. She squinted down at him.

"You look exhausted. Did you sleep at all?"

He glanced up. "Cindy's gone."

She let the coat drop, and twisted out of her thermal underwear T-shirt.

"Good. I need to be alone with you this morning."

Chapter Twenty-one
Choices

Mike was inside Tanya Kriel when the phone rang. He knew who it was instantly and his mind spun through array of possible responses: let the machine pick it up? At almost two in the morning? If he didn't answer the phone that would only lead to more questions and confrontations. Answer it and act as if she had just awakened him? But he couldn't fool Cindy and he knew it. He could just hear her: "Why the fake 'sleepyhead' stuff? Is someone there with you?"

The phone rang again. It seized him up inside like a police siren, like the flashers in his rearview mirror. Tanya was staring up at him. He had lifted himself off her by the full extension of his arms. He looked like he was doing some kind of stretch in yoga class. He looked down at her face. She was baffled and frustrated, but also concerned. She didn't know what was going on yet, and a call this late usually meant trouble of some kind—a heart attack or a car crash.

Mike eased out of her with the familiar physical tug of reluctance. He pushed himself off to her side and sat up at the edge of the bed. The phone rang again. If he didn't pick it up before the next ring, Tanya would get to hear Cindy's grating late night message. That would be bad.

He picked up the phone.

"Mike?"

"Cindy, where are you? What's going on?"

"Are you alone?"

"Of course I am. It's two in the morning."

Cindy was crying.

"What's happening? Are you all right? Where are you calling from?"

"I'm—I decided to…I'm at the Logan Airport Hilton. I'm taking the first flight tomorrow."

He put it together. She must have fled the party, and rushed home to pack. Then the mad rush to the airport to make the last flight out. He had been upstairs with Tanya when her plane was lifting off. He forced himself back to moment.

"The first flight?"

"To New York."

"Wait a second—I don't…What's going on?

Mike heard Tanya shifting on the bed behind him. His furnace kicked on. The wind was steady against his house. The phone line was alive with the imminence of the unspoken.

"Cindy?"

"I have a date with Mark Toland tomorrow. I've been dreaming about him for years. Now there's no reason not to see him."

"Except your marriage."

"Are you going to lecture me about fidelity? It would never have occurred to me if you hadn't—"

"So this is revenge?"

"It's reality. You changed the rules. Things have to be different after that. This is the way things are now. If Mark Toland had wanted to undress me last year I would have told you about it and it would have been exciting. You always liked the idea of other men being attracted to me. I might have even flirted a little, let him look down my dress or at least say I did, just to get you revved up. But to actually let him do anything…"

"Jesus."

"Please, Mike."

"What—I can't have a reaction to this?"

"You can react. But you can't make me feel guilty and you can't expect anyone to sympathize with you. No one's going to do that. It's like watching a mugger get robbed. People cheer when that happens."

"So you're doing it to hurt me?"

"No, Mike, it had nothing to do with you. I've been in love with Mark Toland since the ninth grade."

"Why call me, then? Why wake me up at two in the morning to tell me about it?"

"I don't know. But I didn't wake you up."

He expelled a long breath. "No. You didn't."

"I hate this."

"Don't do it."

She sighed. "I mean all of this."

"Come home."

"Give me a reason."

Tanya walked around the bed. Mike noticed she had gotten dressed, but she was barefoot. She held out her hands, elbows tight to her body, and let her palms curl up as if tugged by her eyebrows. She might as well have said, "What the hell is going on, how long is this going to take?" He answered with a lifted arm, one finger up, miming "Give me a little more time, I'll explain later."

"Cindy—"

"Forget it. I have things to do in the city anyway."

"What things?"

"Just—appointments. I don't really feel like going into it."

He squeezed the phone so hard his knuckles hurt. This was much worse than the planned adultery. He mashed his eyes shut.

"You don't want to tell me? Fine. I'll tell you."

But Tanya chose that moment to give up on him. She raised her arms again but the gesture this time was different. She might have been throwing two crumpled pieces of paper at him. She shook her head and bent down to grab her shoes. Her back was to him as she started for the door. Mike covered the phone with his hand.

"Wait—"

She gave him a thin, tired smile. "You're a little too married for me, Mike. Sorry."

Then she was out the door. When he put the phone to his ear again, Cindy said, "She's there."

"What?"

"That girl. She's there with you."

"She's leaving."

"You were with her in our bed."

"Cindy—"

"You better go after her, Mike. Don't let her leave angry. Tell her you're getting a divorce. It will be interesting, telling the truth for a change."

She hung up.

Mike heard the front door close. A minute later he heard Tanya's truck start up and pull out of the driveway.

He fell back on the bed. For the moment he had no energy, but he knew what he had to do. First thing: wash these sheets. Then he had to try and sleep for a couple of hours. He dug his fingertips into his forehead, staring up at the ceiling, which definitely needed to be taped, spackled and repainted.

He sat up, swiveling the Rubik's cube of logistics. He hadn't gotten the chance to say it, but he knew the appointment Cindy was talking about. She was going to see her family doctor, who worked with Planned Parenthood and enjoyed a profitable sideline in clean safe abortions.

Mike was pacing now, hyperventilating. He had to stop her. And he would, he'd talk her out of it. He just needed to think. It was early Sunday morning, that was a huge advantage. She couldn't see the doctor until Monday. Mike had time to get into the city. Billy's check wouldn't clear until Tuesday at the earliest, but that was okay. He could dip into the thousand dollars he had stashed in case the IRS attached his bank account. He could show her a nice time in the city if he got the chance,, and replace the cash out of Billy's check next week. And he had an old Hy-Line ticket left over from the summer, when a some emergency had forced him to cancel a trip off-island. Those tickets were good for a year.

The first boat was 7:45. He'd be on the road by 9:30.

His clients Josh and Emily Levin kept an old Acura sedan in the Steamship Authority parking lot for just this sort of occasion. They always spent the month of December in Nevis, some little island in the Caribbean. He had the key to their brownstone on West Seventy-fifth Street. He knew their alarm code and they had long ago given him an open invitation to use the house when they were away. He had painted the place top to bottom five years before.

He could stay over and be at the doctor's office bright and early, well-rested. The office was on Eighty-second and Madison, with a coffee shop across the street: an excellent surveillance post. And the coffee was pretty good.

This was doable.

Mike took a breath. He had good friends. More than that, he had allies. He had partisans. People like Josh Levine and Billy Delavane would always come through for him. What was that phrase? It took a village—to raise a kid or keep your marriage going or stay solvent. Well, fuck the village.

He had a platoon.

And he had hope. Cindy couldn't have decided yet. She would never contemplate some random sexual dalliance on the eve of such a huge step. Maybe she was using Mark Toland to help her decide. Either way, Mike would be there to keep her from making the mistake.

Mike felt infallible that morning, as he got ready to leave. But he wasn't. In fact he was making a terrible mistake, one in a long string of accidental blunders. Every move Mike had made for the last month, now including this trip to Manhattan, taken together and viewed with the cold eye of the law, would combine in the diabolical machinery of circumstance to cast him as the primary suspect in Nantucket's most gruesome and notorious murder, ever. In less than a week he'd be in jail and facing the very real possibility of life in prison. If he'd known all that, he would have gone anyway. But he would have left a paper trail.

He was going to need one.

Part Two: Post Mortem

Chapter Twenty-two

Suspects

The Nantucket police station was occupied and under siege at the same time. Inside, every jail cell and office, as well as all the common rooms were filled with witnesses and suspects. The C-pac team from off-island had commandeered the upstairs conference room and filled it with high-tech computers and low-tech chalk boards, boxes of files and half a dozen serious technicians who were working everything from background checks to forensics.

Haden Krakauer was interviewing one of the girls from Fiona's maid service in the second floor interrogation room when I arrived.

Outside, gathered in the big parking lot off Fairgrounds Road, the press was turning my domain into a familiar off-island circus of vans with gaudy logos and microwave antennas, lights and microphones, snaking cables and of course the jostling crowds of reporters. The Boston newspeople were the most visible and self-important, but there were network correspondents and cable news stringers, too, just as Lonnie Fraker had predicted.

A busty, Botoxed blonde was clutching a microphone as she finished her report, staring down the red light above camera lens. "…and so, with no clues, leads, or suspects in custody, the local police remain baffled at this hour by the death of one of this tiny, privileged island's most prominent citizens. All we know for sure, this cold December morning: a powerful man lies brutally murdered, and his killers are still on the loose."

"And the press will milk the story until they've made every last possible cheesy dime out of it," I muttered under my breath as the reporter identified herself and wrapped up her story. "Or until something sleazier comes along to distract people from all the unpleasant *actual news* going on in the world."

"Or you solve it, Chief. That would really spoil everything." I turned. David Trezize was standing next to me, squinting into the crowd. "Hey—they're still cashing in on those JonBenet Ramsey stories. Everyone loves a mystery."

I had parked my cruiser in the rear security lot and normally I would have walked in through the garage entrance, but I was curious this morning. I was wearing my uniform, I looked like one more cop. David was the only reporter who recognized me. I headed back around the corner. I didn't want this pack chasing me, not at eight o'clock on a Monday morning.

"Come on inside with me," I said to David. "I need to talk to you."

I was already walking. Trezize hurried to catch up. "Am I getting an exclusive? It better be for this week's edition because I might not have a newspaper next week."

"I'm sorry to hear that, David."

"Care to take out an ad? I could use the revenue."

We pushed through the throng into the main lobby. For the moment I was alone with the pudgy reporter.

"I need to talk to you about last night," I said. "And we should do it with a lawyer present."

"What, I'm a suspect?"

"You have the right to remain silent. If you choose to waive that right anything you say can be used against you in a court of law. You have a right to legal representation. If you can't afford a lawyer—"

"Chief—"

"Let me finish, David. This is serious. If you can't afford a lawyer, one will be appointed for you by the court. Do you understand these rights as I've explained them to you?"

"Of course I do, but—"

"Then you might not want to talk to me right now."

"You can't seriously believe I could have done this."

"I believe anyone could do anything, under the right circumstances."

"I was trying to take a splinter out of my son's hand last week and my fingers went limp. I couldn't do it. Does that sound like a murderer?"

I sighed. "That's not the right question, David. The right question is, where were you between the hours of eleven and midnight last night?"

"I was—I don't know, let me think for second."

"This is exactly what I'm saying. That's an answer you need to get right the first time."

"I was—I was driving around."

"Just driving? At midnight?"

"I—it's embarrassing. I drove over to, to talk to my wife, my ex-wife. About the kids, there's been a problem and I thought if we just sat down and discussed it we could clear things up. We used to be able to talk."

"How did it go?"

"That's my point, she wasn't there. Midnight on a school night. The sitter's car was in the driveway. She drives a used Volvo. I can tell you this much, Chief—if I had left the kids with a sitter on a school night and I was still out that late, Patty would have crucified me. Normally, I would have gone in and checked with the girl, found out where Patty was. But I knew. She was with Grady Malone. Grady's ex-wife has the kids on Sunday, so where else would they go?"

"David—"

"I drove to Grady's house. Her car was sitting there, you could see it from the road. She didn't even bother to park in the back."

"So what did you do?"

"I just sat there."

"You didn't go in?"

"And do what? Start a fight? I couldn't even snoop at the windows. They would have seen my tracks in the snow. He shoveled the driveway but that's it. So, yeah, I just sat there. I saw a shadow move across the blinds occasionally. Then the lights went out."

"What time was that?"

"One in the morning, 1:30, I don't know. Late."

"Did anyone see you there?"

"I don't think so."

"Did anyone drive by while you were parked? Anyone you know?"

"No, nobody."

"So no one can verify your whereabouts for the hours in question."

"No, but—who'd make up a story like that?"

"A writer?"

"Chief—"

"Let's finish this with your lawyer in the room, David. I think we'd both be more comfortable."

"Listen, I just—"

"This afternoon if possible. Tomorrow at the latest."

I badged myself into the operations room before Trezize could answer. The noise level jumped as I opened the door. Central dispatch was crowded with people waiting to be interviewed. I saw one of the girls on Fiona's cleaning crew with Haden Krakauer and thought, Fiona. I have to deal with Fiona.

Upstairs in the conference room, Lonnie Fraker introduced me to Ken Carmichael from the Mass D.A.'s office. Carmichael was tall and scholarly-looking, with glasses and a worn tweed jacket. His jutting nose and bald head gave him a raw, scoured look, like someone who'd just stepped out of a windstorm. But he had a good smile and a firm handshake.

He introduced himself and said, "I'm running theC-Pac team for the D.A., which is basically by the book for any 'unattended death.' That's how the statute's written."

"I don't think witnesses are the issue here. With a guy like Lomax, you'd be on the case if they'd whacked him in the Fleet Center during a Celtics game."

"Point taken. So you'll appreciate—this is the top priority team. We have two detectives and a detective lieutenant along with the forensic unit and as many warm bodies as we can scare up to do the footwork. But don't get me wrong. We're not here to push anybody around. I mean that. We just want to help."

I nodded. "Great, we can use it. Any word on those DNA samples?"

"Nothing yet. All the labwork should be back by tonight, though. How about you? Anything?"

"We're just running down names. Business associates, friends, family. The wife, kids. People at the party, people who worked on the house. A lot of people."

We were all silent for a few seconds. The room bustled around us. Someone elbowed past us with a pile of faxes. Someone else was bringing coffee upstairs. Cell phones were ringing with a uniquely modern electronic discord: the Nokia default tones clashing with "Mission Impossible," rap downloads and "The Blue Danube."

Carmichael grabbed a cup of takeout coffee, pulled off the plastic lid, and took a gulp. "You want hot coffee, you gotta make it yourself. I'm getting a pot up here." He set the coffee down on top of a file cabinet and glanced around the room. "I hate this part, you know? When everything's out and nothing's coming back in. It's all questions and loose ends and unchecked alibis and pissed-off people and nosy reporters—"

"The reporters are his problem, boss," Lonnie Fraker grinned. "He only sneaked in here today because they didn't recognize him. But after the first press conference he's going to be famous. You're going to be a star, Kennis. You're gonna be getting some serious fan mail now. Just be sure you share it around if the girls enclose pictures. Sharing information is vital on a case like this."

"Very funny, Fraker," said Carmichael. "Didn't you have some depositions to transcribe?"

"Yes, sir."

Fraker disappeared.

"Nice trick," I said. "I have to learn how to do that."

"Perk of the job," Carmichael said, "Anyway. You know what I'm saying. This is the messy part."

I saw Haden Krakauer coming up the stairs. "It's like cleaning a kid's room, Ken. You make it look worse first, so you can get all the junk organized."

"You got kids?"

"A boy and a girl."

"Jesus. What do you tell them about this stuff?"

"Nothing. They're too young, they couldn't care less. My daughter hates the uniform. My son thinks the flasher bar is cool. That's about it."

Haden walked up to us. "Sorry…Chief? You should take a look at this Irish girl's interview tape. Molly Flanagan her name is. Something's bugging me but I don't know what. And Nathan Parrish is downstairs demanding to talk to you."

"Demanding?"

"Have fun, Chief," Carmichael said. His cell phone was ringing: The worst one yet. A robotic female voice kept repeating "You have an incoming call. You have an incoming call." He slid his finger across the bottom of the screen. "This is Carmichael," he said as I headed for the stairs. Haden followed me.

"Any thoughts?" I asked.

"Couple. First off, no tradesman did this. The screwdriver thing is cute, but it doesn't fool me for a second. Scattering a little dog hair around would have been better. None of these guys go anywhere without a dog in the truck. And they wouldn't leave that kind of money behind, no matter what. They might have thought about it, maybe had a laugh about it later. But no contractor I ever met is gonna leave close to a grand stuffed down some dead guy's throat. No way."

"Unless that's what he wants us to think," I said. "It actually sounds fairly cost-effective to me."

"Yeah. I guess. Another thing. There was a benefit party the night of the murder, fifty bucks a head. Some plasterer with MS, family's trying to raise money for the hospital bills."

"He wasn't insured?

"I guess he never got on board with the personal mandate."

"Too bad."

"Yeah, well. We get our hands on the guest list, that'll clear some alibis."

"Good idea."

Fiona was at that party, I remembered now. She had invited me, but I'd had the kids that night. The knowledge gave me an almost physical relief, the way touching your toes could ease a stitch in your side. A clear alibi would save both of us a lot of questions and malicious gossip, a lot of accusations about conflict of interest and impartiality. Investigating my girlfriend was a nightmare I was grateful to avoid.

Upstairs, Nathan Parrish was pacing the corridor outside my office.

"Chief Kennis!" he called out. "Chief Kennis!"

Haden shook his head with his mouth turned down contemptuously: This was the real reason he had never wanted to be chief. He headed downstairs and left me alone to deal with the burly real estate mogul.

"Mr. Parrish." We were blocking the corridor. I led him into my office and gestured to the chair facing the desk. I leaned against the edge, the heels of my palms braced against the flat surface. The office was big and lavish, like a corporate executive suite. It still embarrassed me a little. The big windows showed snowy trees across Fairgrounds Road. Parrish took out a cigarette, caught my look and slipped it back into his pocket.

"What can we do for you, Nathan?"

Parrish stared at me as he no doubt stared at his own employees when they said something unusually dense. "What can you do for me? You can find out who committed this atrocious crime and bring them to justice! That's what you can do for me."

"Well, we're working on it."

"You're 'working on it'? That's not good enough."

I shrugged. "What do you suggest?"

"Look—sorry. I'm not here to tell you how to do your job. I'm not a policeman. But I want to help. I can contribute if you need to hire temporary personnel, if you need new equipment…just let me know. Preston Lomax was more than a business associate, Chief. He was a friend. Whatever the gossip sheets might say about him and despite his occasional high-handed attitude—I know he could be abrupt sometimes when the world didn't move as fast as he did, you had to run to keep up with him and he didn't have much patience for laggards. But Preston Lomax was one of the good guys. As everyone seems to know by now, I was about to close a major deal with Preston's company. That deal may still be salvageable, I don't know. Frankly, no one even wants to think about it at the moment. But this isn't about the money or the opportunity I may have lost. It's about a man who didn't deserve to die. And it's about justice. I don't want to live in a world where people can commit a crime like this and get away with it."

"Then you're living in the wrong world, Mr. Parrish. In this one, more than half of all homicides are never solved."

"How do you live with that?"

Before I could answer, the office door opened and Lonnie Fraker stuck his head in.

"Got something, Chief."

"What?"

I stood as Lonnie slipped inside and shut the door behind him, closing off the little wedge of noise from the hall. He grinned as the clatter subsided. "Neighbor driving by around midnight. They saw a big van and a gray Ford Escape in the driveway. The guy had never seen those cars before. He thought they were renters, until we talked to him."

"What type of van?"

"He had no idea. Big. What the hell does a guy like that know about vans?"

"Okay, good—run the plates of everybody we're talking to, see who drives an Escape. As to the van ..."

"I know, I know. Every tradesman on the island has one. I'm all over it, Chief. I don't know what your guys are doing today, aside from the coffee runs. But we've got this one all sewn up."

"The Escape?"

He grinned. Parrish sat forward, listening. I had forgotten all about him.

"Tell me," I said.

"Okay, four gray Escapes. Two off-island, one in the shop."

"Who's left?"

"Your friend David Trezize. Does he have an alibi?"

"He says he was 'driving around'.."

Lonnie snorted humorlessly; you couldn't really call it a laugh. "Among other things. You can throw some meat to the dogs out there. We'll get this little prick into custody. And then we can check out his shoes—see if they match the footprint casts we made in the driveway."

"He's coming in with his lawyer tomorrow. Let's hold off until then."

"What if he runs?"

"He won't."

"What is that? A feeling?"

I nodded.

"Is that what you used in L.A.? Feelings?"

"As a matter of fact, yes it was."

"Right. Well, you play it any way you want. But there's a guy from the BBC out there now. There's even some chick from Al Jazeera English. This story is going global, Chief. So don't choke."

"I know that David Trezize person," Parrish said, jumping to his feet. "He's been hounding Preston for weeks! He threatened the man's life two nights ago. The man's a lunatic."

"I don't know, Mr. Parrish. He sounded upset at the party. He'd been drinking. But I know the guy and he's not dangerous. Anyway, most killers don't advertise their intentions beforehand."

"Well, this one did. You said you don't want to go press with the story? If you don't have Trezize in jail this time tomorrow, I'm going to the press myself. Then *you'll* be the story, Chief. The cop who let his cronies get away with murder. You'll never live that one down, believe me. You'll wish you'd never left Los Angeles."

Then he bulled past me and out the door. Lonnie shrugged and followed him. I kicked the door closed and just stood there for a long moment, in the dense comfortable privacy of my oversized office. After a while, I tipped forward until my head touched the cool hard surface of the door.

It was only nine o'clock. In the morning. I was already exhausted.

Chapter Twenty-three
The Best Thing Ever

At that moment, Mike Henderson was sitting in the coffee shop at Eighty-second Street and Madison Avenue, staring out into the final assault of Winter Storm Iago. The snow was blowing horizontal and the wind whined like a tablesaw. He had driven into the city through the storm yesterday, found a parking space down the street from the Levine's house and gotten a good night's sleep in their guestroom. But he had woken up anxious at six in the morning.

Mike sat at the table nursing his coffee, staring out at snow-frosted street. "Clean it up with paint," his first boss had always said: no scrubbing or sanding, just a heavy layer of latex. "Don't make it right—make it white." That's what the upper East side looked like this morning: dirt and garbage covered over with pristine crystal. The snow itself would be filthy enough soon.

Mike waved the waiter away. He needed to think about what he was going to say this morning. Everything depended on that. And his mind was a blank.

How had things gotten this bad? They had wanted a baby for years. Cindy had gotten pregnant two years before, but she had miscarried. That tragedy had revealed every weakness in their marriage. Cindy had been inconsolable and Mike had been shut out completely. It was her tragedy, it had happened inside of her. Mike had nothing to do with it. He could only intrude. When he tried to understand, he was presumptuous. When he tried to cheer her up, he was shallow. When he ignored her, as she seemed to want, he was heartless.

But it was even worse than that. Over time, she blamed the way they lived. She hated the seasonal panic of housepainting on Nantucket, as everyone scurried around looking for interior work like woodland creatures trying to get inside for the winter, and waited for final payments and groveled to imperious general contractors. The constant stress had killed the baby, that was Cindy's theory. It infuriated Mike. The doctors had no idea what might have happened, the best minds in modern medicine were baffled, but Cindy knew it was his fault. It was her body. That made her the final authority.

Mike didn't know; maybe she was right. The stress never let up. Even now he could feel it, like pressure on a bruise. Things had been the same two years ago, they'd been going through some other crisis: a lawsuit, a lost job, a late check. They always pulled through, Billy Delavane helped them make it through until the phone call came, and it always did, and he went from no work to hiring extra people overnight. But the constant uncertainty was corrosive. Painters got hypertension and ulcers and colitis from it. They had nervous breakdowns. They became alcoholics. Why not their wives?

Cindy had held her grudge, clutched it tightly, a little kid holding her bus fare, hurrying through a bad neighborhood. It had helped for a while, but she couldn't keep it up forever. Something like normal life resumed eventually. The wall stayed up, though. Mike couldn't reach her. They still talked, but the talk was more and more superficial; they made love, but less and less often. Still, somehow she had gotten pregnant again. It was a small miracle, really. Maybe it was fate.

Mike had been in her doctor's office once, when Cindy had come down with stomach flu on a visit to her parents. He remembered sitting for more than an hour in the dark wood paneled waiting room. P.S. 6 got out for the day sometime during the wait. He had listened to the shouts and laughter of the newly liberated kids across the street, loving the sound, wanting kids of his own.

Well, that's why he was here today.

He should order breakfast. But he couldn't eat. He ordered more coffee instead, checked his watch: ten after eight. Office hours didn't start until nine.

The waiter returned with a visible sigh. But the place was still uncrowded, so at least Mike wasn't taking up a table where real eaters and big tippers might be sitting, not yet. It was warm. He pulled off his coat and took a sip of coffee. It was strong and hot and it went down all right.

A cab pulled up across the street: the office nurse. The rest of the staff arrived over the next half hour. Mike drank two more coffees. He was getting wired. He asked for the check. He didn't want any delays when Cindy finally arrived. He watched the traffic, yellow taxis and buses half obscured by the gusting snow. The windows were steaming over; he'd be lucky to see her at all.

Finally, he couldn't sit still anymore. He paid the check, left an extra five dollar tip, and walked out into the blizzard, zipping up his coat.

Her cab pulled up ten minutes later, just as he was considering going back inside. The light was green but it was about to go red. He sprinted across Madison Avenue. Cindy sensed the bulky figure moving toward her and looked up blankly. He hit a patch of ice on the sidewalk and skidded into her. They grabbed each other to keep from falling, an awkward little dance that ended with him sitting in the snow.

She helped him up. "Graceful as always." Her smile softened the words.

"Thanks."

They stood holding each others' arms lightly, snow blowing between them, traffic coursing through the slush behind them.

"What are you doing here?"

"Can we go somewhere and talk?"

"I have an appointment—"

"With Doctor Mathias. I know. 47 East 82nd Street."

"I don't understand. How did you—?"

"I know what's going on, Cindy. I figured it out. I'm not an idiot. And I know you."

"Mike—"

"Can we go somewhere? Get out of the cold?"

"Let's just walk."

She stuck her hands in her coat pockets and started across Madison toward Fifth Avenue. Mike followed, looking around him at the heavy green copper-roofed old buildings, the snow gathering on their ornamental stonework. These were think tanks now, embassies, foundation headquarters. But they had been residences once. They had been built when the details of craftsmanship mattered and no expense was spared. The wealth they represented made the Nantucket trophy houses look cheap and suburban by comparison. There were co-op buildings of the same pre-war vintage lining the avenues behind them that would never have let Preston Lomax into their lobbies, much less their owners' associations. It was a different world, and Mike couldn't help feeling it was a better one. It was solid at least, rooted in generations of privilege and civic responsibility. But it made him feel like he was trespassing. These old buildings dwarfed him and his proletarian difficulties. But he rebelled against the feeling. He was lucky in a way: he could enjoy the formal elegance of the neighborhood with a comfortable detachment. He let it buoy him up for a moment. It was actually the perfect location for this dispute. It embodied tradition and history. It had its own persuasions.

He took Cindy's arm and began. "I was thinking about the last time we were in the neighborhood. You were sick, we thought they were going to take you to Lenox Hill. But Dr. Mathias took care of you. I remember sitting in the office, waiting, thinking how much I wanted to have kids."

"That was a long time ago."

"No it wasn't. It feels that way but it wasn't."

"Mike, I'm going to be late if I don't—"

He wanted to say, "Forget it, you're not seeing the doctor today," but he knew that would backfire. Besides, he was on to something now and he wanted to finish it. "Just listen to me for a second. This is important. Sex felt different after that, it felt pure, like there was nothing between us and the consequences of what we were doing. Like, the consequences were what we were doing. The orgasm almost didn't matter. It was just the starter's gun. You know? It was scary. But it was good. It was like skydiving without a parachute, except when we hit the ground we weren't going to die. Someone else was going to be born."

Cindy looked down. "Well, it didn't work out that way."

"No. I know that."

"I wish you'd said some of this stuff then."

"I tried to. But it was just a jumble. I needed time to think about it."

"Things were different then, Mike. We were different."

He stopped walking, took her hands, faced her down.

"I want this baby, Cindy."

She looked away, watching a Great Dane pulling a slim man on a taut leash. A woman was coming around the corner with a pair of King Charles spaniels. The dogs sniffed each other, the leashes tangled.

"That's not your decision to make," Cindy said.

"Yes it is. This is happening to both of us. Just like it happened to both of us before. I lost a baby, too, Cindy."

"Mike—"

"I lost a baby, too."

Impulsively, she hugged him. She flung herself at him and knocked him back a step, into a big car, its make and model anonymous under a great loaf of snow. They held each other tight through their heavy coats. She was crying. "I'm sorry," she said. "I'm sorry."

"Hey, it's okay. I love you. Cindy—it's okay."

She pulled away and looked up at him, tears glittering in her eyes, snow glittering in her hair.

"What a pair of ridiculous fuck-ups we are."

He kissed her. "I know. But we'll stop. We'll be better. We'll have to be better. We're going to be setting an example now."

"Oh God."

"We can do it. Our parents did."

She smiled. "Don't set the bar too low, Mike."

They pushed off the car and walked on, across Fifth Avenue, past the museum and along the park wall.

"It doesn't matter about Mark Toland," he said after a while. "I deserved that. And so did you."

"Well, I needed it, anyway."

"As long as it's over."

"It barely began."

"Good. It balances things. It settles the score."

"Not really. I didn't sleep with a co-worker, or make you the subject of choice for every malicious gossip on the island. You never had to stand making small talk with Mark Toland at a party."

"No. But it still hurt."

"Did it really?"

"Thinking of you with that guy? Jesus."

"You were jealous?"

"Come on."

"Unbearably jealous?"

"Actually, I found the whole thing strangely erotic."

She punched his arm. "You're sick."

They walked along quietly for another block. The snow was coming down more heavily now, muffling their footsteps and cutting them off from the gauzy buildings across the street and the Christmas card shadows of the park.

"There are just two things you have to do for me," Cindy said as they crossed the transverse entrance at Seventy-ninth Street.

"Tell me."

"First, just keep talking to me." She grabbed a handful of his hair, shook it. "I want to know what's going on in there. I know I can be a jerk. But tell me so from now on. Don't just nod and go off to work another seventeen-hour day. Whenever some painter's wife tells me her husband is on the job until nine every night, all I can think is, your marriage is in trouble, Honey. If it wasn't, he'd be home. No one has to work until nine o'clock every night, unless they're on some corporate fast track. And you're not."

"No."

"So come home early and talk to me. If I take your head off, I'll make it up with sexual favors. I promise. At least until the baby arrives."

"Fair enough," Mike said. "What's the other thing?"

"It's about Tanya Kriel."

"What about her?"

Cindy gave him her sweetest smile. "Fire the bitch."

"Done," Mike said. "As soon as we get home. But right now, since this is the first time we've been off-island together in six months, I'd like to take you to a fabulous breakfast and a tour of the new Museum of Modern Art and maybe even an early movie before we drive back."

"Lunch at Papaya King?"

"Absolutely. Five star all the way."

She stood on her tiptoes to kiss him. "Thanks, Mike," she said. "I mean it. Thanks for coming. It's the best thing anyone's done for me since…I don't know. Since my dad drove all the way up to Maine to take me out of that horrible Outward Bound summer camp. God, I was so happy to see that old Dodge Caravan coming up the camp road. I started crying right on the spot. No, this was better than that. This may be the best thing ever."

"Throw in a plate of pesto scrambled eggs, some great art, and a drastically maudlin chick flick with all the popcorn you can eat, and we may never top this."

"Just wait six months."

Then she took his hand and they started east through the curtain of snow, toward breakfast and the rest of their day.

Chapter Twenty-four
The Widow

I woke up in the dark. Fiona was kissing me. She had taken off the flannel pajamas she wore to bed in the winter, pushed my T-shirt up and pulled my boxers down; she was easing them clear of my ankles with her foot. I felt the dry tight sweetness of her naked body. I was more than ready, I was bursting. At first I thought I was dreaming: the long warm thighs sliding across mine, the breasts pressed to my chest, the firm bare ass filling my palms in the inchoate darkness. In fact I had experienced this exact dream many times as an adolescent, always with embarrassing results and an extra load of laundry in the wash before school.

But this time I was awake. I kissed her open mouth and we rolled free of the covers. She shivered and reached behind her to retrieve them. I had never known a woman before who liked to make love in the morning. It had been an unbroken run of bad luck, from Kathy Jablonski, my first girlfriend in high school, to my ex-wife, Miranda, who could never stand any human contact until her third cup of coffee and acted like "morning mouth" was a venereal disease. I didn't care about it and neither did Fiona. Our circadian rhythms matched perfectly, a Utopian compatibility I had never even known existed. Though, like the possibility of other inhabited planets in the galaxy, or ever getting a good-looking haircut, logic had always indicated that it must.

I lunged up into her, feeling her come. Then she leaned down, brushing against me and whispered, "Let go." So I did. I rolled both of us over, and the covers were on the floor and neither of us cared anymore. She pulled me down to her and said "Shhhh," though there were no kids in the house to hear me.

We lay side by side afterward, catching our breath, and she said, "You really did it, didn't you?""

She had told me the night before she would come to the station and answer any questions and cooperate in any way she could—sign depositions, testify in court, make stew for the state police. All I had to do in return was stop thinking about the case for one night.

I kissed her cheek. "I'm still doing it."

"Not thinking about Preston Lomax at all?"

"Who?"

"I've heard of this before. Sexually induced amnesia. A very serious condition."

I laughed. "Yeah, because no one wants to get cured."

But I remembered everything perfectly. The clock was ticking in my head: Lomax had been dead for thirty-one hours and the need to solve the case was multiplying exponentially every minute. Fiona sensed the urgency. By the time I was out of bed and dressed she had the coffeemaker dripping and a pot of McCann's steel-cut oatmeal cooking on the stove. The sound of her moving in the kitchen drew me out of bed. I pulled on my bathrobe and a pair of socks, glanced out the window at the crusted snow. There was no warmth in the pale morning light. The sky was white. The cold bleached the color out of everything. But the house was warm and the smell of coffee made it warmer.

I took a deep breath. The murder investigation could wait until I finished breakfast. These few moments at the beginning of the day belonged to me. I stood still for a second, caught in a domestic fantasy. This was our actual life together, not just an occasional night fitted into the jigsaw of child custody. It was so easy to imagine. A tiny shift of thought changed everything. I could actually feel it: the exotic privilege of an ordinary moment.

I shrugged. Maybe someday. And then the trick would be not taking it for granted.

Seeing her standing at the stove barefoot, wearing a pale blue Provisions T-shirt, her red hair tangled around her shoulders, I had to doubt even that small reservation. Anyone who took this for granted deserved to lose it. She turned and smiled, still stirring the oatmeal. The kitchen looked southeast and caught the sunrise. The light from the big windows was dazzling.

I walked up behind Fiona and wrapped my arms around her waist. She had just showered and I could smell the herbal shampoo she used along with her own scent. I kissed her neck.

"Breakfast is almost ready," she said. "Take a cup of coffee and sit down. Go on now. I'll bring it to you."

I took a scrap of paper and a pen off the kitchen counter and sat down at the rickety blue table in a dazzle of sun, thinking about the soft lilt of her County Cork accent. I scribbled the rhyme as she put the oatmeal into a pair of blue flower patterned bowls.

The sound of your voice
Is my drug of choice.

I folded the piece of paper and slipped it into my pocket as Fiona set breakfast in front of me. I poured maple syrup and a little cream into the oatmeal, sipped my coffee.

Fiona sat down across from me, touched her mug to mine. "To the future?"

I nodded. "The future."

It was her favorite toast, but only in the morning, and only over coffee. The thought of a future with her always cheered me, no matter how nasty the weather was, or how grim the day ahead promised to be. I took a first taste of oatmeal.

"Good?"

"Perfect. Everything is perfect. I'm trying to enjoy it because twenty minutes from now this day is going over the cliff. I wish we could spend some real time together."

"But we can't. The *Times* came while you were getting dressed. You should take a look at it."

She got up and took it off the counter. I slipped the front page under my bowl, using it like a placemat. I saw the article instantly: top right, above the fold, next to a photograph of a wounded Yemeni sheepherder killed in a drone strike. The Mosul car bomb story ran below the picture. Beside it, there was another headline:

Deceased Executive Indicted for Fraud, Grand Larceny

New York State Attorney General Alan Fichter disclosed today that an ongoing investigation into financial malfeasance at the LoGran Corporation will proceed despite the untimely death of the principal subject of the inquiry, LoGran CEO Preston J. Lomax.

"The truth has to come out," Fichter said yesterday in a brief press conference at City Hall. "The man's death doesn't change that. The stockholders of LoGran and the citizens of New York State deserve to know what went on in those corporate offices and what crimes, if any, were committed."

Lomax, who owned numerous properties up and down the East Coast, including a recently completed multi-million dollar mansion on Nantucket Island, Massachusetts, was about to be indicted on more than twenty felony counts including grand theft, conspiracy, violating general business laws, and falsifying business records. Lomax allegedly paid himself unauthorized bonuses and forgave loans to himself, an ongoing pilferage of company funds that may amount to as

```
much as fifty million dollars.
   J. Thomas Allbright, CFO of the com-
pany, pledged all assistance and coop-
eration to the investigation. "LoGran is
a stable and dynamic organization on the
cutting edge of the global economy," he
affirmed yesterday, in a prepared state-
ment. "This scandal extends no further
than the isolated mendacity of one rogue
executive. We hope to put this disgrace-
ful episode behind us. The company is
looking to the future." Allbright, who
joined LoGran three years ago after
                            CONTINUED C3
```

I lifted my bowl and set the paper aside. I had no desire to read the rest of it. I glanced up. Fiona was watching me quietly. "What do you think?"

I finished my coffee. "I don't know. It just seems like more. More people who hated Lomax, more suspects, more complications, more publicity, more scrutiny. More trouble. Nathan Parrish was in business with Lomax. I'm going to have to talk to him again."

Done with breakfast, I took the dishes to the sink and let the water warm my whole body through my hands. The grumble and beeping of the earthmovers brought my eyes up to the frost-rimed windows. The crew next door was at work already, excavating a new foundation. The old house, or the partial shell of it that the Historic District Commission insisted the builders preserve, was sitting on a pair of metal beams supported by four towers of wooded brackets. The old structure had been gutted from the inside out. It seemed sad and startled, like a bird frightened off its nest.

Fiona got up and stood beside me "They're everywhere," she said. "There must be at least ten houses like that around town. It would be far more sensible to just demolish them. What do they think they're preserving?"

I shrugged. "As little as possible."

"The same thing happened in Ireland, before people like Lomax destroyed the world economy." I gave her as sidelong look "Well, all right, but he did his best. It was booming for a while, easy money and low interest rates, and new people building new houses. My mother always says, human beings are like the worm in an apple. Everything ahead of us is green and fresh. And everything behind us is brown and rotten."

"Wow. Really? My mom said 'Turn a frown upside down.'"

"Well, she was a fortunate woman leading an easy life." She kissed me on the cheek. "I've got to get dressed."

I finished putting the dishes away, found Fiona in the bedroom, and gave her a kiss meant to last until we were alone together again.

Twenty minutes later I was talking to Nathan Parrish, with the jostling noise of the press corps still ringing in my ears, all my phone lines on hold, a pile of interrogation transcripts on my desk, and a message log in front of me that was going to take all morning to clear.

"Businessmen are criminals," Parrish was saying. "Of course they are! Criminals built this country. They didn't call J. P. Morgan and Andrew Carnegie 'robber barons' for nothing."

I tilted back in my chair. "So you suspected Lomax was not quite on the up and up?"

"From time to time. But it didn't matter. This wasn't personal. I was doing business with LoGran and I still am. It's a straightforward corporate investment. I mean…obviously the indictment complicates the deal, at least from a public relations perspective. But Tom Allbright is a good man and he has a great team over there."

"You mentioned all this when we spoke yesterday. You also said the deal was in question now."

"No, no, absolutely not! Everyone was in a state of shock, that's all. But no one wants to abandon an extraordinary venture like this because of one man's excesses. Or his death. We're putting it behind us."

"It's been less than two days."

"Time moves swiftly in the business world, Chief. We don't have the luxury of outrage or mourning. The man did good things and bad things. Then he died. We can't change that. But the meters are ticking, the interest is adding up, and LoGran stockholders want to see results."

"You mention outrage. Was that how you felt?"

"Not really. But I'm an old cynic. Nothing Preston did could surprise me."

"Did he have enemies inside the company?"

Parrish snorted. "He does now. They're all coming out of the woodwork. But that doesn't make the Moorlands Mall a bad investment. I'm the one they're dealing with, and I know Nantucket."

I made a note on a slip of paper, looked up. "Mrs. Lomax is on-island right now. I've asked her to come in this morning. She should be at the station in a few minutes."

"Is that really necessary?"

I shrugged. "You're a friend of the family. How is she handling this?"

Parrish shook his head. "Not well. You can imagine. He was everything to her. She's a beautiful woman and she's going to be very wealthy one. But I don't envy the man who has to follow Preston Lomax. She's not going to recover from this and she doesn't even want to. She'll probably spend the rest of her life alone, like Mary Todd Lincoln or Yoko Ono."

I stood. "Thanks, Nathan. I may need to talk to you again, but for now..."

"Any time, Chief." He pulled out his wallet and removed a card. "You can always reach me on my cell, unless I'm in 'Sconset. There's hardly any reception in Polpis either, come to think of it. Or Madaket. Well, let's face it, the thing is basically useless. But it takes excellent pictures."

"I use a camera. And a landline."

"Cunning of you, Chief. Anyway, feel free to call the home number or the office. My answering machines are always on."

I took the card and slipped it into my pocket. "Can you find your way out?"

"Like a bird dog."

He flashed a grin and was gone.

Haden Krakauer edged into the office and shut the door. He hadn't shaved in two days and he was starting to look like a revolutionary fanatic skulking around St Petersburg in 1920—or maybe one of those crazy guys living under the Pacific Coast Highway footbridge in Santa Monica. He had a cold and he blew his nose loudly as he came in.

"Don't give me that," I said.

"You never get sick. You're a genetic immune. You ought to get the flu for once. It would humanize you for the men."

"I'd rather stay remote and godlike."

"So—Mrs. Lomax is like Yoko Ono?"

"Eavesdropping again?"

"Monitoring the interrogation, Chief. Just like the regulations specify."

"In other words, eavesdropping."

"Well, yeah. But that's what I love about this job. I'm *explicitly required* by strict *department policy,* to be a nosy, officious snoop. Which I've always been anyway. Mrs. Lomax is waiting to talk to you. And FYI…in the dignified widow category, I wouldn't call her Yoko Ono. More like Courtney Love."

"Hey—"

"I'll go get her. See for yourself."

While I waited for Diana Lomax, I began to sort through the papers piling up on my desk. I had typed records of most of the interviews pertaining to the case; top copies were in the crime binder upstairs. The state police had brought two stenographers from off-island to keep up with the volume of work. I was falling behind, myself. I liked to read everything. Sometimes not being present at the interrogation actually helped. You could see things in the text that the officer conducting the examination missed. Body language and intonation could be revealing if you were skilled and experienced, but they could distract a small town neophyte.

I took a page at random. Helen Sandler. She had thrown the benefit party on the night of the murder. She had just bought an expensive digital camera and an Apple G4 Powerbook. She had spent the whole night taking pictures, and at Haden Krakauer's suggestion she had e-mailed them to the station. I put the paper aside and pulled my computer toward me. I logged onto the NPD site, found the note with the attached photos, opened the file and scrolled down through the pictures.

They were useful, if only for the time references built in: a stove clock visible in the kitchen in some of them, a TV tuned to the local news in others. Some of them gave solid alibis for their subjects: the coroner had estimated the time of the murder at around 11:15. Kathleen Lomax had gone out to her second round of parties at 10:30. I had done the drive from Eel Point to the house in Squam several times in the last few weeks. Squam Road was a dirt track that ran along the east coast of the island, between Wauwinet and Quidnet. The mid-point was about as far as you could get from the Lomax house without a boat. There was a lot of construction going on out there and trucks had dug deep ruts in the mud that had frozen into ice-hard ridges and gullies. It wasn't an easy drive. I figured it would have taken more than an hour that night, round trip. It took me forty-five minutes in broad daylight.

Fiona, Bob Haffner, and two other people from Mike Henderson's paint crew were posed next to a grandfather clock in the living room that showed 10:55. That cleared them; and the local news cleared the people in the picture with the TV in the background. The kitchen stove digital read-out showed 9:55, which didn't prove much of anything. Other pictures, which included the family's kids, were equally useless for my purposes. The oldest girl was in bed by ten.

There was a knock on the door.

"Come on in." I clicked the file closed.

Haden was right. There was something vulgar and oversized about Diana Lomax that I hadn't seen in her darkened car when I pulled her over. The flower pattern on her dress, the gold belt-buckle that cinched it at the waist, her great mane of teased-out hair. She used the most expensive perfume and make-up, but way too much of both. The blue of her eyeliner matched her eyes exactly. A lot of thought had gone into her presentation, but no taste.

She was like a woman walking a straight line for the highway patrol. It wasn't just her stiff, careful gait, it was her whole presence. She was pacing out that tightrope in her mind, clenched and dizzy with the effort to appear calm and stay vertical. Most of it was grief and alcohol and the forbidding venue of the crowded police station. I felt sorry for her. I stood up.

"Mrs. Lomax. Thanks for coming in. Sorry to keep you waiting. Please, have a seat. This won't take long."

"Thank you." Her voice came from the back of her throat, choked and thin.

"First of all, my sincere condolences."

She let out a breath that might have been a laugh if she had put a little energy behind it. "No one knows what to say. Even my friends. I suppose that will do as well as anything else. Sincerity is so important at a time like this."

"Mrs. Lomax—"

"I'm sorry. I don't seem to have any patience left for formalities and niceties. So let's cut to the chase. You're far too nice a young man to say this, but I am the obvious primary suspect in my husband's murder. The spouse is always the first choice, and for obvious reasons. Certainly I had mine. If I was capable of such a thing. Apart from Preston's defects of personality, even a cursory investigation will reveal that our pre-nuptial agreement is voided by an override in his will. If I survived him and we were still married at the time of his death, I proved my loyalty and I got everything. If that seems uncharacteristically generous and decent, it was. But don't worry—he was planning to change his will on the first of the year. I was to be cut out almost completely. That's the Preston Lomax I knew. He actually challenged me to kill him before he could send the document to his lawyers. That will seems to have disappeared. It may never have existed. It's natural to assume I destroyed it, like some harridan in a Victorian novel. Certainly, I do very well under the terms of the current document. Not to mention the life insurance benefits, which are far greater in the case of 'unnatural death,' as this was. That's enough motivation for two murders. My mother was immensely wealthy but she left everything to my children to evade the estate taxes. I didn't receive a penny from her estate. I would have been destitute if the new will had been formalized. So I say, investigate to your heart's content. If you want to subpoena my e-mails and depose my friends, feel free. Turn my life inside out." She smiled. "See if you hate it as much as I did."

"Past tense?"

"It's over. What begins now, I have no idea. The body is being shipped to New York tomorrow. The memorial service is next week. After that…"

"You're free."

"But I don't feel that way. Isn't that peculiar? I read an article the other day about the Berlin Wall coming down. People had hoped for it all their lives. But it made life ten times worse for everyone."

"I'm sure you'll be fine."

"I hated him, Chief Kennis. And now I can't seem to function without him. I'd laugh at that but I've lost my sense of humor, also."

"It will come back. Let me just say this, if it helps at all. You're not a suspect. You're free to come and go as you please. And once again, I'm truly sorry for your loss."

"I—I don't have to stay here? I don't have to testify or whatever it is people do, when they—"

"No. I may call you if I have a question, but I think the sooner you get away from this island, the better."

I stood up and walked around the desk. "Let me show you out."

She stood and slipped into her coat. "How can you be so sure about me? I was off-island when it happened but I could have hired someone, some thugs, to do the job."

"Thugs? Could you really?"

She looked down. "Well…no. I suppose not."

"I'm not sure you'd even recognize a thug if you saw one."

"My mother made that exact point when I got married."

I opened the door and she stepped into the hall.

A second later she backed up into me. "I'm sorry," she said. "I just…I have to—" She peered out the door again and then jerked her head inside with a look of utter of horror and confusion. She stared at me for a long moment before she was able to speak.

"That woman out there," she said. "Standing in the hallway. It was her. She did it. She murdered my husband."

Chapter Twenty-five
Voices of Nantucket

I led Diana Lomax back to the chair facing my desk, took her elbow to guide her down. She sat heavily. The shock and anger scarcely registered on the surgically tightened mask of her face. But her whole body was trembling.

"Mrs. Lomax?"

It took her a moment to look up. "That woman in the hall out there," she said. "The tall blonde, her name is Tanya Kriel. She's a killer. She's dangerous. She should be in a holding cell. Instead she's slouching around like this was a *Vogue* photo shoot."

"Are you all right?"

"I feel ill suddenly. I have to take this coat off."

She was struggling with it. I pulled at one of the arms to help her disentangle herself.

"I'm sorry, but this is so strange and horrible and sick. It's like seeing a ghost. Like Anna had come back. They look so much alike. She's come back for revenge. There's no other possible—have you arrested her? Is she going to jail?"

I leaned back against the desk. "Tell me about her."

"She's a killer, Chief. She swore to kill Preston and now he's dead, and she's standing there with that cocky attitude, like no one can touch her, and—"

"Please, Mrs. Lomax. Tell me what happened."

She took a breath. "I'm sorry. This is quite upsetting. All right…Preston had an affair with a girl named Anna Kriel. She was working for us. This was two years ago. Light housework, some secretarial duties. A 'gal Friday' position. But she dressed provocatively. I thought she was flirting with my husband. I confronted him and he laughed at me. Of course I was right. They were sleeping together. They got careless and I actually—I caught them. I found e-mails later. And—photographs. She was very photogenic. I wouldn't normally discuss this, but…I—"

"It's all right. Can I get you some water? Or tea? We make a mean cup of Earl Grey tea here. We even have decaf."

She tried to smile. "I'm fine. Really. I just needed to catch my breath. I'll be quick. Anna got pregnant. Preston insisted she have an abortion. There were complications. The girl died. And now the sister is here. Do you think that's a coincidence?"

I shook my head slowly. "I don't like coincidences. I can't use them."

"She killed him, Chief Kennis. She came here to kill him and she did it, in cold blood like an assassin. What other reason could she have for being here? How long has she been here? How long has she been planning this? It wasn't some heat of the moment thing, you can be sure of that, some crime of passion. Oh no. Not this girl. She organized all the details, and when the moment was right, when she knew my husband was alone and helpless…"

"Please, Mrs. Lomax. Try to stay calm. This is good information. I mean that. It's an excellent lead. Thank you. You've been tremendously helpful. But you've done all you can. It's police business now. We'll take it from here."

"Are you going to arrest her?"

"If I have reason to believe she killed your husband, yes I will."

"But I'm telling you—"

I reached over and put a hand on her shoulder.

"We'll handle it. You've got a memorial service to organize. And a daughter to take care of. And a new life to begin."

She started to say something else, she was half on her feet; then she gave up and subsided back into the chair. "I'm sure you'll do what's right."

I stared at her for a second. "I can't promise you anything else," I said. "I hope it's enough."

I took her outside through the rear of the station to avoid all but the most enterprising reporters. When I got back to my office, Lonnie Fraker was waiting for me.

"You want the good news or the bad news on your friend Trezize?"

"Start with the good news."

"The Escape in the driveway? The family just called it in. Apparently someone took it for a joyride that night. They thought their son had it. Someone abandoned it on the shoulder of Rugged Road, just off Milestone. One of our guys found it, and called it in. And that was that. We have forensics on it. There may be some trace DNA. We'll see. So it that would get Jimmy Olsen out there off the hook. If not for the bad news."

I made a little beckoning gesture with my hand. "Go on."

"One set of tracks in the mud match these fancy orthopedic sneakers Mindy Levin sells out of her chiropractic office. Guess who wears them."

My eyebrows went up and the corners of my mouth went down, riding a slow nod of appreciation. "Nice job, Lonnie."

He shrugged. "You just have to work the databases, Chief. Scan in the picture, find the company, track the sales outlets, isolate the one vendor on-island, vector that with Mindy's customer records and the medical files of everyone who bought a pair of sneakers in the office, looking for the shoe size. And boomp, you're done. Takes about twenty minutes, tops. That's the advantage guys like me have, you know, guys who live in the twenty-first century? Over dinosaurs like you. No offense."

"So what's your conclusion?"

"Trezize was smart enough to use a different car. But he's the kind of guy who never wears boots in the snow and he was too angry to care about wet feet."

"How did he get into the house?"

"He's friends with the daughter. Maybe he had the alarm code."

I walked around behind my desk and sat down. "Here's where you twenty-first century cyber cops strike out," I said. "Real detectives study people, not computer screens. No offense."

"And your people powers tell you Trezize couldn't have done it."

"They tell me…dig a little deeper and you'll find the real reason David was there."

"You gotta be kidding me."

"Go on your computer again. Check the duration of that little thaw we had. Build a simple chronology for the mud. How long was it soft enough to take a print, when exactly did it freeze up again? Then you'll have a real time line for David's trip to the house. David or anyone else."

"You do it. I got a killer to book."

So Lonnie Fraker solved the Preston Lomax murder. It was his first solution—but not his last one. If he could have somehow gotten credit for the number of times he cracked the case, Lonnie would have been running the state police by New Year's.

I called Tanya into my office a few minutes later. I remembered her from the bar fight at the Chicken Box. She was hard to forget.

She wore the same faded jeans today, with a black turtle neck sweater that offset her thick blond hair. She slouched down in the chair, legs crossed, assessing and dismissing me simultaneously. The fact that she was a suspect in a capital crime and I was a high-ranking police officer investigating her connection to the deceased apparently had no effect on her. Her own effect on me was all she cared about, yet she contrived to seem indifferent. It was a neat trick. She crossed her legs again. The pants were impossibly tight, more like a full body tattoo than an article of clothing. I looked away, out the window.

"Yeah, I wanted to kill Lomax," she said. "Can you arrest me for that?"

I swiveled the chair back to face her. "A lot of people wanted to kill Lomax. I can't arrest all of them. Where were you the night of the murder?"

"At the benefit party, along with half of the rest of the people in the station today. Helen, the hostess, she was taking pictures constantly. It's got to be the best documented party ever. Plus, at least a hundred people saw me there. I think I danced with most of them." She paused.

"What?"

"I just…I left early. That's all."

"How early?"

"I'm not sure. When was the murder?"

"I can't tell you that, Tanya. Just think. Did you watch television when you got home? Did you hear the church bells? Maybe someone called you?"

She half closed her eyes, put a fist to her mouth, and bit down on a knuckle. Then she cheered up. "It had to be before eleven; 'Arts and Ideas' was on the radio. On WCAI. They were just starting some new segment. So maybe…ten fifteen? Does that clear me?"

It didn't, not even close. But I didn't want to alarm her and I didn't want to arrest her—not yet. "Mrs. Lomax thinks you came here to avenge your sister."

"How shrewd of her."

"But someone beat you to it?"

"I got distracted. Fell in love with a married man. I guess it runs in the family."

"It would have been almost impossible to pull off. You were bound to be a primary suspect."

"Motive and opportunity."

"That's right."

"I knew that. When I came here it didn't bother me. Actually I liked the idea. If I killed Lomax I'd want everyone to know. I'd be proud of it."

"And jail?"

"Three meals a day and a clean bed? All the books I could read? It sounded pretty good, Chief. You should see my apartment in the East Village. Jail is nicer. Free rent and you learn a trade. Supposedly."

"Cold."

"Practical."

"Yeah. But then you fell in love with the married man."

She nodded.

"Going down in flames lost its appeal at that point."

"Until I got dumped."

"Recently?"

She nodded.

"I'm sorry to hear that."

"I should have seen it coming."

"So what now? Lomax is already dead. Anyone else you want to kill?"

"No, I only had one sister."

"How about Mrs. Lomax? She certainly hates you. She wanted your sister to get rid of the baby. She was jealous. She was angry. She had a strong influence on her husband."

"Are you trying to talk me into it?"

"I'm trying to decide whether or not to put you in custody until this case is solved. One murder at a time during the holiday season, that's my policy."

"Sounds good. It could be a new slogan for the Chamber of Commerce."

I smiled. "I'll run it by them. But I need an answer."

"I'm not going to do anything to anyone, Chief Kennis. I barely have the energy to get out of bed in the morning. I might not swerve to avoid hitting a rabbit in the road. That's about the extent of the threat I pose right now. I can't pay my rent because I just got fired from my job. I may go back to the city."

"Not until the case is resolved. I'm sorry."

"Whatever. Fine, I'll stay. I may do some carpentry. There's an all-girl crew that's hiring."

"Sounds good."

"Okay…so are we finished? Can I go?"

"Sure. Thanks for coming in. I'll be in touch if I need to talk to you again."

When Tanya Kriel was gone, I sat back and took a few deep breaths. I turned on my police monitor and listened to the soft crackle of calls and dispatcher's instructions. The room, with its essential atmosphere of purpose and sanity and virtue, reasserted itself. The click of the shutting door dissolved the intricate, geometric tension that Tanya carried with her. It melted like a snowflake on a window pane.

I picked up the internal phone line and asked for a cup of coffee. Then I got down to work.

I spent the rest of the morning going through the transcripts, highlighting quotes that struck me as odd or significant.

Molly Burke:

I don't know anything about that murder, and why should I? I cleaned his house but I've cleaned a hundred houses, haven't I? And I never wanted to kill anyone. I don't even know why you're asking me these things. I don't know anything and I'm glad I don't.

Kathleen Lomax:

I came in late from dinner, we'd been at The Pearl and we had a few drinks—what? Oh, just friends from grad school and Barry Hewitt, he just got engaged to Annette Moore and he took us all out to celebrate. It was like, nine when I got home. I took a shower and talked to my dad. That was the last time—I'm sorry. You don't need to—but it just keeps kind of coming at you from behind, you know? You think you're doing okay and then it surprises you. Anyway, sorry, I'm okay. Really. I'm fine now. I guess I left the house about eleven fifteen or so. There was a party, this benefit thing I wanted to go to. I reset the alarm and locked up. Dad was a little whacked about that alarm. We used to argue about it, I mean this is Nantucket after all, but I guess he was right. Not that it makes any difference.

Kevin Sloane:

Of course my fingerprints were on the headboard! That doesn't make me a killer. I had a thing with Diana Lomax, all right. The chief knew it. He pulled us over one night and he don't miss much.

Anyway, she liked doing it with me in her own bed. I just used the headboard for traction. There's probably a dent where her head slammed it, too. Anyway, I wasn't the only one up there.

Billy Delavane:

Actually, my brother Eddie once asked me about Folger's keys. The guy caretakes at least a hundred houses. What did I say? Frankly, I told him to go fuck himself, Officer. Ed's always been screwed up about money. Our parents made me the executor of the estate because they knew I wouldn't sell it out. I mean—hey, I've unloaded a few parcels. There was a two-acre lot in Madaket last year. But Ed's always looking for some way to make a fast buck. He's no killer, though. I mean—sure, he killed people in the war. But aiming a carbine into a dust storm and squeezing off…that's not cold blooded murder. Trust me. Ed's a little crazy and he's got a temper like a snapping turtle. Especially when he's drunk. But you could say that about half the rednecks on this island. People used to say that about me in the old days. Before I mellowed out.

Derek Briley:

Only a matter of time, mate. Someone was going to kill the bloke. End of the day, you can only ask for it so long. Someone's going to oblige, aren't they? But it wasn't me. I did my bit, ratting him out to the newspaper. I like to work behind the scenes. That's my style.

Bob Haffner:

Hey, I was totally out of it that night. I went to the benefit, but I had dinner at the strip first and I was sick as a dog. That's all I was thinking about, OK? Bad clams. I actually got to the benefit though. They gave me something to make me puke at the emergency room and everything was cool. I'm like a dog, man. I barf and I'm fine. Hey, at least I don't try to eat it, like my dog does. So anyway, I got to the party late, someone was watching Leno's monologue in the back room, but the place was still jumping, so that was cool. You should check out the guest list, man. Everybody was there.

Mike Henderson:

Listen, the guy owed me money. I could see threatening him. But I've never understood killing people over stuff like that. Or even hurting someone. Like the mafia. Some longshoreman owes them money, so they break his legs. How is he supposed to earn the money to pay them at that point? It's crazy. I did spread the news about Lomax skipping out. I overheard him, and I just thought…People should know this. It occurred to me that someone might try to do something to the guy. Sure, I admit it. And I guess they did. But it's nothing he didn't deserve, believe me. Lomax was a bad guy. You got in his way, you were roadkill. He wouldn't step on the brakes. He'd step on the gas. That's how I see it.

Cindy Henderson :

Of course Mike hated Lomax. Everyone did. But he would never have done anything violent. Mike's not that way. He breaks up fights, he doesn't start them. He was off-island the night Lomax died. He came to meet me in New York. It had nothing to do with the murder. It's private. We had private business there. I really don't think it's relevant.

Pat Folger:

Sure, I was in his face at the party. People like Lomax make you want to get out of this business, I swear to God. They make it a goddamn misery. Ten years later, a pipe bursts and they'll sue you into the poor house. Meanwhile they change their minds every ten minutes, and you have to videotape them asking for the extras if you ever want to get paid. And the checks bounce, or they left their goddamn checkbook in New York. Who travels without a checkbook? But if I killed every one of these people who deserved it, I'd be more famous than Son of Sam, all right? And just for the record—whoever got in there, they didn't use my key. I keep those suckers locked up tight. I'm old school, sonny. I take my responsibilities seriously.

Jesse Coleman:

Yeah, I know Ed Delavane. I spend time at his house. But I don't sell drugs and neither does he. If he did, I'd bust him. This whole line of questions pisses me off, if you want to know the truth, Lonnie. I'm a cop. I have ambitions. Busting that turd would make my career. From summer special to detective in two years, man. I could write my own ticket after that. No, I'm not scared of him. He can try all the karate tricks he wants. I'm licensed to carry a firearm in this state and all that ninja stuff don't mean shit unless you're bulletproof.

Rick Folger:

I just worked for my dad. I was at the bottom of the food chain, man. I didn't know any of the customers. He would have killed me if I even said hello to them. The rule was, whatever they asked, I had to say, "You'll have to talk to my dad." I mean—anything. "How's the weather? What about them Sox last night?" You'll have to talk to my dad. "You and that girlfriend of yours still together?" You'll have to talk to my dad. He loved that one. That was his idea of a joke. Anyway, the point is, I never met Lomax or his family. I couldn't pick them out of a lineup. By the time they had their big party I had quit. So there was zero socializing, I hate those parties anyway—you know, put out some food for the morlocks. Give 'em a drink and pretend they're human for the night. Fuck that. I was long gone, anyway, like I said. I even got rid of my tools. I don't own a hammer anymore. Can you believe that? And it feels great. I'm never going to bang a nail again. My dad always said I hammered 'like a cobbler.' Anyway. The one time I took a good swing, I smashed my thumb. The nail was black for a year. Ask him about it. He loves to tell that story. Hey, I know he's an asshole, but he'd never kill anyone. Let's get that straight. He doesn't even hunt anymore.

When I set the last page aside, I finished my coffee. It was cold, but I liked cold coffee. My notes reminded me of the "Voices of Nantucket" column in the *Inky Mirror*, man-on-the-street sound bites about the issues of the day. "How do you feel about the Lomax murder?"

I glanced at the clock: almost twelve. I should have left five minutes ago. I was going to be late picking up Fiona for lunch. I started to rise, changed my mind, and pulled the chair up to my desk. There was something in those transcripts, some organizing detail that would resolve all these random voices into a coherent story. I didn't have it, and it was giving me a headache.

Chapter Twenty-six
Dirty Laundry

I set the files aside. I had more immediate problems, and the first one was David Trezize, sitting in a holding cell downstairs. It wasn't just that he was innocent, which I firmly believed. Cobbling together circumstantial evidence against him was wasting valuable time. Plus the process had to be annoying David, and one thing I learned in Los Angeles was—don't gratuitously annoy journalists if you can avoid it. They write their stories anyway, and people read those stories, and the words shape people's perceptions and negative perceptions can make the day-to-day business police work, on the ground, talking to witnesses, panning the swift stream of a neighborhood gossip for a nugget of useful information, almost impossible. Conversations that start "Fuck are you doing here, pig?" rarely turn out well.

The Shoals was a small paper, but its circulation was growing and in any case every big newspaper in the country had sent reporters to the island, and David was the obvious local contact for them. He'd be telling a story, and I didn't want that story to be one of arrogance, harassment, and incompetence.

Besides, I liked the guy. I admit it.

"So what were your footprints doing in the mud?" I asked him. He looked more rumpled and miserable than usual, sitting on the edge of the concrete slab. He needed a shower and a shave.

He looked up. "Funny, no one bothered to ask me that, Chief. I guess they figure it's obvious. I mean, I threatened the guy in front of all those witnesses. Including you."

"No offense, David, but weak people make threats. Killers just get the job done. And they don't advertise it beforehand."

He managed a smile. "Thanks. I guess."

"Still. You came to the house. I'm betting it was the earlier in the day."

He nodded. "I was returning Kathy's inhaler. She has asthma and she wears glasses and she takes the antidepressant and she's always losing her inhaler and leaving her glasses and forgetting to fill her prescription. Personally I think it's because she'd like to be a happy person with strong lungs and 20-20 vision and some part of her just rebels."

I sat down next to David on the slab. "So she's in denial."

"That's what we were fighting about. She was at my apartment and I was trying to explain…well, it's private."

"Not during a murder investigation. Nothing's private during a murder investigation."

A lot of people were going to find that out in the next few days.

He sighed. "All right. It had to do with her boyfriend. This painter kid, Kevin Sloane."

"He was having an affair with her mother." David looked up, startled. "Diana Lomax was driving the car that night. Remember? You picked up the traffic stop on your scanner. Kevin Sloane was with her."

"Makes sense. Wish I'd known that. Anyway, she didn't want to hear it and she took off. I found the inhaler the next morning— after the big party. She threw herself at me when I brought it back, sobbing and sniffling and apologizing and calling herself an idiot."

"She found out the truth?"

"She caught them in bed together."

"Jesus."

David bit his lip, shaking his head. "Terrific little present for the Advent calendar, huh? Must make you all giddy about what you're getting the next day."

I stood. "But we know what she got the next day."

"Yeah."

"Sorry about this David. I'll expedite the paperwork, get you out of here. If you remember anything else that might be useful, call me." I dug out my card—the one with my private cell number, the old number with the 323 area code.

He took it. "I will."

I dismissed Kevin as a suspect—he was a pilot fish, not a shark, and three other people's depositions placed him at the benefit party until dawn, long outstaying his welcome, still drinking Bud Light and chowing down on whatever food was left, but not helping to clean up, or even bus dishes back to the kitchen. Kevin had a clear idea who the party was going to benefit and it wasn't some stranger with multiple sclerosis. It was Kevin Sloane. That was his MO, but that didn't make him a murderer, especially when it came to the powerful husband of one of his many disposable girlfriends. Kevin was the type to cut and run, not make some romantic last stand with a fistful of cash and a bloody screwdriver.

He wore boots the same size as the prints in the snow, and with the same vibram sole. But the prints were too deep for him to have made them. I guessed that the person wearing those shoes had to weigh at least a hundred pounds more than the skinny painter. Hal Loomis, the taciturn SID guy from the state police, reluctantly agreed with me. I think he was surprised that I noticed. Local cops were supposed to be bumpkins. "I guess you picked up a thing or two with the LAPD," he muttered.

That was as close to a compliment as I was going to get.

For Diana Lomax, innocence wasn't so clear-cut. Despite her apparently solid alibi, her genuine-seeming shock and her plausible suspicion of Tanya Kriel, her genuine upset at the sight of the girl, we weren't quite done with Diana.

There was still some of her privacy left to violate.

"You're not gonna believe this," Lonnie Fraker said to me as I walked into the station the next morning.

I patted his shoulder. "You're probably right."

He led me into the conference room, shut the door and took out a small digital recorder. "Listen to this."

Then the two disembodied voices filled the room. I recognized Diana's raspy contralto immediately. The guy I had never heard before.

"Hello?"

"Hello, Paul."

"You sound awful. Are you drunk?"

"No, but thanks for the suggestion."

"What's going on? Did something happen?"

She laughed. "No, don't worry about that, Darling. Nothing ever happens. That could be my whole autobiography. At least I don't need a ghostwriter. I am a ghost. The autobiography of a ghost. Three words. Nothing ever happened."

"You are drunk."

"Just high on life. Isn't that what we used to say?"

"Diana, you have to get out of there."

"Really? And how do you propose I should do that?"

"Go to the airport. Buy a ticket. I'll meet you at LaGuardia."

"And then what? We live in your tiny apartment on a music teacher's salary? We'd be at each other's throats in a month."

"Divorce Preston. Than you can live any way you want."

The room went silent. Fraker held up one finger to say "just wait." So we waited. I felt a sickly voyeuristic thrill listening to these intimacies, and I began to understand what motivated the spies who operate our surveillance state. The sense of power was overwhelming. We were omniscient at that moment, just like God, listening in on the most private moments of these hapless creatures.

But what petty and mean-spirited little gods we were.

"Diana? Are you there? These fucking dropped calls! Every time you try to—"

"I'm still here."

"Then talk to me. What's going on?"

"I signed a prenuptial agreement, Paul. I would have thought you'd have figured that out by now. Everyone assumed I was a gold digger. I suppose I was a gold digger. What they don't tell you is, it's much easier to actually *dig gold* out of the ground than to live with Preston Lomax."

"Diana—"

"If I leave him, I get nothing. Even the gifts he gave me. He makes me sign 'gift vouchers.' I have to return everything if we break up. Even the clothes I bought. I'd be left with a two shirts and a pair of blue jeans. And my old sneakers."

"We'd survive."

"That's an attractive prospect. Survival. Between your ex-wife and my ex-husband, we could barely afford groceries."

"So what are you saying?"

"I don't know. I don't see the point anymore. This isn't even fun. Sometimes I don't even remember why I loved you, or if I did. It's all just talk. I hate the telephone anyway. It's fake, it turns a whole person into this little quacking in your ear. And my ear gets sore. It's uncomfortable. And it seems…I don't know. I don't know what I'm talking about."

"I want to see you. I'll come there."

"You can't afford a plane ticket. You can't afford cab fare. You told me yourself."

"I'll take the bus and walk onto the boat. That's cheap."

"Paul—"

"Then we could be together and—"

"That's two full days of travel, and all you have is the weekend."

"I have a sick day coming."

"Stop. Please just stop talking about this. It's all too shabby and sad."

Another silence.

Fraker perched over it eagerly, waiting to pounce.

"Listen, Diana—"

"You know what's funny? Preston's left me everything in his will—all the property, all the stocks, all the cars and cash. Nothing to charity, nothing to the kids. Everything goes to me. The problem is he's healthy as a horse. He's going to outlive all of us. Both of his parents are still alive. His Dad is ninety-three—and he drinks! Preston isn't even a teetotaler. He allows himself exactly enough red wine every day to clean the platelets out of his arteries."

"Well, at least you're taken care of, that's something."

"Oh, yeah. I'm taken care of all right. When I've served my life sentence I can wear mink in the retirement home. It'll be the snazziest retirement home money can buy, but I'll be too senile to notice."

"Come on. That's just—"

"You know what I need? I need someone to kill him for me. Can you do that, Paul? Can you kill him for me? Or will I have to do it myself? Because that's the obvious solution."

"Diana! Cut it out. This is a cell phone, for God's sake! It's illegal to even talk about this stuff, don't you know that? It's called conspiracy."

"So you don't want to talk about it."

"Goddamn right I don't! I'm hanging up right now!"

The recorder went silent.

Fraker stared at me, grinning. "This Paul knows what he's talking about when it comes to conspiracy, Chief. Looks like we just found ourselves a killer."

"What about David Trezize? You found him yesterday."

"I didn't have this recording yesterday."

I started pacing the big room. My queasiness was firming up somehow, coalescing into simple indigestion, the heartburn of uncomplicated rage. I stopped walking and drilled Fraker with an unblinking stare. "How did you get it?"

"Excuse me?"

"The recording. That's a private cell phone transmission from one American citizen to another, within our borders, with no discussion of a terrorist act."

"No, just murder."

"But you couldn't know that until you heard the tape. Diana Lomax was no more under suspicion than anyone else. Do you have recordings of everyone involved with the case? Because that's a lot of talk and ninety-nine-point-nine percent of it is none of your goddamn business."

"It's the point-one percent we care about, Chief. And we always look at the wife first—even she knows that. She said so herself."

"Then why would she incriminate herself on the telephone?"

He shrugged. "I've never understood women. Ask my ex-wife."

We had veered off the subject. "The state police don't have the authority for this. How did you get the recording?"

"Well, I'll tell you, Chief. I went to an old friend of yours from your West Coast days."

"What are you talking about?"

"Jack Tornovitch. You remember good old Jack Tornovitch, don't you? He ran the FBI investigation that saved your ass and solved one of your cases for you. Just before you got fired. That's how the newspapers painted it. I Googled you—and him. It's all online for anyone to see."

"This is unbelievable."

Jack Tornovitch. Three thousand miles and five years later, I thought I was finally done with Jack Tornovitch. But maybe we're never really done with anyone in our lives. They linger. They may be dormant, like the shingles virus after a bout of chicken pox. But they can flare up anytime.

Fraker was still talking. "Hey, you're not the only detective around here, Chief. Tornovitch moved up. He's a big wheel at Homeland Security now. So I called him and used your name and explained the situation. I told him some push with the FISA court could help the state police solve this thing while you were stumbling around trying to get DNA reports on old cigarette butts. He liked that idea. In fact I think he liked the idea of making you look bad more than he liked the idea of solving the case. You've got a way with people, Kennis. Too bad it's not a good way. Tornovitch may hold a grudge, but I don't. I'll let you stand on stage with me when I announce the arrest."

Well, there was no arrest. He brought Diana Lomax in, and he made her cry, but she was in the city with the boyfriend Paul on the night of the murder, with lots of witnesses and an impressive paper trail of credit card receipts and ATM withdrawals to prove it. Her phone log showed no contact with contract killers or anyone else even remotely sinister.

In the end she was just one more unhappy cheating wife who had contemplated killing her husband. If we made that illegal we'd have to arrest half the married women in America, and clear out the prisons to make room for them. It would be a good excuse for legalizing marijuana, but none of it was ever going to happen. It might comfort Diana Lomax to know she wasn't the only one to have her dirty little secrets flushed out by the investigation. There were plenty more to come. But Lonnie Fraker chose to lay low for a while after his pair of overreaching blunders.

That left the next round of embarrassing revelations to me.

Reading through the interview transcripts I marked down every person of interest with a weak or nonexistent alibi. That gave me a short list of suspects, and I didn't need to violate anyone's civil rights in the process.

First up was the landscaper, Jane Stiles. Her "I was at home all night" soon clarified itself. There were some minor details that Charlie Boyce had skimmed over. It turned out that she was indeed at home, but she wasn't alone. She was with her little boy, and her ex-husband had called several times on her landline, a comforting anachronism she maintained so she could still have phone service in a blackout. "Also, once in a while it's kind of fun to actually hear what people are saying. And I don't really need to go online or play Angry Birds while I'm talking to my mother in the nursing home." It was easy to access her phone records and verify the calls. "Besides," she said. "No matter what I wanted to do, I couldn't just leave Sam alone. I mean—who gets a babysitter so they can commit murder?"

That made me laugh.

She said: "You should do that more often. It makes you look about ten years younger."

"But I want to look older. I want to look intimidatingly mature."

"No chance. I'd say you were going to go directly from boyish rogue to kindly old geezer. No transition at all. Kind of the way we skip spring on Nantucket—late winter, straight into summer."

In her bright astringent way, she was flirting with me. It was fun but I was taken. And I had a long day ahead of me. I walked her out to the parking lot and went back to my list.

The three most obvious candidates for investigation: electrician Tom Danziger, plumber Arturo Maturo, and painter Derek Briley. The first two had the standard motivation—Lomax was ripping them off catastrophically. Briley was a crank. He had leaked the Moorlands Mall story to the newspaper. He hated Lomax, as a person and as a species. "They're parasites," he told me in the interrogation room. "Like deer ticks, blowing themselves up like great balloons on other people's blood. I was in Spain, on the Costa Del Sol, working on houses there, when that bubble burst. The big boys were all long gone when the *shite* came down, Chief. The rest of us were swimming in it, weren't we? Useless buggers."

It didn't take long to unearth the tough little cockney's whereabouts on the night of the murder. Nathan Parrish ran a high-end poker game out of his house and anyone who could afford the five hundred-dollar table stake was welcome. The game provided a utopian model of social equality: Parrish and a few wealthy friends, a retired executive recovering from knee surgery, a Chinese hedge fund mastermind, along with people like Tom Danziger, Derek Briley, and the groundskeeper for the Sankaty Head golf course. Briley didn't like admitting he hung out with the "toffs" as he called them; and his girlfriend thought he was attending AA meetings.

Danziger's wife was a trickier problem: a hard-line Jehovah's Witness who hated gambling. She thought Tom had joined the reading club at the Atheneum, and he was working his way through *Moby Dick*. Tom faked it easily, as he read everything he could get his hands on—including a stray copy of the Lola Burger employee handbook he found on the counter as he waited for his Wagyu hot dog, and the annual Town Meeting Warrant he found in the post office, while standing on line to mail a package. His wife Judy read nothing but her personal translation of the Bible and the *Watchtower* magazine.

I had to ask. "How did you two wind up together?"

He shrugged. "She was the prettiest girl at Nantucket High School. She could probably still qualify as the prettiest girl at Nantucket High School." I watched him quietly across the chipped Formica tabletop. He knew he had to give me more. "And she's a good person, Chief. She helps people. She volunteers at the food bank. She nursed her sister in our house for two years when she was dying, She had Ewing's Sarcoma. It's like bone cancer. The parents had disowned her and she had no insurance."

"That sounds tough."

"If Jill had been a great person it would have been tough. But she was a nasty little bitch and being in pain all the time didn't help her personality any."

"You sound like the hero to me, Tom. Jill wasn't your sister."

"Yeah, well. I wasn't as nice about it as I could have been. I recall saying something like 'If that troll doesn't die soon I'm going to shoot myself just to get the fuck out of here.' But Judy made it work. And she has a sense of humor. You don't normally associate Jehovah's Witnesses with a sense of humor. She came back from her door-to-door visiting thing a couple of nights ago and said, "The Pomeroys' marriage is in trouble, Tom.' I asked her how she knew and she said. 'They let us in. They'd rather talk to the Jehovah's Witnesses than to each other! That's scary. They seemed really interested in Armageddon. After being in that house for an hour I can see how they might be looking forward to it. They even invited us for dinner. I thought they were going to make up the guest room.' She got me laughing, Chief. She does that a lot. So I'd like to stay with her and I'd really appreciate it if you kept this poker thing to yourself."

David Lattimer was a regular at that poker game, too, lucky for him. Lonnie had found out he'd been some kind of Delta Force elite combat soldier in Vietnam ("He wears long sleeve shirts all the time, even at the beach. Know why? He's got military tattoos all over his arms!"). Of course the Lattimers loathed the Lomaxes, as old money always loathes new money, but the clincher was that one of Lonnie's men found a pack of Camel Regulars in the Lattimers' freezer when they went in for a follow-up interview. He told them they were for emergencies only, but it didn't matter. The DNA would set the record straight one way or another. In any case he'd been losing at poker—ineptly bluffing his way out of more than a thousand dollars—at roughly the moment Lomax was being stabbed with a screwdriver, four miles away.

His wife had no philosophical problem with poker in particular or gambling in general, but she hated how tragically bad at it her husband was, and it broke her heart to see him lose. I agreed to keep David's secret as I had agreed to keep Tom Danziger's.

I did the same for Arturo Maturo. His secret was much bigger and potentially much more damaging than the others', but it was no more relevant to the matter at hand. I was beginning to feel like a priest, taking all these confessions. No one was confessing to murder, though. That was the real problem. About eighty percent of major crimes are solved that way. But no one had come forward in this case so far, and I had a feeling that they weren't going to.

Meanwhile, I spent my days uncovering the sad and sordid hidden lives of my new neighbors.

Arturo Maturo represented the pinnacle of his type: the arrogant, greedy, inconsiderate Nantucket plumber. Plumbers reigned as the kings of the local trades—uniquely skilled, high-priced, state-licensed, over-booked, indispensable, careless, tactless and smug. They looked down on everyone else—except the equally elite electricians. They stomped into houses and left chaos behind them—dust and chunks of plaster where they cut through a wall or ceiling, water stains where they had cut a PVC pipe, boxes, and packing materials for faucets and sinks piled behind them when their work was done. It was generally understood that the painters would clean up after them, or at least that was what I understood from Derek Briley and Mike Henderson.

Maturo was willing to go face to face with any of the lower orders, and had been known to punch out the occasional plasterer or floor-finisher in the heat of the moment at the end of a job. He was tough. He was macho. He was a legendary cocksman, also—notorious for sleeping with other people's wives, and stealing their girlfriends. He had verbally threatened Lomax on numerous occasions. He was in the Chicken Box when Mike Henderson announced that the tycoon was about to run out on all his bills. Arturo had motive and opportunity. He had the right personality profile. He also had an air-tight alibi.

He just didn't want anyone to know it.

Arturo Maturo was bisexual. On the night of the murder, he was with his gay lover in the kid's family house in Monomoy. That he'd managed to keep that side of his life a secret for this long, among the prying eyes of his neighbors, was something close to a miracle. I didn't want to wreck that for him.

I gave Arturo the news, and a vow of silence, a few days after our first interview.

"I owe you one, Chief," he said, pumping my hand. "Just name it."

"Sorry. Cops are like EMTs. We can't take a tip, even if we really want to."

He squinted at me. "I don't get you. Cops are supposed to be hard-ass pricks."

"Like plumbers?"

He laughed. "Yeah."

"The trick is knowing when to be a hard-ass prick, Arturo. That's helpful for plumbers, too."

"Hey, I'm not turning into a nice guy just because you got me off the hook for this."

"You don't have to. But you might think about cleaning up after yourself on the job, time to time."

"Oh yeah?"

"That's what you can for me. Think about other people. Promote harmony."

"I don't know about you, Chief."

"Give it a try."

He nodded but I didn't think there was much chance that he'd follow through. Still, it was worth a shot.

All my other efforts were going nowhere.

I was sitting in my office late on a Thursday afternoon going through the Lomax file one more time, trying to figure out what I'd missed, when Lonnie Fraker barged in, like a cat with a dead mouse in its jaws. He had found another culprit to lay on my doorstep.

"I got a movie for you, Chief."

I looked up, set the file aside. It was almost quitting time and I was thinking about taking a long weekend. Sometimes the best thing you can for a case is ignore it. The fussy left side of your brain goes to the beach or the barbecue and the secret intuitive part, the corpus callosum, can get some real work done. But it looked like Fraker was ready to put in another shift.

"What are you talking about, Lonnie?"

He reached into his jacket pocket and pulled out a DVD in a plastic lined paper cover. "You know how Lomax paid for the kid's apartment off Bartlett Road? Eric?"

"Sure. So what?"

"Well he had it wired for surveillance—state-of-the-art stuff. There's a rig just like it at the Eel Point pile, but they were still installing it when he died."

"So he was filming his son all the time?"

"HD video and surround sound, baby. "We were searching the place and we found the whole setup. We copied the files, burned them to a DVD—and boomp, it's a done deal."

"Boomp?"

"I say boomp, you got a problem with that?"

"It's fine, Lonnie. What's on the disc?"

"Wait and see."

"Let me guess. The brothers murdered him there and dragged the body back to the house."

"Very funny."

"What then?"

He walked over to my Blu-ray/monitor set up, grabbed the remote and set the DVD on the sliding tray. "This shit is definitely NSFW—not safe for work. But this is our work, you know what I mean? Which is one of the main reasons that we love our work! Am I right?"

I swiveled around in my desk chair to face the flat screen TV. "Let's take a look at it."

The screen went blue for a second, then we were watching a freeze-frame of Tanya Kriel and the Lomax brothers, sitting in the cramped living room of Eric's garage apartment. She was wearing a jeans and a Cutting Edge Painters T-shirt, that sported Mike Henderson's company logo: two brushes crossed under a bucket of paint

"The camera was hidden in the bookshelf," Lonnie informed me. "Built into a dummy copy of *1984*. You can't say Lomax didn't have a sense of humor."

"I'm surprised they had books at all."

"What a snob! Lots of killers read books. Some of 'em even write books. Mao was a pretty good poet when he wasn't slaughtering everyone who looked at him funny."

"Okay, okay."

"Check it out."

He hit "play" and Tanya said "You're stuck, both of you. You're going to talk about killing your father until you die and he goes to your funerals."

"So what do you suggest?" Eric said, walking into the frame.

"Just do it."

"And how are we supposed to get away with it?" Danny asked. He was sitting in a ratty armchair sideways to the couch where Tanya lounged, legs parted, one foot on the pillow.

"There are lots of poisons. I've been doing some research—poisons that take an hour or ten hours to do the job, poisons that break down in the bloodstream and ten hours later it looks like he died of a heart attack."

Eric:"And where do get this stuff?'

"Online, obviously."

Danny: "Poisons.com?"

"There are sites. If you know how to find them."

"What are they?"

She shook her head. "Not yet. I don't trust you yet."

Eric: "I don't know."

Tanya stood. "Fine, whatever. You're right. I don't know what I was thinking about. This isn't fair. It's like asking a pair of paraplegics to carry me upstairs. It's pointless and it's mean… Sorry, boys. I'm outta here."

She uncoiled herself from the couch and started for the door. Danny said, "No! We can do this."

"You can act. You can be bold."

"Yes."

"You can take charge of a situation."

Eric said "Fuck, yeah."

"You can work together."

Together: "Yeah."

"You can stay out of each other's way."

"Yeah."

"You can have a three-way without crossing swords?"

Silence.

Danny, finally: "Wait, what?"

"Sex is the marker. It tells you everything about a person. That's why I do one-night stands, not first dates. You can bullshit on a date, show off, throw your money around, do your patented cool guy act. Everybody's got four or five hours' worth of that shit. But it all goes away when you're naked. Sloppy kissers are sloppy. Rough boys are bullies. If he calls you a bitch and a whore, chances are he means it. If he comes too soon don't count on him to keep it together any other time. If he won't go down on you, he's not going to come up with anything else you need. Trust me."

Eric: "So then…I mean—what are you—?"

She pulled off her T-shirt. Fraker was watching me so I kept my expression blank.

"So let's see what you've got. And what you can do. Get me off—then we'll off your father together."

She grabbed Eric by the belt and unbuckled it.

Fraker froze the frame.

"You don't need to see the rest, Chief."

"And you have it memorized."

He grinned. "I'm working on it."

I blew out a breath. "Wow."

"It's not a confession, but it's the next best thing."

"It's inadmissible."

"They made the tape themselves—the father did, anyway. It's all in the family and we had a signed warrant to search the premises. Boomp, over and out."

But something still bothered me. "When was the tape made?"

"Who knows? Who cares? Before Lomax got killed, that's all we need to know."

I pushed the intercom button on my phone console. "Betty? Could you track down Haden Krakauer for me?"

"Sure, boss."

Lonnie frowned in irritation. "What do we need him for?"

"I have a question for him. He's knows about this stuff."

"What stuff? Not sex, I bet."

I ignored that remark. "Electronics, video. He was quite a geek, back in the day."

"He's still a geek."

"But now he's on our side. No more black box phone calls and hacking escapades."

Haden came in sneezing, still fighting the cold he picked up at Thanksgiving. We showed him the same piece of video.

"There's something missing," I said.

Haden nodded. "No, it's there. It's hidden. We just have to find it."

I turned to Lonnie. "Police work, in a nutshell."

"What the hell are you two talking about?"

Haden said, "The time code. It's obviously keyed-in on this video. You need an electronic device to read the digital time code information from the tape and generate the numbers to be temporarily keyed—superimposed—over the video. The problem is that you can only see the code if you've got special equipment, like the right editing system."

"Do we have it?"

"I think I can find something, kicking around here somewhere. Give me a couple of hours."

Well, he found the proper equipment and keyed the time code onto the video: date and time. But that was the problem. Tanya and the boys were planning Dad's murder on the precise date and time that someone else was actually murdering him. I took Lonnie to lunch at Kitty Murtagh's and broke the news

"It's the perfect alibi," I said.

Lonnie grabbed his hair with both hands and pulled it hard. "Fuck this. I give up."

Thomas Edison once answered an interviewer's question about the frustration of his thousand failed efforts to invent a working light bulb: "No, no, It was wonderful! Now I know a thousand ways not to make a light bulb." Same with police work. I knew it, even if Lonnie didn't.

Every wrong guess and dead end and failure was bringing us closer to the truth

Chapter Twenty-seven
The Interrogation

Haden Krakauer grabbed me as I walked back into the lobby.

"I think we may have something, Chief."

"What?"

"It's Mike Henderson. The painter? I went back and talked to him and his wife. I followed up on the alibis, checked with people, examined his bank records, did some print comparisons. It's all here." He hefted the file folder in his hand. "I think you need to talk to this guy. Seriously. He looks good for the murder."

Haden had the victorious look I had last seen when he found a double-crested cormorant roosting at Stump Pond. Birding—though he was teased for it around the station—had made Haden tireless, patient, and detail oriented—the trifecta for good police work.

I took the folder. "I'll check it out," said. "See how bad it looks."

As it turned out, it looked very bad indeed—at least for Mike Henderson.

For me the day had brightened considerably.

Mike Henderson was sitting in the main interview room off Central Dispatch. Charlie Boyce, Haden Krakauer, and I stood next door in the dark, watching him through the one-way mirror. Mike glanced at his watch, stood, paced, ran a hand through his hair, jammed his palm against his forehead. The body language sandwich sign: "I'm nervous, I'm scared, what the hell am I going to do?"

I turned to the others in the official twilight of the viewing room, spoke softly. "What do you think?"

"Guilty, Chief," Charlie said. "Guilty as hell."

Haden sighed. "Just because you're innocent, that doesn't make you happy in there. The police pick you up for something you didn't do—that's America's number one nightmare."

"I thought showing up at work naked was America's number one nightmare,' Charlie said.

I jabbed my palm at the air between them. "Finish this chat off-duty, boys. I'm going in. And you need to pay attention."

I took the file from Haden and walked out.

Mike Henderson jumped up when I opened the door. "What's going on, Chief? I mean—why did—I'm at work this morning, I'm talking to a customer and a cop car pulls up! These two goons cuff me and take me away—"

"They shouldn't have cuffed you, Mike. That was a mistake."

"Tell that to Ed Powers! Now he thinks I'm some kind of felon or something and he was about to sign off on a winter's worth of work. I guess I can kiss that one goodbye."

"I will talk to him. But right now we have to go over a few things."

"Do I need a lawyer?"

"Didn't they Mirandize you?"

"They did, but…I just—I don't understand what's happening, Chief. What do you think I did? Am I some kind of suspect?"

I gestured him back to his chair and sat down across the table from him. "Can I get you some coffee or something? Water?"

"No, no. I'm—just tell me what's going on. I have to get back to work."

I took a breath, let it out slowly. "Let's back up," I said. "First of all, can you tell me where you were four nights ago? That would be last Sunday night. The sixteenth of December."

Mike's face bunched up in thought for a second, then cleared. He pushed back away from the table eyes wide, like I was going to attack him. "Wait a second. That's the night Lomax was killed."

I nodded.

"You can't possibly—are you saying that I—"

"We're just looking at everyone who had a motive, Mike."

He laughed. It sounded more like a cough. "That would be everyone who ever worked on that house! Everyone who ever met the guy. I mean, what a total—"

"Mike."

"What?"

"Before you go much further, this might be the time to get your lawyer in here."

"I don't need a lawyer! I didn't do anything! Getting a lawyer, that's like pleading the Fifth Amendment, it's like saying 'I'm guilty'."

"No, Mike. Not all. It's merely a way of—"

"Forget it." We stared at each other. "Like I could afford a lawyer anyway."

"I thought they explained this. The court will appoint one for you if—"

"Yeah, they're motivated. They fall asleep during the trial."

"Okay, that was bad. But it happened a long time ago, in Texas. Any attorney chosen to represent you here will be fully professional. I guarantee that. Lester Rowlands is on call today. He's a good man."

"I painted his house five years ago."

"Okay, then. Shall I call him?"

"Are you trying to frame me? Or sweat a confession out of me?"

"Of course not."

"Then let's just get this over with."

I shrugged. "So where were you Sunday night?"

"At a client's house in Manhattan."

"Can they vouch for your whereabouts?"

"They weren't home."

"And they just let you stay in their apartment whenever you want?"

"They like me. And they trust me. And it's not an apartment. It's a house, a sort of row house. A brownstone. On the upper West Side."

I stood up. "So no doorman?"

"No."

"Any neighbors see you?"

"Not that I'm aware of. But you should check with them."

"We already did, after Assistant Chief Krakauer's initial interview."

"So you already know all this! What the hell are you trying to—"

"We need it on the record Mike, in your own words." I walked around and sat against the edge of the table. "How did you get off-island?"

"Hy Line fast boat. I used an old ticket."

"So they have no record of you at the counter."

"No, but—"

"Did you see anyone you knew on the boat?"

"No."

"How about the Hy Line guys? Would they remember you?"

"I doubt it."

"So you disappear off the island Saturday morning?"

"I guess."

"You're in Hyannis. Did you take a bus to the city? Or did you go by plane, because if you did they'd have a record—"

"I drove. In my customer's car. They keep one off-island in the Steamship Authority lot."

"Nice customers."

"They're friends of mine."

"What were you doing in the city?"

"I had—I was—that's private."

I walked around, sat down again and opened the file. I turned over a few pages. "Your wife says more or less the same thing. It seems she had a doctor's appointment."

"How would you know that?"

"Phone records."

"You can just grab my phone records now? Just because you suspect something? Just because you're curious? Just start pulling my life apart and nosing through the pieces because you have a hunch?"

"It's the law now, Mike. Let's try to work through this. Cindy made the appointment on Saturday night. That was unusual. We checked it out. Apparently she called this Dr. Mathias at his home number. She told him it was an emergency. He suggested she go to the ER on Nantucket, but she insisted that she had to see him, as soon as possible. He gave her an appointment on Monday morning, the 17th. Any idea what that was about? It would help us to know. So we can put together a viable picture of your trip."

Mike slumped in his chair. "She was getting an abortion. All right? Happy now? And I had to stop her."

"She didn't keep the appointment."

"Because I stopped her! I talked her out of it."

"And then?"

"We spent the day in the city, drove to Hyannis, and got the last flight back. The eight-thirty flight. Nantucket Airlines."

I turned a page. "The problem is, we have no record of you on that flight."

"We used Cindy's coupon book."

"Yeah, well...okay, but—no one remembers a couple boarding the aircraft."

He sat forward. "Cindy was in the bathroom. She almost got left behind. And they didn't seat us together because they have to distribute the weight on the plane. You know that."

I nodded. "Was the flight crowded?"

"I don't remember. Yes—I think so. Yes it was."

"Well it would be, this time of year."

"So I'm guessing?"

"I don't know. Are you?"

"What are you trying to say?"

"Try and see it from my point of view, Mike. You manage to get on and off the island, all the way to New York and back, without a trace. That's very convenient."

He jumped up and lurched behind the chair, grabbing the seat-back. I half expected him to lift it up like a lion-tamer. But he just stood there. "Convenient? For who?" he yelled. "Convenient? For the guy who wants to go to jail? For the guy who wants to make sure he has no alibi for a crime he didn't commit? Or maybe it's convenient for you, so you can have an arrest, and look smart and get the fucking media off your back."

"Sorry. You're right. That was out of line." I tried a different tack. "Maybe you can clear up some of the other questions that keep cropping up. The murder weapon was a 'four-way' screwdriver with removable tips. People we spoke to told us it was your favorite tool. You even joked about using it as a murder weapon. I found the page, the quote highlighted in red by Haden Krakauer. 'It would have to be someone you hated enough to kill with one strike,' you said, presumably because the tip would lodge in the body."

"That's ridiculous! I never said that. Why would I say that if I was actually going to kill someone that way?"

"I don't know. Maybe…so you could say 'Why would I say that if I was actually going to kill someone that way?' It's classic misdirection."

"What so now I'm some weird psycho who likes to play head-games with the police? I'm a housepainter! I like four-way screwdrivers. So what?"

Time to move on. "We found your fingerprints on the headboard in Lomax's room."

Mike was studying his hands on the table. "I had sex there."

"Would your wife verify that?"

"It wasn't with her."

I made a note on the file. Kevin Sloane had said he "wasn't the first" to fool around on that bed. Maybe he knew something about his boss that could help us. "Who then?"

"I'd rather not say."

"Let me tell you. It was a woman named Tanya Kriel. She came here to kill Lomax—to avenge her sister's death. I'm sure you know the story. We heard it from the widow. Tanya comes here, gets on the crew painting the Lomax house and when she finds out Lomax is going to cheat everyone out of their final payments, she tells you and she has an instant accomplice. You were both stalking him, your cars were seen there. And the night before, you were seen in the house after the party, eavesdropping while Lomax boasted about ripping everyone off. An hour later you're at the Chicken Box, telling everyone to go out and kill him. Then you disappear into the no-alibi zone. You took a thousand dollars out of your account in cash over the last month and that's the exact amount that wound up in the victim's mouth. Ten Nantucket sawbucks, as they say. The amount rich guys hand out as petty cash. But it wasn't petty to you."

"Goddamn right it wasn't! I'm broke. I took that money out so I'd have some way to buy groceries if the IRS attached my bank account."

"Or you wanted to make a statement and the price didn't matter. It makes sense—you were going to be ruined anyway."

"Did you find my fingerprints on the cash?"

"No, you wiped it clean. Then you knocked him out, stuffed his mouth with money and stabbed him with a screwdriver. Nice symbolic touch there. The working man's murder weapon."

"You didn't find my prints on it."

"No, of course not. You were wearing gloves."

"So how did I leave a print on the headboard?"

"You didn't, not that night. But the print proves you were there, that you trespassed on the man's property, that you had an unhealthy, sinister interest in him, that you had in fact been stalking him. It's ironic. The gloves gave you a false sense of security. If you had been bare-handed you would have wiped off every surface and removed all your fingerprints, even the old ones. We'd have no evidence of your history with Lomax, no way to prove your obsession with him. Of course there were all those witnesses at the Chicken Box. Some of them thought you were going to go back and kill Lomax that night, yourself. But you waited until you knew he was alone. You made the mistake of using your work van—a gray Ford Econoline. Maybe you thought it would be inconspicuous. But someone saw it at the house on the night of the murder."

Mike seemed to have shrunk into himself. His voice lacked conviction. "I told you. I was in New York City on the night of the murder."

"With your wife, supposedly. Well, she in fact spent the night at the Sherry Netherland Hotel. But she was with another man, a filmmaker named Mark Toland. Name ring a bell?"

"Yes, but…I told you I was staying at the Levines' that night, and I—it's not possible, I couldn't have—I'm not—"

It was time to close this down. "Sorry, Mike. You had motive and opportunity. You had the murder weapon in your possession. You had the thousand dollars in cash we found in the victim's mouth. You left fingerprints at the crime scene. Your van was observed there at the coroner's estimated time of death. You had keys to the house. You knew the alarm code. You had an equally motivated partner, but she has an alibi for the night in question and you don't. I think you got played, Mike." I stared at him. "It doesn't look good."

Mike pushed his chair away from the desk and stood facing me. "Talk to my wife. She'll tell you what really happened. She'll defend me."

"Of course she will. But if she claims to be with you on the night of the murder, she'll be facing perjury charges of her own. I hate to do this, Mike, but I'm placing you under arrest for the murder of Preston Lomax."

"This is crazy."

"We picked up Tanya Kriel an hour ago. She wasn't happy with you. It looks like you've burned that bridge. She might wind up being our key witness. As a first-time offender, an impressionable girl under the sway of a Svengali-like sociopath, she'll get off with a light sentence if she testifies against you. Maybe a year's probation."

"I don't believe this! I didn't do anything! I not only didn't kill anyone, I saved someone! I talked Cindy out of the abortion! Then I come back here and go on trial for murder? It's a right-to-lifers nightmare. It's almost funny. And here's the best part. I get to be in the *Inky Mirror* police log, accused of killing one of my customers! That should do wonders for my business. Pay-or-Die Painters, that can be the new company name!"

"Listen, Mike—"

"Are you going to call a press conference and apologize publicly when you finally clear my name? Or should I just sue the town for defamation of character, loss of income, and hardship when the business I've spent twenty years building goes down the tubes?"

I walked to the door, but turned back with my hand on the knob. "Let's take it one step at a time, Mike."

He gave a me a twisted little smile. "I guess I should have called my lawyer after all."

I took a last look at him before I left the room. I knew everyone at the station and the state police headquarters would be celebrating. The reporters would be scrambling all over each other to file first and get the scoop on what they would inevitably refer to as the "crime of the century." I'd be famous for a while. I could probably ride this master-stroke of police work all the way back to L.A., and reclaim my old position in the Robbery-Homicide division. Nantucket had proved it could take care of itself. Our humble police force could track down criminals and punish them without hesitation, even when they presented themselves as upstanding members of the community. The island had emerged from the publicity storm as a safe haven again—for tourists and wealthy homeowners alike. It was a win for everyone.

The only problem was, I didn't believe it.

Something was off-kilter in the case we'd built. And Mike Henderson didn't project the defiant chagrin of a bad man run to ground. I saw something very different: a good man fighting a run of bad luck. I felt sorry for him. There was nothing I could do to help, though.

At least not yet.

Chapter Twenty-eight
Chain of Evidence

Mike Henderson didn't spend much time in jail.

Billy Delavane posted bail, which Judge Perlman had set at ten thousand dollars. "He's hardly a flight risk, Mr. Carmichael," the judge remarked to the state's attorney at the bail hearing. "If these allegations hold up, Mr. Henderson's only trip off-island in the last year took place entirely in his imagination. A flight of fancy, at best. You can't have it both ways."

Billy caught up to me in the street outside the town building. "Mike's innocent, Chief. You trust me. I trust Mike."

I nodded. "I think I do, too. And he can do himself some good now that he's back on the street. Post a request in the forums at Yack On—maybe someone saw him on the boat. And he could get the mileage off the Levines' car. They might keep a log, especially when lots of different people are driving the vehicle. If the new mileage matches up with a trip to New York that would help. And get him a decent lawyer. Lester Rowlands is a good guy, but he's a lazy drunk. There's two kinds of people in the world—the ones who do the most they can and the ones who do the least they can. Lester is group two all the way."

Billy nodded. "Anything else?"

"Have your guy check the traffic cams on I-95. If Mike was speeding they may have taken his picture. That would solve the whole problem right there. He told Haden Krakauer he waited for his wife in some coffee shop near the doctor's office. Those places have regulars. They might remember a stranger. The waiter might recall a guy who came in for breakfast and only ordered coffee."

"That's a stretch, Chief."

"Yeah, well Mike needs a stretch right now. Or a miracle."

But as it turned out, all Mike really needed was for the NPD to arrest someone else for the murder.

And that happened before the court clerk finished processing the bail papers.

It began with a dirty ashtray in Fiona Donovan's living room.

I was late picking her up for lunch after a morning crowded with impatient reporters and squabbling cops. Lonnie Fraker was just as certain as Billy Delavane that my suspect was innocent. They had played Whalers football together. Haden called Lonnie's latest new theory the "Lomax Love Nest," in honor of the various tabloid writers who were covering the story.

In this version of events, Kevin Sloane conspired with Diana Lomax and her daughter to kill the old man so they could live out the rest of their incestuous love triangle on the money he left behind. The only evidence they had for any of this was Diana's "hinky" demeanor. I told them with a rigorously straight face that city cops just said "suspicious" these days. "Hinky" was so twentieth century. Kevin Sloane's fingerprints on the headboard fed the in-house frenzy, along with a fervid belief that this was exactly the kind of stuff that rich people were doing all the time.

"These guys watch too much TV," I told Haden Krakauer.

Haden shook his head. "Not me, but I just read *The Wings of the Dove*, Chief. And let me tell you—these sleazy shenanigans have Henry James written all over them."

I wasn't happy with my own theory either, so I kept quiet. I shrugged at the other cops and said "No comment" to the reporters. The only refuge in my day was lunch with Fiona. We usually ate at the airport. I actually liked Crosswinds, and no one ever thought of looking for me there. The tang of jet fuel, the view of the runways, the sound of planes taking off and the periodic flight announcements all gave me the illusion that I was in transit myself, killing time before a trip to Boston and points east—London, Belgrade, Beijing. I was thinking about the pleasant anonymity of travel, wondering if there was a poem in it, when I walked into Fiona's house, and everything changed.

I didn't notice anything at first. I stood waiting for Fiona in the living room—more of a common room really, since the house served as a dormitory for the girls who worked for her—studying the books on the shelves. I had the bad habit of judging people by their books, but I knew that none of these belonged to Fiona. She never read novels. She preferred popular history and science. She had inhaled Nathaniel Philbrick's complete works, and was currently reading Richard Dawkins, so that she could marshal the necessary arguments to crush and humiliate anyone who argued in favor of "intelligent design"—primarily the members of her own family, good Catholics all. In any case, she never purchased a book. They were nothing but an extravagant source of clutter to her, and a pointless one if there was a decent library available. Ebooks? She liked reading in the bathtub too much. These volumes had to belong to the girls on her cleaning crew. They were all paperback romances and they had the creased and grimy look of the "take it or leave it" shack at the dump.

I pulled one off the shelf, opened it at random. "Marcella swooned at his touch. Edward pulled her to him roughly, and kissed her as the storm raged on outside and the ocean dashed itself against the cliffs."

I shook my head, turned the book over and read the blurb on the back. No woman had ever swooned at my touch. But then again, I wasn't "mysterious" or "sinister" like this Edward guy, and I definitely didn't own a castle on the Scottish coast. Maybe I should look into that—buy a chunk of craggy real estate, hire a cute governess with father issues, make a few cryptic comments, and let the fur fly. Of course, I'd need a dark secret to be "tormented" by, if the back cover could be trusted. That was a problem. I am strictly a what-you-see-is-what-you-get. My past was as dull as my present, at least from a romance novel point of view. I set the book back on the shelf.

"Broadening your horizons?"

I turned around. Fiona had just walked into the room.

"I'm not sure. How come you never swoon when I kiss you?"

"Low altitude and sobriety. Get me drunk at the Mount Everest base camp and I'll swoon like a Bronte character."

"Very romantic."

"Oh, so it's romance you're looking for?"

"You know it is."

She grabbed my belt and tugged me closer. "Glad to hear it, Chief Kennis. I could use a little myself."

I kissed her—a long, deep kiss, and when we pulled our mouths apart, I said "Swooning yet?"

"Just the opposite: wide awake like a badger in heat."

I grinned. "Even better."

I kissed her again and we wound up wrestling each other's clothes off and making love on the couch. It was a narrow couch. At some point we fell off and finished on the floor. When we were done, she rolled over and showed me her chafed elbow.

"Rug burns," she said. "Now that's romantic."

"It's a badge of honor—like a hickey on your neck. We used to flaunt them when I was a kid. Girls would wear open shirts even if it was freezing out."

"And when I was a girl, we were embarrassed. We'd wear turtlenecks, even if it was the middle of summer."

"Yeah, I knew some girls like that. Others wore turtlenecks so people would think something had happened. That way they could show off and pretend to be modest at the same time. Which is kind of like my friend Doug in L.A. He drives around in his car with the windows closed so people will think he has air-conditioning."

Fiona was distracted. She was looking up, over my shoulder across the room.

"What?"

"Damn it. How many times do I have to tell them?"

"Tell them what?"

"I don't know whether they can't actually think at all, or they just can't be bothered."

I propped myself up on one elbow. "They?"

"The girls. They've broken two Baccarat crystal glasses which they were forbidden to use in the first place, and now they're using my silver bowls as ashtrays. I've told them over and over, but it makes no difference. I don't even like them smoking in here. They're incorrigible."

Fiona stood and walked over to the end table next to the corduroy-covered armchair that faced the hearth. I stood and joined her. There was indeed a scattering of ashes and a cigarette butt in the silver bowl next to the lamp.

Fiona was about to pick it up to clean it.

My voice stopped her. "Don't touch that."

"Excuse me?"

"I mean it, Fi. Just step aside for a second."

She tilted her head questioningly in that almost canine way she had sometimes, but she took a step toward the fireplace.

I was staring down at the cigarette, the single gold circle above the filter. I was so absorbed by the sight that I started reaching into my pocket for tweezers and an evidence bag before I remembered that I was naked.

Fiona watched quietly while I got dressed. I walked back to the table, picked the butt up delicately with the tweezers and held it out to her.

"Who smokes these?"

"I—"

"Think, Fiona. It's important. Who was here last night?"

"How should I know? I was with you. You got here before I did today."

"Sorry. You're right."

"What's going on, Henry?"

"Do any of these kids smoke Camel Lights?"

"Molly's boyfriend, Jesse. I bought him a pack last week. I was going to Cumberland Farms and he—"

"Jesse Coleman?"

"That's right."

"He's a cop, Fiona."

"I know that. Are they not allowed to smoke? I had no idea that there was any—"

"This cigarette may be evidence in a capital murder investigation, as well as a number of grand larceny felony cases. I don't know how many, yet. But I'm going to find out."

"I—"

"They told me cops were involved in this. But I didn't believe them. I didn't want to deal with it. I thought things were different here."

"Who told you this?"

"Different people. Haden Krakauer. David Trezize over at *The Shoals*. Even a kid who writes for the goddamn high school newspaper told me. A high school kid. What an idiot I am."

She put an arm on my shoulder. "You're not an idiot. You just trust other cops. You want to believe the best about them."

"Really? Do you really think that? Because as far as I can tell, that completely disqualifies me from doing my job. That's a firing offense. People want a naive police chief about as much as they want a wise-cracking airline pilot. And they're right."

I started for the door. I felt a quick twinge of relief—this was one piece of evidence that didn't tie in to Mike Henderson. He was an aggressive non-smoker. He'd gone to town meeting to get cigarettes banned on the outside decks of the Steamship Authority ferries.

"Henry, wait a minute."

I turned back. She was standing in front of me, still naked, pale and beautiful, her body gleaming like a pearl in the early afternoon light, one curling strand of red hair touching her neck. In another world, or some better version of this one, I could take her hand, walk her upstairs to the proper bed in her room, make love all afternoon, and then buy her the steak she'd be craving at Kitty Murtagh's.

In this world I had to leave. "I'll call you later," I said.

But by the time I got around to calling her, I was flat on my back, staring up at the fluorescent lights in the ceiling of Nantucket Cottage Hospital.

I took a long, circuitous route to the emergency room that afternoon. Jesse Coleman was the first step. The kid was furious at being interrogated. "I'm a police officer," he said. "I deserve some trust. And some respect."

"Get some perspective, Jesse," I told him. "You were a rent-a-cop summer special six months ago. Seniority isn't your strong suit. Punctuality, maybe. I'll give you that. But getting up on your high horse and saying 'You can't do this to me! I've shown up mostly on time since September!' doesn't really sound that impressive."

We were sitting in the interrogation room, a stigmatized venue most of the cops called "the hole." My cell phone rang. I turned it off without checking the number. "My Lieutenant in Los Angeles, a classic tough guy named Chuck Obremski, said something to me at my going away party. He said I was going to have it easy here, because small town crooks were stupid. 'The smart ones go to the city'. That's what he told me. Then he winked and added, 'but so do the smart cops.' So he'd say we were evenly matched."

Jesse sat forward, looking even more aggrieved. "Wait a minute, Chief, what exactly are you trying to—"

"It's just too easy out here, for everyone. Mainland standards don't apply."

"What's this about? The fuck are you saying?"

"Hey! Station house rules, remember? No swearing." I let Mike Henderson get away with it, but I had different rules for civilians—and friends. "The town doesn't permit smoking, either."

"I never smoked in the station."

I watched him steadily. "No, that's true. But you do smoke everywhere else. Including the alley outside. And every house you've robbed for the last two years."

"I never robbed anybody."

I sighed. "At this point I have to Mirandize you, Jesse."

"What?"

"You know the drill. You have the right to remain silent. If you chose to talk, anything you say may be used against you in a court of law. You have the right to a lawyer. If you can't afford a lawyer, one will be appointed by the court."

"Chief, this is crazy. I have no idea—"

"Do you understand these rights as I have explained them to you?"

"Come on."

"Do you understand your rights?"

We stared at each other. "Okay, yeah fine. Of course I do. Now what the hell are you—"

"Jesse, please. Don't say anything for a minute. Just listen. Okay? Before you call a lawyer, before I have to book you, before we file on this. Hear me out."

Jesse nodded.

I took a breath. "I found a Camel Light cigarette butt at Fiona's house today. She bought you the pack. I found the same type of butt, smoked down to the same point, at the Lattimers' house in 'Sconset last week. They had some furniture stolen. So did Lomax. And I found another butt on the floor under Lomax's bed, the morning after he was murdered. Same brand, smoked down to the same point."

"So what? Camel is the most popular brand in America. Go to Lucky's and ask them how many packs they sell a week."

"You're right. I smoked them myself."

"That's what I'm saying."

"We have the DNA workups on the first two cigarettes, Jesse. They match. And your butt is being processed right now. The state police are putting a rush on it, through the lab in Fall River. They'll have the results by tomorrow. But we both know what those results will show. It was you, Jesse. I know it. You know I'm right."

"That's bullshit!"

"Cooperate with me. You don't have to go to jail for this. No one's accusing you of murder. But you have information we need. The people who did these robberies with you, were they selling drugs? Lomax was a user. He owed them money. They came to collect, things got out of control. You weren't there but you knew what was supposed to go down that night."

"I can't go to jail, Chief. I can't do that."

"There's a way out, Jesse. Just talk to me. Tell me about Ed Delavane."

Jesse tensed in his chair as if he was thinking of making a run for it. But he didn't move. He spoke to the arm of his chair.

"I can't tell you anything about Ed Delavane. I don't even know the guy."

"Jesse. Come on."

"I've heard the name, okay? I'm sure I'd know the face. But this is Nantucket, Chief. You can go years before you put the name and the face together."

"Small town life, right? It makes things difficult sometimes. Like meeting someone for a drink at the Chicken Box every Saturday for six months and trying to keep it secret."

"Chief—"

"He orders shots and beers. Canadian Club and Bud Light. You pay for them."

"Not always. Sometimes he…shit."

"Don't worry about it, Jesse. Lots of people have seen you there. Haden Krakauer, Dietz. They're regulars. Copeland and Drake play pool every night. I saw you there myself a few weeks ago. You met your girlfriend there. She works for Fiona Donovan. If you want to keep things private, stay home."

Jesse slumped in the chair. "Fucking fishbowl."

"Jesse."

"Friggin' fishbowl, okay?"

"Yeah. Except nobody really watches a fishbowl. Nobody cares. Fish are boring."

"Christ."

"So is Delavane dealing drugs, or just stealing furniture?"

"I'm not talking about Ed Delavane."

"Or was it both? That would make sense. One-stop shopping."

"Maybe it's time to get a lawyer in here."

I sat forward. "Give me Delavane and you'll walk on this. I promise."

"But I won't be a cop anymore."

"Your dad's a plumber. Get your license and work with him."

Jesse smiled grimly. "No thanks."

"It doesn't matter. Do what you want. Finish college. Study Russian cultural history or marine biology. Put this behind you. Get away from Delavane and—"

"You don't just 'get away' from Ed Delavane."

"You do if he's in jail."

"He has friends. And there's such a thing as parole."

"Not for Murder One. Not in this state. Not for a three-time loser. Which he will be."

"Yeah? Well, people escape. I heard someone busted out of Norfolk a couple of years ago."

"They were caught in two days."

Jesse snorted. "Ed Delavane wouldn't need two days."

"Jesse, come on."

"I mean it. You don't know this guy."

"Okay, if he's that bad? All the more reason to put him away."

"You put him away, then. Just leave me out of it."

Jesse slouched down in his chair. I took a long breath and blew it out. "Here's what I'm getting from this conversation. You know Delavane. You worked with him. You sold drugs and ripped people off with him. You were pretty sure he was capable of murder, even before he killed Lomax. And now you're so scared of him you'd rather spend the rest of your life in jail than wind up on his hit list. But he isn't going to be hitting anyone when he's doing solitary in a maximum security cell. In fact if you don't help us arrest him, he may come looking for you to shut you up in advance. People like that don't like loose ends. Or witnesses."

"Sounds good. You're very persuasive, Chief. Can I see a lawyer now?"

I sat forward. "Give me something, Jesse. Before the DNA report comes in. Give me a chance to help you. Show me you're on my side."

Jesse looked down, away from my stare. He was studying the edge of the desk. "You want something? Talk to Rick Folger. He gave us the keys."

I found Folger in the basement apartment he'd been renting since he left home. It had started raining, and most of the snow was gone, except for a few dirty piles in the back yard. But the wind was wet and stinging. I hunched into the collar of my coat, walked down a short flight of cement stairs and knocked on the door. Folger answered it with a book in his hand. He blinked at me, adjusting his eyes to the sharp glare of daylight.

"Chief? Am I in trouble?"

"I don't know. Can I come in?"

"Do you have a warrant?"

"Do I need one? I don't want to search your house. I just want to talk to you. I could stay outside, but it's cold. The wind is really picking up out here."

Folger shrugged. "Sorry. Come on in."

I took one more step down into the gloom of the little apartment. The small living room held a corduroy couch and a yard sale armchair with a reading lamp in the angle between them. There was an expensive-looking sound system, but no television. I looked twice as my eyes adjusted. There was a cable wire poking out of the chipped baseboard; Folger chose to ignore it. I liked him for that.

The little room opened onto the kitchen. To the left, an open door led into the bedroom.

"You keep the place neat," I said.

"It's like living on a boat," Folger answered from the kitchen. "You want some coffee? I just made it."

"Thanks."

"Cream? Sugar?"

"Just milk."

There was some noise from the little galley and then Folger emerged with two steaming white mugs. He handed me mine by the rim and we took a sip.

"Starbuck's," Folger said. "I hate to admit it, but they make excellent coffee."

"You hate to admit it?"

"You know—corporate giant, taking over the world, forcing little guys out of business. All that. I was raised to believe a company like that had to suck. Now I don't know what to think."

We drank some more coffee. Music filtered down from upstairs, a Bach piano variation. It wasn't a recording.

"Who's playing?"

"Old Mrs. Tolliver. My landlady. She's actually pretty good."

We listened for a few moments. The music resolved itself, stopped and then started again. I sat down and put my mug on the plank coffee table in front of the couch. Folger sat down on the chair.

"Listen, Rick. Let me tell you what I know and what I need from you. Okay? I know you used your father's keys for a string of break-ins going back at least two years. You and Jesse Coleman and Ed Delavane. There were a couple of high school kids involved. They sold drugs for you at NHS."

Folger started to speak, but I held up my hand. "I've been thinking about how you could have gotten involved with all this. You were younger. Delavane was cool. You were bragging about the keys at the Chicken Box. You wanted to impress him, but he called you on it. Suddenly you were involved. He scared you and you didn't see any way out."

"I got out, Chief. I told him it was over."

"But he still had the Lomax keys. And now you're an accessory to murder."

"I didn't kill anybody!"

Folger jumped up so fast he spilled his coffee and banged his shins into the edge of the table. "I didn't know he was going to do that! Lomax owed us a lot of money. I mean…a lot of money, man. You start smoking coke and it adds up fast. I thought they were just going to scare him—maybe steal some stuff, that's all. If I'd thought that—I mean, I knew he was crazy, but…if I'd known Ed was going to…Jesus, Chief. I'd have gone to the cops myself. I swear."

"But you didn't."

Sleet rattled against the window that looked out on the pavement. The temperature was dropping as the band of storm clouds moved across the island. It was still morning but it felt like late afternoon. Folger sat down heavily and picked up his coffee mug. He stared at it for a second and then put it down again.

"Oh, man, I am so fucked."

"Maybe not. I can get you immunity. All you have to do is testify against Delavane."

"What good would that do? He's got an alibi. He was in Boston, supposedly. No one else'll say shit. You think Jesse Coleman would testify against Ed Delavane? Guess again."

"I talked to Jesse already. But every little bit helps. This would show where you stand. You feel remorse. You want to make things right. You're young, you've got no record. Judges care about that. And you can place Delavane at three other crime scenes at least. That's a multiple felony indictment that adds years to his sentence. That's valuable, Rick. You can bargain with that."

"And I get what?"

"Five years probation. Maybe only three. If you don't screw up, you can start over. That sounds good to me."

He shrugged. He seemed to crumple into the chair. "Yeah, okay, whatever."

"I'm not sure what that means. Was that a positive statement? Will you do it?"

"Yeah, I'll do it. But I'm still fucked. I still have my dad to deal with. When this comes out, he's gonna kill me. I wish he would kill me and get it over with. That would be easier."

"You'll work it out with him."

"Yeah, right."

Before I could conjure some answer to the bitter despair in the boy's voice, my cell started ringing again. I winced an unspoken apology and unfolded my little Nokia. Lonnie Fraker was on the line.

"You're not gonna believe this, Kennis. And you know why? Because it's goddamn unbelievable, that's why. This one goes in *The Guinness Book of World Records*. I just don't know whether to submit it under suicidal or stupid. Maybe there's a joint listing, like for Kamikaze pilots who forgot to put gas in the tank."

"Slow down, Lonnie. What happened?"

"Okay. We get a call from Milo Torrance over at Sun Island. Some guy with a big storage locker over there was six months behind on his rent. So they snap the lock and get ready to empty the place out. That's the policy, right? But this shed is stuffed floor to ceiling with antiques. It looks like a dealer's warehouse, but this guy ain't no antiques dealer, at least not the legal kind. Milo knows him. It's Ed Delavane, Chief."

"Ed Delavane."

"Milo called it in and we came over to check it out."

"You're telling me Ed Delavane robs houses, keeps all the stolen property at Sun Island, and then *doesn't pay his rent?*"

"He's high most of the time. He didn't pay his phone bill either. I called out there. It was disconnected a month ago. But listen—this is the best part. The stuff he stole from Lomax is right in front, just sitting there. That big desk and some other pieces. I checked with the insurance photographs. Anyway, there's credit card bills and checkbooks in the drawers. Lomax all the way."

I fought to round up my thoughts. It was like getting a bunch of rowdy kids into a school bus. "This is nuts."

"Hey, you gotta get a break sometime."

"Yeah. But this fills our quota for the next ten years, Lonnie. Milo just called you and that was it."

"Like winning the lottery."

"But better. When people win the lottery the first thing they say is "I have this lousy job and I'm quitting." I hear this and I'm thinking to myself, this is the best job in the world and I'm doing it forever."

"Yeah. It's been a pretty good day. But it ain't over yet. I sent a cruiser out to his house. Nobody was home, but we had a warrant, so we searched the place. Guess what we found? Hiking boots with the exact vibram sole footprint we found at the crime scene. And Delavane is heavy enough to leave a deep track."

"Great work, Lonnie."

"Wait a second, it gets better. Krakauer talked to Jesse a few minutes ago, just after you left. Nice double-teaming, by the way. Were you the good cop or the bad cop?"

I smiled. "I'm always the good cop, Lonnie."

"Yeah, right. Anyway, Jesse gave us the word—Delavane's doing some kind of drug deal out on Hinsdale Lane, out by the airport. We're setting up a perimeter right now."

"I'll be there in five minutes. Keep everybody back. And no sirens."

I closed the phone.

"Did you catch the guy?" Folger asked.

"No. He caught himself. We just have to bring him in. Thanks for your help, Rick. I'll be in touch."

I reached down and shook his hand, then I was out the door and gone.

Chapter Twenty-nine

Ed Delavane Conducts Business

At that moment, Ed Delavane was demonstrating the new drug trade business model he had learned from the late Preston Lomax. With his usual talent for elegant phrase making, Ed referred to it as "not paying for stuff."

A drug connection might not like it, but what was he going to do? Call the cops? Delavane had cops on his payroll. A dealer could go back to his supplier, of course; that was why you had to make sure he was more afraid of you than he was of them. And Ed Delavane had a talent for making people afraid. He enjoyed it; torture had been his hobby since grade school. You could feel it the first moment you met him. It steamed off him like the pheromones that attracted women. Even Lomax had begged, and not at the end, either, when you were supposed to beg. No, with Ed Delavane you did it at the beginning, because you knew what the end was going to be. You could see it in his eyes.

This Joe Rafferty kid could see it there. He'd seen it before. Rafferty's nose had been broken a few times, and so had the jaw. With the scar tissue around his eyes and the burn slag on his neck, Rafferty looked pretty bad. Delavane grinned, the natural bare-fanged salutation of the happy predator. Rafferty was going to look a lot worse if he didn't go along with the program today.

They were standing in the raw squalor of the kid's apartment on Hinsdale Lane. It was all rusting metal cabinets and peeling veneer and missing baseboard; crooked shelves on metal racks screwed off-center into the cracked plaster. The place stank of ancient cigarettes. It was almost sweet. It was like breathing flypaper. The brown carpet was frayed at the edges; the speckled linoleum in the messy kitchen was buckled. It was the lair of the lifetime small-timer. This kid was going nowhere.

Delavane slipped the six plastic bags into his coat pockets and turned to go.

"Hold it, Cap." Rafferty grabbed his shoulder. "That's a grand you owe me."

"Not anymore. The new system is, you find the money somewhere else."

"What the fuck—"

Delavane turned in a feral blur, grabbed Rafferty's wrist and knocked his left leg out from under him with a single swift kick. Delavane punched him hard in the chest as he fell. The kid hit the floor on his back. It sounded like someone dropped a bag of cement. The breath blasted out of him. Before he could move, Delavane's muddy boot was pressed to his throat.

"Rob a bank. Jack a Range Rover. I don't care what you do. Just make it right with your supplier somehow, because this is how things are going to be. From now on."

"Fuck you—"

Delavane pressed down harder on Rafferty's throat to shut him up. But the kid managed to twist himself around and slam the side of Ed's knee with his elbow. The force of the blow rocked him. Ed staggered sideways into the kitchen counter as Rafferty scrambled to his feet. The Mister Coffee machine shattered. Ed grabbed the handle and swung the jagged glass carafe as the kid charged. Rafferty ducked and rammed into Ed with his head. It hurt. Dizzy with rage, Ed plunged both elbows down onto the kid's shoulders, once, twice; the third time, Rafferty stumbled back a step with his guard down. Ed launched himself off the counter and clocked him with a roundhouse right just above the ear. The blow had all his weight and momentum and the whiplash energy of his hips behind it. The kid spun around and dropped face-first onto the filthy rug. Ed could hear that nose breaking again. It gave him a snarling moment of animal satisfaction.

"Motherfucker," he croaked. "Try that again and I. Will. Kill. You. Set aside a weekend for me, shitbag. Because that's how long it's gonna take."

There was blood in Rafferty's mouth. But he still managed to choke out the words, "I want…my thousand bucks. You owe me—"

"Here's what I owe you."

Delavane kicked him hard in the ribs, then again. The second time he got the shriek of pain he was looking for.

He was aiming the next kick at Rafferty's head when he heard the pounding on the front door.

"Open up! Police!"

Chapter Thirty
Reasonable Doubt

Lonnie Fraker and I were on either side of the door, with Kyle Donnelly and another Statie named Huff behind us. The noise stopped from inside. Lonnie was about to knock again when the door ripped open. We had a split-second view of Rafferty on his knees in the living room, then Delavane was bounding into us like a pit bull into a crowd of taunting children. A lunging blow to the throat dropped Lonnie. I threw myself backward as Delavane jack-hammered Huff with a series of punches and threw him into Kyle Donnelly. The two cops went down in a thrashing tangle of arms and legs.

I got my balance, jumped the pile and took off after Delavane.

Behind us, Donnelly staggered to his feet just as Rafferty sprinted out of the apartment. The two collided and I heard them go down.

I burst out into the street, twenty feet behind Delavane, both of us running hard. Delavane tore across Arrowhead Drive and into the Toscana complex.

The big excavation firm had bought up all this land a few years ago. There had been a nursery here and some apartment buildings. They had bulldozed the greenhouse and gutted the buildings for storage space. It was a bleak industrial landscape now, with rows of big green trucks, stacks of concrete forms, piles of tires, hillocks of gravel and dirt. Delavane darted between two rows of pipes and vaulted a steel I-beam held off the ground by a block of wood at either end. I was right behind him. Various Toscana workers leapt out of our way.

I didn't shout out "Halt" or "Freeze" or even "You're under arrest." I knew that was pointless. I didn't un-holster my gun, much less shoot it as a movie hero might have. This was real life. There were innocent bystanders all around us and in any case, actually hitting what you aimed at with a handgun while running was physically impossible.

This was a footrace, plain and simple.

I had a few advantages. I was in the best shape of my life and I didn't smoke anymore—cigarettes, much less weed or crack. I knew Delavane did all three. I could hear the breath tearing in and out of the big man's lungs as I closed the distance between us. I also knew the territory, and it held some surprises for the uninitiated. Delavane was clambering over a hurricane fence. Just past it gaped a massive sandpit, a giant L-shaped crater, thirty feet deep and as big as couple of football fields, dotted with humps of dirt and excavating machinery, a grim and forbidding gash in the earth, the rim edged by the airport's chain-link fence at one end and a series of marine storage companies at the other, the white shrink-wrapped pleasure boats stacked ten high on metal racks.

This side of the pit was overgrown with brambles. They blocked the view and slowed you down. Before Delavane realized where he was, I had leapt onto a pile of lumber and hurled myself over the fence at the ex-Marine's back.

We hit the brambles together and rolled, spiked stems tearing at our ankles and wrists and faces. Then the bushes ended and we hurtled over the edge, rolling down the steep dirt slope. We couldn't get to our feet or even slow ourselves down. Sand abraded our faces though the sleet had packed it a little. After a bruising ride, I landed at the bottom flat on my back. Delavane could have taken me out if he had noticed, but he had already jumped up running.

I struggled to my feet and launched into pursuit again, skirting the big eight-foot cones of dirt that covered this section of the pit in even rows, right to the edge. The sand was soft and the footing was bad. We couldn't really run until we hit the packed flats, but once we did I started gaining.

Finally, I was close enough. I took a dive and connected with Delavane's knees. The big man pitched into the packed dirt with an explosive grunt. The freezing rain, which had let up briefly, started again now, pushed horizontal by the wind. We grappled briefly, then Delavane threw a punch at my jaw. I reared back and the massive fist just grazed me. Even so, pain detonated inside my head and I stood helpless for a second or two. Delavane jumped to his feet and pulled me toward him. My vision cleared and I saw the .38 Special stuck into the drug dealer's pants. Then an uppercut rammed into my stomach and I buckled to my knees.

I had a moment of clarity. I was alone in this stark manmade crater with a desperate criminal who outweighed me by thirty pounds of muscle. Delavane had been trained to kill. He was armed. He had nothing to lose. His two punches had made me stupid, turned my bones into concrete. My whole body was vibrating. It felt like that last punch had done some real damage. The pain and nausea came in waves with my pulse. The ground was tilting. I was in no condition to fend off the next blow, and when it landed I'd be helpless. After a couple more I'd be unconscious. But that wouldn't stop Delavane. I was going to die here. This sociopathic drug dealer was going to kill me.

Delavane turned away, digging into his waistband for the gun. Through the clanging tinnitus in my head I heard a shout and thought, "Lonnie, thank God." But it wasn't Lonnie.

It was Rafferty. He'd gotten loose and followed us. "You owe me a thousand dollars, you motherfucking piece of shit!"

That was his battle cry. He was a psychotic vision of torn clothes, wild hair, and dirt-caked blood, brandishing a kitchen knife over his head. Delavane worked the gun loose and started shooting. The first three shots missed, echoing off the sandpit walls. But the fourth shot took Rafferty in the shoulder and the fifth one shattered his knee. He fell and the knife went flying.

I had my own gun out now. I had stumbled to my feet behind Delavane, some dense speckled fog in front of my eyes. There were actually three of Delavane for a second, then two. I chose one and brought the butt of the big Glock nine-millimeter down on the back of his head. Delavane staggered forward but got his legs under him, turning, bellowing with rage. There were two shots left in his gun maybe more.

I hit him again, harder. I felt the blow from my wrist to my elbow and all the way up to my shoulder. This time Delavane went down.

I fell to my hands and knees beside him and vomited into the sand.

Things went hazy for a while. Lonnie called the ambulance, they cleared everyone out of the pit. Ed Delavane, dazed but otherwise unhurt, was taken directly to jail. Donnelly and Huff got patched up in the emergency room. Rafferty was waiting there for knee surgery.

I needed some surgery of my own, it turned out. Delevane's punch had ruptured a hernia in my stomach wall. It was an inherited condition, Tim Lepore assured me, and he was the only doctor on the island I trusted. I'd been born with it, just like my father. My son probably had one, too. Fixing it was a minor operation. I would have to stay overnight at the Cottage Hospital, but only because of the anesthetic. Lepore, a veteran of Vietnam MASH units and Boston inner-city emergency rooms, was dismissive about my worries, but his brusque bedside manner was oddly reassuring.

"You'll live, Chief," he said on his way out the door.

The arrest was on the Boston news, and Lonnie Fraker came in while I was watching it.

"It was touch and go for a while there," Lonnie was saying on the television, perched on the brink of the sandpit, a cute reporter's microphone in his face. "But the state police are trained for this kind of thing. And the local police were very helpful.

We appreciate their support…even if all it means sometimes is getting out of our way and letting us get the job done."

I turned off the TV with the remote. "You look good on TV, Lonnie."

"Listen, Chief—"

"Don't worry about it. We caught the guy. That's all that matters. Besides, you came up with the final lead."

"That Sun Island stuff got dumped in my lap. I happened to be there and I answered the phone. That's all I did and you know it."

"Lonnie—"

"I'm sorry, Chief. Things got out of hand with those TV people. They were interviewing me and they assumed that I was, you know—that I had—"

"Let it go, Lonnie. It's fine. We all have an interest in the state police looking good. And it's a nice boost for you. You deserve it. You worked your ass off on this case."

"But you—"

"I have a glass ceiling on this job. You know what I mean? I'm not going to get a promotion. I give out the promotions. And I have to tell you, the last thing I want is more TV coverage."

"Not everybody feels that way. Kyle Donnelly was saying this afternoon—"

"I'll talk to Donnelly. We have to close ranks right now."

Lonnie stepped up and shook my hand. "Thanks, Chief. You gonna be okay?"

"I'll be out of here in the morning. Hold the fort till then."

"No problem. See you tomorrow."

I had other visitors: Haden Krakauer and a couple of other cops who were concerned and awkward and brief. My ex-wife who managed to both make it into her story ("I was so worried, I cancelled my whole afternoon. This is such a mess. God, I hate hospitals. They make me feel sick, as if there was something *contagious* in that awful disinfectant they use.") and find the real estate angle ("The bright side is, with the drug dealers cleared out of there, the whole Hinsdale Lane area is going to get gentrified fast. It may be the new Naushop.")

My kids came, and their reactions were predictably diverse. Caroline wanted to know all the details of the operation—where they were going to cut and how long I'd be under and why I had to stay overnight. She was worried about everything from the cuts on my face to the hospital food and offered to bring me a bagel and coffee in the morning. Tim wanted to know about the arrest, the chase, the fight with Delavane. He was especially interested in the sand pit and I promised to take him out to the Toscana yards so he could see it for himself.

Fiona came in next, after an uncomfortable moment passing Miranda and the children in the corridor outside.

"So how do you like your quiet small town life now, Chief Kennis?"

"I've been thinking about that. It occurred to me the other day that this place has most of the disadvantages of a city, and none of the advantages. You've got crime, traffic jams, dirt, noise, construction going on next door, terrible parking."

She smiled. "But no traffic lights."

I winced. A rope of pain tightened around my stomach, squeezing my ribs together. Fiona reached down and stroked my cheek.

"Are you all right, Henry?"

I took her hand and kissed it. "I'm fine. Apparently I should have had this operation twenty years ago. Delavane did me a favor."

"What a horrible creature. Were you frightened?"

"Terrified."

"But it's over now."

"Except the adrenaline goes sour like old beer. Ever sniff a can of Bud Light that's been sitting out in the sun too long? It smells like skunk spray."

She stroked my hair. "Ahh, that mind of yours. Always working. Always looking for the right word. Even here."

"Especially here. There's nothing else to do but read old magazines and wait for nasal fatigue to set in." I waved a hand to include the whole room, which was already crowded with bouquets from concerned friends and citizens. "Whoever said 'stop and smell the roses' never spent much time in a hospital room."

"I should have told you I decided not to bring flowers, for that very reason."

"No, no. I like the fact that it never occurred to you."

"You're a strange one, Henry Kennis." She leaned down and kissed me. "Be strong. I'll see you in the morning."

Ken Carmichael, the prosecutor from the Mass D.A.'s office, was the last visitor and he only had a few minutes before they wheeled me into the operating room. He looked rumpled and exhausted, wearing the same brown suit he'd been wearing since he arrived on island. He needed a shave. But he was obviously in a good mood.

"Nice work, Chief," he said.

"Thanks."

"I guess your pal Mike Henderson is off the hook."

"Looks that way."

"Sounds like you got lucky in the sand pit. I have a little rule of thumb I'll pass on to you. Don't go one-on-one with an armed psychopath in some dirt trench in the middle of nowhere. Especially when your back-up is Lonnie Fraker."

I smiled. "I'm sure that comes in handy a lot."

"And people say I'm overly specific."

We were quiet for a moment or two. A gurney rolled by on the waxed linoleum outside the room. On a television next door, Dr. Phil was haranguing someone to lose weight. We listened and Carmichael shook his head. "That guy could skip a few meals himself, Chief."

"Yeah."

"So anyway...we're pretty much wrapped up on this one now. It's open and shut. I wish they were all this easy."

"Yeah."

Carmichael squinted at me. "What?"

"I don't know. I just got my head rattled and my teeth feel like they're off-kilter. Maybe my brains are scrambled, too."

"But?"

"There's still a piece missing, Ken."

"Tell me."

"It's Kathleen Lomax. I've been thinking about her. She told me she turned the alarm on when she left the house that night. But no alarm went off when Delavane and his crew broke in. That means either they had the alarm codes, and I want to know how they got them, since now we're figuring it wasn't from Mike Henderson. Or someone else turned the alarm off for them, and I want to know who. The Lomax house had just been hooked into the station. Most houses aren't and none of the other places these guys ripped off were. This alarm was going to bring the cops, bored cops with nothing else to do. Every cruiser on the island would have showed up in the first five minutes. You see what I'm saying? If the alarm was turned off, whoever did it had to know about the new set-up. That's a good place to start."

I struggled to sit up. Carmichael took a step back and raised his hands, palm out as if to stop me from leaping off the bed. "Down boy. We're ahead of you. I talked to Kathleen Lomax myself. Turns out she didn't reset the alarm. She and her dad had always disagreed about it. She thought it was crazy to treat a house on Nantucket like a fortress. But he insisted. Sometimes she turned it on and sometimes she didn't. This time she didn't. And she felt bad about it. She felt guilty. She virtually let those guys into her house. She might as well have given them the key. She was distraught. She didn't want to deal with it, much less admit anything to the cops. But I made her realize that coming clean now was the only way we could sew up the case against these fuckers. Okay, she did something bad. But lying about it would make it worse. Martha Stewart went to jail for perjury, not stock fraud."

"You told her that?"

"I thought she could relate. And I was right. She's on board now. She'll testify if she has to. So don't worry about it. Those boys are going away for a long time. You just get healthy and let us take it from here."

I eased myself back against his pillows. "Okay. Thanks Ken. Nice work, yourself."

Carmichael left and in the few minutes before the orderlies rolled me down the hall to the operating room, my mind kept coming back to the case. The puzzle was complete, for the second time in one day, for the fifth time in one week. Once again, the cops were happy. The State's attorney was happy. The victim's family was happy. There would be commendations and promotions, just as I had suggested to Lonnie Fraker. It looked like we had finally invented the light bulb that worked. This was clean efficient police work that made everybody look good. In a week they'd all forget the bungled arrest of Mike Henderson. We had the real bad guys now. Still, in two different interviews, Kathleen Lomax had said she reset the alarm system on the night of the murder. I had believed her both times.

And I still did.

Chapter Thirty-one
Discrepancies

I came out of the hospital to find that Christmas spirit had taken over the Nantucket Police Department.

There were wreaths on the doors and someone had put up and trimmed a Christmas tree. There were even presents piled under it. One of the dispatchers, Madeline Kelly, had brought her boombox and her collection of seasonal CDs to work. The selection of politically correct and culturally diverse carols (sung by Bing Crosby, Jorma Kaukonen, and Ladysmith Black Mambazo) combined with the smell of pine to create an air of festivity at the station. It felt like the last days of school before the winter vacation, with the midterms finished and the last papers turned in. My people had passed a tough test, and there was more than enough credit to go around. The state police and the local cops were hanging out together. Ken Carmichael took everyone out for dinner at Kitty Murtagh's, a private party that required the whole upstairs dining room as well the gloomy basement tables.

Over a slice of key lime pie, as the evening wound down, Ken boasted to me that the Lomax case was going to be a career-maker for him. I pointed out that there was only one slot above his at the D.A.'s office, which he'd get by attrition when Joe Tosco retired next year.

"No, Henry. I'm running for office. After these convictions I'll be a shoo-in as a law-and-order governor, and that's what the Republican Party needs right now. We have to clamp down. We're at war. People forget that sometimes."

All I could think was, what an awkward way to find out someone's a Republican. I was a Democrat who believed in fewer laws and more disorder. This complicated my life as a cop, but I liked it that way. Poets were the first ones to go when things got as orderly as Carmichael liked them.

The only small pothole in Ken's road was something Ed Delavane had said to him about a "big shot" who had supposedly hired him to kill Lomax. They had spoken on the phone, but they had never met face to face. Delavane had what he called proof of the man's involvement: twenty thousand dollars stuffed into a suitcase in his closet. This potential complication didn't bother Carmichael. A drug dealer trying to deflect blame with a sack of cash? It had become a joke around the station. Delavane was like a poacher defending himself with a bunch of deer carcasses.

The lie was pointless, anyway, since Delavane couldn't identify this mystery man, or turn him in. There was no bargain he could strike with the prosecutor's office. The information was too vague. It didn't even make him look good. The merciless and vengeful drug lord suddenly reduced to a small time killer working for chump change and taking the fall.

"He's desperate," Carmichael had shrugged. "He'll say anything. Hopefully the next thing he says will make some sense."

The Lomax murder trial was going to be held on Nantucket despite an attempt by Ed's lawyer to get a change of venue. That meant the media were going to be sticking around for a while, some of them at least—E! and Court TV and Fox News; stringers from the *Globe* and the *New York Times*. I had noticed that attitudes about the press were changing. When they had been outside the station clamoring to be told why "no progress was being made" and the killers were still "at large," calling Nantucket "a town under siege" ("Yeah," Haden Krakauer had pointed out, "by *them.*"), everyone complained bitterly. Now that the press was running stories about the "dogged small-town crime fighters" who broke the case, things were different. Cops were giving interviews and starring in TV "newsmagazine" features about the "dark side" of small town life and the "criminal underbelly" of their famously elite resort community. *People* magazine had even approached me, inviting me to appear in the next "Fifty Most Beautiful People" issue—"In the required 'nobodies' section," Miranda remarked when she heard about it.

My face had been on television, which made people assume an alarming intimacy with me. People I had never met stopped me on the street to discuss the murder. Tourists wanted to be photographed next to me. But at the same time, no one at the station was paying much attention as I poked and scratched at the edges of the case. I read through the case binder several times, printed out and pored over the photographs from the MS benefit party.

A couple of the people who knew about the alarm changeover had been there. One, the guy from Inter-city alarm, was in Fiona's group, posed by the clock; the other, an electrician, had apparently gotten into a drunken fight with someone about the proposed wind farm in Nantucket Sound, around eleven. Numerous people remembered it. He was in favor of the alternate energy technology and anyone who wasn't was an oil-squandering, Saudi-loving not-in-my backyard hypocrite terrorist by default. And a fag. Or something. The resulting fight ended with a fractured jaw, a sprained thumb, and two broken lamps.

The rest of the people privy to the alarm system, including Pat Folger, had unbreakable alibis elsewhere, with lots of witnesses and no real motive for the killing. I sorted through the pictures several times. But nothing jumped out at me.

Finally I gave up and took Kathleen Lomax out to lunch.

It was a breath-stoppingly cold day, with new ice glazing the Christmas trees on Main Street. Met on Main was hot and steamy and crowded. We took a table in the back. Kathleen had cut her hair severely. She wore a black turtleneck sweater under her pea coat. It matched the circles under her eyes. We ordered coffee.

"I like this place," she said, glancing around. "It's like a bar in SoHo. Hip and cool."

"And expensive."

"That, too."

The coffee arrived and we sipped it quietly, cocooned in the sociable noise of a busy restaurant.

"I know this is hard for you," I said.

"Not really. I'm in total denial. I say that and it feels like I'm kidding, like I'm even in denial about being in denial. Which I totally deny, by the way. I just deny everything. I'm like a politician. Hey, it works for them. Denial is way underrated. I'd recommend it to anyone."

"I know what you mean. I still refuse to admit that my grandmother died and that was five years ago. I keep meaning to call her, just like when she was alive. I'm not getting the twenty dollars at Christmas anymore, though. I can't really explain that one."

"Do all grandmothers give twenty dollars at Christmas?"

"I've heard the modern ones give fifty."

"You should tell that to my grandmother. Strictly twenties, since I was six years old."

We sat and listened to the Roches singing Handel's "Hallelujah Chorus" a capella on the sound system.

"Who is that? And how many are there?"

"The Roche sisters," I said. "And there's just three."

"King of Kings," the Roches sang. "Lord of Lords. And he shall reign forever and ever."

"Why haven't I heard of them?" Kathleen asked.

"I don't know. They haven't done much lately. But they were great, back in the day."

The waiter came back and we ordered cheeseburgers.

"I have to ask you about the alarm system again," I said.

"But that's all settled. I explained it. I told everyone already. I forgot to reset the alarm and the…the people got in, but if I testify and explain what happened they'll all go to jail and—and even though I was a part of it, I can still do something to make things right."

"Is that what Ken Carmichael told you?"

She nodded.

"Because it sounds almost exactly like what he told me."

"It's true."

"All of it?"

"He told me they were going to jail for life, Chief Kennis."

"Probably. But that's not what I meant."

"I don't understand."

"You told me you reset the alarm. You told me that twice."

"I was confused."

"Did Mr. Carmichael confuse you? An interrogation can be intimidating."

"No, no, he was very nice. I just—I couldn't be sure, when I thought back. And the way he described it, it made so much more sense if I had just forgotten. What happened was my cell went off just as I was leaving. Margie was calling me, about some—some stuff I was supposed to bring to this party."

I raised an eyebrow. "Stuff?"

"Yeah, just—it doesn't matter. I didn't have it anyway. In fact we had a fight about it. I wound up being late, and Margie's boyfriend—Dane Collier? Do you know him? He was totally losing it because—"

"Kathleen."

"—he had no idea that—what?"

"I need you to concentrate for a minute. How close to the keypad were you when the phone went off?"

"I was at the front door. So I was right next to it."

"And the phone was in your purse?"

"That's right."

"So you pulled it out with your right hand."

"I guess."

"That means your left hand was next to the key pad. Was your purse strap over your shoulder?"

"I don't know. I think so. Sure. Usually."

"So your left hand was free. Did you set the code while you were talking?"

"I—maybe. I don't know. I could have."

"How long did you talk before you left the house?"

"Not long. We were still, like, going at it in the car. I know you're not supposed to drive and talk on the cell phone."

"Especially at night. On icy roads."

She looked down. "Sorry."

Our food came and we ate quietly for a few minutes.

"You told me you fought with your dad about the alarm," I said.

"That's right."

"But you also said he'd won that war. You do it more or less automatically now."

"I guess…I don't know. If I reset it, why didn't it go off when those people broke in?"

I sighed. "I don't know, Kathleen. That's what I'm trying to figure out, myself."

We turned to other subjects. Kathleen was trying to write a eulogy for the memorial service. She was fighting with her mom and still reeling from some nightmare with her boyfriend she didn't want to discuss. She had broken up with him, but missed him and wanted to call him and hated herself for that. She was looking for PhD programs in Political Science and studying for the GRE. She had missed several days of work at the gallery she managed in Boston. I was able to help her there.

"Your father just died," I told her as I paid the check. "They'll cut you some slack. Which is just about the only upside to the whole thing. I mean it. I've been there. You can get away with pretty much whatever you want, those first few weeks. It's tough, though—you don't want to take advantage, and it's tempting sometimes."

She shook her head. "You don't talk like a cop, Chief Kennis."

"I'm just telling you the truth."

"That's what I mean."

"Cops tell the truth."

"But not the whole truth. And there's always an angle."

I shrugged. "Well, in my other job all I do is look for interesting ways to be as honest as I possibly can."

"Your other job?"

"I write poetry."

"That's a job?"

"Well, it doesn't pay much. And the benefits package is bad. No dental plan. I guess the idea is, artists are supposed to suffer."

She looked up at me. "Since we're telling the truth…my father really was a drug addict, wasn't he?"

"I'm afraid so."

"He was a bad person. A cheater and a liar and a thief."

"I don't know if—"

"I've read the articles. I saw the segment on CNN. I've heard people talking. It's true isn't it? He was a bad person."

I nodded. "Apparently. I'm sorry."

"And supposedly he bankrupted *The Nantucket Shoals?*—because he was angry about an article, which he said was a lie but…I guess it wasn't. When he choked that waiter at Topper's?"

"There were witnesses."

"So he got all his cronies to pull their ads, and now …"

"It's looks like we're going to be a one-newspaper town again."

"That's so unfair. It's so—just so mean."

"He lashed out. He was angry."

"I worked for the paper when I was in college. I was supposed to be an unpaid intern but David—David Trezize, the editor?—he paid me anyway. This was before I got my inheritance. I was totally broke all the time. David let me use his charge at Daily Breads. I practically lived on their pizza that summer. David's a good person and a good writer. He doesn't deserve this. He loved that paper."

"A lot of us did."

"I guess he made my dad angry. But I never saw that side of him. He never got angry at me. Ever. He read *The Catcher in the Rye* aloud to me when I was twelve years old. I was exactly Phoebe's age, she's Holden Caulfield's sister, that was why he wanted me to hear it then. He used to take me out of school for lunch at this little dim sum restaurant called HSF? On the Bowery, in Chinatown. Just him and me, just for fun. I guess I was his favorite. Parents aren't supposed to have favorites but I was always his little girl."

"I'm sorry, Kathleen."

"And now I find out he was this whole other person. Eric and Danny were right about him. All the things people are saying about him…I don't know what I'm supposed to do."

"There's nothing to do. Just…remember him the way he was to you. It sounds like you got the best of him. Keep that. Don't let anyone take it away—even Eric."

She nodded. "Thank you, Chief Kennis. I really…you've been very nice through all this. Not like some people. I appreciate it. I have a feeling policemen only hear about it when they do something wrong or someone complains. So anyway—thanks."

Outside on Main Street, we went our separate ways. I had an appointment the middle school in twenty minutes. I had volunteered to give a D.A.R.E. lecture to the seventh graders. My speech to the high school had been a great hit, supposedly. The Drug Abuse Resistance Education program struck me as a waste of time and money. But the Selectmen liked the program and it was good diplomacy to participate. We called it SCARE around the cop shop. The program wanted to terrify kids, but equating marijuana with crack seemed foolish to me. I saw D.A.R.E. T-shirts around the school, but only the hard-core drug-users wore them. The program amused them.

The slant-parking in the school's access lane was all taken. I parked my cruiser against the curb in the tow-away zone.

It struck me as I walked inside and out of the wind that Kathleen Lomax might enjoy my speech; it wasn't going to be the usual propaganda. For one thing, I didn't think Not Doing Drugs was a particularly positive or useful focus for a kid's life. Steely-eyed drug haters had at least one thing in common with the stoners they reviled: drugs were their number one priority. I thought drugs should be marginalized, treated as a peripheral annoyance. That's what I told the seventh graders. I told them that weed would make them forgetful and stupid. It would give them the munchies and make them gain weight. You see a fat, pimply kid who can't keep a train of thought going for more than two sentences? Probably a stoner. Yeah, he's cool—but only to other stoners. The problem is, they're also fascinated with wallpaper patterns and the endless lame solos on bootleg Grateful Dead concert albums.

I got a few laughs, told a few self-deprecating anecdotes—I had smoked enough weed in college to know it was a depressing waste of time—and got out. The teachers looked at me strangely but at least a few of the kids were receptive. The perils of addiction, lung cancer, and brain damage may have meant nothing to them. Pimples, they could understand.

I was walking to my car, buttoning up my coat against the cold, when Alana Trikilis skidded up to me on the icy sidewalk. She must have been waiting behind the front doors of the high school. She had run the twenty-yard distance, out of breath and carrying a flat, wrapped package in her hand.

"I want to give you this," she said. "It's a present, I made it myself, like we always do at Christmas. I mean, in my family. We never buy presents. We have to make them. It's kind of stupid, but I wanted you to have this. Unwrap it."

She handed me the package.

"This is very nice." I tore off the paper and saw it was a framed pencil sketch of me. I seemed very serious in the drawing, looking back over my shoulder at something I didn't like. The drawing was good, slashed out in a matter of seconds, with very few lines, like a Duchamp sketch I had seen at the Museum of Modern Art years before. Its casual vitality had impressed me far more than all the urinals, hat racks, and nudes descending staircases put together.

"It's just a thank you," Alana was saying. "For being so kind to Rick Folger. He's not a bad person. He's a good friend of Mason's—and mine…and—I don't want to see him just kind of sucked under by a bunch of creeps, you know?"

"You don't have to worry. Rick will be fine."

She smiled faintly. "I hope so."

I stared at the drawing. "This is extraordinary. You have to get out of here. I know that sounds bad. But you have to go someplace where people can appreciate this."

She looked away. "I'm working on it."

"Good."

She glanced around nervously. "I'm not really supposed to even be here today. I'm not allowed 'on school grounds.' I got suspended for doing a stupid drawing, but that's a long story and anyway…I just—I heard you were going to be here and I wanted to give you this."

"Could I ask you where you did it?"

"At the VFW Hall. At the auction. Osona's auction? Two weeks ago."

"Oh, right, of course."

"You were only there for a few minutes. You were really upset about something."

I hefted the picture gently. "I can tell."

"Well, anyway—thanks again. Bye."

She darted away, almost slipping as she turned, running lightly back toward Surfside Road, half skating over the patches of ice. She crossed the street and then I was alone at the edge of the big pavilion.

I looked at the drawing in my hands, thinking about the auction. I remembered being upset, but the face in the picture was angry and determined—a man with a mission. It didn't matter, though. It was over, we had resolved the problem, Fiona's explanation made sense. I had the pen she'd bought me that day in my pocket. I always carried it, though it was impractical for everyday use. I touched it now, through my coat.

After a while, I climbed into the car and put the picture on the passenger seat. I needed to get back to the station, but I found myself driving out to the ocean. I kept thinking about the auction and the glimpse it had given me of Fiona's hidden life. She and Parrish had been bidding on a Thomas Donovan porringer. That explained the bidding war. But they still lost out to Preston Lomax. You could never win, playing the I-get-what-I-want entitlement game with someone like that. He was too willful, too relentless and too rich.

The thought struck me—I felt it in my chest, as if I'd run over a rabbit in the road. I pulled over onto the dead grass between the bike path and the street.

Where was the porringer? Where was it?

It hadn't been listed in the insurance inventory, but that made sense. That list had to have been compiled before the auction. But I didn't recall it on the stolen property sheet for the robbery, either. Nothing had been reported stolen but some big pieces of furniture. I'd double check it but I was pretty sure. Was the porringer in the Sun Island locker? I hadn't seen it, but I hadn't been looking for it, either.

I did a U-turn and headed out to the storage facility.

A sparse, icy snow had started falling. I put on the windshield wipers. I took a quick right onto the boulevard and drove the back roads through the sprawling tree-screened subdivisions west of the airport. There was never much traffic on Lover's Lane or Skyline Drive and for some reason I wanted to be seen by as few people as possible.

Sun Island Storage was off Nobadeer Farm Road, a bleak airport tributary far from Nobadeer beach, with no farm in sight anywhere. Instead there was a scattering of commerce: an automobile repair shop, a car parts store, retail warehouses, and contractor's offices, a lot of new construction and raw shingles. Sun Island itself was a big building with loading bays and offices, standing above a fenced plot of the prefab storage spaces. I found the alley between rows three and four, parked and got out.

It was colder here and the lines of corrugated steel bunkers channeled the wind. Ed Delavane's space was open, sealed with a strip of yellow police tape. I ducked under it into the musty jumble of old furniture. I found the light switch and fluorescents cut the gloom. The piles of antiques were daunting, like the improvised barricades that blocked the streets of Paris during the French Revolution. I spent two hours sorting through the chairs and desks and highboys and end tables, the chests of drawers and footstools and headboards. I found paintings and bookends and lightship baskets and sets of antique silver in brass-bound boxes. I found Tiffany lamps, ivory-topped canes, commemorative teacups, candlesticks, and wood-trimmed telescopes.

But no porringer.

I leaned against a dresser with a hinged mirror. It started to tip over. For a second I thought the whole teetering jagged mass was going to collapse in an avalanche of cherry wood and rusting casters. There were some ominous creaking noises, but after a few seconds it stabilized. The storage space smelled like old houses and the icy snow beyond the big bay door made it feel almost cozy. I stood quietly, thinking back, trying to remember if Lomax had actually bought the porringer. I had been angry that afternoon. The details of some stranger's bidding transaction wouldn't necessarily have registered on me. Someone else could have made the highest offer. That would be the simple answer, and simple answers were often the right ones. I needed to check Osona's records. I glanced at my watch. It was a little before two in the afternoon, and Osona's office was just down the street.

Five minutes later, I was upstairs in the auctioneer's office, going through the receipts. It didn't take long. I knew the date. And Osona remembered the sale; he rarely forgot one. A copy of the invoice was stapled to the sheet:

Item #224. *hammered silver porringer, circa 1840. Some tarnishing, small dent in the handle. Makers mark on bottom. Sold to Preston Lomax, 89 Eel Point Road. Final sale price, $5,000, plus twenty percent tax, total of $6,000.*

Osona was leaning over my shoulder. "Anything else I can do for you, Chief?"

I almost asked for a copy, but thought better of it. There would be time enough for that later, if it turned out to be necessary.

"No, I'm fine," I said. "Thanks."

"If you think of anything, just let me know. I'm always glad to help."

"I appreciate that."

We shook hands and I left. The office was overheated; it was good to get outside. I stood by my cruiser for a few seconds, feeling the icy speckle of snow on my face. I was thinking about the rearranged silver cupboard in the Lomax foyer. Someone with a good eye and a light touch had pulled off that piece of work. There was an obvious suspect. Fiona's crew had been cleaning the day before the party, I recalled from the depositions.

She was home when I got there.

"Is everything all right, Henry?" she said when she saw my face.

"I'm not sure," I said, walking past her. "Give me a second."

She was cooking something good; the house smelled of braised meat and red wine. The porringer was still on the living room end-table, though no one was using it for an ash tray this afternoon. The handle was dented, just as the bill of sale specified. Fiona came up behind me. I felt her hand moving up and down my back. She did it to relax me, but I needed to stay tense now. I pulled in a tight breath.

"What is it, Henry?"

"Tell me what happened. I need to know the truth."

"What happened?"

I turned. "Fiona. Don't do this. You stole the porringer from Lomax. I need you to tell me exactly how and when you did that."

"Are you going to arrest me?"

"No. I don't know. Probably not. It depends. First, tell me what happened. What did you do? And when did you do it?"

"Not why?"

"I know why." I picked up the porringer and turned it over. The tiny TD mark was sunk into the bottom of the bowl. I lifted it a little. "Thomas Donovan."

She smiled. "Himself."

"So?"

"So, I took it on the last day we were cleaning the house."

"You didn't think anyone would notice?"

"I was going to replace it with another one, nowhere nearly as valuable. And I didn't think anyone would see the difference, no."

"So why didn't you do it?"

"It was foolish. I was procrastinating. I couldn't decide which one to part with. I finally did decide, though. There was one Nathan Parrish gave me, a lathe-turned bowl from much later. I knew we were coming in on Monday to clean up after the weekend. And with everyone hung-over from the party, I assumed I was safe. I would have been, too. It was a quick switch and they're a great lot of ignorant swine."

I took a breath and set the porringer down on the table. "I'll tell you what," I said. "When are you supposed to be cleaning the Lomax house next?"

"Mrs. Lomax wants me in there before Christmas. I think they're putting the house up for sale and the real estate people want it looking perfect."

"All right. Put the porringer back when you're there, and we'll just forget about it."

"Does it matter which porringer?"

"Yes, it matters."

"And why would that be?"

"Because I'll be checking on it. And I know what to look for."

"You're a bastard, aren't you?"

"No, Fiona. I'm a cop."

"And cops are all the same."

"Only criminals think that."

"In Ireland everyone's a criminal then. Because everyone feels just the same way I do."

"Right. The Ireland card. Most people hate cops here, too. But there's nothing holy and virtuous about it. It's not a religious war. They're just cheaters and liars who don't like to get caught."

We stared at each other.

"Take care of this, Fiona. I have to go."

The snow had tapered to the occasional flake, spinning on the wind, as I walked to the car. Growing up in California I had always assumed that snow came in big blizzard slabs of

city-paralyzing white. Snow only made it into the *L.A. Times*
when buses were slewed across New York City streets and people
were using cross-country skis to get to work. This stuff annoyed
me. It was indecisive weather. I was feeling stymied and defeated.
A whiteout would give me an excuse to stay home.

Maybe it was time to admit I was on the wrong track. Viewed
from that angle, things were great. We had closed the case—Ed
Delavane was going back to jail. My girlfriend had sticky fingers,
but she seemed to have learned her lesson. Even Rick Folger was
on the right track, and with Jesse Coleman gone, any hint of
corruption in my cop shop was scrubbed clean.

I might as well face facts. This was a time to celebrate, not
brood.

But I couldn't help brooding. Miranda would say it was my
natural state. Her biggest complaint about me had always been
"You think too much." She might have been right, but the fact
remained—I was still missing something. It was right in front
of me, like the arrow shaped by the space between letters in the
FedEx logo.

I was just looking at it wrong. I decided to go home and
read through the crime binder one more time, from page one.
The kids were with their mother tonight, they were leaving for
Tortola tomorrow morning early. I didn't expect to hear from
Fiona and all my really good friends lived three thousand miles
away, so barring some police emergency, I could pretty much
count on having a night to myself.

I finished out the day, picked up some drunken noodles with
shrimp from Thai House, settled in at home with the food and
a beer, watched the news on TV. I even found myself looking
at a few minutes of insipid celebrity gossip in the purgatorial
half-hour before primetime began. I hadn't watched any of those
programs since my divorce. Miranda had always loved them,
though she called them her 'dumb shows.' I was startled to realize
that I had absolutely no interest in the famous people on screen.
Someone was pregnant, someone was in rehab, someone had
gotten into a fight. It might as well have been the court report

section of some Midwestern newspaper. I turned off the TV and silence settled on the house. The snow was coming down heavily outside, and it seemed to make things quieter. I brewed a pot of coffee, cleared the dining room table, set out the crime binder and all the photographs from Helen Sandler's benefit party.

I had just started going through the reports on the crime scene and the interviews with neighbors when my landline phone rang. I let the machine pick it up. After the familiar sound of my own voice saying, "This is Henry. If I'm home, I'll pick up. If I'm out, I'll be back. If I'm late, I'm on my way. Leave me a message," I heard a voice say:

"I know what you're doing. Drop it, if you want your family to stay healthy."

I pushed my chair back and leapt across the room, grabbed the receiver. There was nothing to hear but a dial tone.

Chapter Thirty-two
The Missing Piece

I was sitting in the snow between Miranda's house and Polpis harbor, on a waterproof sheet with my back to a pine tree. The wind blew steady off the water. After countless Nantucket winters, the spindly trees in this little forest had permanently bent to the south. Clumsily through my heavy gloves, I pushed back the sleeve of my parka and pressed the button on my watch. The face glowed blue: twenty to four.

I exhaled and watched the breath steam away from my face in the moonlight. The coffee in my thermos had run out two hours ago. Miranda's lights were out and nothing moved in the woods. They were catching an early flight to Boston. They'd be gone for the whole Christmas vacation which meant spending the holiday alone. We'd have another celebration when they got back. I'd gotten Billy Delevane to build Caroline a gorgeous dollhouse, complete with dormer window and strip oak floors. This might be the last Christmas when there was any chance of her still believing in Santa Claus and I wanted to keep the myth alive for as long as I could. The gorgeous inexplicable dollhouse would help. For Tim I had bought a new iPod, loaded with all the music my father had loved and passed on to me: The Beatles, early Dylan, Led Zeppelin, Pink Floyd, Jackson Browne. Neil Young, Joni Mitchell, and, Paul Simon. Laurie Anderson, Talking Heads and The Mountain Goats could wait for another season. I knew he'd have no problem believing the music came from the North Pole. Elves didn't make electronic equipment, but everyone else outsourced their manufacturing jobs—why not Santa?

I checked my watch again. Another two or three hours and it would be over. I could make it. I was dressed warmly and it wouldn't even be that cold if the wind let up. I felt the comforting weight of the Glock nine-millimeter in my coat pocket. There was something absurd about packing heat in this Christmas card town. But someone had conspired to commit murder here, and whoever it was had just threatened my family.

Lots of bad things had happened to me in Los Angeles: I'd been punched and sideswiped and shot at. But never anything like this. Big city cops were anonymous. I'd felt like a faceless cipher so often back then, just a threat behind a badge. I'd hated that, but it was starting to look pretty good around about now. You might take your work home with you sometimes; but it didn't show up at the door uninvited. It didn't stalk you.

I shrugged. Nostalgia was funny. I even missed my wife sometimes. I had thought about calling Miranda and warning her, but decided against it. She would have laughed it off and dismissed me, either as paranoid, "We're not in L.A. anymore, Henry," or as manipulative, an excuse to sneak back into her life.

The wind picked up, sending a whirling cloud of snow against my face. I tucked my head into the hood of my parka. I might have actually succeeded in scaring Miranda, but that would have been even worse. Caroline seemed to absorb through the pores of her skin any emotion her mother felt. The fumes of ordinary bitterness and anger were bad enough. I didn't want a smog-alert of gratuitous panic to wreck their vacation. No, this was better: a quiet vigil that affected no one but me. I had left the crime binder open on my dining room table and I was longing to get back to it. But that was all right. A little extra distance might help me focus.

I glanced at the house again and turned away from the wind. There was no change. I could imagine them all: Miranda, lying at the very edge of the bed on her right side, with her neck-support pillow and the Lanz flannel nightgown she'd been wearing since high school. Tim would be thrashing and snoring and talking in his sleep ("Americanos!" he had said in a weird Mexican accent one night recently. "Always bring gifts! Shirts.") Caroline would be surrounded by her stuffed animals, the Gund monkey and the Steiff lion were her long-standing favorites, probably wearing the Coldplay t-shirt I had paid thirty dollars for at the Fleet Center at Thanksgiving. And heavy wool socks. Her feet froze no matter how many quilts and comforters she had on the bed. Miranda kept the heat low. She said it was for political reasons, but I knew she was just cheap.

My mind wandered. It occurred to me suddenly, as if for the first time, that my father was dead. Despite my own best efforts at Kathleen Lomax's denial technique, the treacherous thought kept slipping up behind me. It was always a chilly surprise. It gave me the same queasy sense of imbalance each time: one of the great cables attaching me to the Earth had been cut and I was swaying dangerously in the wind, like these trees.

I had no unresolved issues to torment me, I just missed my dad. One of his friends had said to me at the memorial service, "No one's going to call me 'dear boy' anymore." I could only nod. David Kennis had been a Hollywood screenwriter of the Old School, but he never took it very seriously and was delighted with his son's choice of career. "Well, what do you know? Someone in this family is finally going to have a real job," he had remarked on the day when I graduated from the academy.

Details of police procedure had intrigued him and he had enjoyed knowing the inside scoop on various high profile crimes. He had edited the crime novel that got me fired, trimming it into a lean if somewhat generic action piece. "You're writing a thriller," he had explained breezily when he handed back the much-thinner manuscript. "I took out everything that wasn't thrilling. But don't feel bad. I could cut a minute-thirty out of the Book of Genesis if I really had to."

Dad had always wanted to go on a stakeout. I could never convince him of how boring they were. LAPD policy forbade ride-alongs in any case. But I set the policy at the Nantucket PD and it would have been good having Dad here with me tonight. The cold would have gotten to the old man, but his ghost didn't care.

So I sat with that spirit and the spirits of all the Indians who had hunted here and all the other lives I could have chosen and didn't, and I was just starting to doze off when I heard a sound from the bushes on the other side of the house.

I sat up, fully awake, listening.

I heard it again: a rustle of low branches. Whoever it was must have parked near Wauwinet Road and cut through people's back yards, skirting the harbor, using the woods as cover.

I struggled to my feet, stiff and cramped. My heart was pounding, fear and anger and outrage clenching in my chest. They were really doing it. Some hired thugs from Boston or Fall River were closing in on my family, deciding whether to go in through a window or a door, maybe checking their picking tools. That would really mark them as off-islanders. Miranda had never locked her house and didn't even own a key. One turn of the knob and these goons could be inside, cocking their weapons, choosing who to take out first.

I crouched low and sprinted through the trees. I couldn't stuff my bulky gloves into my coat pocket. I pulled them off as I ran, my feet thudding softly in the untouched snow. I had the Glock in my hand when I reached the side of the house. I stood with my back to the shingles, my mouth held open, breathing quietly, giving the air the widest channel I could.

I listened, my whole body flexed in the effort. I heard the wind rasping against the snow, nudging the high branches. A solitary car passed on Polpis Road. But there was nothing from the other side of the house. I edged my way toward the corner, straining for a single unnatural sound.

Nothing.

They must have heard me. That meant they were waiting, too, guns out, leveled at the spot where they expected me to appear. I checked the safety on the Glock and brought it up to my chest, clutched in both hands. I was outnumbered. One or two of them were probably moving around the house right now, to take me from behind in a flank attack. Whatever tiny advantage I had, I was about to lose it.

I had to move.

I took a breath and then swung around the corner of the house in a single step, crouched low, with the gun in front of me.

Standing ten feet away in a patch of rosa rugosa was a huge and stately white-tail buck, complete with nine point antlers. It looked like it weighed at least a hundred and fifty pounds. The deer was staring at me with feral indifference. I stood still, watching the big animal, feeling the adrenaline crash of relief and self disgust.

So this was the gang of hit men from the big city. The only big city creature in these woods was me, standing with slack-jawed urban awe in front of this beautiful animal, who had clearly sized me up perfectly. Despite the gun in my hand, I was no threat at all.

We stood ten feet apart, our breath condensing on the icy air. I slipped my gun back into my coat pocket. The deer cocked its head slightly at the movement. I took a step forward and the deer pawed the ground with his foot. It was like a dance. I had a piece of a Fast Forward oatmeal cookie wrapped in plastic next to my wallet, left over from a hasty lunch a few days before. I had been intending to feed it to the ducks at the Union Street pond. This was better.

I reached under my coat, took out the cookie and unwrapped it. My fingers were stiff and numb from the cold. The buck seemed content to watch me at first. But when I extended my hand, I broke the fragile intimacy between us. Maybe I moved too fast. The deer tossed his head once, as if he had caught more interesting scent, twisted sideways, launched himself off his hind legs and bounded away into the woods. There was a diminishing clatter of branches, and then silence.

I was alone. I leaned back against the side of the house, let the frigid air burn my lungs. I pushed my parka sleeve back easily, having dropped my gloves as I approached the house, and checked my watch again: 5:15. I jammed my hands into my coat pockets and looked around.

There were no footprints, no surveillance litter, no cigarette butts or take out coffee cups, no sign of human life at all. The woods breathed in the winter night as they had for ten thousand years. No one was here and no one was coming. All I had to show for my vigil was a near case of frostbite and a funny anecdote to tell at the cop shop. "How I almost shot a deer out of season."

It would be dawn in another hour. If I moved fast I could get home, have a hot shower, and see my family off at the airport.

I found one of my gloves, and gave up on the other one as I trudged back to the car, shivering and annoyed with myself. The cold had finally eaten through my clothes. The gun banging against my hip made me feel absurd. I half expected to get lost on the way back to my car. But I found it all right. The drive home was uneventful, the shower was hot and long, the farewell predictable: Tim begged me to come with them, Caroline told me she was proud of me for working so hard. Miranda looked at my still-wet hair, red nose, and bloodshot eyes, shaking her head with weary fatalistic contempt.

"Where have you been all night?" she whispered to me as the bags were being weighed and tagged at the Cape Air counter. She held up a hand as I started to speak. "Please. Don't tell me. I don't want to know."

I hugged the kids and watched the plane take off, feeling bereft and relieved at the same time. There was more air on the island with Miranda gone; but watching my children sealed into a metal tube and vanishing into the cloud-wracked December sky weighed me down.

I turned away from the window. Everything evened out.

I had breakfast at Crosswinds, chatted with my Bulgarian waitress and took a second cup of coffee to go. Fifteen minutes later I was sitting at my dining room table, with the Lomax case binder open in front of me.

I pulled the rings apart, took out the interview transcripts and stacked them on the table. The problem was here, in the things people said, the way they described what had happened on the night of the murder. Someone was lying. There was a contradiction and I was going to find it. I had all day.

You searched differently when you knew the thing you were looking for had to be there. A missing wallet, car keys, an incriminating statement, it didn't matter. Questions made you falter. When you were sure, you didn't give up. And I was sure. That was the one unintended benefit of last night's wild goose chase. Someone thought I was close enough to try and scare me off. That was a fatal miscalculation. I might have actually walked away from the case if I had never gotten that phone call.

I took the first page and started reading.

It took me three hours to find the answer. I had shuffled the pages, hoping that reading them in random order might trick me into seeing something fresh. If Bob Haffner's deposition had come up on top of the pile, I would have been done in the first five minutes.

It was so obvious. When I finally saw it, I felt like a fool. I had highlighted the passage with a yellow marker and still missed it. I arranged the rest of the pages in their proper sequence and slipped them back into the binder.

Then I read Haffner's statement again:

Hey I was totally out of it that night. I went to the benefit but I had dinner at the strip first and I was sick as a dog. That's all I was thinking about, okay? Bad clams. I actually got to the benefit, though. They gave me something to make me puke at the emergency room and everything was cool. I'm like a dog, man. I barf and I'm fine. Hey, at least I don't try to eat it like my dog does. I got to the party late, someone was watching Leno's monologue in the back room. But the place was still jumping, so that was cool. You should check out the guest list, man. Everybody was there.

I rummaged through the photographs, found the one I wanted and set it next to the sheet of paper with Haffner's statement.

I had felt this before, when cases came together and everything was suddenly clear. It was a triumph and a letdown at the same time. Mysteries seemed so obvious and banal once they were solved. And at the same time, you knew your leaps of perception were partly luck; and you had to wonder if you'd ever get lucky again.

But there was something else, this time. It was like watching the film of a shattered vase in reverse. I kept running the film forward and backward—the ball smashing the vase into a million pieces and then retreating, pulling the cloud of fragments in its wake, the shards sealing themselves together, creating the seamless reality of how things looked before. This is what happened. This is how it happened.

And this is who did it.

I knew everything now except the details. But there was no exhilaration, no thrill of victory—just the opposite. I felt trapped and defeated and sick, achy and nauseous as if I had actually caught pneumonia sitting in the snow all night. I was shivering. My hand was shaking. I lifted it off the table and watched it tremble. I was dizzy when I stood. I should call in sick, go to bed, sleep for the rest of the day. But I was perfectly healthy. And I had to finish this thing.

I pulled on my coat and left the house, slamming the door behind me.

Chapter Thirty-three
The Whole Truth

I drove to the hospital, to see the emergency room records for the night of the murder.

I had to do my job. I held onto that lifeline as I always had before. That was what kept me going. Miranda had never understood that—to her it was the job itself that poisoned my life. Maybe she had been right, after all. I spent every waking hour trying to find the truth and the truth was toxic. It was ugly. It ratified your suspicions and justified your fears. It made your most cynical moment look naive. People didn't hide the pretty parts of themselves.

"I prefer the surface of things," Miranda had told me once. But not me. No, I had to dig things up and turn them over and see what was squirming in the crumbling filth on the underside.

I didn't need a warrant at the hospital. They were glad to print out the material for me. In L.A. it would have taken an extra three hours, finding a judge and convincing him to issue a court order.

"Are you sure you don't want to see a doctor, Chief?" the duty nurse asked me.

"I'm fine. Thanks."

The records verified Haffner's story, but I had known they would.

I walked back out into the frigid late morning, climbed into my cruiser and set the papers on the seat beside me. I was reluctant to start the car. There was a finality about turning the ignition key. Once the engine was on, I was either driving or idling. I couldn't idle now and there was only one destination, once I started to drive.

When I got there, I parked in the dirt and walked around to the side door. Various pieces of snow-clad lawn furniture cluttered the deck, and a muddy track led to the sliding door. It opened into the big sunny kitchen. Fiona was at the table with her ledgers and her adding machine, writing up the month's invoices for the cleaning company. She was wearing blue jeans, heavy wool socks and a Rory Gallagher t-shirt ("The First Irish Rock Star"), which a friend of hers had designed when Gallagher died.

I watched her for a few seconds before she looked up. She smiled and pushed her chair back, stood and opened the door. I could feel the warmth of the house, the smell of recently toasted bread billowing out toward me invitingly. But I wanted to stay on the deck. I wanted to do this in the cold. It was childish. I dreaded going inside, like a kid in a Grimm's fairy tale. I jammed my eyes closed for a second. There was no gingerbread here, just shingles and peeling white paint. Fiona was no witch. There was nothing to be afraid of. But still I hesitated.

"Henry? Are you all right?"

That voice, that lovely accent, broke the stasis.

"I know what you did," I said. "And I know exactly how you did it. But I don't know why."

"Henry, what are you talking about, what are you trying to—"

"We can do this here or we can do it at the police station. It's up to you. But if we do it there, you won't be leaving for a long time. I won't be able to help you. If I even decide I want to. Once you're in custody it's out of my hands."

"I—"

"It's over, Fiona. Just tell me the truth."

She stepped back and I followed her into the house. She walked with her arms crossed in front of her chest, fingertips pressed to her elbows, binding herself together. We wound up in the living room. Neither of us sat down.

"I'll go first," I said. "So there won't be any misunderstanding. You disabled the alarms at the Lomax house on the night of the murder. It took longer than you thought because Kathleen came back from dinner and you had to wait for her to leave. When you got back to the benefit you set the grandfather clock to 10:55 and made sure you were photographed in front of it. That was a shrewd idea and it would have worked except that one of the people in the picture with you didn't get to the party until eleven thirty. I have the emergency room records to prove it. None of the other people in the picture had access to the alarm codes, and two of them got into a fight while you were gone. That's what I know. What I think is this. You were having an affair with Nathan Parrish. You lied about it and I believed you. He tried to scare me off the case last night, but it backfired. He wanted Lomax dead and he paid those punks to pull the trigger. He got you involved and now you're looking at an accessory charge in a first-degree murder indictment. How am I doing so far? Pretty close? Because we're talking twenty years to life if you're convicted. I'd love to hear you say I'm wrong, but we'd both know you were lying. And one more lie is all it would take to end this conversation and this conversation is all you have left."

I stared at her. She looked away. An ambulance passed on Bartlett Road, heading for the hospital. We listened to the diminishing two note wail. Someone was sick, someone was dying. And inside me, the final doubt fell, like the last frail tree in a fire-gutted forest, tipping soundlessly into the ash. Even hectoring her just now, I had half-expected a flash of that Irish temper, an angry rebuttal that would have set things right.

But her voice was quiet when she spoke. "I don't know where to begin."

"Start with Parrish and Lomax. They were in business together. What was the problem?"

She looked up at me at last. I could see she was going to talk now. I had seen the look before. I had no tape recorder. I hadn't Mirandized her. She hadn't availed herself of an attorney and no attorney had been appointed for her. Nothing she said could be used against her in a court of law.

That was all right, though. I just wanted to hear it.

"Nathan knew Lomax was in trouble," Fiona began. "He had to do something about it. Ten years ago, Nathan was about to close a major deal, a hotel chain that was supposed to be fronted by a famous quarterback. The deal hinged on this athlete, but he died in a plane crash and the deal went down with him. Nathan lost millions. Or so he says. Anyway, he was determined not to repeat that catastrophe. "Only new mistakes," that's one of his favorite expressions. Once I told him, "There are so many mistakes, you could make a dozen a day and never repeat yourself. I was right about that."

She shrugged. "This conversation proves it."

"Go on."

"The deal he wrote insured that if Lomax was dead or incapacitated, the Moorlands Mall project would revert to LoGran's corporate control. If Lomax was arrested, if he was a fugitive, the deal would have collapsed in the blink of an eye. LoGran has stockholders to answer to. Well, something Lomax said at the party set Nathan off. I don't know what it was. You'll have to ask him. He slipped upstairs "for a little recon," that's how he put it, and indeed all the bags were packed. The mortgage button that Lomax was so proud of, the one that was supposedly being inscribed with the family crest? It was in one of the suitcases, in a jewelry box. That tore it. Lomax was about to bolt. And if he escaped we were finished."

"We?"

"Henry, please. Do we have to—"

"Just tell me, Fiona. No, no, forget it. I'll tell you. Parrish was your ticket out. He was going to save you and your whole crazy family. But he needed the Moorlands Mall money to do it. Then I came along and that was inconvenient. Whatever you felt for me, you knew I couldn't pay off the debts and pony up the legal fees. I wasn't going back to Ireland. I had my own family to take care of. I was the wrong guy. Maybe you loved me, but it didn't matter. You had one shot to get what you wanted, and that shot was Parrish. You were in too deep to say no. He needed some muscle and one of your girls was dating a crooked cop. Jesse was part of Delavane's gang and you'd overheard enough in the last few weeks to know that Lomax owed Delavane some serious drug money. Everyone who knew Delavane knew he was capable of murder. It was a perfect match. You hooked him up with Parrish. Let me guess. Lomax owed Delavane twenty thousand dollars."

Fiona sat down at the edge of the couch. He voice was so quiet I could hardly hear her. "No. It was ten. Nathan paid him double."

"Lomax must have told Parrish about hooking the alarm into the police station. It's rich guy chitchat. My alarm is bigger than your alarm. So he knew it had to be turned off. And you had the codes. You took the porringer that night, but that didn't screw things up. You knew the only person who cared about it would be dead by the next morning. And if anyone noticed it was gone, you had your cover story all worked out. It was a neat little story. I believed it."

"Because you wanted to. That's the clever liar's trick, don't you know? Be sure to tell people something they want to hear."

I pushed on. "So, you and Parrish worked out the plan on the fly, but it was pretty good. If Jesse had quit smoking like he kept swearing he was going to, and Bob Haffner had ordered a burger instead of clams that night, you'd have gotten away with it. Then when the Moorlands Mall deal closed, it would have been off to Ireland as Mr. and Mrs. Parrish. That would have been quite a homecoming. The Prodigal Daughter returns, with the rich white knight in tow. They say money doesn't solve problems, but you know better, don't you?"

"I—"

"When you disabled the alarm that night, you knew you were helping to kill a man. How could you do that? What goes through your mind? I don't get it."

Fiona looked up. "People die every day, Henry. And this one won't be missed."

The urge to slap her pulsed through me like a wave, rising and subsiding. I stood very still. "Yes he will. He will be missed. His daughter misses him. You're a daughter. How tough is that one to figure out?"

"He hurt her, he would have hurt her again. Lomax wasn't ashamed. He bragged about it. He was a bad man, Henry. The world is better off without him."

"Really? Well, that's exactly the logic Lomax would have used. That's the way his mind worked. Welcome to the club, Fiona. Your fellow members have been turning this world to shit since the first Neanderthal killed the last Cro-Magnon, just because he could."

Fiona pushed at the tops of her thighs, squeezing the knees of her jeans. She seemed to be trying out answers and discarding them. Twice, three times, she looked like she was about to speak, but she said nothing. I felt the walls closing in on me, the mustard yellow paint starting to flake around the windows, the white shades closed against the winter sunlight and the constant buzz of traffic from Bartlett Road, the shelves of shabby romance paperbacks with their lurid artwork, their simplicities and shameless, pandering happy endings, the air of tired melodrama and contrivance they exuded along with the smell of old glue and yellowing paper; the bad paintings of whaling ships and seascapes hanging slightly crooked, always. It was suffocating. It was giving me asthma. Maybe there were mold spores under the rug. The place was old. You could keep it neat but you could never get it clean. The dirt was ingrained. The silence was impacted.

I had nothing more to say. I turned to leave.

"What are you going to do?" she asked me.

I paused at the door." I don't know."

And then I walked out.

Chapter Thirty-four
The Verdict

I drove through the drab mid-island clutter, past the gas stations and the Stop & Shop, around the rotary and out the Milestone Road, my cruiser aimed at the east end of the island. People slowed when I came up behind them. No one could drive properly with a police car in their rearview mirror. No one wanted to be pulled over. Everyone was guilty about something. They weren't inspected or they weren't registered or they weren't insured. They all had unpaid traffic tickets and parking tickets jammed into their glove compartments.

A Range Rover Discovery was right in front of me now, with sand in its tire-treads and no beach permit sticker. Probably no rope or boards in the back, either. I wanted to arrest them all, revoke their licenses, impound their cars, and lock them up.

I finally put my flashers on, stamped on the gas, and snarled past a long line of SUVs crawling behind a front-end loader. It was heading for a job site, probably one of the new lots out on Rugged Road. More forest leveled, more suburban sprawl, more properties for real estate brokers to sell each other. I kept the flashers on and drove fast until the procession was no longer visible behind me. Several people pulled over, adrenaline spiking sourly no doubt, hoping to be let off with a warning for whatever it was they knew they shouldn't have been doing. Good.

Let them sweat. Let them fear the law for a few seconds. They might learn something from it.

I turned on to New South Road. It only stretched for a couple of hundred yards, and high school kids routinely used it as a drag strip, pushing the speedometer needle as far as they could before Milestone Road at one end or the chain link airport gate at the other forced them to slow down. It was a tempting stretch of dead-end asphalt, and I gave in to it now, hitting eighty before I had to touch the brakes, just another scofflaw. Part of me wanted to keep the gas pedal pressed to the floor, drive through the fence and keep on driving, until I buried the big cop car in the sea.

Instead I took a left onto the rutted dirt road that led into the Madequecham Valley. It was almost impassable at this time of year; they wouldn't bother to grade it again until the wealthy homeowners showed up in the spring. The Crown Victoria bucked and undulated over the gullies and craters. It took me almost twenty minutes to reach the turn-off that led to the beach.

I thought of Fiona on the Squam Road, the night Lomax was killed. This kind of driving took patience. She had probably rushed, leaving the party, racking the suspension on some of the deeper furrows of frozen mud. She would have taken her time on the way back, though, her mission accomplished and her plan all figured out, with the porringer, her little trophy, on the seat beside her. All she was going to need was a few seconds unobserved to reset the clock. Everyone was drunk by then. It would be easy. And it had been. Everything had gone perfectly. The fall guys had taken the fall. The trial was set to begin just after the New Year.

This line of thinking wasn't getting me anywhere. What was done was done. The mistakes were permanent. The consequences were non-negotiable. Rehashing it all could only distract me and I had to think clearly now.

I parked in the dirt lot and walked the narrow beaten path through the brambles and bayberry to the edge of the cliff. I loved this view. The bluff was only twenty feet above the sand but it seemed higher. You could see the broad beach in both directions and the wind-scoured ocean stretching away to Portugal. The waves were big today and the water was an unwelcoming gray under the milling sky. There were no picnickers, no surfers, no one clamming or fishing. The few houses I could see were closed for the season, boarded up against the northeast wind. It was a harsh place this time of year, solitary and abandoned. I was the only living presence, the single ember of human consciousness at the edge of the world.

I thought about Parrish and Fiona. I could turn them both in, give the new evidence to Ken Carmichael, send them to jail and disgrace them. They certainly deserved it. I could let Carmichael and the Lonnie Fraker take the credit. They'd owe me big-time then, and if Ken Carmichael rode this case into the governor's office the value of that debt would be multiplied a hundredfold, for me and for Nantucket. We'd have a little savings account of goodwill in the State House for as long as Carmichael held office.

It was one of those rare moments when duty and self-interest coincided, and you could actually be rewarded for doing the right thing.

But arresting Parrish and Fiona wouldn't help the people Lomax cheated, or protect the island from the Moorlands Mall. I was in a unique position at this moment. I could do much more than attend to the formalities and complete the paperwork of punishment in triplicate.

I could dispense justice.

I had earned the right by working the case harder than anyone else. They had settled for the easy answers, I hadn't. Closing was all they cared about, getting the conviction, putting the notch in their belts, beefing up the solved-case statistics. One more in the plus column, as they inched closer to their end-of-the-year bonus. But it wasn't just that. The courts performed the simple tasks they were designed for—indict, convict, sentence…and eventually parole. It wasn't enough. The law was designed to punish perpetrators, that was the real problem. And it was useless now, because the perpetrators didn't matter anymore. This wasn't about them, it was about everybody else. It was about this town and the people who lived here. My job was to take care of them. And I was going to do it. That was all I cared about.

Everything else was covering your ass and smiling for the cameras, the easy way out and the route of least resistance.

I watched one more massive wave reach up until it was concave. The thick gray ledge thundered down and the white water churned toward the shore.

It was time to find Nathan Parrish.

It took me a while. Parrish was with a surveying team at the south east edge of his parcel in the Shawkemo Hills, deep in the Middle Moors just east of the Pout Ponds. These vast expanses of rolling heath made the claims that Nantucket had been overbuilt and developed to death seem absurd, ignorant, arrogant. This was truly wild land. Even the narrow dirt roads seemed always on the verge of being swallowed by the dense bushes that crowded them and scraped the sides of your car, if you tried to avoid potholes. I had the "Nantucket pinstripes" on my Jeep—now the moors were going to mark my police cruiser, also.

I was still driving too fast. One particularly deep gouge in the dirt slammed my head into the roof as the big car bottomed out. I slowed down, and skidded a little on a patch of ice.

Parrish was standing in a froth of bearberry and false heather in a cleared section of brush near the eastern tip of the smallest of the Ponds. Spray-paint marked this corner of the property; the surveyors had their tripods set up and were taking laser scan measurements. Cars were parked tilted sideways off the narrow road. I found a spot behind a new Jeep Grand Cherokee. Everyone looked busy and professional except Parrish, who was hovering behind the surveyors and probably just annoying everyone.

Parrish saw me and waved. I walked over.

"Chief Kennis," Parrish bellowed. "Good to see you. The stuff you're walking on is called poverty grass. Fitting name for it, don't you think? The first thing we're going to do is plow it all under. You see what I'm saying? It's a symbol, Chief. You know, the Indian lore says these ponds were made by some mystical giant. They're his footprints, filled with water, supposedly." He waved his arm to include a vast swath of land. "Well, this is my footprint. I'm the new giant. And I'll have a new legend. That's what progress means, my friend. My footprint is going to be filled with money."

I stared at him. "Like your friend's throat?"

"What?"

"That was your idea wasn't it? I don't give Delavane that much credit."

"I don't know what you're talking about."

"You'll have to do better than that, Parrish. The crime scene was described in the newspaper. Everyone on this island knows what I'm talking about."

"Yes, but you seem to be implying—"

"Wrong. I'm not implying anything. I'm stating the facts."

"Wait one moment. You can't just show up out of nowhere and start—"

"Of course I can. Let's take a walk. You're going to want the privacy."

I started back along the packed dirt, away from the parked cars. After a few seconds, Parrish followed me.

"Fiona told me everything," I said. "But I still have a few questions. Why did a mortgage button clinch it for you that Lomax was running?"

"You talked to Fiona?"

"Her alibi didn't hold up. Possibly for the first time ever, it was actually in her best interest to tell the truth. So she did. But there are still some gaps, some things she couldn't tell me. Why the mortgage button?"

"I don't have to talk to you."

"But you are. You're talking to me, Parrish. Because you think there's some way out. And maybe there is. But first I need some answers."

Parrish stopped walking. "You're wearing a wire."

I coughed out a contemptuous laugh. "Don't be paranoid. I'd need a court order to record this conversation. It would all be on the record and there'd be no point in having it. No, this is just between you and me. At least for now."

We started walking again, eyes on the rutted path in front of us, walled on either side by the dense, thorn-spiked bushes. You didn't see too many tourists out here. Once was usually enough for them. Well, that was going to change, if Parrish had his way: this whole area was set to be cleared and paved for the Moorlands Mall parking lot.

"Come on," I said finally. "The mortgage button. Explain it to me."

I wasn't watching the other man but I could feel him shrug. I knew this moment; it happened in every successful interrogation. The subjects gave up.

"That button meant a lot to him," Parrish said. "Maybe he had started to buy his own bullshit, lord of the manor, country squire with the account at The Pearl, and the Hummer in the driveway. Like he had arrived finally. It was a trick, a con game. I know that. He knew it, too. But the place had started getting to him. It gets to people, Chief. They come for a weekend and never leave. That button was who he wanted to be. Listen to this. A year ago, he paid some hotshot genealogist more than fifty thousand dollars to research his family tree. He didn't like the results so he fired the guy and stiffed him on the last payment. Sound familiar? He was a vengeful little prick and the biggest fucking snob I ever met. I knew he wouldn't leave here without that button. Maybe I was wrong. But he'd been giving me the runaround all night, and the way he lied about the scrimshaw and all that bothered me, too. It was so slick. He'd worked it all out. You see what I'm saying? Why bother? If it wasn't important. So I gave Fiona her marching orders, and you know the rest."

"How did you know I was still on the case?"

Parrish raised his eyebrows inquiringly, then nodded. "Oh, the phone call. I was talking to Rafael Osona…one of those 'it used to be nice on Nantucket' conversations. He used you as an example. He couldn't imagine the police going through his auction records in the old days. I knew what you had to be looking for. I saw you at the VFW Hall. When I found out Fi had taken that porringer, I lost it. All right? I screamed so hard I went hoarse. But she came right back at me and it was all just talk anyway because we couldn't put it back. But you were sniffing around. So I thought I'd throw a scare into you. Make you back off." He shrugged. "It was worth a try."

We walked in silence for a while. I watched a pair of ringtail hawks, circling above us.

"So what's the deal?" Parrish said at last.

I said nothing. I had been on some kind of high when I conceived this plan, but I was coming down hard.

"It's okay," Parrish said. "I have a pretty good idea. This is the end-game. There aren't too many options left, for any of us. So how about this—I pay off the people Lomax stiffed, and drop the Moorlands Mall and we all walk away happy."

I was startled into silence.

Parrish read my look perfectly." Come on, Chief. I'm not psychic. What else was it going to be? I'm a businessman. I know how to do business. So, anyway, as far as the case goes— it looks like a classic 'he-said-she-said' between me and Fiona, but I have a motive. I wrote it into contracts myself. I knew about the alarm changeover. And Delavane might recognize my voice. Not to mention your testimony. Even if I got a great lawyer and managed to walk, I'd still be ruined. I mean, let's face it, this is America, where you're guilty until you're proved innocent. And even after you're proved innocent. DeLorean was acquitted of those narcotics charges. But everyone remembers him as the creep who sold drugs to finance his car company. They'd know I did it, too—and they'd be right. If it comes to trial, I'm fucked either way. So how about it? We do this deal, nobody gets hurt. Fiona walks. All the little people get rescued. No Moorlands Mall. And you get the pleasure of seeing me in bankruptcy court. But I can start again, which might be tough from a prison cell. And don't believe what you hear about those 'country club' prisons, Chief. It's impossible to get a decent tee time and they're letting in just about anyone these days. Kind of like the Nantucket yacht club." He grinned at his little joke, and stuck out his hand. "Do we have a deal? Cause if we do, let's shake on it. I'm busy today and you've got me running behind."

We stood like that for perhaps twenty seconds, facing each other across the dirt path, the air between us dense and cold, grained by the thin snow. I saw myself in the mirror of the other man's smile. There was an assumed understanding there: we were both part of the same casual fraternity of corruption, above the law or just beyond it, writing our own rules.

This was business as usual for Parrish, but I knew then that I couldn't go through with it. These things didn't stop. They multiplied, they colonized you like a virus. For instance—I would have to destroy the incriminating photograph. I would have to get the negative and all the other copies from Helen Sandler. It would be easy to do under some official pretext. But lie would follow lie, a murderer would go free and when he murdered again, it would be partly my fault.

This was impossible. I wasn't above the law—just the opposite. I was below the law, toiling away like an ant at the base of a pillar. I was just a cop who performed his duties and filled out the forms in triplicate, exactly as I had thought so dismissively on the cliff an hour ago.

I was a humble minion of the law. And I was proud of that.

For one fevered moment, I had imagined that I could do anything I wanted. In fact I could do nothing. I couldn't prevent the murder, or stop Fiona's betrayal, or even make myself see her clearly. I couldn't fix anything, even my own judgment.

I was over-matched. I couldn't perform these labors and I wasn't supposed to. The law would do it for me. It was so obvious. The Moorlands Mall couldn't survive Parrish's indictment. The people Lomax had defrauded would get paid with no help from me. They all had liens on the house. The executors would have to sell it to settle the outstanding liabilities. The process would take time, but there was more than enough money to go around. As for Fiona, what had my plan been there? Was I going to save her, help her redeem herself, marry her, and live happily ever after?

It was laughable. I laughed at myself, a short bark of self contempt.

"Well, Chief? Yes or no?"

"What?"

"Do we understand each other?"

I shook my head. "I understand you. That's what matters."

I turned and started walking. Parrish trotted after me, grabbed my arm. "Hey! Stop! Where are you going? Chief! Hold on a second. What do you think you're doing?"

The answer was easy. "My job."

"Listen, Chief, we have to—"

I pulled his arm away. "Get a lawyer, Parrish. You're going to need one."

I met with Ken Carmichael the next morning, in the temporary cubicle he had set up on the second floor of the police station. Two folding screens gave the illusion of privacy. It was quiet: just the occasional ringing phone and the heat pipes grumbling. I laid out everything. It was more than enough to indict, and Carmichael was sure he could get a conviction. He'd strike a deal with Fiona. She'd get immunity from prosecution for her testimony but she'd be extradited back to Ireland. No more green card, no rich husband. She wouldn't be able to do anything for her family. She'd be returning in disgrace, probably facing at least five years' probation over there.

"Is that a problem for you?," Carmichael asked

I met his level stare. "Not at all."

"Okay then."

He took a sip of his takeout coffee and winced. It was cold. He set the cup down. "So why are you giving me all this?"

I shrugged. "It's Christmas, Ken."

"Seriously."

"I don't want it. And the town doesn't need it."

"But you figured this out on your own. Take some credit. You deserve it. We're not making quilts here."

I smiled. "First of all, I'm not sure any of that's true. And I certainly don't want people thinking about me that way. This job is a lot easier when people assume you're a little slow."

"Yeah, right. Good luck with that."

"Just remember Nantucket when you get to the State House."

"Hell—when I get to the White House I'll declare Nantucket a National Park and make you attorney general."

"I'll have retired by then."

Carmichael grinned. "Don't count on it."

I stood to go.

"Christmas plans, Chief?"

"Not this year. The kids are away. I didn't even get a tree. I think I'll just lay low. I may go to Hyannis on the 26th. Stay at Heritage House, see some movies, eat breakfast at Pain D'Avignon. Maybe pick up a book at Tim's."

"Sounds pretty good."

"Yeah."

"One more thing. The Donovan woman's going to be held at Barnstable Corrections until the trial. We're taking her over on the Island Airlines ten thirty flight tomorrow. We're keeping her isolated. Her lawyer doesn't want her talking to anyone until the immunity deal is finalized. But at the airport…you know, people run into each other. I just thought you should know. In case—"

"Thanks, Ken. I appreciate it."

I drove out to the airport the next day. It was a clear blue morning. The sun glittered on the dry crust of snow that lined the roads. All the X5s and Escalades and Navigators were wearing wreaths on their grills. The town was dressed for Christmas in garlands and lights that looked like strings of dime-store jewelry in the glare of the morning sun. Like many other commercial enterprises (prostitution and casino gambling came to mind), Christmas looked much more attractive at night.

Couples were everywhere in their bright coats and hats. It felt odd to be alone. I had declined a dinner invitation from Haden Krakauer the night before and stayed home with a turkey pot pie from Bartlett's and a couple of bottles of Sankaty Light. There had been a late showing of *Casablanca* on TCM.

My father had made me watch *Casablanca* for the first time when I was in high school. I had no interest in old movies then and hated anything shot in black and white. But Dad had intrigued me by saying, "This movie will teach you everything you need to know about being a man. Study Rick Blaine and you'll never go wrong." So I had watched the movie, mainly to see what my amusingly cryptic and evasive father actually thought about manhood and all its mysterious ramifications.

I had seen it many times since then, and it always helped. I had done the right thing today, acted as Rick would have acted, behaved the way a man should behave. No airport farewell was necessary. It would have been more *Maltese Falcon* than *Casablanca* anyway: "You're taking the fall," not "We'll always have Paris."

I had nothing with Fiona. Every moment between us was tainted now. But the fact remained—the problems of two little people didn't amount to a hill of beans in this crazy world. I was nowhere as good at being noble as Rick was, and nowhere near as modest. But at least I got the point.

Despite everything, I was still in love with Fiona. But that changed nothing. Love wasn't blind, as people liked to say; just stupid. And over-confident, like a drunk teenager racing his father's BMW, like the kid driving in front of me now on the airport road, passing on the left, barely avoiding a head-on collision, then running the stop sign on Lover's Lane.

I was reaching out to hit the flashers when I remembered I was in my jeep this morning, wearing street clothes on a private errand, just another citizen thinking *There's never a cop around when you need one.* I memorized the license number and noted the time. I'd take care of this later. A word to the kid's parents might be enough.

I got to the airport and parked at the curb across from the terminal. The security guy, Jerry, recognized me and waved. I lifted my arm in return. Jerry had a cup of takeout coffee in his hand and I realized I wanted one, too. I sat back and shut my eyes for a second. This wouldn't take long. I wasn't going inside, I didn't want to see Fiona. I just wanted to know she was gone. Watching the plane take off would make it official.

The flight was late. Finally I heard the steepening whine of the engines and watched the little Cessna lift up above the airport buildings. I got out of the Jeep to watch it bank over the ocean and straighten out north for Nantucket Sound and the mainland. Eventually it was just a speck, glinting in the hard sunlight. Then it was gone. I climbed back into the Jeep. The clock on the dash said 10:45. Most of the morning was used up already. There was a pile of paperwork waiting for me on my desk. I went home, changed into my uniform, took the Crown Vic to the station. But first I got that coffee, and sat in the warm Jeep and drank it.

I lifted the cup to the windshield and made a silent toast: to the future.

Then I let the day begin.

Epilogue

Balancing the Egg

As usual, summer took Nantucket by surprise. Winter had lingered through May, chilly and damp. The Daffodil Day parade had been marred by freezing rain and thirty-mile-per-hour winds. The crocuses that had poked their heads up tentatively at the end of April were killed by the late frost. Still, the island's hardy native plants had managed to greet the change of seasons in the proper order.

Cindy Henderson had paid close attention in the final days of her pregnancy, waiting impatiently for her water to break: first, the peace pipes and snow drops hidden in the woods, then the gaudy exploding yellow of the forsythia bushes and the white shad, like a memory of snow. The ornamental cherry trees downtown were next, with their storms of pink blossoms, then the swamp iris and the daisies in every yard and pasture. The roses appeared last, perfumed royalty at the end of the long parade, covering the cottages in 'Sconset, garlanding Rose Sunday at the Congregational church.

That took her as far as the birth of her baby girl Katherine Jane (six pounds, nine ounces) on the day before the vernal equinox. But she fell asleep that night with the baby on her chest and Mike lying beside her, thinking about the hydrangeas that were on their way, and the day lilies and the rose-of-sharon as fall approached. Finally the weedy chicory plants would appear at the side of the road, and the joe pye weed in the meadows, and the summer would be over. It had saddened her in the past, but this year she found the cycle comforting. She was part of it now.

By the next morning they were ready for visitors. Billy Delavane brought a slow-cooker of soup. Mike's whole crew stopped by, and she heard their news. Derek Briley was going into business for himself. Bob Haffner was grazing the fields of pretty girls who seemed to bloom with the hydrangeas in the high season. He was living in the one house he did caretaking for (the people showed up two weeks a year, in August), driving the owners' Lexus SUV and wearing the husband's wardrobe (a perfect fit). Cindy had to smile. At least some things never changed.

The newest member of the crew stayed the longest. They had known each other since high school.

David Trezize leaned down over the bed to hug her. The baby was in the crook of her arm.

"Congratulations, Honey. You look great."

"I feel like I just had a baby."

"It becomes you."

"Thanks."

"Any word from Mark Toland?"

"God, no."

"I hear he finished his movie."

"I don't have to see it, do I?"

"Not if you behave."

She took his hand. "How was the big high school reunion?"

"I never went. I didn't feel like lying and I certainly wasn't going to tell those jerks the truth."

"Good for you. I hate reunions anyway. All the people you really want to see wouldn't be caught dead there."

"All the people you really want to see, you never lost touch with in the first place. Like us."

"It's true."

He stroked the baby's hair, kissed her and Cindy on their foreheads and left. He could tell they were both about to fall asleep.

"Anything I can do, let me know," he said to Mike on the way out.

Mike patted him on the back. "Work some extra hours. That would help. I want to get the north side finished by the end of the week."

David still hadn't adjusted to his new life, though he had done some painting in high school and he had a knack for glazing windows. *The Shoals* remained in a state of suspended animation, with the staff scattered and lease paid through September. He hadn't been able to raise the funds to start the little newspaper up again, but he hadn't quite been able to give it up either. He could have sold the computers and printers and the office furniture for a much-needed cash transfusion, and he thought about doing it every day. It was hard to make ends meet on Nantucket, earning twenty-five dollars an hour.

The next day, at lunch, David was sitting on a stone bench in the customer's garden trying to balance a hardboiled egg upright, when Kathleen Lomax, strolling up Main Street, ducked through the gate and walked up to him. She had gained a little much-needed weight and lost the harrowed look of the previous winter. Her hair was cut short; it fell just to her shoulders now. Her flower-patterned summer dress fluttered against her bare legs in the breeze from the harbor.

"Hello, David," she called out.

"Hey."

Kathleen had gotten into the Public Affairs doctoral program at Princeton's Woodrow Wilson School. That would keep her busy—and off-island. But it looked like she was back for the summer.

She stood above him, looking down. "What are you doing?"

"It's the vernal equinox. You can balance an egg upright today, while all the planets are lined up perfectly. I've never managed to do it, though."

"That's a myth, you know."

"I don't think so. I've seen people do it."

"No, I mean about the equinox. You can do it any time. The trick is not giving up."

"I'll try to remember that."

"I wish you hadn't given up your newspaper. I loved *The Shoals*. I loved being part of it. I'll miss your editorials. They were so passionate."

David looked up at her. How was the human race supposed to propagate itself when it was this hard to talk to beautiful women? "Thank you," he said.

"The island needs a voice like that."

"Tell it to Marine Home Center and Bailey Real Estate. A little of their ad revenue might get the paper up and running again."

She stepped back, assessing him. "What you really need is a patron."

He laughed. "Everybody needs a patron."

"No, but if *The Shoals* had some real money behind it, you wouldn't have to worry about getting in trouble for telling the truth. People like…like my dad—they couldn't hurt you. Or shut you up."

"I'm not easy to shut up."

"You know what I mean."

He nodded. The egg fell over again.

"I'm very rich," she said quietly. "It has nothing to do with my father. My grandmother's family have always been rich. My great great-grandfather helped finance Eli Whitney. His brothers were cotton brokers and they made a lot of money…before the Civil War. I think there was some slave trade going on there, too. So we have a lot to make up for. Lots of bad Karma. My grandfather sold short just before the big crash in 1929. Then he bought back all the stock at pennies on the dollar. He wasn't a very nice man, either. Dad must have felt like a natural choice for my mother. Anyway, I have all this money and I'm trying to figure out what to do with it."

David sat up. "Kathleen …"

"I don't mean like Wendy Schmidt, with her matching funds and boutique bakeries and that awful new Dreamland Theater. I mean putting real money where it can really help."

"Are we talking about what I think we're talking about?"

She sat down on the bench and twisted a little to face him. The dress rose up on her thighs. Her legs were tanned and firm; but the challenge in her voice was far more provocative than her body. "Let's get back into the newspaper business."

He looked up into her eyes. "I could go after the Land Bank. And those assholes who run the dump."

She smiled. "You be Ben Bradlee. I'll be Katharine Graham. Except they were never linked romantically."

"Are we…linked romantically?"

"Anything's possible. This is a terrible town for gossip. Why don't you come over to the house tonight? Talk about everything, get organized, make our plans. 52 Baxter Road. Seven o'clock?"

"Uh—great."

"I'll cook. Do you have any dietary restrictions, any vegetables you hate? Beets or Brussels sprouts?"

"No, I eat everything."

She reached out and squeezed his knee. "I'm so happy to hear that." She stood. "Try it again. The egg."

Feeling her eyes on him, David rolled it vertical, gingerly pulled his fingertips away. The egg trembled for a second. But it stayed upright.

"Look at that," Kathleen said.

"It gives you hope."

She plucked the egg off the bench. "I'm keeping it. As a souvenir."

"Not for too long, I hope."

"Just until tonight, how about that? Bring champagne, we'll celebrate."

"Okay."

"See you then."

She walked back across the lawn, and out the gate. Bob Haffner emerged from behind a hedge, grinning. He had obviously been listening.

"You are a god," he said, grinning. "I bow down to you."

◇◇◇

On the other side of town, Rick Folger was hanging the "Open" sign on his antique store. It was his first day of business, his screw-up brother Douggie was helping out, and the way it had all happened made all his careful planning seem absurd.

At one time or another, he had planned on taking over his father's business, going back to college. More recently, he had penciled in a five-year jail term. But his father had disowned him, and his college transfer forms were still lying neglected in a drawer in his bedroom in his family's house, where he couldn't get at them even if he wanted to. Dad had changed the locks.

As for jail, Chief Kennis had saved him from that nightmare. He was on strict probation now after testifying against Ed Delavane, and that was fine with him. He had become almost comically law-abiding lately. No bounced checks or parking tickets. He didn't even litter anymore. His little brother was just out of rehab for Oxycodone and he was keeping Doug straight, too, cracking the whip. It was a lot of work, but he was too grateful to begrudge the effort.

The store had come about through a series of serendipitous flukes, most of them engineered by his primary guardian angel, Billy Delavane. Billy was glad to see his brother Ed sent away and he was grateful to Rick for testifying. They still surfed together and during one of their winter sessions, Billy had suggested a job at the dump. He knew people at the DPW and he made a few phone calls on Rick's behalf. The only other available jobs were in retail and construction.

Rick hated the new over-organized landfill, with its officious off-island managers and the air of apocalypse it exhaled in the smoke from its trash fires and its piles of rusting junk.

Ironically it was one of his father's big dump trucks that changed Rick's life. He was working at woodpile #2 on Valentine's Day, when Ethan Daniels pulled in and started off-loading the trash from a house that Folger Construction was gutting in Shawkemo. Ethan heaved a Chippendale end table out the back of the truck. It hit the snow-crusted ground and one of the legs snapped off. The crack of breaking wood couldn't have been more shocking if it had been a living bone.

Rick sprinted toward the tailgate. "Hey Ethan!" he shouted. "Let me give you a hand with that stuff!"

In half an hour he had rescued three Windsor chairs with their layered impasto of milk paint, a Queen Anne tea table and a nineteenth century tabletop with an inlaid chessboard barely visible under decades of dust. He set the stuff aside and took it home with him that night. You had to laugh—his penny-pinching father was throwing away thousands of dollars of antique furniture out of ignorant greed. Rick had spent months with Ed Delavane stealing bad reproduction junk from fancy new houses when the really valuable pieces were right here for the taking, on the trash heap. Most of all, the dead end job he had dreaded opened up his future.

Over the next weeks he found more treasures. There was a Handel lamp in the take-it-or-leave-it pile whose painted shade had gotten separated from the base. He had found the finial after two hours of rummaging through boxes of old silverware and chipped china. There were Creamware jugs and Slipware china plates with the distinctive red glaze and curling yellow line, stuffed carelessly in with the broken orange pots from someone's gardening shed.

Soon he had enough to open a shop and when he told the story to Billy Delavane, Billy offered him one of his family's rundown properties off Orange Street at the edge of town. He didn't want to charge rent. All he wanted was ten percent of the profits. He and Billy had fixed the place up, rushing to be ready for summer like everyone else on the island. They had hoped to be done by Memorial Day, but nothing was ever done on time and at least they had the satisfaction of blaming the traditional culprits, the plasterer and the plumber.

It was only three weeks late, anyway. Rick had quit the dump with his probation officer's blessing. But he still had friends working the trash piles, keeping an eye out for him. Any item they managed to rescue was pure profit.

He stood outside in the bright June sunlight now, waiting for his first customers. Some of the nicer pieces—including that Chippendale table; Billy had helped him repair it—were set up outside near the front door. He was officially in business. Maybe he'd be asked to join the chamber of commerce by this time next year. Why not? It might have been the silky touch of the summer air on his face—giddy optimism felt like common sense.

His first customers arrived a few minutes later: a fat white-haired man and his impeccably thin wife. The man had an ivory-handled cane; the woman carried a lightship basket. They were saying things like "Charming piece," and "It would be perfect in the guest bedroom."

He followed them into the store.

I sat in my office holding a letter from Fiona Donovan in my hand.

It was the first letter I'd received from her since the deportation. I had been happy not hearing from her, or so I would have said, if anyone had asked me. Yet I found myself going through the mail every day with an eagerness I detested. What was I hoping for? The same thing I had wanted on that last day, some explanation or denial that would exonerate her? That was impossible. Nothing she said could change anything. But love persisted. You couldn't say much for it, but you had to give it that. It held on, like a chest cold in a wet autumn.

I had given up on hearing from her, finally, with a mixture of sadness and relief. And then the letter arrived, unmistakable with its green and purple Irish stamps, the angular right slanted handwriting and the County Cork return address. It was thick, too. She obviously had a lot to say. Maybe she had sent pictures. I wouldn't mind having a picture or two of her tucked away in a drawer to indulge myself in my weaker moments. I weighed the letter in my hand for another second or two. I knew I was better off without it, pictures and all.

I threw it into the trash can beside my desk and turned back to the night watch log on the blotter in front of me. I read the same sentence three times—something about a three-car crash on Polpis Road. I tried it for a fourth time and then gave up. I let out a sigh so deep it turned into a shudder, and bent over to retrieve the envelope.

I was staring at it, still not quite willing to open it, when Haden Krakauer stuck his head in the door.

"You have to hear this, Chief. Somebody's threatening to set off a bomb at the Pops concert this year. It's on tape. The guy says he's going to take out the whole financial ruling class of this country with one brick of C-4."

I looked up. "Jesus."

"Come on, check it out. This guy is serious."

I dropped Fiona's letter into the trash can for the last time, jumped to my feet and followed Haden Krakauer out the door.

To receive a free catalog of Poisoned Pen Press titles, please contact us in one of the following ways:

Phone: 1-800-421-3976
Facsimile: 1-480-949-1707
Email: info@poisonedpenpress.com
Website: www.poisonedpenpress.com

Poisoned Pen Press
6962 E. First Ave. Ste 103
Scottsdale, AZ 85251